The old servant Hildegarde took me to my room. 'Goodnight,' she said; 'bolt the door when I have gone. It is not always safe in the heart of the forest.' I did as she asked, then stayed by the door, my heart pounding with excitement. I heard a footstep on the stair. Hildegarde spoke. 'No, Master, I'll not have it. Your women if you must, but not a young and innocent girl from the convent.'

I was trembling. Then I saw the door handle slowly turn. A voice—his voice—whispered: 'Are you there?'

An inexplicable impulse to draw the bolt began to rise in me . . .

VICTORIA HOLT

On the Night of the Seventh Moon

Collins

FONTANA BOOKS

First published in 1973 by William Collins Sons & Co Ltd
First issued in Fontana Books 1974
Twelfth Impression August 1980

© Victoria Holt 1972

Made and printed in Great Britain by
William Collins Sons & Co Ltd Glasgow

CONTENTS

The Forest Idyll

1859-60

ONE

Now that I have reached the mature age of twenty-seven I look back on that fantastic adventure of my youth and can almost convince myself that it did not happen as I believed it did then. Yet sometimes even now I awake in the night because, in my dreams, I have heard a voice calling me, and that voice is the voice of my child. But here I am, a spinster of this parish – at least those who know me think of me as such – though deep within me I believe myself to be a wife even as I ask: Did I suffer some mental aberration? Was it really true – as they tried to convince me – that I, a romantic and rather feckless girl, had been betrayed as many had been before and because I could not face this fact, had fabricated a wild story which none but myself could believe.

Because it is of the greatest importance to me to understand what really happened on the Night of the Seventh Moon, I have decided to set out in detail the events as I remember them, in the hope that by so doing, the truth will emerge.

Schwester Maria, the kindest of the nuns, used to shake her head over me. 'Helena, my child,' she would say, 'you will have to be very careful. It is not good to be as reckless and passionate as you are.'

Schwester Gudrun, less benevolent, would narrow her eyes and nod significantly as she regarded me. 'One day, Helena Trant, you will go too far,' was her comment.

I was sent to the *Damenstift* to be educated when I was fourteen years old and had been there for four years. During that time I had been home to England only once, which was when my mother had died. My two aunts had then come to look after my father and I disliked them from the first because they were so different from my mother. Aunt Caroline was the more unpleasant of the two. The only thing she appeared to enjoy was pointing out the shortcomings of others.

We lived in Oxford in the shadow of the college in which my father had once been a student until circumstances – brought on by his own reckless, passionate conduct – had forced him to give up. Perhaps I took after him; I was sure I did, for our adventures were not dissimilar in a way; though his were never anything but respectable.

He was the only son and his parents had determined that he should go to the university. Sacrifices had been made by his family – a fact which Aunt Caroline could never forget nor forgive, for during his student days he had, in the company of another student, taken a walking holiday through the Black Forest and there he had met and fallen in love with a beautiful maiden, and after that, nothing would satisfy them but marriage. It was like something out of the fairy tales which had their origin in that part of the world. She was of noble blood – the country abounded in small dukedoms and principalities – and of course the marriage was frowned on from both sides. Her family did not wish her to marry a penniless English student; his had scraped to educate him for a respectable career and it was hoped that he would make that career within the university, for in spite of his romantic nature he was something of a scholar and his tutors had high hopes for him. But for both, the world was well lost for love; so they married and my father gave up the university and looked around for a means of supporting a wife.

He had made a friend of old Thomas Trebling who owned the small but lively little bookshop just off the High Street, and Thomas gave him employment and rooms over the shop. The young married couple defied all the evil prophecies of sarcastic Aunt Caroline and Cassandra-like Aunt Matilda and were blissfully happy. Poverty was not the only handicap; my mother was delicate. She had in fact when my father met her been staying at one of her family's hunting lodges in the forest for her health's sake. She was consumptive. 'There must be no children,' announced Aunt Matilda, who considered herself an authority on disease. And of course I confounded them all by making my existence felt almost as soon as they were married and appearing exactly ten months afterwards.

It must have been considered tiresome of them to prove

everyone wrong, but this they did; and their happiness continued until my mother's death. I know that the aunts disapproved of fate which, instead of punishing such irresponsibility, seemed to reward it. Crusty Old Thomas Trebling who could scarcely say a polite word to anyone – even his customers – became a fairy godfather to them. He even conveniently died and left them not only the shop but the little house next door, which he had occupied until then; so that by the time I was six years old, my father had his own bookshop, which if it was not exactly a flourishing concern provided an adequate living; and he lived a very happy life with a wife whom he continued to adore and who reciprocated that rare brand of devotion, and a daughter whose high spirits it was not always easy to curb, but whom they both loved in a remote kind of way because they were too absorbed in each other to have excessive affection to spare for her. My father was no business man but he had a love of books, particularly those of an antiquarian nature, so he was interested in his business; he had many friends at the university and in our small dining-room there were often intimate little dinner parties when the talk was often learned and on occasions witty.

The aunts came now and then. My mother called them the greyhounds because she said they sniffed about the place looking to see if it had been properly cleaned, and on the first occasion I remember seeing them at the age of three, I burst into tears protesting that they weren't really greyhounds but only two old women, which was very difficult to explain and did not endear me to them. Aunt Caroline never forgave my mother, which was characteristic of her; but she didn't forgive me either, which was perhaps less reasonable.

So my childhood was passed in that exciting city which was home to me. I can remember walking by the river and my father's telling me how the Romans had come and built a city there, and how the Danes had later burned it down. I found it exciting to see the people scurrying through the streets, scholars in scarlet gowns and the students in their white ties, and hearing how the Proctors prowled the streets at night preceded by their bulldogs. Clinging to his hand, I would go with him southwards down the Cornmarket right into the very heart of the city. Sometimes the three of us went on a picnic into the meadows; but I always preferred to be with one or the other alone for then I could have the attention I could never capture when the three of us were

9

together. When we were by ourselves my father would talk to me of Oxford and take me out to show me Tom Tower, the great bell and the spire of the Cathedral, which he proudly told me was one of the oldest in England.

With my mother it was different. She would talk of pine forests and the little schloss where she had spent her childhood. She told me of Christmases and how they had gone into the forest to get their own trees with which they would decorate the house; and how in the *Rittersaal*, the Hall of the Knights, which was found in almost every schloss large or small, the dancers came on Christmas Eve and when they had danced, sang carols. I loved to hear my mother sing *Stille Nacht, Heilige Nacht*; and her old home in the forest seemed to me an enchanted place. I wondered that she never felt homesick and when I asked her once and saw the smile on her face I knew how deep was the love she bore my father. I believe that it was then that I convinced myself that one day there would be someone in my life who would be to me as my father was to her. I thought that this deep, unquestioning, unshakable devotion was for everyone to enjoy. Perhaps that was why I was such an easy victim. My excuse is that, knowing my parents' story, I expected to find a similar enchantment in the forest and believed that other men were as tender and good as my father. But my lover was not like hers. I should have recognized that. Tempestuous, irresistible, overwhelming, yes. Tender, self-sacrificing – no.

My happy childhood was overshadowed only by the visits of aunts and later the need to go away to school. Then followed holidays and a return to the exciting city which never seemed to change – indeed, said my father, it had been the same for hundreds of years; that was its charm. What I remember from that time is the wonderful sense of security I felt. It had never occurred to me that anything could change. I should always take walks with my father and listen to his accounts of the days when he had been a student; and it was such a joy to listen because although he spoke of them with pride there was no regret. I loved to listen to him as he talked reverently of his days at Balliol; I felt I was as familiar with the college as he was; and I could clearly understand his absorption in the life as he planned to spend the rest of his days there. He would proudly tell me of the famous people who had studied there. My mother talked of her childhood and sang *Lieder* to me, fitting her own words to melodies

10

from Schubert and Schumann which I loved. She made little sketches of the forest and they seemed to have a fairy-tale quality which has always haunted me; she would tell me stories of trolls and woodcutters and some of the old legends which had been handed down from pre-Christian days when people believed in the gods of the North such as Odin the All-Father, Thor with his hammer, and the beautiful Goddess Freya after whom Friday was named. I was enthralled by these stories.

Sometimes she would tell me about the *Damenstift* in the pine forest where she had been educated by nuns; she talked sometimes in German so that I became moderately conversant with that language, although never quite bilingual.

It was her dearest wish that I should be educated at that convent where she herself had been so happy. 'You will love it there,' she told me, 'high up in the pine-clad mountains. The air will make you strong and healthy; in the summer mornings you will eat breakfast out of doors – fresh milk and rye bread. It tastes good. The nuns will be kind to you. They will teach you to be happy and work hard. It is what I have always wanted for you.'

As my father always wanted what she wanted, I went to the *Damenstift*, and when I had recovered from my home-sickness I began to enjoy it. I was soon under the spell of the forest, though I had in fact been so before I had set eyes on it; and as I was at that time the sort of girl who has few inhibitions I was able to accept the new life and my companions with no great difficulty. My mother had prepared me, so nothing seemed very strange. There were girls from all over Europe. Six of them were English, including myself; there were just over a dozen French, and the rest were from the various little German states of which we were in the midst.

We mingled well. We spoke English and French as well as German; the simple life was good for us all; the discipline was intended to be stern, but of course there were those indulgent nuns who could be wheedled and we were quick to find them.

I was soon happy in the convent and I spent two contented years, passing even the vacations there, because it was too far and too expensive to return home. There were always six or seven of us who did this and some of the happiest times were when the others had left and we decorated the hall with firs from the forest and sang our carols, or decorated the chapel for Easter, or took picnics in the forest during the summer.

I had come to accept this new life; Oxford with its towers and spires seemed far away until that day when I heard that my mother was dangerously ill and I was to go home. Fortunately it was in the summer and Mr and Mrs Greville, friends of my father, who were travelling in Europe, collected me and took me home. My mother was dead when I arrived.

What a change I found. My father had aged by ten years; he was vague as though he could not drag himself away from a blissful past to face an intolerable present. The aunts had descended upon the household. At great self-sacrifice, Aunt Caroline told me, they had given up their *comfortable* cottage in Somerset to come and look after us. I was sixteen years old, time to stop wasting my time on a lot of foreign languages and habits which would be of no use to me; I should make myself useful in the home. They could find plenty for me to do there. Young girls should be able to cook and sew, keep a stillroom and perform other domestic tasks which she doubted were taught at outlandish foreign convents.

But Father roused himself from his apathy. It had been *her* wish that I should complete my education at the *Damenstift* and should stay there until I was eighteen years old.

So I went back and I often thought that if the aunts had had their way that strange adventure would never have taken place.

It happened two years after my mother's death. I had forgotten so much of life in Oxford and only rarely did I think of walking down the Cornmarket to Folly Bridge and St Aldate's, of the castellated walls of colleges; of the hollow silence of the Cathedral and the fascination of the Murder of St Thomas à Becket in stained glass in the east window. But the reality was the convent life, the secrets shared with girls as we lay in our cell-like dormitory where a thick stone buttress divided one cell from another.

And so there came that early autumn after which nothing would be the same again.

I was nearly eighteen – perhaps young for my years. I was frivolous yet in a way dreamily romantic. I have no one but myself to blame for what happened.

The most gentle of the sisters was Maria. She should have been a mother of children; perhaps she would have been

12

over-indulgent, but how happy she would have been and would they! But she was a virgin nun and had to content herself with us.

She understood me more than any of the others. She knew that I did not wish to be wayward; I was high-spirited; I was impulsive; my sin was thoughtlessness rather than wilfulness. I know she had constantly explained this to the Mutter.

It was October – and we were enjoying an Indian summer, for the autumn was long coming that year. It was a pity to waste the golden days, said Schwester Maria, and she was going to choose twelve girls whose conduct warranted the privilege to accompany her on a picnic. We could take the wagonette and go up to the plateau; and there we would make a fire and boil a pan of water and make coffee and Schwester Gretchen had said she would bake a few of her spiced cakes as a special treat.

She chose me to be among the favoured twelve rather in the hope that I might mend my ways than because of past good conduct, I was sure; but whatever the reason I was in the party on that fateful day. Schwester Maria drove the wagonette as I had seen her so many times before, looking like a big black crow in her flapping black robes, sitting there holding in the horse with a masterly touch which was surprising. Poor old horse, he would have known the road blindfolded, so it did not really need very much skill to lead him there. During his lifetime, he must have taken the wagonette full of girls up to the plateau many times.

So we arrived; we made the fire (so useful for the girls to learn these things); we boiled the water, made the coffee and ate the spiced cakes. We washed the cups in the nearby stream and packed them away; we wandered around until Schwester Maria clapped her hands to call us to her. We were leaving in half an hour, she told us, and we must all assemble at that time. We knew what this meant. Schwester Maria was going to lean against the tree under which she was sitting and for half an hour take a well-earned nap.

And so she did while we wandered off, and the feeling of excitement which being in the pine forests always gave me began to creep over me. In such a setting Hansel and Gretel were lost and came upon their gingerbread house; in such a wood the lost babes had wandered to lie down and sleep and be covered by the leaves. Along the river, although we could not see them here, castles would appear to hang on the edge

13

of the hillside – castles such as the one in which the Beauty slept for one hundred years before she was awakened by the kiss of a Prince. This was the forest of enchantment, of woodcutters, trolls, princes in disguise and princesses who must be rescued, of giants and dwarfs; it was the fairy-tale land.

I had wandered away from the others; no one was in sight. I must watch the time. Pinned to my blouse was a little watch with blue enamel decorations which had been my mother's. It would not be fair to be late and upset dear kind Schwester Maria.

Then I started to brood on what I had found when I last returned home; the aunts in possession and my father grown indifferent to what went on around him; and it occurred to me that I would have to go back soon, for girls did not stay after nineteen at the *Damenstift*.

The mist comes suddenly in the mountainous forests. We were very high above sea level. When we went into the little town of Liechtenkinn which was the nearest to the *Damenstift* we went downhill all the way. And as I sat thinking of home and wondering vaguely about the future the mist descended and when I got to my feet I could only see a few yards ahead of me. I looked at my watch. It was time to be going. Schwester Maria would already be rousing from her slumbers, clapping her hands and peering about for the girls. I had climbed a little and the mist might be less thick where she was resting, but in any case the fact that it was there would alarm her and she would certainly decide that we must leave at once.

I started off in what I thought was the direction in which I had come; but I must have been wrong, for I could not find the road. I was not unduly alarmed. I had five minutes or so to spare and I had not wandered very far. But my concern grew when I still could not find the way. I believed I could be wandering round in circles but I kept assuring myself that soon I would come upon the clearing where we had had our picnic. I would hear the voices of the girls. But there was no sound in the mist.

I called out: 'Cooee!' as we did when we wished to attract each other's attention. There was no response.

I did not know which way to turn and I knew enough of the forest to realize that one could be deceived by direction in a mist such as this one. A horrible panic came to me. It might thicken. It might not lift all night. If so how could I find my way back to the clearing. I called again. There was no answer.

I looked at my watch. I was five minutes overdue. I pictured Schwester Maria fussing. 'Helena Trant again!' she would say. 'Of course she didn't mean it. She was just not thinking . . .'

How right she was. I must find my way back. I could not worry poor Schwester Maria.

I started off again, calling: 'Coo-ee. It's Helena. Here!'

But no answer came out of the implacable grey mist. The mountain and forests are beautiful but they are also cruel, which is why there is always a hint of cruelty in the fairy tales of the forest. The wicked witch is for ever waiting to spring, the spell-bound trees are waiting to turn into the dragons they become when darkness falls.

But I was not really frightened although I knew I was lost. The wise thing was to stay where I was and call. So I did.

I looked at my watch. Half an hour had passed. I was frantic. But at least they would be searching for me.

I waited. I called. I abandoned my decision to remain where I was and began to walk frantically in several directions. An hour had passed since the time for our rendezvous.

It must have been half an hour after that. I had called until I was hoarse; and then I was alert, for the sound of a displaced stone rolling and the crackle of undergrowth indicated that someone was near.

'Cooee!' I called with relief. 'I'm here.'

He loomed up out of the mist like a hero of the forest on his big white horse. I went towards him. He sat for one second regarding me, then he said in English: 'It was you who called. So you're lost.'

I was too relieved to be surprised that he spoke in English. I began to talk quickly: 'Have you seen the wagonette? And Schwester Maria and the girls? I must find them quickly.'

He smiled slowly. 'You're from the *Damenstift*.'

'Why, yes, of course.'

He leaped down from his horse. He was tall, broad and immediately I was aware of what I could only describe then as authority. I was delighted. I wanted someone who could get me back to Schwester Maria with all speed and he gave an impression of invincibility.

'I'm lost,' I said. 'There was a picnic.'

'And you strayed away from the fold.' His eyes gleamed.

They were very bright topaz colour, I thought, but perhaps that was the strange light due to the mist. His mouth, which was firm and full, turned up at the corners; he had not taken his eyes from me and I was a little embarrassed by his scrutiny.

'Sheep who stray from the fold deserve to be lost,' he said.

'Yes, I suppose so, but I didn't exactly stray far. But for the mist I should have found them easily.'

'One must always expect mist at these heights,' he reproved.

'Well, yes, of course, but will you take me back to them? I'm sure they are still searching for me.'

'If you can tell me where they are, most certainly. But if you knew that important fact you would not need my help.'

'Couldn't we try and find them? They can't be far.'

'How could we find anyone in this mist?'

'It's more than an hour since I was supposed to be there.'

'Depend upon it. They've gone back to the *Damenstift*.'

I looked at the horse. 'It's five miles. Could you take me there?'

I was rather startled to be promptly lifted up and set sideways on the horse. He leaped into the saddle.

'Go on, Schlem,' he said in German.

The horse walked cautiously forward while the stranger kept one arm about me; he held the reins with the other. I could feel my heart beating very fast. I was so excited I had stopped worrying about Schwester Maria.

I said: 'Anyone could get lost in the mist.'

'Anyone,' he agreed.

'You were lost, I suppose?' I asked.

'In a manner,' he said. 'Schlem –' he patted the horse – 'would always take me back.'

'You're not English,' I said suddenly.

'I am betrayed,' he replied. 'Tell me what did it.'

'Your accent. It's very faint, but there.'

'I was educated at Oxford.'

'How exciting! My home is there.'

'I believe I have risen somewhat in your estimation. Am I right?'

'Well, I hadn't started to make an estimation yet.'

'How wise of you. One never should on a very short acquaintance.'

'I'm Helena Trant, studying at the *Damenstift* near Liechtenkinn.'

16

I waited for him to introduce himself, but all he said was: 'How interesting.'

I laughed. 'When you loomed out of the mist I thought you were Siegfried or somebody like that.'

'You are very complimentary.'

'It was the horse. Schlem. He's magnificent. And you looked so tall and commanding seated up there, just as he must have looked – Siegfried, I mean.

'You are well acquainted with our heroes?'

'Well, my mother comes from these parts. As a matter of fact, she was at the same *Damenstift*. That's why I'm there.'

'How very fortunate.'

'Why do you think that?'

'Because if your mother had not gone to this particular *Damenstift* you would not have come and you would never have been lost in the mist and I should never have had the pleasure of rescuing you.'

I laughed. 'So it is a pleasure?'

'It's a great pleasure.'

'The horse keeps going. Where is he taking us?'

'He knows his way.'

'What! To the *Damenstift*?'

'I doubt he has ever been there. But he will take us to some shelter where we can make plans.'

I was contented. I suppose it was that air of authority which gave me the impression that whatever the proposition it would not be too difficult for him to solve it.

'You haven't told me your name,' I said.

'You've already named me,' he said. 'Siegfried.'

I burst out laughing. 'Is it really? Well, that is a coincidence. Fancy my hitting on the name. I suppose you are *real*. You're not a chimera or something? You're not suddenly going to disappear.'

'Wait and see,' he said. He held me tightly against him, which aroused in me a strange emotion which I had never felt before and which should, of course, have been a warning.

We had been climbing a little and the horse suddenly changed direction. A house loomed out of the mist.

'Here we are,' said Siegfried.

He dismounted and lifted me down.

'Where are we?' I asked. 'This is not the *Damenstift*.'

'Never mind. We'll find shelter here. The mist is chilling.'

He shouted: 'Hans!' and a man came running out from

17

stables which I discerned at the side of the house. He did not seem in the least surprised to see me; calmly he took the reins which Siegfried threw at him and led the horse away.

Siegfried then slipped his arm through mine and drew me towards the stone steps which led up to the portico. We were facing a heavy iron-studded door which he pushed open and we stepped into a hall with a big fire roaring away in the grate; there were skins of animals in the form of rugs, over the polished boards of the floor.

'This is your home?' I asked.

'It's my hunting lodge.'

A woman came into the hall. 'Master!' she cried and I saw the dismay in her face as she looked at me.

He spoke to her in rapid German explaining that he had found one of the young ladies from the *Damenstift* lost in the forest.

The woman seemed even more disturbed. '*Mein Gott! Mein Gott!*' she kept muttering.

'Don't fret so, Garde,' he complained. 'Get us some food. The child is chilled. Find her a wrap or something so that she can get her damp clothes off.'

I spoke to her in her own language and she replied in a scolding voice, 'We should get you back to the *Damenstift* soon.'

'We might let them know I'm safe,' I temporized, for I had no desire for my adventure to end so quickly.

'The mist is too thick,' said Siegfried. 'Wait awhile. As soon as we can get her back we will.'

The woman looked at him reproachfully and I wondered what that meant.

She bustled me up a wooden staircase into a room with a big white bed and a great many cupboards. She opened one of these and took from it a blue velvet robe lined with fur. I exclaimed with pleasure at the sight of it.

'Take off your blouse,' she said. 'It's damp. Then you can wrap this round you.'

I did so and when I glanced at myself in the mirror I seemed transformed. The blue velvet was so magnificent. I had never seen anything like it.

Could I wash my hands and face, I asked. She looked at me almost fearfully. Then she nodded. After a while she came back with hot water.

'Come down when you're ready,' she said.

I heard a clock strike seven. Seven o'clock! What would be happening back at the *Damenstift*? I felt sick with anxiety at the thought but even that could not curb the wild excitement which was possessing me. I washed thoughtfully. My cheeks were pink; my eyes bright. I undid the plaits which Mutter insisted were worn and my hair fell about my shoulders; it was thick, dark and straight. Then I wrapped the blue velvet robe about me and fervently wished the girls in the convent could see me now.

There was a knock at the door and the woman entered. She gasped when she saw me. She seemed as though she were going to say something but refrained from doing so. It was a little mysterious, but so exciting.

She took me down the stairs to a small room where a table was set. There was wine and cold chicken with fruit and cheeses and a big crusty coburg loaf.

Siegfried was standing by the fire.

His eyes sparkled as he looked at me. I was delighted. I knew it meant that the robe suited me – as indeed it must suit anyone; and of course my hair was more becoming loose than in plaits.

'You like the transformation?' I said. I always talked too much when excited. I went on exuberantly: 'I look a more fitting companion for Siegfried now, than with my plaits and school blouse.'

'A very fitting companion,' he said. 'Are you hungry?'

'Starving.'

'Then let us waste no time.'

He led me to a chair and very courteously held it while I sat down. I was unused to such attentions. He filled my glass with wine. 'I shall wait on you tonight,' he said.

I wondered what he meant for a moment and then I said: 'Oh, servants.'

'They would be a little redundant on such an occasion.'

'And hardly necessary when we can help ourselves.'

'This wine,' he said, 'is from our Moselle valley.'

'We don't have wine at the *Damenstift* – only water.'

'How abstemious.'

'And what they would say if they could see me sitting here now with my hair loose, I can't imagine.'

'So it is forbidden to wear it so?'

'It's supposed to be sinful or something.'

He was still standing behind me and suddenly gathered my

19

hair up in his hands and pulled it so that my head was jerked back and I looked full into his face. He leaned over me and I wondered what was going to happen next.

'You do strange things,' I said. 'Why do you pull my hair?'

He smiled and, releasing it, went to the chair opposite me and sat down.

'I suppose they consider it would arouse temptation in unscrupulous people. That's how they would reason. And quite rightly.'

'Hair, you mean?'

He nodded. 'You should keep it plaited except when you are completely sure of your companions.'

'I hadn't thought of that.'

'No. You are somewhat thoughtless, you know. You wandered from the fold. Don't you know that in the forest there are wild boars and equally wild barons? One could rob you of your life; the other of your virtue. Now tell me, which would you consider of the most value?'

'The nuns would say one's virtue of course.'

'But I wanted your opinion.'

'As I have never lost either it is hard for me to decide.'

'The nuns haven't either presumably, but they came to a decision.'

'But they are so much older than I. Are you telling me that you are one of the wild barons? How could you be? You're Siegfried. No one with a name like that could ever rob maidens of their virtue. All they do is save them from wild boars or wild barons perhaps.'

'You are not very sure of that. I sense you have a few misgivings. Have you?'

'Well, a few. But then if I hadn't this wouldn't be an adventure, would it? If it was another nun who had found me it would be rather dull.'

'But surely you should feel no misgivings with Siegfried.'

'If it were really he, no.'

'So you are doubting me.'

'I think you may be rather different from what you seem.'

'In what way?'

'That remains to be discovered.'

He was amused and said: 'Allow me to serve you some of this meat.'

He did so and I took a piece of rye bread which was hot and crusty and delicious. There was a mixture of spicy pickle and a kind of sauerkraut such as I had never tasted before. This was something more than the usual layers of white cabbage and spice seeds; it was quite delicious.

I ate ravenously for a while and he watched me with all the pleasure of a good host.

'So you were hungry,' he said.

I frowned. 'Yes, and you're thinking that I really ought to be worrying about what's happened at the *Damenstift*, not enjoying this.'

'No. I'm glad you can live in the moment.'

'You mean I should forget about going back and facing them at all?'

'Yes. I mean just that. It's the way we live. We have met in the mist; you are here; we can talk together while the mist lasts. Let us not think beyond that.'

'I'll try,' I said. 'Because quite frankly I find it very depressing to contemplate all the fuss there'll be when I get back.'

'Then you see I am right.' He lifted his glass. 'Tonight,' he said. 'The devil take tomorrow.'

I drank with him. The wine warmed my throat and I felt the colour flushing my cheeks.

'Although,' I said severely, 'it is not a philosophy of which the nuns would approve.'

'The nuns are for tomorrow. We mustn't let them intrude tonight.'

'I can't help thinking of poor Schwester Maria. Mutter will scold her. "You shouldn't have taken that Helena Trant," she will say. "There is always trouble where she is".'

'And is there?' he asked.

'It seems to work out that way.'

He laughed. 'But you are different from the others. I'm sure of that. You were telling me that your mother was here.'

'It was a beautiful story; and now it has become a sad one. They met in the forest and they fell in love and lived happily ever after . . . until she died, that is. There was great opposition to the marriage but they overcame it, and it all turned out so right. But she is dead now and Father is alone.'

'He has you when you are not far away at the *Damenstift* or roaming the forest in the mist.'

I grimaced. 'They were always lovers rather than parents. Lovers don't want intruders and even children can be that.'

'The conversation is growing a little sad,' he said, 'and this is a time for gaiety.'

21

'What! With me lost and the nuns frantic and wondering how they are going to break the news to my father that I am lost in the forest.'

'You'll be back with them before they have time to send the message.'

'But I hardly think we should be gay when they will be so worried.'

'If we can do no good by worrying we should be gay. That's wisdom.'

'I suppose you are very wise, Siegfried.'

'Well, Siegfried was, wasn't he?'

'I'm not so sure. It could all have worked out so much better with Brynhild if he had been a little more clever.'

'I suppose your mother told you the legends of our forests.'

'She talked about it when we were together sometimes. I loved the stories of Thor and his hammer. Do you know the one where he went to sleep with his hammer beside him and one of the giants came and stole it and they said that they would only give it back if the Goddess Freya became the bride of the Prince of the Giants? So Thor dressed up as the Goddess and when they laid the hammer on his lap, he grasped it, threw off his disguise and slew them all. So he came back to the land of the gods with his hammer.'

He laughed with me.

'It was not strictly honest, I must say,' I went on. 'And those giants must have been rather blind to have mistaken Thor for a beautiful goddess.'

'Disguises can deceive.'

'Surely not to that extent.'

'Do have some more of this. It's Hildegarde's very special sauerkraut. Do you like it?'

'Delicious,' I said.

'I'm delighted that you have such a good appetite.'

'Tell me about yourself. I've told you about me.'

He spread his hands.

'You know that I was in the forest hunting boar.'

'Yes, but is this your home?'

'It's my shooting lodge.'

'So you don't actually live here?'

'When I am hunting in this area I do.'

'But where is your home?'

'Some miles from here.'

'What do you do?'

'I help look after my father's lands.'

'He's a sort of landowner with an estate to look after. I know.'

He asked me about myself and I was soon telling him of Aunt Caroline and Aunt Matilda.

'The ogresses,' he called them. He was amused about the greyhound story.

He talked about the forest and I knew that it fascinated him as it did me. He agreed that there was an enchantment about it which comes through so clearly in the fairy stories. From my childhood I had been aware of the forest through my mother's accounts of it and he had lived near it; so it was agreeable to be with someone who understood my feelings as he so clearly did.

He was interested that I could recount stories of the gods and heroes who, long, long ago, legend had it, lived in the forests when the lands of the north were one and the gods ruled in the days before Christ was born and brought Christianity to the world; then the heroes of the north lived and died – men like Siegfried, Balder and Beowulf, and one could often believe that these spirits still existed in the heart of the forest. His conversation fascinated me. He told me the story of Balder the beautiful who was so good that his mother the Goddess Frigg made every beast and plant of the forest take an oath not to harm him. There was one exception – the evergreen plant with the yellow-green flowers and white berries. The mistletoe was hurt and angry because the gods had condemned it to be a parasite and Loke the mischievous god had known this, and had thrown the twig of this parasite sharp as an arrow at Balder. It pierced his heart and killed him. The lamentation of the gods was great.

I sat drinking in his words, glowing with the excitement of the adventure, a little light-headed from unaccustomed wine and more excited than I had ever been in my life.

'Loke was the God of Mischief,' he told me. 'The All-Father often had occasion to punish him, for Odin was good and it was only when his wrath was roused that he was terrible. Have you visited the Odenwald? No? Then you must one day. It's Odin's Forest and in this country we have this Lokenwald which is said to be Loke's Forest. And here in this neighbourhood only we celebrate the Night of the Seventh Moon when mischief is abroad and is routed with the coming of dawn. It's an excuse for one of our local cele-

23

brations. You're getting sleepy.'

'No, no. I don't want to be. I'm enjoying it all too much.'

'You have ceased to fret about tomorrow, I'm glad to notice.'

'Now you have reminded me.'

'I'm sorry. Let's change the subject quickly. Did you know your Queen quite recently visited our forest?'

'Yes, of course. I believe the forest enchanted her, but this is the home of her husband. She loves the Prince as my father loved my mother.'

'How can you know – you who are so young and inexperienced?'

'There are things one knows instinctively.'

'About devotion?'

'Love,' I said. 'The great love of Tristan and Iseult, of Abelard and Heloise, of Siegfried and Brynhild.'

'Legends,' he said. 'Real life may not be like that.'

'And my parents,' I continued, ignoring him, 'and the Queen and her Consort.'

'We should consider ourselves honoured that your great Queen married one of our German princes.'

'I believe she felt herself honoured.'

'Not by his position, by the man.'

'Well, there are so many German princes and dukes and little kingdoms.'

'One day there will be one mighty Empire. The Prussians are determined on that.' He went on: 'But let us talk of more intimate matters.'

'I have the wishbone,' I cried. 'Now we can wish.'

I was delighted that he had not heard of the custom, so I explained it to him. 'You each take an end by your little finger and pull. You wish and the one with the larger portion gets the wish.'

'Shall we try it?'

We did. 'Now wish,' I said. And I thought, I want this to go on and on. But that was a stupid wish. Of course it could not go on and on. The night had to pass. I had to go back to the convent. At least I could wish that we met again. So that was what I wished.

He had the larger piece. 'It's mine,' he cried triumphantly. Then he reached across the table and took my hands; his eyes were very brilliant, almost tawny in the candle light. 'Do you know what I have wished?' he asked.

'Don't tell me,' I cried. 'If you do it won't come true.'

He bent his head suddenly and kissed my hands – not lightly but fiercely and I thought he was never going to release them.

'It *must* come true,' he said.

I said: 'I can tell you what I wished because I lost, so mine doesn't count.'

'Please tell me then,' he said.

'I wished that we should meet again and we should sit at this table and talk and talk and I should wear a blue velvet robe and have my hair loose.'

He said: 'Lenchen . . . little Lenchen . . .' very softly.

'Lenchen?' I said. 'Who is that?'

'It is my name for you. Helena is too cold . . . too remote. For me you are Lenchen . . . my little Lenchen.'

'I like it,' I said. 'I like it very much.'

There were apples and nuts on the table. He peeled an apple for me and cracked some nuts. The candles flickered; he watched me from across the table.

And suddenly he said: 'You have grown up tonight, Lenchen.'

'I feel grown up,' I said. 'Not a schoolgirl any more.'

'You will never be a schoolgirl again after tonight.'

'I shall have to go back to the *Damenstift* and be one.'

'A *Damenstift* does not make a schoolgirl. It is an experience. You *are* sleepy.'

'It's the wine,' I said.

'It is time you retired.'

'I wonder if it is still misty.'

'If it were, would you be reassured?'

'Well, then of course they would know I could not get back and it would be stupid to worry because there wouldn't be anything I could do about it.'

He went to the window and drew back the heavy velvet curtain. He peered out. 'It is worse than ever,' he said.

'Can you see it then?'

'Since you came down in your blue robe I have seen nothing but you.'

The excitement was almost unbearable, but I laughed rather foolishly and said: 'Surely that's an exaggeration. When you were pouring the wine and serving the chicken you saw that.'

'Precise, pedantic Lenchen,' he commented. He rose: 'Come, I will take you to your room. I can see the time has come.'

He took my hand and led me to the door.

To my surprise Hildegarde was there. She was fussing with a candle.

'I will show the young lady the way, Master,' she said.

I heard him laugh and mutter something about her being an interfering old woman from whom he endured too much.

But he let me go with her. She led the way to the room in which I had changed, where a fire was now burning in the grate.

'The nights are chilly with the mist about,' she said.

She set down the candle and lighted those in their sconces over the dressing-table. 'Keep the windows closed against the mist,' she said. I saw that a white nightdress was laid out on the bed and I wondered vaguely why they had such a thing because I did not believe the pretty silk garments belonged to Hildegarde.

She looked at me earnestly. Then she drew me to the door and showed me the bolt. 'Bolt it when I have gone,' she said. 'It is not always safe here in the heart of the forest.'

I nodded.

'Make sure,' she said. 'I shall be uneasy and unable to sleep if you don't.'

'I promise,' I said.

'Good night. Sleep well. In the morning the mist will have cleared and you will be taken back.'

She went out and listened while I bolted the door.

'Good night,' she called.

I stood leaning against it, the excitement making my heart pound. Then I heard a footstep on the wooden staircase.

Hildegarde spoke. 'No, Master, I'll not have it. You may turn me out. You may have me flogged but I'll not have it.'

'You interfering old witch,' he said, but he said it indulgently.

'A young English girl . . . a schoolgirl from the *Damenstift* . . . I'll not have it.'

'*You'll* not have it, Garde?'

'No, I'll not have it. Your women . . . if you must, but not a young and innocent girl from the *Damenstift*.'

'You're worried about the old nuns.'

'No, about innocence.'

26

There was silence. I was afraid and yet expectant. I wanted to run away from this place and yet I wanted to stay. I understood. He was one of the wicked barons. He was no Siegfried. He had not told me his real name. This was his hunting lodge. Perhaps his home was one of the castles I had seen high above the river. 'Your women if you must,' she had said. So he brought women here and, finding me in the mist, he had brought me here to be one of them.

I was trembling.

Suppose Hildegarde had not been there. In the fairy tales the wicked giants kept the Princess captive until she was rescued and emerged unscathed. But this was not a castle, it was a hunting lodge; and he was not a giant, he was a virile man.

I took off the velvet robe and looked more like myself. I undressed and put on the silken nightdress. It was soft and clinging, so different from the flannelette we wore at the *Damenstift*. I lay down and could not sleep; and after a while I thought I heard a step on the stair. I rose and went to the door and stood there listening. That was why I saw the handle slowly turn. If Hildegarde had not insisted on my locking the door it would have opened then.

I stared at it in fascination; I listened. I could hear breathing. A voice – his voice – whispered: 'Lenchen . . . Lenchen . . . are you there?'

I stood there bewildered, my heart thumping so that I was afraid he must hear. I was fighting an inexplicable impulse to draw the bolt.

But I did not. I kept hearing Hildegarde's voice: 'Your women . . . if you must . . .' And I knew that I dared not unlock the door.

I stood there trembling until I heard his footsteps die away. Then I went back to bed. I tried to sleep but it was a long time before I did.

I awoke to a hammering on my door and Hildegarde calling 'Good morning.'

I opened my eyes and saw the sunshine streaming into the room.

I unbolted the door to find Hildegarde there; with a tray on which was coffee and rye bread.

'Eat this and dress immediately,' she commanded. 'We must get you back to the *Damenstift* without delay.'

The adventure was over. The bright morning had dispelled

it. Now the music had to be faced.

I drank the hot coffee and swallowed the bread; I washed and dressed and in little more than half an hour I went downstairs.

Hildegarde was wearing cloak and bonnet and outside was a trap drawn by a strawberry roan.

'We must go at once,' she said. 'I sent Hans off as soon as it was light with a message to say that you were safe.'

'How good you are!' I said, and I thought of what I had heard last night and how she had saved me – though I am not sure that I had wanted to be saved – from the wicked Siegfried.

'You are very young,' she said severely, 'and should take great care not to get lost again.'

I nodded and we went out to the trap. 'It is almost eight miles,' she said, 'so quite far to go. But Hans will have explained.'

I looked around for Siegfried but he was not there. I felt angry. He might have come to say goodbye.

I got into the trap rather lingeringly but Hildegarde was brisk. I gazed back at the house – it was the first time I had seen it clearly. It was of grey stone with latticed windows – smaller than I had imagined it. I had seen similar houses before and had heard them referred to as shooting lodges.

Hildegarde whipped up the horses and we took to the road. Progress was slow, for the way was often steep and the road sometimes rough. She did not speak much but when she did I gathered that she was anxious for me not to talk about my adventure. She managed to convey discreetly that I should not talk of Siegfried. Hans had delivered a message. The implication would be that Hildegarde's husband had found me in the mist and taken me home. They had looked after me until I could be taken back. I understood what she was implying. She did not want the nuns to know that a wicked baron had found me and had taken me to his shooting lodge for the purpose of seducing me. There! I had faced the true facts, for it was really obvious that that had been Siegfried's intention. But Hildegarde had saved me.

She clearly adored him while disapproving of him. I could understand that too, and I agreed that it would be wiser to tell my adventures from a slightly different angle.

So we reached the *Damenstift*. What a fuss there was! Schwester Maria had clearly spent the night weeping.

Schwester Gudrun was silently triumphant. 'I told you that it was no use expecting good behaviour from Helena Trant.' Hildegarde was warmly thanked and blessings showered upon her and I was seated for a long time in Mutter's sanctum but I scarcely heard what she said. So many impressions crowded into my mind that there was no room for anything else. Myself in the blue robe; the way his eyes had glowed when we pulled the wishbone and the sound of his voice vibrating and passionate outside my bedroom door. 'Lenchen . . . little Lenchen.'

I continued to think of him. I would never forget him, I was sure. I thought: one day I shall go out and find him waiting there.

But nothing like that happened at all.

Three barren weeks followed, lightened only by the hope that I should see him and made wretched by the depressing fact that I did not, and then news came from home. My father was seriously ill. I must go home at once. And before I could leave came the information that he was dead.

I must leave the *Damenstift* altogether. I must go home at once. Mr and Mrs Greville who had brought me home on that other occasion had kindly offered to come and fetch me and take me back.

In Oxford Aunt Caroline and Aunt Matilda were waiting for me.

TWO

Back in England it was the beginning of December with Christmas almost upon us; in the butchers' shops there were sprigs of holly round the trays of faggots, and oranges in the mouths of pigs who managed to look jaunty even though they were dead. At dusk the stall-holders in the market were showing their goods under the flare of naphtha lights and from the windows of some shops hung cotton wool threaded on string to look like falling snow. The hot-chestnut seller stood at the street corner with his glowing brazier and I remembered how my mother could never resist buying a bag or two and how they used to warm our hands as we carried them home. She liked best, though, to bake our own under the grate on

Christmas night. She had made Christmas for us because she liked to celebrate it as it was celebrated in the home of her childhood. She used to tell us how there would be a tree for every member of the family lighted with candles and a big one in the centre of the *Rittersaal* with presents for everyone. Christmas had been celebrated for years and years in her home, she used to say. We in England had also decorated fir trees when the custom had been brought from Germany by the Queen's mother and later strengthened by Her Majesty's strong association with her husband's land.

I had looked forward to Christmases but now this one held no charm for me. I missed my parents far more than I had thought possible. It was true I had been away from them for four years, but I had always been aware that they were there in the little house next to the bookshop which was my home.

Everything was changed now. That vague untidiness which had been homely was lacking. Aunt Caroline would have everything shining as she said 'like a new pin'. In my unhappy mood I demanded to know why there should be such a desirability about a new pin, which was what Aunt Caroline called 'being funny'. Mrs Green, who had been our housekeeper for years, had packed her bags and left. 'Good riddance,' said Aunt Caroline. We only had young Ellen to do the rough work. 'Very well,' said Aunt Caroline, 'we have three pairs of hands in the house. Why should we want more?'

Something had to be done about the shop, too. Obviously it could not be carried on in the same manner since my father's death. The conclusion was reached that it would have to be sold and in due course a Mr Clees came along with his middle-aged daughter Amelia and bought it. These negotiations went on for some time and it emerged that the shop and its stock would not yield so very much once my father's debts had been paid.

'He had no head, your father,' said Aunt Caroline scornfully.

'He had a head all right,' replied Aunt Matilda, 'but it was always in the clouds.'

'And this is the result. Debts . . . I never saw such debts. And when you think of that wine cellar of his and the wine bills. What he did with it all, I can't imagine.'

'He liked to entertain his friends from the university and they liked to come,' I explained.

'I don't wonder at it, with all the wine he was fool enough to give them.'

Aunt Caroline saw everything in that way. People did things for what they got, never for any other reason. I think she had come to look after my father to make sure of her place in heaven. She suspected the motives of everyone. 'And what is he going to get out of that?' was a favourite comment. Or 'What good does she think that will do her?' Aunt Matilda was of a softer nature. She was obsessed with her own state of health, and the more irregular it was, the better pleased she seemed to be. She could also be quite happy discussing other people's ailments and brightened at the mention of them; but nothing pleased her so much as her own. Her heart was often 'playing her up'. It 'jumped'; it 'fluttered'; it rarely achieved the required number of beats per minute for which she was constantly testing it. She frequently had a touch of heartburn or there was a numb freezing feeling all round it. In a fit of exasperation I once said: 'You have a most accommodating heart, Aunt Matilda.' And for a moment she thought that was a new kind of disease and was quite cheered.

So between the self-righteous virtue of Aunt Caroline and the hypochondriacal fancies of Aunt Matilda I was far from content.

I wanted the old security and love which I had taken for granted; but it was more than that. Since my adventure in the mist I would never be the same again. I thought constantly of that encounter, which seemed to be growing more and more unreal in my mind as time passed but was none the less vivid for that. I went over every detail that had happened: his face in the candle light, those gleaming eyes, that grip on my hand; the feel of his fingers on my hair. I thought of the door handle slowly turning and I wondered what would have happened if Hildegarde had not warned me to bolt it.

Sometimes when I awoke in my room I would imagine I was in the hunting lodge, and was bitterly disappointed when I looked round my room and saw the wallpaper with the blue roses, the white ewer and basin, the straight wooden chair and the text on the wall which said 'Forget yourself and live for others', and which had been put there by Aunt Caroline. The picture which had always been there still remained. A golden-haired child in a flowing white dress was dancing along a narrow cliff path beside which was a long drop on to the rocks below. Beside the child was an angel. The title was *The Guardian Angel*. The girl's flowing dress was not unlike the nightdress I had worn in the hunting lodge; and although I did not possess the pretty features of the child and my hair was not golden, and Hildegarde did not resemble the angel in the least, I associated the picture with us both. She had been my guardian angel, for I had been ready to plunge to disaster – ably assisted by my wicked baron who had dressed himself up in the guise of Siegfried to deceive me. It was like one of the forest fairy tales. I would never forget him. I wanted to see him again. If I had a wishbone again, my wish – in spite of my guardian angel – would still be: Let me see him again.

That was the main cause of my discontent. There was a quality about him which no one else had. It fascinated me so much that I was ready to face any danger to experience it again.

So how could I settle down to this dreary existence?

Mr Clees had come next door with Miss Amelia Clees. They were pleasant and kind and I often went into the bookshop to see them. Miss Clees knew a great deal about books and it was for her sake that Mr Clees had bought the shop. 'So that I shall have a means of livelihood when he is gone,' she told me. Sometimes they came to dine with us and Aunt Matilda was quite interested in Mr Clees because he had confided to her that he had only one kidney.

That Christmas Day was dreary. The Clees had not yet taken possession of the shop and I had to spend the time with Aunts Caroline and Matilda. There were no trees, and our presents to each other had to be useful. There were no roasted chestnuts, no ghost stories round the fire, no legends of the forest, no stories of my father's undergraduate days; nothing but an account of the good deeds Aunt Caroline used to perform for the poor in her Somerset village and from Aunt Matilda the effects of too rich feeding on the digestive organs. I realized that the reason they were more intimate with each other than they were with anyone else was that they never listened to each other and they carried on a conversation independently of each other. I would listen idly.

'We did what we could for them but it's no use helping people like that.'

'Congestion of the liver. She went all yellow.'

'The father was constantly drunk. I told her that the child must not go about in torn garments. "We've got no pins, ma'am," she said. "Pins," I cried. "Pins! What is wrong with a needle and thread?" '

'The doctor gave her up. It had led to congestion of the lungs. She lay like a corpse.'

And so on, happily pursuing their individual lines of thought.

I was amused and then exasperated; I would take my mother's book called *Gods and Heroes of the Northlands* and read of those fantastic adventures of Thor and Odin and Siegfried, Beowulf and the rest of them. And I fancied I was there with that unmistakable scent of the fir and pine trees, the rushing of little mountain streams and the sudden descent of the mist.

'It's time you took your nose out of that book and did something useful,' commented Aunt Caroline.

'Bending over books will send you into a decline,' Aunt Matilda told me. 'It stops the expansion of the chest.'

My great solace at that time was the Grevilles. They could talk of the pine forests. They had a feeling for them. They had spent a holiday there some years ago and often went back to visit them. It was they who had brought me back and forth from the *Damenstift*, for they had been great friends of my parents. Their son Anthony was studying for the church. He was such a good son, the delight of his parents, who were so proud of him. They were very kind and sorry for me. I spent Boxing Day with them and it was a relief to escape from the aunts. They tried to make it gay for me and there were little individual Christmas trees just as my mother had arranged them.

Anthony was there, and when he spoke his parents listened in a hushed silence which amused me while it endeared me to them. We played guessing games, and games with paper and pencil, but Anthony was so much more learned than the rest of us that we came nowhere.

It was quite pleasant and Anthony walked home with me and said rather shyly that he hoped I would visit his parents' home whenever I wished to.

'Is that what you would like?' I asked.

He assured me that he would.

'Then they would want it too,' I said, 'because they always want what you do.'

He smiled. He had a quick understanding and was very pleasant, but not in the least exciting to be with and it was

33

impossible for me now to avoid comparing any man with Siegfried. If Anthony had found a girl in the mist he would have taken her straight back to where she belonged, and if he could not, to his mother; and she would have no need to utter warnings and to take on the role of guardian angel.

I would be pleased to go to the Grevilles and see them and their son; but the desire to be again in that hunting lodge sitting opposite my wicked baron was so intense that it was sometimes like a physical pain.

There were more visits to the Grevilles. The Clees came to the shop and I heard that I had fifteen hundred pounds clear when all debts were paid.

'A nest egg,' said Aunt Caroline; and invested wisely it would give me a small income which would enable me to live like a lady. I would continue under their care and they would teach me how to become a good housewife, an art in which it was obvious to them I was by no means accomplished. I was disturbed. I saw myself growing like the aunts; learning how to run a house, speaking to Ellen so that she cringed, making rows of jams, preserves and jellies and lining them up in chronological order with labels on them denoting that they were blackberry jelly, raspberry jam or orange marmalade of the 1859, 1860 variety and so on through the century, while I grew into a good housewife with banisters which held not a speck of dust and tables in which I could see my reflection, making my own beeswax and turpentine, salting my own pork, gathering my blackcurrants for jelly and brooding over the quality of my ginger wine.

And somewhere in the world Siegfried would be pursuing his adventures and if we met again after many rows of jars in my stillroom he would not know me – but I should always know him.

Escape was at the Grevilles' house where I was always welcome, and sometimes Anthony was there to talk about the past, for he was as enamoured of the past as I was of the pine forests; I found it interesting to learn what the Queen's marriage had meant to the country, how the Consort had ousted Lord Melbourne, what he had done for the country – of the great Exhibition in Hyde Park which Anthony described so vividly that I could see the Crystal Palace and the little Queen so proud beside her husband. He talked of the war in the Crimea and the great Palmerston and how our country was growing into a mighty Empire.

34

I should have been very unhappy during that period but for the Grevilles.

But Anthony was not always there and I found it tiring to hear an account of his virtues, which his parents never failed to give me; and I was restless and unhappy and felt sometimes as though I were in limbo, waiting . . . for what I was not sure.

I told Mrs Greville that I wanted to do something.

'Young girls really have plenty to do in the house,' she said. 'They learn how to be good wives when they marry.'

'It seems very little,' I replied.

'Oh no, being a housewife is one of the important jobs in the world . . . for a woman.'

I didn't take to it. My jam burned the pans; the labels came off.

Aunt Caroline tut-tutted. 'This is what comes of going to outlandish schools.'

'Outlandish' was a favourite word, to be applied to anything of which she did not approve.

My father had made that 'outlandish' marriage. I had 'outlandish' notions about doing something in life. 'What could you do? Go and be a governess to children? Miss Grace, the vicar's daughter in our old home, went as a companion when her father died.'

'She went into a decline soon after,' added Aunt Matilda grimly.

'To that Lady Ogilvy. She was the one who stopped giving soup to the poor because she said they gave it to the pigs as soon as her back was turned.'

'I knew what was wrong with her long before,' put in Aunt Matilda. 'She was that transparent colour. You can tell. "You'll go into a decline, my girl," I said to myself. "And it won't be very long before you do either." '

I was thoughtful. I didn't fancy looking after children or being a companion to some fratchetty old lady who might well be worse than Aunt Caroline and Aunt Matilda; at least the incongruity of their conversation and the predictability of their views gave me a little amusement.

I was drifting. It was as though I were waiting. Life was dull; my high spirits were taking a waspish turn because I was frustrated. I provoked the aunts; I refused to learn what Aunt Caroline was so desperate to teach; I was flippant over the ailments of the body. Yes, I was frustrated. I yearned for something and I was not sure what. I felt that but for that adventure in the forest I might have felt differently. If Siegfried had not robbed me of my virtue (as he had put it), he had robbed me of my peace of mind. I felt that I had glimpsed something which I would not have known existed if he had not shown me; and now I could never clearly be content again.

When the Clees came in the spring life was more tolerable. They were as serious as Anthony Greville. I went into the shop quite a bit and grew very friendly with them. The aunts quite liked them too. I was nearly nineteen – not yet of age; the aunts were my guardians; and life seemed to promise me very little.

And then the Gleibergs appeared in Oxford.

I was helping Aunt Caroline make strawberry jam when they arrived. There was a knock on the door and Aunt Caroline cried: 'Who on earth is that of this hour of the morning?'

It was about eleven o'clock and I was surprised afterwards that I had no premonition of how important this meeting was going to prove.

Aunt Caroline stood, her head on one side listening to the voices in the hall, to make sure that Ellen was making the necessary enquiries as to the visitors' identity in the correct manner.

She came into the kitchen. 'Oh Mum . . .'

'Madam,' corrected Aunt Caroline.

'Madam, they say they're your cousins so I put them in the drawing-room.'

'Cousins!' cried Aunt Caroline indignantly. 'What cousins? We have no cousins.'

Aunt Matilda came into the kitchen. Unexpected callers were an event and she had seen them arrive.

'Cousins!' repeated Aunt Caroline. 'They say they're our cousins!'

'Our only cousin was Albert. He died of liver,' said Aunt Matilda. 'He drank. We never heard what became of his wife. She was as fond of the liquor as he was. Sometimes it affects the heart and she was always a funny colour.'

'Why not go and see them?' I said. 'You'll probably find they're some long-lost relations who have suffered all the diseases that flesh is heir to.'

Aunt Caroline gave me that look which meant that I was

showing signs of my outlandish education; Aunt Matilda, who was more simple, never tried to analyse the workings of my mind; although she kept a close watch on my physical condition.

I followed them into the drawing-room because after all, if the cousins were theirs they were probably some relation to me also.

I was unprepared for the visitors. They looked foreign. 'Outlandish' I knew Aunt Caroline was thinking.

They were a man and a woman. The woman was of middle height and carried herself well; the man, of the same height, was inclined to rotundity. She wore a black gown and elegant bonnet on her fair hair. The man clicked his heels and bowed as we entered.

They were both looking at me and the woman said in English: 'This must be Helena.' And my heart began to beat fast with excitement because I recognized her accent; I had heard it many times while I was in the *Damenstift*.

I went forward expectantly and she took my hands in hers and looked earnestly into my face. 'You have a look of your mother,' she said. She turned to the man: 'It is so, don't you agree, Ernst?'

'I think I see it,' he replied rather slowly.

Aunt Caroline said: 'Won't you sit down?'

'Thank you.'

They sat. 'We are here for a short visit,' said the woman in rather laborious English. 'Three weeks or so. We came to London. My husband has seen a doctor.'

'A doctor?' Aunt Matilda's eyes glistened.

'It's a complaint of the heart. So he came to London and I thought while we are in England we must go to Oxford and see Lili. We have called at the bookshop and they tell us this sad news. We did not know, you see, that she was dead. But at least we can see Helena.'

'Oh,' said Aunt Caroline coldly, 'so you're relations of Helena's mother.'

'Would it be the valves?' asked Aunt Matilda. 'I knew somebody who was born with valve trouble.'

Nobody was listening to her. In fact I doubted the visitors knew what she was talking about.

'Soon after her marriage when she came to England,' said the woman, 'we began to lose touch. There were a few letters and then – nothing more. I knew there was a daughter,

37

Helena.' She smiled at me. 'I felt we couldn't be so near and not look you up.'

'I'm glad you did,' I said. 'Where do you live? Near my mother's old home? She talked about it a good deal.'

'Did she ever mention me?'

'Tell me your name.'

'Ilse . . . Ilse Gleiberg now, but not then of course.'

'Ilse,' I said. 'There were some cousins, I know.'

'There were several of us. Oh dear, it seems so long ago. And then everything changed when she married and went away. People should never really lose touch.'

'Whereabouts do you live?'

'We have just taken a little summer place temporarily. It's in the Lokenwald.'

'The Lokenwald!' There was a lilt in my voice. Aunt Caroline would notice it and think it unbecoming. Aunt Matilda would be aware of my high colour and think I was developing heart disease. I wanted to laugh; I was suddenly so light-hearted.

'I was educated at a *Damenstift* near Liechtenkinn.'

'Really . . . well that's quite close to the Lokenwald.'

'Loke's forest!' I said gaily.

'Ah, you know something of our old legends.'

Aunt Caroline was restive. These people seemed to forget that she was the mistress of the house, because they were so excited to have discovered me.

To turn the attention from me Aunt Caroline suggested that the visitors might like a glass of her elderberry wine. They accepted and Aunt Caroline summoned Ellen and then, afraid that she would not dust the glasses or in some way not carry out the order to her liking, went off to superintend the ceremony. Aunt Matilda cornered Ernst Gleiberg and talked to him about hearts, but his English was not as good as his wife's, which didn't worry Aunt Matilda who never needed replies, only an audience.

Meanwhile I turned to Ilse, more excited than I had been since I came home. She was about the age my mother would have been and she talked of life at the *Damenstift* and the games they had played in the little schloss where they had lived and how my mother's family had visited hers and how they had ridden their ponies in the forest.

I felt a deep sense of nostalgia.

The wine was brought – last year's brew which Aunt Caroline reckoned would be ready for the drinking, and the fresh wine biscuits which she had baked the day before. She glanced significantly at me to make sure that I was realizing how important it was to be prepared with wine and biscuits for unexpected visitors.

Ilse then turned her attention to Aunt Caroline, praised the wine, which pleased her, and asked for a recipe for the biscuits.

So altogether the three of us were pleased with the visit.

That was a beginning. They had taken lodgings in the town and the aunts and myself were soon invited to dine with them. This was exciting and the aunts enjoyed it, although Aunt Caroline did think they had some outlandish ways.

I enjoyed most the times when I could be alone with them. I talked constantly about my mother and how she had met my father when he was on his walking tour. They were very interested. I told them about the *Damenstift* and the different nuns; in fact I realized that I talked a great deal about myself – far more than they did about their lives. They did, though, bring back to me very vividly the enchantment of the forest; and I could sense the change in myself. I was more like the girl I had been before I came back to find my life so sadly changed. Not a word did I say of my adventure in the mist but I was thinking of it; and the night after that first day of their arrival I dreamed of it all so vividly that it was like living it again.

The days passed all too quickly and not one of them without a meeting with the Gleibergs. I told them how very sad I was that they would soon be leaving; Ilse said she would miss me too. It was Ilse to whom I had grown so close – identifying her with my mother. She began to tell me stories of their childhood together, all the little jaunts and customs which my mother had mentioned; and little incidents concerning Lili, as she called her, of which I had never heard before.

About a week before they were due to leave she said to me: 'How I wish you could come back with us for a visit.'

The joy in my face seemed to startle her. 'Would you really like it so much?' she asked, well pleased.

'More than anything on earth,' I said vehemently.

'Perhaps it could be arranged.'

'The aunts . . .' I began.

She put her head on one side and lifted her shoulders; a

39

gesture she used frequently.

'I could pay my fare,' I said eagerly. 'I have some money.'

'That would not be necessary. You would be our guest, of course.'

She put her finger to her lips as though something had occurred to her.

'Ernst . . .' she said. 'I am concerned about his health. If I could have a travelling companion . . .'

It was an idea.

I broached it to the aunts during luncheon.

'Cousin Ilse is worried about Ernst,' I told them.

'I don't wonder at it. Hearts are funny things,' said Aunt Matilda.

'It's travelling. She says it's a burden for one.'

'She might have thought of that before she left her home,' said Aunt Caroline, who thought every adversity which befell others was their own fault and only those which came to her due to unavoidable ill fortune.

'She brought him to see a doctor.'

'The best of them are here,' said Aunt Matilda proudly. 'I remember Mrs Corsair's going up to London to see a specialist. I won't mention what ailed her, but . . .' She looked significantly at me.

'Cousin Ilse would like someone to help her on the journey. She suggested I go.'

'You!'

'Well, it would be such a help and in view of Cousin Ernst's complaint . . .'

'Hearts are very funny things,' from Aunt Matilda. 'Unreliable . . . more so than lungs, though you can't be sure of lungs either.'

'Well, I've no doubt it would be a help to her but why should you go tramping out to outlandish places?'

'Perhaps because I'd like to. I'd like to be of use to her. After all, she is my mother's cousin.'

'That's what comes of marrying foreigners,' said Aunt Caroline.

'Someone who understands hearts would be very useful now,' said Aunt Matilda speculatively. Good heavens, I thought. She's not suggesting she should go?

She was. Her love of disease would carry her even to such lengths. Aunt Caroline was horrified and this was fortunate, for I was sure that because of this veiled suggestion of her sister's she viewed my departure with less dismay.

'How would you get back?' demanded Aunt Caroline triumphantly.

'By train, by sea.'

'Alone! A young girl travelling alone!'

'People do. And it's not as though it's my first visit. The Grevilles might be coming out again. I could wait for them and travel back with them perhaps.'

'It all seems very outlandish to me,' said Aunt Caroline.

But I was determined to go; and I think that Aunt Caroline realized that I had my mother's determination – 'stubbornness,' she called it – and once I had made up my mind I would go. Aunt Matilda was in a way on my side because she was certain that when you travelled with a 'heart' more than one pair of hands would be needed if things went wrong. So it happened that at the end of the month of June when the Gleibergs left England I was with them.

THREE

I was in a state of exultation. Some strange transformation had come to me on that night in the hunting lodge and I would never be quite the same again. I sometimes believed that I had supped with the gods – or one of them at least. He belonged in Asgarth with Odin and Thor; he would be as bold and brave and as wicked and ruthless as any of them. He had taken possession of my mind so that I was like the knight-at-arms who had met the *belle dame sans merci*. 'Alone and palely loitering' I would wander the earth ever more until I found him.

How foolish one could be! Yet on the other hand if I could retrace my steps in some ways, if I could prove to myself that what I had met on that night was not a god but a man who was not very scrupulous and might have submitted me to that to which I am sure people like my aunts would think death preferable, I believed I might throw off this spell which now bound me. I would return to Oxford and learn to be a good housewife. I might be a spinster who looked after the aunts for the rest of their lives; or I might marry and have a family and bring them up to be respectable citizens. My daughters should never be sent to a *Damenstift* in the pine forests for fear one day they should be lost in the mist and captured by a wicked baron, for who could be sure that the good angel in the guise of a Hildegarde would always be there?

We travelled through the familiar country and as I smelt the pines my spirits rose. At length we came to the little station of Lokenburg. A trap took us and our luggage to their house.

How excited I was to be in Lokenburg – a typical south German town. There were a few new houses which had been recently built on the outskirts in the *Altstadt*. It seemed to have come right out of a fairy tale – with its arcaded streets and look of the middle ages.

'It's beautiful!' I cried, gazing at the high roofs and gabled houses, with little domes capping the turrets and the window-boxes on the window-ledges overflowing with flowers. There was the market-place with a pond in the centre and in which a fountain played; and from the shops hung iron signs creaking in the wind with the quaint pictures on them indicating the various trades.

'You must visit our *Pfarrkirche*,' Ilse told me, pointing out the church. 'The Processional Cross is locked away but it will be brought out to show you, I dare say.'

'It's so exciting to be back,' I told her.

'We're just in time for the Night of the Seventh Moon,' she said.

I could hear his voice then distinctly.

'The Seventh Moon,' I cried, 'when Loke, the God of Mischief is abroad and routed by the All-Father Odin.'

Ilse laughed delightedly. 'Your mother made you aware of our legends, I see,' she said. 'This, though, is rather a local one.'

We had passed through the centre of the town and had reached its outskirts. The house was a mile or so from the *Altstadt*. We turned in at a drive, where the fir trees which lined it were thick and rather stubby and pulled up before a porch.

The house was about the same size as the hunting lodge and not unlike it; there was the hall, on the walls of which hung spears and guns, and a wood-staircase led to a landing on which were the bedrooms. I was taken to mine, and hot water was brought; I washed and went down to a meal of sausages, sauerkraut and rye bread which Ilse and I took alone. Ernst was resting. The journey had been so exhausting for him, Ilse explained. I was probably a little tired too, more so than I realized.

I had never felt less so.

Ilse smiled indulgently. She was delighted by my pleasure. I wondered what she would think if she knew its true source and that my excitement was due to the fact that I was hoping to meet Siegfried again.

That afternoon we went in the trap for a trip into the forest and I was enchanted by the mist of blue gentians and pink orchids. I wanted to gather them but Ilse said they would soon die if I did. So I left them.

I slept little that night. I was so excited. I couldn't get out of my mind the belief that I was going to see him again. He would come hunting and we would meet in the forest. We must. It couldn't possibly happen that we never met again and I could not stay here for ever, so it had to happen soon.

I looked eagerly about me during the ride but we saw hardly anyone – only an old woman collecting sticks for firewood and a cow-herd with his cows whose bells about their necks tinkled melodiously as they walked.

The next day I went into the market, which was being decorated with flags because this was the night of the full moon – the seventh of the year; the night of festivities when the god Loke was supposed to be abroad.

'You'll see the girls in their red skirts and white embroidered blouses and yellow tasselled aprons,' Ilse told me. 'Some of the men will be masked; they may be dressed as gods in doublet and hose and light capes; they'll be masked and wear horns on their heads. You've probably seen the pictures of the gods in your mother's books. They'll dance and play tricks. The idea being that none will know which represents Loke and which the All-Father. You must see it. We'll go into the market-square as soon as the moon rises.'

I had not seen Ernst all day. He was very self-effacing and so quiet that one could almost believe he was not there. 'He has changed a great deal since his illness,' explained Ilse. 'He suffers a great deal more than he admits.'

So Ernst stayed in his room and Ilse and I were together most of the time. We talked a great deal – I more than she. I suppose Aunt Caroline was right when she said I talked too much; Ilse was the perfect listener; and I did not notice that she was not so much exchanging chatter as being an audience for me.

And so came the evening of that second day – the prelude to the Night of the Seventh Moon. We had eaten what she called the English high tea as it was too early for dinner and she did not wish us to be out too late when the excitement was supposed to warm up and the fun might get too fierce.

After this high tea she came to my room, her face grave.

'I can't allow Ernst to go out,' she said. 'He's not well enough.'

'So there'll be just the two of us.'

'. . . I hardly think we ought to go.'

'Not . . . go!'

'Well, on occasions like these . . . two women on their own . . .'

'Oh, but we *must* go.'

She hesitated. 'Well, we must not stay late. We'll slip out to the market-square and we'll see the start of it. What a pity we haven't a house on the square. Then you could watch from a window. Ernst will be very anxious. He won't rest till we're back.'

'Isn't there some man who could escort us? If we need one.'

She shook her head. 'This is not really our home. We have just taken this house for a holiday. We have been here before but we don't really have friends in the neighbourhood. You understand . . .'

'Of course,' I said. 'Well, we'll go early and not upset Ernst.'

So that was how we came to be standing in the square with the revellers all about us. It was about eight o'clock in the evening. Overhead hung the great moon – the seventh moon of the year and there seemed to be something mystical about it. It was a strange scene; naphtha flares burned from iron jets lighting the faces of the people. There were crowds in the square; people were signing and calling to each other. I caught sight of a man masked, with the horned head-dress which Ilse had described, and I recognized it at once from pictures my mother had shown me. Then I saw another and another.

Ilse squeezed my hand. 'What do you think of it?'

'Wonderful,' I said.

'Keep close. The crowd's thickening and they may become over-excited.'

'It's early yet,' I told her.

44

I saw a girl seized by one of the horn-headed men and go dancing off with him.

'The excitement grows. You'll see.'

'What happens if the sky is overcast and there's no moon?'

'Some say that Loke is sulking and won't come out, others that he's playing one of his mischievous tricks and then one has to be especially careful.'

A group of fiddlers arrived, started to play and the dancing began.

I don't know quite how it happened; it was the way these things do happen in crowds, I supposed. One minute I was standing there by Ilse's side watching the laughing and dancing swirl of people and the next there was chaos.

It began with a sudden splash. Someone had been thrown into the pond; there was a rush towards it and in the mêlée Ilse was no longer beside me.

I was firmly gripped by the hand and I felt an arm about my waist. A voice which made my heart hammer said in my ear: 'Lenchen!' I turned and looked up into that face; I saw the masked eyes and the laughing mouth. I could never be mistaken.

'Siegfried,' I whispered.

'Himself,' he answered. 'Come . . . out of the crowd.'

He kept his grip on me and we were soon on the edge of it. He took my chin in his hands. 'Still the same Lenchen.'

'What are you doing here?'

'Celebrating the Night of the Seventh Moon,' he said. 'But this is an even more important occasion. The return of Lenchen.'

He was drawing me farther and farther away from the crowd and we were in a small street in which there were only a few revellers.

I said: 'Where are you taking me?'

'Let's go back to the lodge,' he said. 'There'll be supper waiting there. You shall wrap yourself in a blue velvet robe and loosen your hair.'

'I must find Ilse.'

'Who?'

'My cousin who brought me here. She will be worried.'

'You are so precious that there must always be those to worry about you. First it is nuns and now this . . . Ilse.'

'I must find her at once.'

'Do you think you will . . . in that crowd?'

45

'Of course.' I tried to withdraw my hand, but he would not release me.

'We will go back and if it is possible to find her, we will.'

'Come then. She was anxious. She thought we might not be able to come because her husband wasn't well enough. She must have visualized something like this.'

'Well, she did lose you and I found you. Surely I should have some reward for that?'

'Reward?' I repeated; he laughed and put an arm about me.

I said primly: 'How shall I introduce you to Ilse?'

'When the time comes I'll introduce myself.'

'There seems to me a great mystery about you. First you appear as Siegfried and now as Odin, or is it Loke?'

'That is what you have to find out. It's part of the game.'

He had some sort of magic which put a spell on me; he was already making me stop worrying about Ilse. But I remembered how anxious she had been about our coming; and now she would be very worried indeed.

We had reached the square; the dancing seemed to have become more frenzied; and there was no sign of Ilse. Someone trod on my heel and my shoe came off. I stopped and stooped. He was just behind me. I told him what had happened.

'I'll get it.'

He stooped but it wasn't there; and the crowd was so great that we were jostled along.

'Now,' he said, 'you have lost both a cousin and a shoe.' His eyes gleamed suddenly. 'What next will you lose?'

I said quickly: 'I must go back to the house.'

'Allow me to escort you.'

'You . . . you have come for the excitement of all this. I don't want to take you away from it.'

'That would be quite impossible. The excitement of this night is where you are.'

I was really frightened. I must get away. Common sense urged me to.

'I must get back.'

'If that is what you really want then you must. Come with me.'

I limped along beside him.

'How far is the house?' he asked.

'It's about a mile from the centre of the town.'

46

'I dare say the road is bad. None of the roads are good in these parts. Something should be done about it. I have a horse in the inn yard there. You shall ride with me as you did on another occasion.'

I assured myself that it would be very difficult walking minus a shoe so I went with him to the inn yard and there was the horse; he placed me on it as he had done on that other occasion and we started off.

He didn't speak as we went along; he held me firmly against him and my excitement was almost unendurable. I felt I was living in a dream but I suddenly suspected that we were not going towards the house.

I pulled away from him.

'Where are we going?'

'You'll know soon.'

'You said you were going to take me back to Ilse.'

'I said no such thing.'

'You said if that was what I wanted.'

'Exactly, but it's not what you want. You don't want me to take you back and say "Here is your cousin, just as you left her apart from the loss of one shoe of course."'

'Put me down,' I commanded.

'Here! We're in the forest. You'd be lost. It's not the night for young ladies to be about alone.'

'What are you going to do?'

'Surprises are almost more amusing than the expected.'

'You are taking me away . . . somewhere.'

'We are not very far from my hunting lodge.'

'No,' I said firmly. 'No.'

'No? But you really did enjoy your last visit.'

'I want to go straight back to my cousin's house. How dare you try to take me away against my will.'

'Be truthful, Lenchen. It's not against your will. Remember the wishbone? You wished that we should meet again, didn't you?'

'Not . . . not like this.'

'How else?'

'This is so . . . irregular.'

'You are talking like those aunts of yours.'

'How could you know? You've never met them.'

'My dear little Lenchen, you told me so much on that night. Do you remember? You sat there with the blue velvet robe about you and you talked and talked. You were so disappointed when we said good night.'

'And you didn't even come to say goodbye.'

'But it was not goodbye.'

'How could you know that?'

'I did know it. I was determined that we should meet again. It would have been such a tragedy if we had not.'

'You are talking to lull me to security. I want to go back. I must go back to my cousin.'

He stopped the horse; and suddenly he kissed me; it was the strangest kiss I had ever received. But then who had ever kissed me before? Father on the forehead; mother on both cheeks; a peck once on my return from Aunt Caroline; Aunt Matilda did not kiss at all; she had heard that it was not a practice to be unnecessarily indulged in as it was a means of passing on germs. But this kiss seemed to drain me of all resistance; it made me feel exalted and expectant all at once. It was cruel and yet tender; it was passionate and caressing.

I drew away and said shakily, 'Take me back . . . at once.'

'You should not have been turned out on *the* Night of the Seventh Moon,' he said; and he laughed rather cruelly, I thought; his eyes gleamed through the mask and the horns made him look like a Viking raider.

I said angrily: 'Whom do you represent tonight?'

'Just myself,' he replied.

'You seem to have the impression that you are some invader who can seize women and carry them off and behave as you like.'

'And don't you think I can?' He put his face close to mine, laughing.

'No,' I cried fiercely. 'Not with me. Perhaps with some . . . but not with me.'

'Lenchen,' he said, 'do you swear that that is not what you want?'

'I don't understand you.'

'Swear by the moon, by the seventh moon, that your greatest wish is for me to take you back to your cousin's house.'

'But of course you must . . .'

He brought his face closer to mine. 'It is dangerous to swear by the seventh moon.'

'Do you think I'm afraid of fairy stories or of you?'

'You are more afraid of yourself, I think.'

'Will you please say clearly what you mean.'

'Lenchen, I have thought of you constantly since that night when we supped together and it ended there.'

'How could you possibly think it could end any other way?'

'Easily – and so did you.'

'I . . . I do not indulge in such adventures, I assure you.'

'The assurance is unnecessary. I know it.'

'But of course you cannot say the same. Such adventures are commonplace with you.'

'There has never been an adventure like that one. You made it unique and now here we are again. Lenchen, stay with me. Don't ask me to take you back to your cousin's house.'

'I must. She will be frantic with anxiety.'

'Is that the reason . . . the only reason?'

'No. I want to go back . . . because . . .'

'Because you have been brought up by the nuns, but if I were your husband you would be very happy riding off alone with me.'

I was silent. 'It's true, Lenchen,' he cried. 'They have instilled these ideas into you. You have chosen the path of respectability – or at least it has been chosen for you; and no matter what ecstasy, what joy, what pleasure I could give you, it would always be incomplete unless you were my wife.'

'You are talking nonsense,' I said. 'Please take me home.'

'It could have been so perfect,' he said. 'I know that, and it must not be less than perfect. Lenchen,' he went on sadly, 'there has never been such a night as that when we met. I dreamed of it; every time the mist fell I wanted to ride out and look for you. It was absurd, wasn't it? But you want to go home so I will take you.'

He turned the horse and we rode in silence. I was held tightly against him and I was happy. I knew now that I loved him. He had excited me as no other person ever had or I was sure ever could; but when he turned the horse towards the village I loved him because although I was inexperienced I was conscious of an almost uncontrollable desire which he held in check by tenderness for me and which seemed to me the very essence of romance – and that was what told me that I loved him.

I could hear the shouts of revellers as we approached the town; I saw the glow from the flares; one or two people passed us – couples mostly, on their way to the forest. We did not go right into the *Altstadt* but skirted it and I directed him

49

to my cousin's house.

He sprang out of the saddle and lifted me down; as he did so for a few seconds he held me in his arms and kissed me tenderly this time.

'Good night, little Lenchen.'

I felt an impulse to tell him that we must meet again, that it was because I was worried about Ilse that I wanted to go in. But it wasn't only that. I did not know who he was; I did know, though, that it was not unusual for him to take a woman to the hunting lodge; I knew that the silk nightdress and the blue velvet robe had probably been put there for one of them, and that he had intended that I should provide him with the same brief amusement as others had.

But my guardian angel had saved me and now I had saved myself – unwillingly, reluctantly, it was true, but I knew that I was right.

He did not suggest another meeting. He let me go; and before I reached the porch I heard his horse's hoofs on the road.

Ilse dashed out of the house.

'Helena! Whatever has happened?'

I told her the story. I had lost her. I had lost my shoe. One of the revellers had brought me home.

'I've been beside myself,' she cried. 'I couldn't think what to do for the best. I roamed about looking for you, then I thought I had better come back here and get a search-party together.'

'It's all right now, Ilse. I was worried about you. I came back as soon as I could.'

'You must be exhausted.'

Exhausted! I was exhilarated and depressed, exultant and frustrated. My feelings were in a whirl.

She looked at me oddly.

'Go to bed,' she said, 'and I'll bring you up some hot milk. It'll make you sleep.'

Nothing could make me sleep that night.

I lay there going over it all. The words he had said; the implications; he had wanted to take me to the hunting lodge. I wondered if Hildegarde was there.

And then as I went over every detail I said to myself: I've lost him now. This is the second time. I shall never see him again.

One thing I knew was that all my life I should be haunted

50

by him. I should never forget him.

I slept late next morning for I had only dozed fitfully throughout the night until dawn and then fallen into a deep slumber.

The sun was streaming into my room when I awoke and a great sadness descended on me. He had gone; he had explained as clearly as he could that since I could not be his companion of a night or so it was better that we should part.

I dressed lethargically and took breakfast on the little terrace at the back of the house but I had little appetite. I said I would go for a walk into the town during the morning and perhaps do a little shopping for Ilse.

When I returned to the house Ilse came to the door. There was a strange look on her face, as near to excitement as I had ever seen her.

She said, 'There is a visitor to see you.'

'A visitor?'

'Count Lokenberg.'

I stared at her. 'Who on earth is that?'

'Go and see.' And she drew me towards the sitting-room, opened the door and pushed me forward. She shut the door on us so that we were alone, which seemed a strange thing for her to do. At home I should not have been left alone with a man – and here the codes of behaviour were as strict as those at home – perhaps more so.

But already I had seen him. He looked incongruous in this little room; he filled it with his presence.

'I've discarded my head-dress,' he said. 'I hope you recognize me without it.'

'You . . . Count Lokenberg! What are you doing here?'

'I am sure Aunt Caroline would be shocked at your manner of greeting a visitor, and you usually set such store on not shocking her.'

I felt the colour rising in my cheeks and I knew my eyes were sparkling, I was so happy.

'I can't think where Ilse is,' I stammered.

'Obeying orders.' He took my hands. 'Lenchen,' he said, 'I've been thinking of you all night. And you, have you been thinking of me?'

'Almost all night,' I admitted. 'I did not sleep till dawn.'

'You wanted to come with me, didn't you? You were calling out for me to abduct you and carry you away to the lodge. Confess it.'

'If it could have happened and then not have happened . . . and could have been a sort of dream . . .'

'Impossible, my darling. But you were frightened, and that was the last thing I wanted. I want you more than I've ever wanted anything . . . but you must be equally eager and willing. It's no use otherwise. You must want to come to me as much as I want you to.'

'Is that one of your conditions?'

He nodded.

I said: 'You didn't tell me who you were.'

'Siegfried sounded so much more to your taste.'

'And then Odin or Loke. And all the time you are this count.'

'A hero or a god is more impressive than a count.'

'But a count is more real.'

'And you prefer reality.'

'If there is going to be any permanency there must be reality.'

'My practical Lenchen, you know I'm obsessed by you.'

'Are you?'

'Your smile is radiant. You know I am . . . as you are with me. *I* make no conditions.'

'Conditions?'

'You understand, Lenchen. If we had made our vows before a priest you would not have said "Go back". You would have said "Go on"; and your eagerness would have equalled my own. Confess it. You don't hide your feelings one bit. I know what you are thinking all the time. It's there in your face . . . your lovely young face. I know every detail. I have dreamed of it every night and seen it every day since I found you in the forest. I love you, Lenchen, and you love me, and love like ours must be fulfilled. That is why we shall make our vows before the priest and then you will have no fears. You will be free to love. You will not see Aunt Caroline in your mind's eye raising shocked hands; there will be no worrying about nuns or your cousin . . . nothing but us – and that's how I wish it to be.'

'You are asking me to marry you?'

'And what do you say?'

I did not have to answer. As I said, I betrayed myself.

'Tomorrow,' I said. 'How can it be tomorrow? People don't marry like that.'

Here they could, he told me. He would arrange it. If he commanded a priest to marry him that priest would obey him. It would be a simple ceremony. The priest would come into the house, either this or the hunting lodge. It had been done before. I could safely leave everything to him.

I was bemused. I could not get rid of the idea that I was in the company of a supernatural being. Perhaps that's how it always is when one is in love. The loved one is unique, of course, but more than that, perfect. Everything had changed; the whole world seemed to be mad with joy; the birds sang more joyously; the grass was greener, the flowers more beautiful; the sun shone with a new warmth; and the moon, honey-coloured, lying a little on its side – still almost full, wise and benign to lovers – seemed to be laughing because Helena Trant loved Count Lokenberg and all difficulties were to be swept aside by the priest before whom they were to make their vows to love and cherish until death parted them.

'But how is it possible?' I asked Ilse and Ernst when he dined with us that night. 'Surely marriages cannot be arranged like that?'

'Ours is a simple ceremony,' explained Ilse. 'It is often performed in the house of the bride – or the bridegroom, if that is more convenient. The Count is a man of great power in these parts.'

A man of great power! I was fully aware of that. Ilse spoke his name with reverence.

'It seems so sudden,' I said, without any real protest and not really wanting to enquire too deeply into the ethics of the matter because I only wanted to be assured that the marriage could take place.

Ilse brought up hot milk when I was in bed; she seemed to think it necessary to cosset me a little. All I wanted was to be alone to think of this wonderful thing which had happened to me.

A message came from the Count in the early morning. The marriage was to be celebrated at the hunting lodge. He had the priest waiting there. Ilse and Ernst were to drive me over. It was a three hours' drive but they made no difficulty about it; they seemed somewhat overawed by him. His name was not Siegfried but Maximilian, in fact. I had laughed when he told me.

'It sounds like one of the Holy Roman Emperors.'

'Why shouldn't it?' he demanded. 'That's what it is. Don't

you think I'm worthy to be named after such people?'

'It suits you admirably,' I told him. 'I could never call you Max. It doesn't fit you. Maximilian, you see, is rather like Siegfried in a way. It suggests a leader.'

'Maximilian!' I said his name to myself a hundred times that day. I kept telling Ilse that I seemed to be living in a dream; I was afraid that I would wake up to discover that I had imagined everything. Ilse laughed at me.

'You are bemused,' she said.

Then I told her how I had been lost in the mist and how Maximilian seemed like some sort of god, quite unreal, but I didn't go into details about that night in the forest and how the handle of my door had turned and the presence of Hildegarde had made all the difference.

I packed my case and we set out for the hunting lodge. It was about four o'clock in the afternoon when we reached it. There was a grove of firs quite near which I remembered vaguely noticing on the morning when Hildegarde had taken me back to the *Damenstift*. We came to the two stone posts on either side of the gate; and as we drove through them I saw Maximilian on the steps under the porch.

He came towards us hurriedly: and my heart leaped with joy at the sight of him, as I believed it always would at the sight of him for the rest of my life.

'I expected you half an hour before,' he said reproachfully. Ilse replied meekly that we had left in good time.

He took my hand and his eyes gleamed as they swept over me; I was so happy because of his impatience.

What happened next was like a dream, which made it easy afterwards for me to wonder whether that was what it really had been.

The hall had been arranged to look rather like a chapel and waiting there was a man whose black garb proclaimed him to be a priest.

'There is no point in delay,' said Maximilian.

I said I would like to comb my hair and change my dress before I was married.

Maximilian looked at me in tender exasperation but I was allowed my own way and soon Hildegarde was taking me up to the room I remembered so well where I had spent that night so long ago.

I said: 'Hildegarde, how good it is to see you again.'

She smiled but she did not appear to be very happy about

54

our meeting. She had a habit of shaking her head so that she looked like some prophet of evil. At least that was the impression I had. I was too excited to think much about her, though. There I was in that room with the window looking out on the pine trees, and it seemed filled with a faintly resinous odour which I never failed to associate with that room in the hunting lodge, and that feeling of almost unbearable excitement which I experienced on that other occasion and which I was to find could only be inspired by one man in the whole of life.

Alone I washed and took a dress from my bag. It was slightly crumpled, but it was my best dress; it was of a green silky material with a monk's collar of velvet of a slightly darker shade of green. Not exactly a wedding dress but more fitting for the occasion than the blouse and skirt in which I had travelled.

I looked into the cupboard and there was the blue velvet robe which I had worn that night.

I went downstairs where they were waiting for me.

Maximilian took my hand and led me to the priest who was standing before a table which had an embroidered cloth on it and candles in tall alabaster sticks.

The service was in German and brief. Maximilian swore to love and cherish me as I did him and he placed on my finger a plain gold ring which was just a little too big for it.

The service was over. I was the wife of Maximilian, Count Lokenberg.

It was evening and we supped as we had on that other occasion; but how different was this. I wore the blue velvet robe and my hair loose and I can say without reservation that I have never known such complete happiness as I did on that night. I could revel in my happiness with no fears that I would be missed. Everything seemed right and natural and it did not occur to me that there could be anything strange about this until afterwards.

We talked; we touched hands across the table; his eyes never left me; they seemed to scorch me with the intensity of their passion. I was bewildered and ignorant but I knew that I was on the threshold of the greatest adventure of my life.

Together we mounted the stairs to the bridal chamber which had been prepared for us.

I shall never forget it; nor any moment of that night. It

was the memory of this which afterwards, I believed, helped me retain my sanity; an inexperienced girl could not have imagined such a night; how could she have imagined Maximilian the lover if she had never experienced loving before?

When I awoke to find him beside me I lay very still for a long time thinking of this wonderful thing that had happened to me, and tears slowly started to fall down my cheeks.

He awoke to see them.

I told him they were tears of happiness and wonder because I had never known there could be anything in the world like marriage to him.

He kissed them away and we lay quietly for a while; then we were gay again.

What can I say of those days? Summer days in which so much happened and which seemed so brief. He said he would teach me to ride, for I had never done anything but amble about on a pony. Riding was not one of the accomplishments the nuns had thought necessary to teach. I was a good pupil, being determined to excel at everything in his eyes. In the afternoons we walked in the forest; we lay under the trees in a close embrace; he talked of his love for me and I of mine for him; that subject seemed to absorb us both.

But I must know more, I told him. The honeymoon would be over. I would go to his home. I wanted to know what would be expected of me there.

'I am the only one who is allowed to expect anything of you,' he parried.

'Of course, Sir Count. Yet presumably you have a family.'

'I have a family,' he said.

'And what of them?'

'They will need to be prepared for you.'

'Had they intended you to marry someone of their choice?'

'But of course. That is the way with families.'

'And they will not be pleased that you have married a girl you found in the mist.'

'It is only important that I should be pleased – and I am.'

'Thank you,' I said flippantly. 'I'm glad I give satisfaction.'

'Complete and utter satisfaction.'

'So you do not regret?'

He held me hungrily against him then and his embrace was as painful as I had found it before, but there was always an ecstasy in the pain.

'I shall never regret.'

'But I must prepare myself for your family.'

'When the time is ripe you'll meet them.'

'It is not ripe yet?'

'Hardly. They know nothing about you.'

'Whom do we have to placate?'

'Too many to enumerate.'

'So it is a large family and your father is an ogre. Or is it your mother?'

'She would be an ogress, wouldn't she? The feminine, you know.'

'How meticulous you have become.'

'Now that I have an English wife I must master the language.'

'You are already a master.'

'In some respects, yes. In language not entirely.'

I began to discover that whenever I tried to talk of his family the talk took a flippant turn. He did not wish to talk of it and for those first few days, which I wanted to be perfect, I did not insist.

I knew that he came of a noble family; his father, whom he mentioned briefly, would probably have wished to arrange a marriage for him after the manner of noble families, and it would be a shock for him to learn that we were married. Naturally we would have to wait until he had warned them and the time, as Maximilian said, was ripe.

So we joked and laughed and made love and that was enough for me.

He told me stories of the forest in which the legends of the past played a great part. I learned more of the mischievous tricks of Loke and the amazing exploits of Thor with his hammer. There was only Hildegarde to wait on us and cook for us and Hans to manage the horses – apart from those two we were alone in our enchanted world.

On the second day I went into one of the rooms and opening the cupboard found a lot of clothes; I knew that the white silk nightdress which I had been given on my first visit to the lodge had come from this store.

Why, I asked myself, were they kept here?

I asked Hildegarde to whom the clothes belonged and she shrugged her shoulders and pretended not to understand my German, which was absurd because I was fluent.

That night when we lay together in the big bed I said:

'Whose are the clothes in the blue room cupboards?'

He took a piece of my hair and wound it round his finger. 'Do you want them?' he said.

'Want them? They must belong to someone else.'

He laughed. 'Someone I knew kept them here,' he said.

'Because she came often?'

'It saved carrying them to and fro.'

'A friend of yours . . .'

'A friend, yes.'

'A great friend?'

'I don't have friends like that now.'

'You mean of course that she was your mistress.'

'My darling, that is over now. I have started a new life.'

'But why are her clothes here?'

'Because someone forgot to take them away.'

'I wish they had not been here. I shall be afraid to open cupboards for fear of what I shall find.'

'I was first Siegfried the hero,' he said. 'After that I was the mischievous Loke, followed by Odin, and now it seems I have become Bluebeard. I believe he had a wife who looked where it would have been better if she had not. I've always forgotten what happened to the meddlesome lady but I believe it was something regrettable from her point of view.'

'Are you telling me not to ask questions?'

'It is always better not to when you have a good idea that the answer is not very pleasant.'

'There have been many women, I believe. You waylaid them in the forest and brought them here.'

'That only happened once and I did not waylay. I found my own true love.'

'But many have come here.'

'It's a convenient meeting-place.'

'And you have told them that you would love them for ever.'

'Without any real conviction.'

'And on this occasion?'

'With the utmost conviction because if it were not so I would be the most unhappy instead of the happiest man alive.'

'So there have been others . . . countless others.'

'There have been no others . . .'

'I can't believe that.'

'You don't let me finish. There have been no others like you. There will never be another like you. Women have been here, yes. Not one but several and it has been . . . agreeable. But there is only one Lenchen.'

'That is why you married me.'

He kissed me fervently. 'One day,' he said earnestly, 'you will understand how much I love you.'

'I know so little.'

'What do you need to know but that I love you?'

'In our everyday life there is more than that.'

'There is never more than that.'

'But I have to prepare myself for our life together. Am I really a countess now? It seems rather a grand thing to be.'

'We are a small country,' he said. 'Do not imagine that we compete with your great one.'

'But a count is a count and a countess a countess.'

'Some are great, others are small. Remember this is a country with many principalities and little dukedoms. Why, there are many people with high-sounding titles which don't count for very much. There are some dukedoms which consist of the big house, and a village street or two and that is the sole domain. In the not very distant days some of our estates were so small and so poor that if there were five or six brothers they would each have had only a pittance. They used to draw lots – or rather straws. The father would hold the straws in his hand – one was a short one, the others all of the same length. The son who drew the short one inherited everything.'

'Have you many brothers?'

'I am an only son.'

'Then they will be particularly eager for you to marry whom they choose for you.'

'They will in time be enchanted with my choice.'

'I wish I could be sure of it.'

'You have only to rely on me . . . now and for ever.'

When I was about to ask more questions he kissed me again and again. I wondered whether it was to silence me.

Three days had passed and the blissful existence continued. I had a strange feeling that I must cling to each moment, savour and treasure it so that I could re-live it in the years to come. Was it a premonition? Did I really have it? Or was it all part of a fantastic dream?

Those summer days were full of excitement and pleasure; the sun shone perpetually; we spent the afternoon in the forest and hardly ever saw anyone. Each evening we supped together and I wore the blue robe which he told me he had bought on impulse.

'To give to one of your friends whom you brought to the lodge?' I asked.

'I never gave it to anyone. It hung in the cupboard waiting for you.'

'You speak as though you knew you were going to find me in the mist.'

He leaned across the table then and said: 'Doesn't everyone dream of the day the only one in the world will come?'

It was the sort of answer he could make so convincingly. He was indeed the perfect lover; he could capture the mood one needed at any particular time. At first he had been tender and gentle, almost as though he withheld a passion which he was aware might alarm me. My experiences in those three days and nights were many and varied and each was more revealing and exciting than what had gone before.

It was small wonder that I preferred to forget the realities of life. Just for a while I wanted to live in this enchantment.

Early on the morning of the fourth day after my marriage we were awakened at dawn by the sounds of horses' hoofs and voices below.

Maximilian went down and I lay listening, waiting for his return.

When he did come, I knew that something was wrong. I rose and he took my hands in his and kissed me.

'Bad news, Lenchen,' he said. 'I have to go to my father.'

'Is he ill?'

'He's in trouble. I'll have to leave in an hour at the latest.'

'Where?' I cried. 'Where shall you go?'

'Everything will be all right,' he said. 'There's not time for explanations now. I'll have to get ready.'

I ran round getting his things together; I put the blue velvet robe over my nightdress, for I had begun to use it as a dressing-gown, and went to call Hildegarde.

She was preparing coffee and the smell of it filled the kitchen.

Maximilian, dressed and ready for a journey, was clearly very unhappy. 'It's unbearable, Lenchen, to leave you like this . . . during our honeymoon.'

'Can't I come with you?'

He took my hands and gazed into my face. 'If only that were possible!'

'Why not?'

He just shook his head and held me close to him.

'Stay here, my darling, until I come back. It will be the very first moment that is possible.'

'I shall be so unhappy without you.'

'As I shall be without you. Oh Lenchen, there are no regrets . . . none at all. There never will be. I know it.'

Questions were on my lips. 'I know nothing. Where is your father? Where are you going? How shall I be able to write to you?' There was so much I wanted to know. But he was telling me how much he loved me, how important I was to him, how once we had met it was clear to him that the rest of our lives must be lived together.

He said, 'My darling, I'll be back with you very soon.'

'Where can I write you?'

'Don't,' he said. 'I'll come back. Just wait here for me to come. That's all, Lenchen.'

Then he was gone and I was alone.

How desolate the lodge seemed. It was quiet, almost eerie. I did not know how to pass the time. I went from room to room. There was the first one in which I had spent that uneasy night. I touched the door handle and thought of his standing outside, wanting me to have left it unlocked. Then I went to that other room in which were another woman's clothes and wondered what she was like; and I thought of all the women whom he had loved or professed to love. They would be beautiful, gay, experienced and clever, probably; I was wildly jealous, and deeply aware of my own inadequacies. But I was the one whom he had married.

I would have to learn a great deal. Countess Lokenberg! Could that grand-sounding title really be mine? I turned the ring on my finger and thought of the paper which I kept carefully in my bag which said that on the 20th July of the year 1860 Helena Trant had married Maximilian, Count Lokenberg, and the witnesses to their union were Ernst and Ilse Gleiberg.

There was the day to be lived through. How desolate the house was; how lonely was I!

I went into the forest. I walked down to the grove of pine

trees; I sat down under one of them and thought of all that had happened to me.

I wondered what the aunts would say when they heard that I had become the wife of a German count. What would the Grevilles say, and the Clees? It all seemed so fantastic when one considered those people. It was the sort of thing that could have happened only in an enchanted forest.

When I went back to the lodge to my surprise Ilse and Ernst had arrived.

'The Count called on us on his way,' they explained. 'He had suddenly made up his mind that he did not want you to stay at the lodge while he was away. He said it was too lonely. He wants you to come back to us. He'll come straight to us on his return.'

I was only too pleased. I put my things together and in the late afternoon we left. It was a relief in a way to get away from the lodge in which I had known such happiness; it would be easier to wait in the company of Ilse.

It was dark when we reached the house.

Ilse said I must be tired out and she insisted on my going straight to bed.

She came to me with the inevitable hot milk.

I drank it and was very quickly in a deep slumber.

And when I awoke of course the forest idyll was over and the nightmare had begun.

The Nightmare

1860-1

ONE

When I awoke it appeared to be late afternoon. For a moment I could not think where I was; then I remembered that Ilse and Ernst had brought me from the lodge yesterday. I glanced at the clock on the bedside table. It said a quarter to five.

I raised myself and a pain shot through my head; I could not think what had happened to me. The walls of the room seemed to close in on me, my head was swimming, and I felt sick.

I'm ill, I thought. Worse still, my mind seemed confused. Only yesterday I had awakened glowing with good health with Maximilian beside me. I must have caught some sickness.

I tried to get up but I could not stand. I sank back into bed. I called feebly: 'Ilse!'

She came in, looking very worried.

'Ilse. What's happened to me?'

She studied me intently. 'You don't remember . . .?'

'But I was all right when we came back here last evening.'

She bit her lips and looked uncertain.

'My dear,' she said, 'don't worry, we'll look after you.'

'But . . .'

'You are feeling ill. Try to rest. Try to go back to sleep.'

'Rest! How can I? What's happened? Why have you suddenly become so mysterious?'

'It's all right, Helena. You mustn't worry. You must try to sleep and forget . . .'

'Forget! What do you mean? Forget? Forget what?'

Ilse said: 'I'm going to call Ernst.'

As she went to the door, a terrible feeling of foreboding came to me. I thought: Maximilian is dead. Is that what they are trying to tell me?

Ernst came in, looking very grave. He took my wrist and felt my pulse as though he were a doctor. He looked significantly at Ilse.

'Are you trying to tell me that I've got some disease?' I demanded.

'You had better tell her, Ilse,' he said.

'You have been in bed since you came back on that night. It is six days since then.'

'I've been in bed for six days! Has anyone told Maximilian?'

Ilse put her hand on my forehead. 'Helena, you have been delirious. It was a terrible thing that happened to you. I blame myself. I should never have allowed you to go in the first place and then to lose you there.'

'I don't understand.'

'I think it would be better if she knew the truth,' said Ernst.

'On the Night of the Seventh Moon,' said Ilse, 'we went out. You remember that?'

'But of course.'

'You remember our being in the square and watching the revellers?'

I nodded.

'We were separated and I was frantic. I searched everywhere for you but I couldn't find you. I wandered round looking over the town for you and then I thought you might have come back to the house so I came back, but you weren't here. Ernst and I went out then looking for you. When we couldn't find you we were frantic with anxiety. We were going out again to search for you when you came back. Oh Helena, I shall never forget the sight of you. That we should have allowed it.'

'But when I came back you understood that I had been brought back by Maximilian.'

Ilse was looking at me shaking her head. 'You came back in a pitiable condition. Your clothes were torn; you were dazed with shock. You were delirious. You were incoherent, but we knew what had happened. It has happened to young girls before on such nights . . . but that it should have happened to you, Helena, in our charge . . . a carefully nurtured girl with little knowledge of the world – I could not face your aunts. Oh, Helena, Ernst and I have been beside ourselves with anxiety.'

I cried out: 'That's not true. Maximilian brought me back

64

here. The next day he called and asked me to marry him. We were married by the priest in the lodge.'

Ilse put a hand over her eyes and Ernst turned away as if overcome by emotion.

At length she sat on the bed and took my hand. 'My dearest child,' she said, 'you must not worry. We will look after you. As soon as you face the truth you will grow away from it. I will tell you bluntly what happened on the Night of the Seventh Moon. You were lost; you were taken into the forest, I believe, and there criminally assaulted. You found your way back to us, so shocked that you didn't seem to remember clearly what happened. We put you to bed and called in an old doctor friend of Ernst's to see you. His advice was that you should be given sedatives until your mind and body had recovered from the shock. He has been to see you every day . . .'

'Every day. But I have not been here!'

'Yes, Helena, you have been in this bed ever since that terrible night when you stumbled in.'

'It's not possible.'

'There!' Ilse patted my hand. 'It has been a nightmare but you're going to put it out of your mind. It is the only way.'

'But he came here,' I cried. 'You know he came here. We were married. You two were witnesses.' I felt for the ring he had put on my finger and turned cold with terror because it was not there. 'My ring,' I said. 'Where is my ring? Someone has taken it.'

'Ring, Helena? What ring is this?'

'My wedding-ring.'

Again those significant looks passed between them.

'Helena, I wish you'd try to rest,' said Ilse. 'We can talk about this tomorrow.'

'Tomorrow!' I cried. 'How can I rest until tomorrow?'

Ilse said: 'We must be clear because I can see that you will have no rest until you have rid your mind of this hallucination.'

'Hallucination . . .'

'Perhaps we were wrong, Ernst. But we thought it best. Dr Carlsberg is a brilliant doctor. He is in advance of his time. He thought that he must do all he could to blot out that shocking memory until your mind had had time to adjust itself.'

'Please, please, tell me what happened.'

'You came home in this terrible condition. Some brute had

found you in the crowd and somehow got you to the forest
. . . close to the *Altstadt*. There he assaulted you. Thank God
you found your way back to us.'

'I don't believe it. Surely I know what happened to me . . .
Maximilian Count Lokenberg brought me back. We were
married at the lodge. You know we were. You and Ernst were
witnesses.'

Ilse shook her head. She repeated slowly:

'When you came back . . . we got you to bed and we called
Dr Carlsberg. We knew what had happened. It was painfully
obvious. He gave you some medicine in order to calm you and
make you sleep. He said you had had a terrible shock and in
view of what we could tell him about your family he thought
it wiser to keep you under his care until you were well enough
to grasp what had happened. You have been under sedation
for the last few days but he did say that this was likely to
produce hallucinations. In fact that's what he hoped.'

It was the second time she had used that word. I was really
frightened now.

She added: 'Helena, you must believe me. Since you came
home on that terrible night you have not left this bed.'

'It's impossible.'

'It's true. Ernst will bear me out, and so will Dr Carlsberg
when you see him. You have been raving about someone
called Maximilian. But you have been here in your bed all the
time.'

'But . . . I am married.'

'My dear, try to rest now. Let's sort it out in the morning.'

I looked from one to the other. They watched me with
compassion. Ilse murmured: 'If only . . . We should never
have gone out without you, Ernst. If we had stayed indoors.
Oh God, if only we'd stayed indoors.'

I thought: I am dreaming. I shall wake up in a moment and
find this is a nightmare.

'Ernst,' said Ilse, 'perhaps you'd better ask Dr Carlsberg to
come and see Helena at once.'

I lay back on my pillow. I felt exhausted yet convinced
that at any moment I would wake up to reality.

I touched my finger believing that my ring would miracu-
lously be there. I had promised when Maximilian had put it
on that I would never take it off.

When I opened my eyes I was alone.

I felt a little better; the dazed feeling was beginning to pass.

Of course I had proof. It was strange about my ring. Could it have slipped off my finger? It had been rather loose and might be in the bed somewhere. But why should my cousin Ilse pretend that I had been in my bed for six days if I had not? Six days! It was impossible. One could not be unconscious for six days. Under sedation? Those words were ominous. And why should Ilse and Ernst, who had been so kind to me, tell such a story? What could be their motive? I had had nothing but kindness from them and they seemed as though they were trying to help me now.

Oh no, I could not believe what they were telling me. I would stand against that. They were saying that instead of the man I loved, the noble count, who to me was the very essence of romance and my own husband, was a man who took women and forced them to submit to him and then abandoned them. I would not believe that. And yet they said I had been here for six days.

It was impossible. Yet Ilse and Ernst said it was so. Why?

If I could find that ring I could prove to them . . . It *must* be in the bed. It *must* have slipped off my finger. But if it had, then my cousin was lying to me. Why?

I got out of bed. The room swam round but I was determined to ignore that. I searched the bed but I could not find the ring. Perhaps it had rolled on to the floor. I could find it nowhere. I was feeling faint but the great need to find this symbol of my marriage urged me on.

What could have happened to the ring?

I was glad to get back into bed because searching for it had exhausted me.

I lay there trying to fight off the terrible drowsiness which was persisting. But I could not and when I awoke it was to find Ilse at my bedside with a strange man.

He was middle-aged, bearded, with piercing blue eyes.

'This is Dr Carlsberg,' said Ilse.

I half raised myself. 'There is so much I want to know.'

He nodded. 'I understand.'

'You would like me to leave you,' said Ilse; and he nodded again.

When she had gone he sat beside the bed and said, 'How are you feeling?'

'That I am going mad,' I told him.

'You have been under the influence of certain sedatives,' he said.

'So they told me. But I do not believe . . .'

He smiled. 'Your dreams have seemed as real as life,' he said. 'That is what I expected. They were pleasant dreams.'

'I don't believe they were dreams. I can't.'

'But they were pleasant. They were just what you wanted to happen. Was that so?'

'I was very happy.'

He nodded. 'It was necessary. You were in a deplorable state when I was called in.'

'You mean on the Night of the Seventh Moon?'

'That's what it is called, yes. You had been out amongst the revellers, lost your cousin and that happened. It had shocked you perhaps even more than a young girl would normally be shocked in such circumstances. It was a mercy you were not murdered.'

I shivered. 'It was not like that at all. I was brought home.'

'That is the result we wanted to achieve. We wanted to blot out the memory as soon as it became unpleasant. It seems that it worked.'

'I can't believe it. I won't believe it.'

'You still find the need to shut out the evil. That's natural, but you can't be kept in that state any longer. It could be dangerous. Now you have to emerge and face the facts.'

'But I don't believe . . .'

He smiled. 'I think we have saved you from a mental collapse. Your condition when you came in on that night was terrifying. Your cousin was afraid for you. That was why she called me. But I think we have managed very successfully and if we can work towards the fact that this was an unfortunate accident – deeply to be regretted, of course – but which has to be accepted since it existed, then we shall get you back to perfect health. Others have suffered similarly; some have emerged and in time led normal lives; others have been scarred for ever. If you will try to put this thing out of your mind, in time it will leave only the smallest scar – perhaps none at all. That is why I took a rather drastic action on the Night of the Seventh Moon.'

In spite of the fact that he looked so calm and professional, I could not stop myself crying out in protest: 'It isn't possible. How could I imagine so much? It's fantastic. I don't believe it and I won't believe it. You are deluding me.'

He smiled at me sadly and gently. 'I'm going to prescribe something for you tonight,' he said soothingly, 'something gentle. You will sleep and tomorrow the dizziness will have passed. Tomorrow you will wake up fresh; then you will be able to see this more clearly.'

'I will never accept this fantastic story of yours,' I told him defiantly; but he only pressed my hand and went out.

Soon Ilse was back with a tray on which was a little boiled fish. In spite of my disturbed state I was able to eat the fish. I drank the milk she brought and before she came to take the tray away I was asleep.

Next morning I felt a little better as the doctor said I would. But that only meant that my terrible apprehension had grown. I could picture Maximilian clearly, the tawny lights in his eyes and hair, the deep timbre of his voice, the sound of his laughter. And yet my cousins and the doctor were telling me that he did not exist.

Ilse came in with a breakfast tray, her eyes anxious.

'How do you feel, Helena?'

'I'm no longer dizzy, but I'm very worried.'

'You still believe that it happened as you dreamed?'

'Yes I do. Of course I do.'

She patted my hand.

'Don't think about it. It will fall properly into place as you become more yourself.'

'Ilse, it *must* have happened.'

She shook her head. 'You have been here all the time.'

'If I could find my wedding-ring I could prove it. It must have slipped off my finger.'

'Dear Helena, there was no wedding-ring.'

I could not speak to her. She was so convinced and alas, convincing.

'Eat this,' she said. 'You'll feel stronger then. Dr Carlsberg had a good talk with us after he saw you last night. He has been as anxious as we have. He's a very clever doctor . . . much in advance of his times. His methods are not always liked. People are old-fashioned. He believes that the mind controls the body to a large extent and he has always tried to prove it. People hate new ideas. Ernst and I have always believed in him.'

'That's why you called him in to me.'

'Yes.'

'And you say he gave me this sedation which produced these dreams.'

'Yes, he believes that if some terrible misfortune overtakes

69

a person the mind and the body have a better chance of recovery if they can be brought to a state of euphoria even if for a short time only. That is briefly his theory.'

'So . . . when this happened, as you say it did, he gave me this drug or whatever it was to let me live in a false world for a few days. Is that what you mean? It sounds crazy.'

' "There are more things in heaven and earth than are dreamed of in your philosophy." Didn't Hamlet say that? It's true. Oh, Helena, if you could have seen yourself when you came back. Your eyes were wild and you were sobbing and talking incoherently. I was terrified. I remembered my cousin Luisa . . . that would be your mother's second cousin. She was locked by accident in the family vault and spent a night there. In the morning she was mad. She was rather like you – rather gay and adventurous – and I thought this could do to Helena what that did to Luisa and I was determined – and so was Ernst – that we would try anything to save you. So we thought of Dr Carlsberg and we called him in. Yours was just a case that he believed he could cure.'

'Ilse,' I said, 'everything that happened is so clear to me. I *was* married in the hunting lodge. I can remember such detail so vividly.'

'I know, the dreams produced in this way are like that. Dr Carlsberg was telling us. They have to be. You have to be torn from this tragedy . . . and this is the only way.'

'I won't believe it. I can't.'

'My dear, why should we, who wish only for your happiness, tell you this if it were not so?'

'I don't know. It's a terrible mystery, but I *know* I am the Countess Lokenberg.'

'How could you possibly be? There is no Count Lokenberg!'

'So . . . he made that up?'

'He didn't exist, Helena. He was created out of the euphoric state into which Dr Carlsberg had put you.'

'But I had met him before.'

I told her, as I was sure I had before, about our meeting in the mist, my visit to the hunting lodge; and how he had sent me back to the *Damenstift*. She behaved as though she were hearing it for the first time.

'That couldn't have been my euphoric dream, could it? I was not under Dr Carlsberg's sedation then.'

'That was the source of your dream. It was a romantic

adventure. Don't you see, what happened afterwards was based on that. He took you to the hunting lodge, planning to seduce you perhaps. After all, you agreed to go with him and he may have thought you were willing. Then he realized how young you were, a schoolgirl from the *Damenstift* . . .'

'He knew that from the beginning.'

'His better nature prevailed; besides, there was the servant there. You were brought home the next day none the worse for your adventure and mentally this had had a great effect upon you. Dr Carlsberg will be so interested when he hears of this. It will bear out his theory. Then came the Night of the Seventh Moon; we lost each other and you were accosted. The man was masked, you have told us. You believed that he was the one whom you had met on another occasion.'

'He was. He called me "Lenchen". It was the name he had called me that first time. No one else has ever called me that. There was no doubt who he was.'

'That could have come up in your mind afterwards. Or it might even have been the man. In any case on this second occasion his better nature did not prevail. I must tell Dr Carlsberg about this meeting in the mist. Or perhaps it would be better if you did.'

I cried: 'You are wrong. You are wrong about everything.'

She nodded. 'Perhaps it is better that for a while you do go on believing in your dreams.'

I did eat a little breakfast and as the physical sickness had passed I got up.

I kept thinking of how I had opened the door of that room below and found him, standing there. I could experience the tingling joy the sight of him had given me. 'We'll be married,' he had said. I had replied that people couldn't get married just like that. Here they could, he had assured me. Besides, he was a count and knew how to get things done.

I thought of riding to the hunting lodge and his impatience and the way he had held me against him and the thrills of excitement he communicated to me. I thought of the simple ceremony with the priest.

The marriage lines! Of course I had *them*. I had put them away carefully. They were in the top drawer of the dressing-table. I remembered putting them with the few pieces of jewellery I possessed, in the little sandalwood box which had been my mother's.

There was the box. I brought it out joyfully. I lifted the

lid. The jewellery was there, but no marriage lines.

I stared at it blankly. No ring. No marriage lines. No proof. It was beginning to look more and more as though they were right and my romance and my marriage were indeed something induced by the doctor's treatment to wipe out the terrible memory of the dreadful thing that had happened to me.

I don't know how I got through the day. When I looked at my face in the mirror I saw another person. My high cheekbones stood out more than ever; there were faint shadows under my eyes; but it was the despair which was so startling. The face which looked back at me was touched with a certain hopelessness and that was when I knew that I was beginning to believe them.

Dr Carlsberg came to see me during the morning. He was delighted, he said, that I was up. He wanted nothing put in the way of my improvement. He was sure that what had to be done now was face the truth.

He sat beside me; he wanted me to talk, to say anything that came into my mind. I explained to him what I had told Ilse, about the meeting in the mist and the night I had spent at the lodge. He did not attempt to persuade me that I had dreamed that.

'If it were possible,' he said, 'I should like to obliterate completely from your mind what happened on the Night of the Seventh Moon. That is not possible. The memory is not like a piece of writing in pencil which can be wiped out with an eraser. But it is over. No good can come by preserving the memory of it. So we must come as near to forgetting as possible. I am glad that you are here . . . away from your home. When you return to England – which I hope you will not think of doing for at least two months – you will go among people who have not heard what has happened. This will help you to push the affair right to the back of your mind. No one will be able to remind you because they do not know what has happened.'

I said, 'Dr Carlsberg, I can't believe you. I can't believe my cousins. Something in me tells me that I am married and that it all happened as I am sure it did.'

He smiled, rather pleased. 'You are still in need of that belief. Perhaps it is better for you to cling to it for a while. In due course you will feel strong enough to be without it and the truth will be more important to you than the crutch these dreams are at the moment offering you.'

'The time works out perfectly,' I said. 'The second day after the Night of the Seventh Moon we were married and on the morning of the fourth day news came to him that his father was in trouble, and he went. Then the next day I woke up in the room above. It's simply impossible that I was there all that time.'

'Yet that is what you will accept in time when you are strong enough to discard your crutch.'

'I can't believe I imagined *him*.'

'You have attached him to this adventurer you met in the mist. You have told me that your mother often recounted fairy stories and legends of the forest. You came here in a receptive mood; you half believed in the gods and heroes. You say you called him Siegfried. This made you an easy subject for this experiment. I am sorry that you were used in this way, but, believe me, it has probably saved your reason.'

'Why should I have thought of such a marriage?'

'Because you were no longer a virgin and you had thought, as a respectably brought-up girl, that this could not be the case without marriage. That's an easy conclusion. Your terror when you knew what was happening to you has to find its opposite so the dreams gave you this ecstatic union.'

'Why should I have thought him to be a count? I never thought of marrying a count.'

'He had seemed all-powerful – rich, a nobleman. That is easily explained.'

'But Lokenberg.'

'Well, we are in the Lokenwald. The name of the town is Lokenburg. Ah, I think I have it. There is a Count Lokenberg.'

My heart began to beat wildly. I cried: 'Then take me to him. I am sure he must be Maximilian. I know he was not lying to me.'

Dr Carlsberg rose; he led me out of the room and took me to a picture which was hanging on the wall. I had noticed it when I arrived but had not studied it particularly. It was a picture of a bearded man, more elderly than middle-aged, in uniform.

'It's the head of our ruling house,' he said, 'you will see his picture in many loyal households. Read the inscription.'

I read: 'Carl VII; Carl Frederic Ludwig Maximilian, Duke of Rochenstein and Dorrenig, Count of Lokenberg.'

'Carl Frederic Ludwig *Maximilian*,' I said dully. 'Duke of Rochenstein and Count of Lokenberg!'

'The Lokenberg title is one of Duke Carl's,' he said.

'Then why did he . . .'

'You had looked at the picture.'

'I had never looked at it closely.'

'You looked at it without realizing you did. The names became fixed in your memory without your suspecting it and in your dream you selected one of them – Maximilian – and attached it to one of the titles you had seen on the inscription.'

I put my hands over my eyes. But he was so clear to me. I could see his beloved face, with the passionate, arrogant eyes that gleamed for me.

I would not believe that I had imagined that. But they had the tangible evidence; for the first time there was a doubt in my mind.

That terrible day seemed interminable. I sat listlessly with my hands on my lap thinking of him. My ears were strained for the sound of horses' hoofs because I believed that I should hear them and that he would come into the house, his eyes alight with passion. 'What have they been trying to tell you, Lenchen?' he would demand, and turn on them in his fury; and they would cringe, as in the dream my cousins had appeared to – well, not exactly cringe, but they had been eager to placate him.

But this, according to them, had not been the case. They had never known each other. How could living people know a phantom? In the dream they had shown respect because that was what I expected them to do. None of it, according to them, had existed.

But it had. I could feel his arms about me. I could remember so many passionate and tender moments.

I knew what Ilse was thinking: 'Could I really believe that a count would suddenly decide to marry an unknown girl with such haste that the day after his decision a priest married them?'

Oh yes, they had reason on their side; and I had nothing but dreams. I could not produce my wedding-ring nor my marriage lines. If I had ever had them, where were they now?

Suddenly I thought: There's the hunting lodge. I must go back there. I would find Hildegarde and Hans, and they

74

would corroborate my story.

I was excited. If I could go back to the lodge Hildegarde would corroborate my story about the marriage. But if she did, that would mean that Cousin Ilse was lying, Ernst too, and the doctor. Why should they? What motive could they possibly have?

If I believed that, I must get away from them as soon as possible for they would be my enemies. They were trying to prove . . . what were they trying to prove?

Sometimes I thought: I'm going mad.

Were they trying to prove me mad? For what purpose? They were trying to save me, they said, from the mental collapse which I had been near when I came in, according to them, the victim of a savage attack in the forest.

Maximilian savage! Passionate he was and fierce at times but he loved me; for he had been tender; and he had said that desiring me as he did, he was determined that I should come to him willingly.

My thoughts were going round in circles. I must know the truth. I must try to be calm. I must face the facts. I must see the truth. Where was my ring? Where were my marriage lines? I could see them clearly now – the plain gold band, the writing on the paper. But they could not be found.

I must know the truth. I had lost six days from my life and I must know what had happened to me, on the Night of the Seventh Moon. Did I meet the one man whom I could love, did I marry him, did I live for three ecstatic days in his hunting lodge as his wife? Or was I attacked by a monster who robbed me temporarily of my sanity?

I must know the truth.

I would go to the lodge. I would see Hildegarde and Hans and if they told me that I had never been there except on that one night when he had brought me there in the mist, I would have to believe them. Then I would see him. And I would then know whether he was indeed my husband.

At the very earliest moment I must go back to the lodge.

Ilse consulted Dr Carlsberg and they all agreed that I must have my way.

'How should we find this lodge?' asked Ilse.

'It is not far from Liechtenkinn – some eight miles, I think. And you remember, Ilse, when you drove me over for my wedding . . .'

75

She looked at me blankly, sadly.

'Well, we'll try to find it,' she said.

Ernst drove the horses; Ilse and I sat side by side; she had taken my hand and pressed it.

'We shall find the lodge you stayed at that night when you were lost in the mist. It will help you if you see the servant whom you saw then.'

I was thinking of Hildegarde. If she told me that I had never been there but once, I should have to believe her. I was afraid and my fear was a sign that I was beginning to waver. When there was so much evidence how could one go on believing in what they were telling me was a dream?

Is it possible? I asked myself. Can such things be done? I kept thinking of Dr Carlsberg's calm, intelligent and kindly face. What point would there be in their trying to confuse me? Yet on the other hand what did I know of Maximilian? He had never really told me anything about his life. I had no idea even where he lived. The more I thought of everything that happened, the more flimsy it seemed.

I could not remember the road. On the first occasion we had taken it when in my dream – if dream it was – I had not noticed any landmarks. That had been my wedding-day. I had been thinking of him and wondering when he would come back and had not noticed the road then either.

Ernst had driven to Liechtenkinn and when we reached the town with its gable-roofed houses clustered round the *Pfarrkirche* we were not far from the *Damenstift*.

I looked at the convent with some emotion, but it was not my schooldays that I remembered but that morning when Hildegarde had driven me back from the hunting lodge and how desolate I had been then because I feared I would never see him again. I was a hundred times more so now; but my spirits were rising. When we found the lodge I would see Hildegarde. She would tell them that I had stayed there three days and nights as Maximilian's bride. But what of Ilse and Ernst? They could surely not be suffering from delusions?

We must find the lodge. I must speak to Hildegarde. And if she said that I had never been there . . .

I felt cold at the thought. Then, I reasoned, I will have to accept what they tell me.

But not yet. I would find the lodge and insist on Hildegarde's corroborating my story.

'Now,' said Ernst, 'we have to find the way from here. You

say it was some eight miles from the *Damenstift.*'

'Yes. I'm sure of that.'

'But in what direction?'

I pointed towards the south. 'I am sure that is the way I remember driving up to the *Damenstift* with Hildegarde from there.'

Ernst took the road, which was straight for some miles as I remembered it. We came to a fork and he hesitated.

'It's a wild goose chase,' he said.

'No,' said Ilse, 'we must find the lodge. It's the only thing that will satisfy Helena.'

I was sure it was the left-hand fork. I seemed to remember the grey farmhouse down the road. We went on.

This was the road Schwester Maria had taken on that fateful afternoon. We climbed and soon were in the pine forest. Here was the very spot where we had picnicked. There Schwester Maria had sat under the tree to doze. And I wandered off into a dream that had become a nightmare.

'Now the lodge you visited on that night could not be very far from here,' said Ernst.

Unfortunately I could not direct him. We took one turning and drove on for a while. We saw a man gathering wood. Ernst pulled up and asked him if he knew of a hunting lodge nearby.

The man paused, set down his bundle and scratched his head.

Yes, there was a lodge. A fine lodge, belonged to a lord or a count or some nobleman.

My spirits began to rise; my heart was beating fast.

Oh God, I prayed. Let this be it. Let me find Hildegarde. Let me come out of this nightmare.

Yes, he could tell us. If we were to go straight on to the end of the road, then take the path that climbed a bit and then a sharp veer to the left, there we would find a hunting lodge.

'They come here in the season,' he said. 'Gentlemen and ladies too. There's boar in the forest. Sometimes it's stags.'

Ernst thanked him and we drove on in silence. I felt it took a long time to climb and I was impatient because we were forced to slacken our pace. And then we reached the top of the hill and I cried out in delight for there was the grove of pine trees that I remembered. The lodge was just beyond them.

Ernst drove on; we were in the grove now because the road ran through them – just as I remembered. There were the two stone posts, beyond them were the grey walls which I knew so well.

I cried out in joy.

'We're here.'

I wanted to leap out of the carriage but Ilse restrained me. 'Be careful, Helena,' she said. 'You're not strong yet.'

Ernst fixed the reins to the post and we alighted.

I ran forward. There was a strange silence everywhere. I noticed that the stables had disappeared. They should have been to the left of the house. It was from them that Hans had come out to take our horses when we had been riding. I could not understand. It seemed different.

Everything was different. This was the lodge; those were the stone posts. Those were the walls. There was no door. I could see through into emptiness.

I was looking at the shell of the hunting lodge where until that moment I had been certain that I had been married to Maximilian.

Ilse was beside me, her arm slipped through mine, her eyes compassionate.

'Oh, Helena,' she said, 'come away.'

But I wouldn't. I ran through that gap where the door had been. I stood inside those blackened walls. There was nothing there – nothing of the room where we had dined; the bedroom we had shared, my little room where I had spent the first night, the blue room which contained another woman's clothes, the hall with its stuffed heads of animals and weapons hanging on the wall – Hildegarde and Hans, all gone.

'This is the place,' I cried.

'Helena, my poor child,' said Ilse.

'But what has happened to it?' I demanded.

'It looks as though it has been burned out at some time. Come away now. Come home. You have had enough.'

I didn't want to go. I wanted to stand there in that ruin and think of it all. How could I remember a dream so vividly? It wasn't possible. I could not bear my misery, because every minute they were convincing me that what had happened had indeed been unreal.

Ilse led me back to the carriage.

We drove home in silence. There was nothing more I could

think of. The evidence against the fact that I had married was overwhelming.

Back at the house I sank into a deep depression. Ilse tried to interest me in embroidery and cooking. I was listless. Sometimes I would let myself dream that Maximilian came back for me; but I was afraid to indulge in too many dreams for fear I should again stray into a dangerous realm of fancy.

Not only was I desolate and melancholy while my heart called out for my husband, but I was afraid of myself. There was a great deal of talk about the powers of suggestion and hypnotism. The fame of the Fox sisters had spread from America to England some ten years ago; they believed that it was possible to communicate with the dead; and although the world was full of sceptics many people were convinced that it was becoming increasingly easier to accept what some time ago would have appeared to be completely incredible, and that certain people were possessed of knowledge and the power to reveal undreamed of secrets. Dr Carlsberg was clearly experimenting with new forms of treatment; and because of my circumstances I was a likely subject for his tests.

I no longer felt that I was uncomplicated Helena Trant. I had had, according to the evidence, a frightening experience, which many believed was the worst which could befall an innocent young girl, or I had enjoyed the exultation which the perfect union between two people can bring. I was not sure which. If they were right, I had lost six days of my life and those were the days during which I had known a state of existence which I could never hope to experience again; I had loved with a deep abiding passion a man whom they told me was a phantom. I could never love again in that way. I had therefore suffered an irreparable loss.

I felt I was a stranger to myself. I often looked searchingly in the mirror and felt I did not know the face which was reflected there. How could I help it when I was not at all sure whether I myself was not in the plot to blot out the fearful memory of a terrifying experience by replacing it with a dream of perfection?

Sometimes I awoke in the night startled because I had dreamed that I was being pursued through the forest by a monster who had disguised himself as Maximilian. I thought in that waking moment – Was that how it happened? We had gone into the forest. There was a moment when he had hesitated. Was that the moment when I started to dream?

I was afraid. I watched everything that I did spontaneously. I had a fear that I was becoming unbalanced. Luisa, my mother's cousin – of whom my mother had never spoken – had gone mad. I was frightened.

I clung to Ilse. There was something so kind and compassionate about her. The manner in which she used to take care of me, to take my mind off my tragedy, was touching. I could see so clearly what she was trying to do.

The days began to pass; I was listless, unless at any time I heard the sound of horses' hoofs; then I would start up expectantly, for I could not rid myself of the hope that one day Maximilian would come to claim me.

Dr Carlsberg came every day to visit me. His care for me was wonderful.

I think it must have been about a week after I awoke to the nightmare that Ilse told me they would have to leave Lokenburg. Ernst's holiday had come to an end. He must return to Denkendorf. He had his work there.

I used to listen idly to their conversation. There had been some plot to replace Duke Carl by his brother Ludwig. They chattered excitedly about it and were clearly delighted that it had gone against Ludwig. They were very loyal to the Duke.

So shortly after that we said goodbye to Dr Carlsberg, who assured me that I would gradually regain my old spirits if I could stop brooding on what had happened and learn to accept it as a regrettable accident. No good could be done by brooding. In fact only harm could come of it.

I said to Ilse as we left, 'What if Maximilian should come here to look for me? He said he would come to the lodge but he wanted me to go to you . . . so he will know . . .'

I stopped. She looked so sad.

Then she said: 'We have taken the house before. The owner knows we come from Denkendorf. If any people come looking for us they could be told where we had gone.'

I was sorry to hurt her by this proof that I believed she had lied to me, but she understood.

She knew that I still had to cling to the dream.

Denkendorf was like so many of the little towns I had seen in this part of the world. The centre of the town had its shops under the arcades; the pavements were cobbled and the aspect medieval; because this was a spa and people came to take the waters there were several inns; and the shops were well stocked, the streets more lively than those of Lokenburg. We were near a river and it was possible to walk out to its bank and see there, perched on the opposite bank, the ruin of a castle in pale silver-grey stone.

I realized when we arrived there that I had grown a little away from my nightmare; I had begun to accept, which I had believed I never could. It was possible, I knew, for people to be drugged to such an extent that they missed days of their lives. It was possible to evoke dreams that seem real. How could I doubt that good kind Ilse was speaking the truth? I should have known that what I had imagined was too wildly and fantastically wonderful to be true.

We had only just settled in to Denkendorf when Ernst left us to go to Rochenburg, the capital city of the Duchy of Rochenstein. This crisis in the affairs of the country meant that in spite of his indifferent health he was recalled to his post in the government, so Ilse and I were alone together.

We grew very close. She would not let me go out without her and each morning we would go into the market to shop. Sometimes she introduced me as her English cousin and I would join in the conversation which ensued somewhat automatically. How did I like the country? How long was I going to stay with my cousin? To these I always replied that I found the country interesting and that I was not sure how long I would stay. I could see they thought me a little dull, perhaps strange. When I thought of what I should have been like a few weeks ago I was appalled. I would never again be that carefree impulsive girl who had attracted Maximilian . . . But how could she have captivated a phantom? In the beginning, I reasoned with myself, he was attracted by me. There was no harm in thinking of that incident which had begun in the mist. That had actually happened.

I wrote to the aunts and in time received letters from them. By that time I had been in Denkendorf for six weeks. Each day was much the same; Ernst paid occasional visits; I learned to embroider and do tapestry work – very fine petit-point – on which we could only work by day. In the evenings we did ordinary sewing or embroidery. I read a great many books on German history and I was particularly interested in the ancestors of Carl, Duke of Rochenstein. It was astonishing how quickly the time was passing.

Aunt Caroline wrote of the affairs which concerned her;

how much strawberry jam she had put down; how many jars of blackcurrant jelly; she implied that she expected me soon to be coming home. She could not understand why I had wanted to go gadding about in the first place. Aunt Matilda wrote of the strange wheezing Aunt Caroline had developed. She got quite breathless; and there was mention of Mr Clees's solitary kidney which had to do the work of two; and Amelia Clees was looking a little pale; Aunt Matilda hoped she was not going into a decline as, she had gathered, her mother had. There was a great deal about Mr Clees in Aunt Matilda's letter. It seemed that a man who had had a wife in a decline and himself possessed only one kidney was very attractive. I heard from Mrs Greville too. They missed me and wondered when I planned to come back. She and Mr Greville might manage a trip out so that I could come back with them. Anthony had said only the other day that it didn't seem the same without me there.

I re-read the letters. That life all seemed so far away. The thought of going back there and trying to pretend that everything was the same as it always had been did not attract me.

Ilse came in suddenly. She had a way of gliding about as though not to disturb me.

'What's the matter, Helena?' she asked. 'You are looking . . . lost.'

'Letters from home,' I explained. 'I was thinking of going back there.'

'You're not ready yet, are you?'

'I don't think I could face them.'

'No, not just yet. It'll change. But there is nothing to worry about. You must stay here with us until you are ready to go.'

'Dear Ilse,' I said, 'what should I have done without you?'

She turned away to hide her emotion. She always liked to keep her feelings in check.

Several more weeks passed. Perhaps I was becoming reconciled. But I seemed to grow more listless; it was as though I had changed my personality. I smiled rarely, and remembering the old days when I had been so often unable to restrain my laughter, I was astonished. And yet I suppose what I had endured – whichever was the truth – would most certainly change one.

As time passed everything seemed to point to the fact that those six days had been spent in my bed. I continued to hope that Maximilian would come to me. I used to look at faces in the streets of the little town and every time I saw a tall man in the distance my heart would leap with hope. Each passing day meant that a little of my hope must fade. If there had really been a marriage, where was my husband? Surely he would have come to claim me?

I suppose when I had seen that shell where the lodge had been I had begun to accept the truth of what Ilse, Ernst and Dr Carlsberg had told me. But I felt as though a part of me had died. I knew I should never be the same insouciant girl I had been before.

Ilse appeared to have no friends in the place so there was no visiting. She explained that she and Ernst had only recently come to live in Denkendorf and the people being rather formal would take some time before they accepted them.

I tried to interest myself in the vegetables she bought in the market or the skeins of silk we chose for our embroidery; but I simply did not care whether we ate carrots or onions, or chose purple or azure-blue for the flowers we were working.

I went about my days mechanically. I was once more in limbo, waiting . . . I was not sure for what.

In the shops we visited people often mentioned Count Ludwig's attempted *coup*. They all seemed delighted that it had failed. I often saw pictures similar to that which Dr Carlsberg had pointed out in the hall of the house in Lokenburg. There was the same face and the inscription, Carl Ludwig *Maximilian*, Seventh Duke of Rochenstein and Dorrenig, *Count of Lokenberg*.

Maximilian, Count of Lokenberg. Those were the words on which my eyes lingered.

It is a strange feeling to know that a part of your life is wrapped in mystery; and that you have been unconscious of what happened to you during that period. You feel apart from your fellow human beings. You are both a stranger among them and to yourself.

I tried to explain this to Ilse, for I was talking to her very freely and intimately now; she said she understood and she knew that in time I would grow away from this.

'Never hesitate to talk to me,' she said, 'that is, if you wish to do so. The last thing I want to do is to force confidence, but I want you to know that I am here if you should need me.'

'I shall have to think about going home soon,' I told her.

'Not yet,' she begged. 'I want to wait until you are quite recovered before you leave us.'

'Quite recovered. I don't think I shall ever be that.'

'You think so now because it is so close . . . later you will see.'

Oh yes, she comforted me a great deal.

Yet each day I awoke I said to myself: I must go home. It was only to be a short visit and it was three months since I had left England.

One morning I woke up feeling ill. I was frightened because I remembered waking in my bed and learning that what I believed had happened had been only in my imagination.

I got out of bed and felt dizzy.

I sat on the edge of the bed wondering whether I had been unconscious for another six days. This time there were no pleasant memories.

I was still sitting there when there was a knock on the door and Ilse looked in.

'Are you all right, Helena?' she asked anxiously.

'Yes, I think so. I just felt a little dizzy.'

'Do you think I should get the doctor?'

'No . . . no. It's passing. You are not going to tell me that I have been in bed for days and didn't go to the town with you yesterday?'

She shook her head. 'No. No. Dr Carlsberg has not been treating you since you have been here. But I'm sorry you feel dizzy. I wonder whether you ought to see a doctor.'

'No, no,' I insisted. 'It is already passing.'

She looked at me intently, and I said I would get up.

We went into the town and it was just such another day as those which had preceded it.

It suddenly occurred to me that if I went home I would be able to think more clearly. I would be able to assess my adventure against the reality of home. Here I still sensed the bewilderment. The very cobbled streets and gabled shops with their creaking signs were like the settings of the old fairy stories. I could not get out of my mind the belief that here, the home of trolls, hobgoblins and the ancient gods, nothing was too fantastic to happen. At home, among the towers and spires of Oxford where I might listen to the prosaic talk of the aunts and enjoy the friendly atmosphere of the Gre-

villes' home, I would reason clearly. I would begin to understand what had happened to me.

One morning I said to Ilse: 'I think I must get ready to go
home.'

She looked at me anxiously. 'Do you really want to?'

I hesitated. 'I think it would be better to.'

'This decision surely means that you are beginning to accept
what has happened. You are getting over the shock.'

'Perhaps. I know that I have to come out of the strange
state into which I have fallen. I've got to go on living. I
would do it best where I belong.'

She touched my hand gently. 'My dear child, you are welcome to stay here as long as you wish. You know that. But
I feel that you are right. In Oxford resuming your everyday
life you will come to terms with what has happened to you.
You will realize that it is not the first time a young girl has
been so cruelly awakened to the cruder aspects of life.'

'It is perhaps the first time a girl has believed herself to
have been married and discovered that she has lost six days of
her life.'

'Of that I am not sure. But I am firmly of the opinion what
Dr Carlsberg did was right and the only thing to do in the
circumstances. He had blotted out an evil thing and replaced
it by something beautiful.'

'But, according to you all, the evil was the truth and the
beauty a dream.'

'Alas . . . but the memory of evil has been obliterated.
While you have suffered, my dear, you have the consolation
of knowing that you have been of great help to Dr Carlsberg.
You have proved his experiment to be so successful that you
cannot even remember the brutality you suffered and you still
persist in believing the dream. It is only the force of tangible
evidence against it that has made you accept it; and I believe
that deep in your heart you still believe that you married this
man.'

How well she had summed up my feelings.

'So I have been a kind of guinea-pig in Dr Carlsberg's re-
searches.'

'Only because the circumstances were as helpful to you as
they were to him. But tell me, Helena, do you still believe in
this marriage?'

'I know everything is against it, but it is clear in my mind as
it ever was. And I believe it always will be.'

She nodded. 'And I believe that is what Dr Carlsberg would wish.' She paused for a moment. 'Helena, I want you to know that as soon as you wish to go I shall take you back. Will you see Dr Carlsberg once more? I should like you to see him before you go.'

I hesitated. I felt a sudden revulsion for the man which I had not felt before. It was wrong. He had been kind to me; he had, according to himself, Ilse and Ernst, saved my reason. Yet I did not want to see him again. I wondered whether if I had faced the truth in the first place I might not have been better able to cope with the situation. Bluntly, I had been assaulted in the most cruel and brutal way. If I had come back that night knowing this, how should I have reacted? I was not sure. But there was one thing of which I was certain. The man whom I had met on the Night of the Seventh Moon was the same one who had found me in the mist. If he had been the cruel ravisher of that night would he have hesitated when I was in his lodge? I thought of the door handle slowly turning. The door was bolted. But would that have been any real deterrent to a man determined to have his way?

If they had let me face the truth I believed I would have done so with courage. I could not believe I had nearly lost my reason. I had been frivolous and impulsive, but never hysterical. How could I be sure what I would have been like suffering under such an outrage? We do not really know ourselves and it is only when we face a crisis that unexpected facets of our characters are betrayed.

Ilse went on: 'I should feel so relieved if he could see you as an ordinary physician this time. I know that he greatly wishes it and I should like to have his advice about your going home.'

I said I would see him, and she wrote to him that day. His reply came. He would be with us in two days' time.

I had had a few more dizzy spells on rising and I was wondering if I was going to be ill. Ilse asked how I was solicitously every morning; she seemed very concerned.

'I think I ought to get home soon,' I said. 'Everything will be different then.'

I was thinking that if Maximilian had really married me he would have come to claim me by now. Each passing day was confirmation that the marriage had never taken place.

If I could get away I would perhaps forget. Home seemed so remote from all that happened; so presumably when I was home, this would be remote.

I could start again.

I wrote to Aunt Caroline and Mrs Greville to tell them I should be coming home shortly. The evenings I had spent at the Grevilles' house had been the most enjoyable of that period. I remembered how amused I had been because of their admiration for Anthony and how Anthony talking above our heads had a pleasant way of assuming that we understood. It was all so cosy. The last word I could apply to this place; and I was beginning to see the virtues of that cosiness from which I had wanted to escape.

Dr Carlsberg came as arranged. I was in the little garden when he arrived and did not hear him come. He must have been with Ilse for a quarter of an hour when I walked into the house and found him there.

When he saw me his face lit up with pleasure. He rose and took both my hands in his.

'How are you?' he asked.

When I told him that I felt I was getting back to normal he smiled with pleasure and gratification. Ilse left us together and he wanted to know every detail of what had happened. What dreams had I had? Had I suffered from nightmares? Every little item seemed of the utmost importance to him.

Then he asked about my physical health and I told him that I often felt unwell on rising.

He said he would like to examine me. Would I agree?

I did.

I shall never forget what followed. It was one of the most dramatic moments in my life.

'I have to tell you that you are to have a child,' he said.

TWO

I was deeply moved by the manner in which Ilse received the news. She was stricken with horror and dismay.

'Oh God!' she cried. 'This is terrible.'

I found myself comforting her, for to tell the truth I could only feel exultation. I was to have a child – his child. I was not mad. He *had* existed. From the moment I realized this I started to emerge from the depth of my unhappiness.

My own child! I did not think of the difficulties which must inevitably lie ahead simply because I could see nothing beyond the wonder of having our child.

I knew then that deep in my heart I must always believe that Maximilian had loved me; I could not associate him with a criminal in the forest; the prospect of bearing his child could do nothing but fill me with a fierce exhilaration.

When the doctor had gone Ilse said to me: 'Helena, do you realize what this means?'

'Yes, I do.' I could not help it if my delight was obvious. I possessed what my father had called a mercurial temperament. 'Up and down,' said my mother. 'Irresponsible,' Aunt Caroline called it. And I was sure Ilse thought me odd and illogical. I had been sunk in depression when I had had every chance of putting an ugly incident behind me and starting a new life; and now that would be impossible because there would be a living reminder. I was rejoicing. I couldn't help it. The wonder of having a child subdued all else.

'This is shattering,' said Ilse at length. 'That this should have happened as well as everything else . . .! What can we do now? You can't go back to England. Helena, have you thought of what this is going to mean?'

But all I could think was: I am going to have a child.

'We must be practical,' she warned me. 'Can you go back to your aunts and tell them that you are going to have a child? What will they say? You would be disgraced. They might not even receive you. If I wrote to them and told them what had happened . . . No, they would never understand. You will have to stay here until the child is born. It's the only way. Yes, we shall have to arrange that.'

I had to confess I had not given much consideration to the months between – only the arrival of the child. I should like a boy but I would not think about that until it came. If it were a girl I should not wish her to think that I was not completely delighted with her.

But I was right. I must try to be practical. What was I going to do? How was I going to keep a child, educate it, bring it up in the best possible way? It would have no father. And what should I do while I waited for the child to be born?

The first exultation had passed.

Ilse seemed to have come to a decision. 'You must stay

with us, Helena, and I shall look after you. I shall never forgive myself for going out that night without Ernst and then losing you in the crowd. Yes, we will arrange something. You'll be all right. You can trust us.'

She seemed to have grown calmer; the first horror had passed and characteristically she was making plans.

The first feeling of triumphant joy had passed. I had had a glimpse of how I should have felt if I had been truly married to Maximilian and he had been with me so that we could have shared the joy of prospective parenthood. I asked myself if there was not something I could do to find him. He was the father of my child. Yet what could I do? If I talked this over with Ilse I would see that sad, patient look come into her face. I had given up trying to make her understand that no matter what evidence they showed me I could never believe that I had dreamed my life with Maximilian. I began to make wild plans. I would travel the country looking for him. I would call at every house seeking information concerning him. Now that I was going to have a child I *must* find him.

I said to Ilse: 'Could I put an advertisement in the newspapers? Could I ask him to come back to me?'

Ilse looked horrified: 'Do you believe that a man who did *that* would answer such an advertisement?'

'I was thinking . . .' I began; and saw how hopeless it was to talk to Ilse, for she insisted that the Maximilian I had known had never existed.

She was patient with me. 'Suppose you mentioned Count Lokenberg. You would be deemed mad. There could even be trouble.'

So whichever way I looked I could do nothing.

I knew that she was right about my not going home. The aunts would be horrified at the prospect of sheltering an unmarried pregnant niece. I could imagine the scandal. No one would believe the story of the attack in the forest any more than they would believe that other version of my unusual marriage.

I needed Ilse's kindnesses and ingenuity to help me in my difficult situation, and I knew I could rely on her. She was very soon her calm and practical self.

'You will certainly have to stay here until after the child is born. Then we shall have to decide from there.'

'I have a little money, but it is not enough to keep us and

educate the child.'

'We'll think about that later,' she said.

Ernst came back. His health seemed much better and when he heard the news he shared Ilse's horror and compassion. They were both very gentle with me and very anxious because they assumed guilt for what had happened.

He and Ilse, I know, discussed my affairs continuously, but for me the state of euphoria persisted and every so often I would forget my circumstances and think solely of the delight of having a child. Sometimes I wondered whether Dr Carlsberg had given them something to put into my food to make me happy. I had a terrible thought once that he might have made me imagine I was going to have a child. I didn't think this was so as Ilse and Ernst seemed to think it such a tragedy. But once one has been the subject of such an experiment one becomes suspicious.

We all decided that for the time being we would not tell the aunts, and during the next months would think very carefully what we should do.

In the meantime an excuse must be made to keep me with my cousin. Ilse took that into her own hands and wrote to Aunt Caroline to tell her that I was staying on because Ernst had taken a turn for the worse and she needed my help.

'A little white lie,' she said with a grimace.

So I stayed on in Denkendorf and the weeks began to slip by. I no longer felt ill when I arose; and I thought constantly of the baby. I bought material and started making a layette. I would sit for hours stitching and thinking.

Dr Carlsberg came to me. He said he was going to pass me over to Dr Kleine, a doctor friend of his who had a little nursing home in Klarengen, not very far away, and soon he would drive me over and introduce me to his colleague. There, in Dr Kleine's clinic, I should have the child.

I wondered about the cost but they wouldn't discuss it and in my present state I was content to let things go.

Ilse said one day: 'When the child is born you can stay with us for a while and perhaps later on you could take a post teaching English in one of our schools. It might just be possible to have the child with you.'

'Do you think there would be such a post?'

'Dr Carlsberg might be able to help. He and his colleagues know a great deal that is going on. They would find out and if there was anything I am sure they would be only too glad to help.'

'You are so good to me, all of you,' I cried gratefully.

'We feel responsible,' replied Ilse. 'Ernst and I will never forget that not only did this happen to you in our country but when you were under our care.'

I was content to allow them to plan for me, which was unlike myself because I had always been so independent. It certainly seemed as though the Seventh Moon had cast a spell upon me and all my actions had become unpredictable.

So I allowed Ilse to cosset me. I was almost unaware of what went on. I stitched at my little garments and delightedly folded them when they were done and laid them away in the drawer I had prepared for them. White, blue and pink. Blue for a boy, they said. So I would have both pink and blue so that I should not have planned for either sex. I knitted and sewed and read. The summer passed and the autumn was with us.

Aunt Caroline wrote that she was surprised that I should enjoy living with foreigners in some outlandish place rather than in my own home but Aunt Matilda, realizing that my cousin Ernst had a 'heart' and hearts being funny things, quite understood that Ilse should want me at hand to help.

Mrs Greville wrote. She had heard that I was staying on to help my cousin nurse her husband. She thought it would be a good experience for me, but she and her husband as well as Anthony were looking forward to my return.

They all seemed so far away in the world of reality where life pursued an even tenor. The fantastic adventures of the last months had sent me worlds away from them.

One day Ilse said: 'Dr Carlsberg has news. He says that the nuns at your old *Damenstift* would take you in to teach English to the pupils. You could have the child with you.'

'You do so much for me,' I said emotionally.

'It's our duty,' replied Ilse solemnly. 'In any case we are so fond of you. We must think of the future, you know.'

I was growing obviously larger. I could feel the movement of my child and whenever I did my heart leaped with joy. How could this be so, I asked myself, if this life within me was the result of an encounter with a savage brute in the forest? I would never stop believing in those ecstatic days –

no matter what evidence they brought forward to try to convince me that they had never existed.

Ilse introduced me to people in the town when it was necessary as Mrs Trant, who had recently suffered a bereavement in the loss of her husband and who was shortly to bear his posthumous child. I was seen as a tragic figure and people were very kind to me.

When I went into the market they called to me to ask how I was; I would stay and chat with them and the women would tell me about their childbearing, the men about their vigils during their wives' ordeals.

Dr Carlsberg came alone one day and drove me into the town where his friend had his nursing home. He thought it was better for me to see the doctor there at this stage.

I did so and Dr Kleine told me that at the beginning of April I should come into his nursing home to be prepared for the birth of the child. He called me Mrs Trant and had evidently been told the story about my recent bereavement.

As we drove away Dr Carlsberg said: 'You can rely on Dr Kleine. He's the best man in his line in these parts.'

'I'm wondering if I shall be able to pay.'

'We are taking care of that,' he said.

'I can't accept . . .'

'It's easy to give,' he said ruefully. 'So difficult to receive. But it is you who must give us the satisfaction of helping you out of this situation. I know your cousin is filled with self-reproach. She and her husband can only regain their peace of mind if they do everything possible for you. As for me, you have helped me in my work tremendously. You have given me an opportunity to prove a theory. I can't thank you enough. Please tell me – have you now come to accept the truth?'

I hesitated and he said: 'I see that you cannot give up your belief in the dream.'

'I lived it,' I said. 'Of the other . . . I remember nothing.'

He nodded. 'It is even better than I thought. And now that you are to have the child you believe that child is the fruit of your marriage, and that is the reason why you feel ready to welcome it. Had you thought . . . but no matter. This is good. Anything we can do for you we shall be delighted to do, rest assured of that.'

Sometimes, looking back, I ask myself: Why did you accept this and that? Why did you not enquire more closely into these strange things that happened to you? I suppose the answer is: I was very young and I appeared to have stepped into a world where strange things seemed the natural course of events.

I was brought down to reality one day in February. I was visiting Dr Kleine once every three weeks and Ilse used to drive me into Klarengen; she would put the trap in an inn yard and shop while I went to Dr Kleine's nursing home.

He was satisfied with my progress and he did pay very special attention to me on Dr Carlberg's instruction. I had had a shock, Dr Carlsberg had told him – Dr Kleine believed this to be the death of my husband – and in the circumstances might have a difficult confinement.

On this February day the sun was brilliant and there was a frost in the air. As I came out of the nursing home a voice behind me startled me as it took me right back to Oxford.

'If it isn't Helena Trant!'

I turned and there were the Misses Elkington who ran a little tea-shop near the Castle Mound, which was only open during the summer months. They sold tea and coffee with home-made cakes, besides egg-cosies, tea-cosies and embroidered mats which they made themselves. I had never liked them. They were constantly apologizing for selling their wares and making sure that everyone knew it was something they were not used to as they had come down in the world, their father having been a General.

'Oh, it's Miss Elkington and Miss Rose,' I said.

'Well, fancy meeting you here of all places.'

Their little eyes scrutinized me. They must have seen me come out of Dr Kleine's nursing home and would be wondering why. But not for long. Although I wore a loose coat my condition could not but be perfectly obvious.

'And what are you doing here, Helena?' Miss Elkington the elder was roguishly censorious.

'I'm staying with my cousin.'

'Oh yes, of course, you've been away some months.'

'I dare say I shall soon be back.'

'Well, well. It is a small world. So you are really staying here?'

'Not exactly. I've come in with my cousin. I'm joining her now.'

'I'm so glad we saw you,' said Miss Elkington.

'So nice to see people from home,' added her sister.

'I must hurry. My cousin is waiting . . .'

I was relieved to get away from them.

I looked at my reflection in a shop window. I didn't think there could be much doubt of my condition.

The weeks had passed and my time was getting near. Ilse fussed over me; often I would find her seated in silence with a worried frown on her forehead and I knew she was concerned for me.

She had consulted both Doctors Carlsberg and Kleine and they had decided that I should go into Dr Kleine's nursing home a week or so before my child was expected. As for myself, I continued in my state of placid euphoria. I could think of nothing but my child.

'You will have to wait until the baby is about a year old before you go to the *Damenstift* to teach English,' said Ilse. 'Dr Carlsberg has not mentioned your name, but on his recommendation no obstacles would be put in the way of your going there.'

How strange that would be! I thought. I remembered the old days (good heavens! It was not two years ago) when I had been a pupil – Helena Trant who had always been in trouble through her irrepressible spirits and love of adventure. How strange that I might go back, a mother.

I pictured Schwester Maria taking sly peeps at the baby and trying to spoil it; and Schwester Gudrun saying: 'Where Helena Trant was, there was always trouble.'

Then sometimes I would think of those three days and my love was as strong as ever, making the longing to see Maximilian unbearable. Only the thought of our child could comfort me and I eagerly waited for the time when I should hold it in my arms.

On a bright April day Ilse drove me to the nursing home. I was taken to a private room, apart from the other patients. Dr Carlsberg had asked that this should be so in view of the circumstances.

It was a pleasant room, everything gleaming white, yet seeming clinical in its cleanliness. There was a window from which I could look down on a lawn, which was very neatly bordered by flower-beds.

Dr Kleine introduced me to his wife, who expressed concern for my comfort. I asked how many other mothers were in the nursing home and I was told that there were several.

94

They were constantly coming and going.

On the first day I looked through my window and saw five or six women walking about the lawn – all in various stages of pregnancy. They were chatting together and two of them sat side by side on one of the wooden benches near the flowerbeds; one was knitting, the other crocheting. They were joined by another woman who took out her sewing; and they talked animatedly together.

I was sorry they had decided to isolate me. I wanted to be down there with those other women.

I had been told that I could use the Kleines' little garden to get some fresh air, but this was not the one where the women met. I went down to the Kleines' garden and sat for a while on a garden seat but there was no one there and I wanted to talk about babies, to compare knitting.

While I was in the garden Frau Kleine came out to me and I told her I had seen another garden from my room. 'There's a lawn and there were several expectant mothers there. I should like to talk to them.'

She looked alarmed. 'I think the doctor doesn't feel that would be wise.'

'Why not?'

'I suppose he thinks it might upset you.'

'Why ever should it?'

'They all have homes and husbands. I think he thinks it might depress you.'

'It wouldn't,' I cried vehemently. And I thought then I would not change the father of my child for any respectable husband these women might have. Then I knew that the reason I could be so happy was that I still believed that one day Maximilian would come back for me and then I should proudly show him our child; and within me there flourished still my childish dream that we should live happily ever after.

When I went back to my room the first thing I did was look out of the window. The lawn was deserted; they had all gone back to their rooms. But I determined to go down to the lawn.

Dr Kleine now knew my story (Dr Carlsberg had thought it wise to tell him) but it had been agreed that for the purposes of preventing gossip – which would have been magnified in any case and no doubt distorted – I was to be known as Mrs Trant, a widow who had lost her husband some months before.

It was early afternoon, the siesta hour, when I decided to find my way down to the lawn. The house appeared to have been built round the garden which contained the lawn, and the women I had seen there had come from a door completely opposite the wing in which I had my room. I would have to work my way round to it so that I could come out by the door through which I had seen the women emerge.

I opened my door quietly. There was not a sound in the corridor. I went swiftly to a flight of stairs, descended it and found myself on a landing. I went along this in what I thought was the right direction and I came to a short flight of stairs which led to a door. As I approached I heard the sound of sobbing. I paused and listened.

There was no doubt that someone was in great distress.

I hesitated, wondering whether it would be better to find out if I could be of use or to ignore what I heard. Then on impulse I went up the three or four stairs and knocked on the door. The sobbing stopped. I knocked again.

'Who's there?' said a high-pitched, frightened voice.

'May I come in?' I asked. There was a sound which could have been an affirmative so I opened the door and entered a room rather like my own but smaller, and hunched on the bed was a girl of about my own age, her face swollen with crying, her hair in disorder.

We stared at each other.

'What's wrong?' I asked.

'Everything,' she replied bleakly.

I approached the bed and sat on it.

'I feel so terrible,' she said.

'Should I call someone?'

She shook her head. 'It's not that. I wish it were. It's long overdue. I know I'm going to die.'

'Of course you won't. You'll feel better when the baby comes.'

Again she shook her head. 'I don't know what I'm going to do. Last night I thought of jumping out of the window.'

'Oh no!'

'It's different for you. You've got a husband and a home and it's all going to be wonderful.'

I didn't answer. I said: 'And you haven't?'

'We should have been married,' she said. 'He was killed six months ago. He was in the Duke's Guard and the bomb was meant for the Duke. He would have married me.'

'So he was a soldier.'

She nodded. 'We would have been married if he'd lived,' she reiterated.

In the Duke's Guard, I was thinking. Duke Carl of Rochenstein and Dorrenig, Count of Lokenberg.

'Your family will look after you,' I soothed.

Again the doleful shake of the head. 'No they won't. They won't have me back. They brought me to Dr Kleine but when it's over they won't have me back. I tried to kill myself once before. I walked out into the river but then I was frightened and they rescued me and brought me here.'

She was small and very young and frightened and I longed to help her. I wanted to tell her that I myself had a future to face which might not be easy; but my story was so fantastic, so different from one of a soldier lover who had come to an untimely end.

She was only sixteen, she told me. I felt so much older and protective. I said it was always wrong to despair. I was of some use to her, I believe, because of my recent suffering. I could recall, because it *was* so recent, the terrible desolation which had swept over me when I had been told that my romantic marriage was nothing but a myth.

At least, I thought, this girl has a plausible tragedy to relate.

I made her talk and she told me about the town of Rochenburg, the chief city of Rochenstein, where she had lived with her grandmother who remembered the day the present Duke's father died, and he became the head of the ruling house. He had always been a good and serious-minded Duke – rather different from his son Prince Carl, who was notoriously wild. Her grandmother had been a great loyalist and she would have welcomed a soldier of the Duke's Guard into the family, but if he had been one of Ludwig's men she would never have accepted him. But that made it all the more terrible because if they had not anticipated their marriage vows, if they had waited, they could have been respectably married in due course. But fate had gone against them. Their child was conceived just before the bomb intended for the Duke had destroyed her lover, leaving her desolate for ever – and with a double burden, for to her grief was added shame. She could not endure it; nor would her grandmother. She had no notion how she was going to fend for herself and the child, and the river had seemed an easy solution.

'You must never do that again,' I told her. 'You'll find a way. We all do.'

'You're all right . . .'

'I . . . I haven't a husband to go to.'

'Oh, so you're a widow? That's sad. But you have money, I suppose. Most people who come to Dr Kleine's have. I don't know why he has taken me in. When I was brought in half drowned and they were scolding me about having done harm to my child he said he would take me in here and look after me.'

'That was kind of him. But I haven't any money either. I shall have to support myself and my child. I may be teaching English at a convent.'

'You are accomplished. I have nothing to recommend me. I'm just a simple girl.'

'What is your name?'

'Gretchen,' she said. 'Gretchen Swartz.'

'I'll come and see you again, Gretchen,' I said. 'We'll talk to each other. We'll discuss what you can do when you have a child and no money. I'm sure there's always a way.'

'You will come back then?' she said.

I promised.

We talked for some time and when I left her I had forgotten about the women on the lawn.

Dr Kleine came to see me later that day. He was pleased, he said, that everything seemed to be going well. He thought the birth was imminent and we must be prepared for that.

I slept well and the next morning I felt comparatively well. After I had breakfasted in my own room I put on my loose dressing-gown and went to the window and there were the women on the lawn again. I immediately thought of Gretchen Swartz and decided to go along and talk to her.

I found my way to her room. I mounted the stairs and knocked. There was no answer so I opened the door and looked in.

There was no one there. The bed was made, and there was an impersonal look about it. The floor was highly polished, the window slightly open; the room looked as though it had been prepared for the next occupant.

Disappointed, I went back to my room. Then it occurred to me that Gretchen must have been taken somewhere to have her baby. Perhaps at that very moment it was being born.

I sat at the window for some little time watching the women below and I could not get poor Gretchen out of my mind.

That afternoon my pains started and for the second time in a very brief period I suffered tragedy.

I can remember the agony; I can remember thinking: It will all be worth while when I have my child . . . everything . . . everything.

I lost consciousness and when I was aware again I was no longer in pain.

'How is she?' I heard a voice say.

There was no answer.

My first thought was for my child, and I held up my arms. Someone was bending over me.

I said: 'My baby . . .'

There was no answer. Then from a long way off I heard someone say: 'Shall she be told?'

And somebody else said: 'Wait.'

I was terribly frightened. I tried to cling to consciousness but it had gone again.

Dr Kleine was at my bedside. Ilse was with him. I saw Dr Carlsberg too. They all looked very grave.

Ilse had taken my hand.

'It was for the best,' she said. 'In the circumstances.'

'What?' I cried.

'My dear Helena, in view of everything you will see in time . . . it will be easier.'

I could not endure the terrible fear. I must know the truth.

'Where is my child?' I cried.

'The child,' said Dr Kleine, 'was born dead.'

'No!'

'Yes, dear,' said Ilse tenderly. 'All the horror . . . all the anxiety . . . it was inevitable.'

'But I wanted my child. I wanted my little . . . was it a boy?'

'It was a girl,' said Ilse.

I saw her so clearly – my little daughter. I could see her in a little silk dress – aged one, aged two . . . and then growing up and going to school. I felt the tears on my cheeks.

'She was alive,' I said. 'I used to smile because she was s
lively. I used to feel her there. Oh no, there is some mistake.

Dr Carlsberg bent over me. 'The shock of everything,' he
said, 'was too much for you. We expected this. Please, do not
fret. Remember that you are free now to live a happy life.'

A happy life! I wanted to scream at them. My lover you
tell me never existed. I *dreamed* of my marriage. But the child
was there – a living thing and now you tell me she is dead.

Ilse said: 'We will take care of you, Helena . . .'

I wanted to cry out: 'I don't need taking care of. I want
my child. How dare you experiment with me! How dare you
give me dreams that are without reality! If I have been
abused I want to know it. There is nothing worse than uncertainty. Oh yes, there is. There is this terrible loss. The baby
who was to have been my consolation has been taken from
me.'

I lay there limply. I had not known such desolation since
they had told me that Maximilian, whom I had believed to be
my husband, was a myth.

I was very weak, they told me. I must not leave my bed. I
did not feel physically weak, only mentally exhausted and in
deep despair.

All these months I had lived for my child. I had made a
dream in which Maximilian came back to me and proudly I
showed him the child. I had believed that . . . just as I had
always really believed in those three days of perfect happiness. It was only when Ilse smothered me with her goodness
that I wavered. But I was never convinced. I could not be
convinced.

'I must see my child,' I said.

Dr Kleine was horrified. 'It would increase your distress.'

I insisted that I wanted to see my baby.

'We were burying her today,' said Dr Kleine.

'I should be there!'

'It is a simple ceremony, and you must not leave your bed.
You have to concentrate on getting well now.'

I repeated that I wanted to see my child.

Ilse came to see me. 'Helena, dear,' she said, 'it is all over.
What you have to do now is forget. You can go back to your
home. You can forget all this . . . nightmare. In a little while
it will be as though it never happened. You are so young . . .'

I said stonily: 'It will never be as though it has not hap-

100

pened. Nothing that can possibly happen to me will ever be so real, so important to me, as this. Do you think I can ever forget?'

'That is not what Dr Carlsberg wants. His object has been achieved. Now he would like you to go back to normality.'

'Dr Carlsberg is too glib with his dream-producing drugs. I want to see my baby.'

'My dear Helena, it would be better not.'

'Are you trying to tell me that I have given birth to some monster?'

'Certainly not. A little girl . . . who was born dead.'

'I was so much aware of her alive.'

'It was a difficult birth. All that you had suffered . . . and you suffered far more than you realized . . . has taken its toll. That is what the doctors feared. In such circumstances it is much better so.'

I said: 'They are going to bury my baby today. I must see her before they do so.'

'It would be better . . .'

I raised myself on my elbow. I cried: 'I will not be told any more what I must do. I will not be the victim of your experiments.'

Ilse looked frightened. 'I will speak to the doctors,' she said.

They put me in a wheelchair because the doctor would not allow me to walk. I was taken into a room in which stood a tiny coffin on trestles; the venetian blinds had been arranged so that a little light came through the slats. And there she lay — my little baby — a small pinched face framed by a little white bonnet. I wanted to pick her up, to hold her to me, to breathe life into that limp little body.

Hot tears were in my eyes and bitter despair in my heart.

They wheeled me silently back to my room. The put me to bed; they smoothed my pillows and tucked in the bedclothes; they did everything they could to comfort me; but there was no comfort.

I lay in my bed; I could hear the voices of the women on the lawn.

It was over. The dream and the nightmare. I was not yet nineteen years old and I felt I had had a greater experience than many people encountered in a lifetime.

Ilse was with me every day. She constantly stressed the fact that I was free now. I could take up my life again as it had been before the Night of the Seventh Moon. She would take me back to England: and there I would find everything was as it had been. It was the best thing for me.

I thought about it a good deal and I could see that it was what I should have to do.

I had to grow away from this mad adventure. I had to forget. I would have to start again.

I stayed in Dr Kleine's nursing home for two weeks and it was almost when I was on the point of leaving – so immersed in my own tragedy had I been – that I remembered Gretchen Swartz.

I told Ilse how I had found her sobbing in her room and Ilse said she would ask the doctor or Mrs Kleine about the girl.

It was the doctor who mentioned her to me.

'You were asking about Gretchen Swartz. So you had a word with her? Did she tell you her story?'

'Yes, poor girl. She was very unhappy.'

'She didn't come through. She died but the child was all right. A fine boy.'

'And what happened to the boy?'

'Her family took him. The old grandmother will look after him and then he will go to an uncle.'

'Poor Gretchen! I was so sorry for her.'

'Now you are going to stop being sorry. You are going to get well and Frau Gleiberg tells me that in a few weeks' time she will be taking you back to your home.'

He seemed almost gleeful. I had an impression that he had ticked my name off a list. A difficult case which has been satisfactorily settled.

And then I felt the tears prickling my eyelids – they had come very easily in the last few days – and I was weeping for the loss of my dream and my child.

The Years Between

1861-9

ONE

A month after I had looked on that little dead face Ilse took me back to England.

How normal everything seemed. If ever I could grow to believe that I had imagined the whole incredible adventure, I could do it there. On the journey Ilse had talked to me of the future and the theme of her discourse was: Forget. The sooner I did this the sooner I should begin to lead a new life. She did not see it as I had seen it. To her it was a horrible misadventure with a climax she could only regard as fortunate. Death, she would say, had solved my problems. She did not know that the ecstatic memory of three days with Maximilian lived on; she did not understand that while a child lives within its mother, love is born.

But I could see that she was right about putting it all behind me. I had to go on living. I had to pick up the threads of my life.

Ilse stayed with us only a few days; then she said goodbye. I fancied there was a certain relief in her attitude. Perhaps she was regretting that she had asked me to accompany her and Ernst on that day some ten months ago, but when I saw her off at the station she made me promise to write to her and tell her how I was getting on and she seemed as concerned as ever.

Everyone agreed that I had changed. I knew that they were right. Gone was the gay, effervescent girl; in her place was a rather withdrawn woman. I looked older too – older than my nineteen years, whereas before I had looked younger than my age.

There were changes at home. Aunt Caroline was slightly different. She had always been critical of society; now she was

103

angry with it. No one seemed right to her; Aunt Matilda came in for a good deal of castigation but I very soon became the butt for it. What I had thought I was doing gallivanting about in outlandish places for nearly a year, she did not know. Improving my German! English was good enough for her and should have been for anyone. I'd come back bone idle, as far as she could see. Had I any new recipes to tell her? Not that she would want a lot of foreign ways of cooking in her kitchen. I developed a talent for appearing to listen to her and not hearing a thing she said.

As for Aunt Matilda, she had changed. Bodily ailments still supplied her main excitement but she had become very friendly with the Clees in the bookshop.

'What I wonder,' said Aunt Caroline sarcastically, 'is why you don't go and live there.'

'You know, Helena,' Aunt Matilda confided in me, 'when you think of all there is to do in the shop they don't get much time for seeing to things about the rooms above it. Amelia's chest isn't what it should be and when you consider Mr Clees's one kidney trying to do the work of two, it makes you think.'

She was happier than she had been when I left and I grew quite fond of her. She was always smuggling in mending from the Clees' house so that Aunt Caroline wouldn't see it. She would sit in her room secretly doing it. It was what Aunt Caroline would call 'making yourself cheap'.

The Grevilles were pleased to see me. I was asked to dinner within a few days of my return.

Mrs Greville embraced me warmly. 'My dear Helena!' she said. 'Why, you've grown thinner!' And she took my face in her hands and looked at it with such close scrutiny that I felt myself flushing.

'Is everything all right, Helena?'

'Why yes, of course.'

'You've changed.'

'I'm a year older.'

'It's more than that.' She looked rather worried so I kissed her and said: 'I haven't settled in properly yet.'

'Oh, your aunts,' she said with a little grimace. Then she added: 'Anthony's so pleased you're back. We all are.'

It was a happy evening. They were delighted by my return. They kept asking questions about my sojourn and I tried to evade them when they touched on my personal experiences and told them some of the legends of the forest.

Anthony could talk very learnedly about this. 'These have come from the pre-Christian era,' he said. 'I believe some of the beliefs still linger.'

'I'm sure they do,' I said; and I was back in the square watching the dancers and I saw a figure in the horned head-dress and heard a tender voice whisper: '*Lenchen, Liebchen.*'

Anthony was looking at me strangely. I must have betrayed something. I warned myself to be careful. So I tried to be very gay and described how the girls dressed on feast days in their satin aprons with bright kerchiefs tied over their heads. Anthony knew something of this because he had visited the forest with his parents before he went to college. He had been fascinated even as I had.

Yes, it was a pleasant evening, but that night I was disturbed by dreams. Maximilian was in them and so was the child, and strangely enough it was not of a dead baby in a coffin I dreamed but of a living child.

The dreams were so vivid that when I awoke next morning I was plunged into deep melancholy.

This is how it will be throughout my life, I thought.

The days passed slowly at first but because one week was so much like another they merged and began to fly. There were the household duties to be performed under Aunt Caroline's never-satisfied authority; there were the occasional visits of friends; sometimes I went into the bookshop and helped when they were busy. I began to acquire a certain knowledge of books. Aunt Matilda, who managed to be there quite often too, was always pleased to see me there. It was such a help for Amelia with her chest and Albert with his solitary kidney.

Aunt Caroline was not so pleased by the friendship. 'What you see in that place, I can't imagine,' she grumbled. 'If they sold something sensible I might understand it more. Books! What are they but time-wasters?'

During the first year of my return, Ilse had written several times. Then there came a letter to say that Ernst had died and she would be leaving Denkendorf. I sent my condolences and expected to be given a new address but I never had another letter from Ilse. I waited and waited but the years passed and there was nothing. It seemed very strange when I remembered how close we had been.

My dreams continued to disturb my nights and haunt my days. Time could no nothing to efface my memories. In those dreams my baby lived – a little girl who so resembled Maximilian that she was clearly his daughter. As the time passed she grew up in my dreams. I yearned for the child; and when I awoke after one of my vivid dreams I suffered the loss of my baby afresh.

We lived perpetually under the cloud of Aunt Caroline's displeasure; and one day when I had been home for a little more than a year she was not up at her usual time and when I went to her room I found her in bed unable to move. She had had a stroke. She recovered a little and I nursed her for three years, with the help of Aunt Matilda. She was an exacting patient; nothing pleased her. Those were three dreary years when I would drop into my bed exhausted every night to dream. And how I dreamed! My memories were as vivid as ever.

I well remember the day when Aunt Matilda whispered to me that she was going to marry Albert Clees.

'I mean,' she said blushing coyly, 'where is the sense of my keeping going in and out. I might just as well live there.'

'It's only a step or two next door,' I reminded her.

'Oh, but it's not the same.' She was bubbling over with excitement like a young bride. I was happy for her because she had changed so much. Happiness suited Aunt Matilda.

'When's the great day to be?' I asked.

'Oh, I haven't told Caroline yet.'

When Caroline was told she was very angry. She talked continually of the folly of old women who ran after men, mending their socks and turning the collars and cuffs of their shirts. What did they think they were going to get out of that!

'The satisfaction of helping someone, perhaps,' I suggested.

'Now, Helena, there's no need for you to come into this. If Matilda likes to make a fool of herself, let her.'

'I don't see that she's making a fool of herself by helping Mr Clees.'

'Perhaps you don't, but I do. You're too young to understand these things.'

Too young! Beside Aunt Caroline I felt old in experience. If she but knew! I thought. If I said to her: But I have been a wife and mother, what would she make of my implausible tale? One thing I was sure of: she must never get a chance to make anything of it.

And that started the yearning again. Indeed, everything seemed to lead back to it.

When Aunt Matilda ceremoniously brought Mr Clees into the house, Aunt Caroline merely sniffed and satisfied herself with contemptuous looks, but I had noticed the hot colour in her cheeks and the way the veins knotted at her temples.

I said that we ought to drink to the health and happiness of the affianced couple and without Aunt Caroline's permission I took out a bottle of her best elderberry wine and served it.

It was rather pleasant to see Aunt Matilda looking ten years younger and I wondered, with a return of my old frivolity, whether she would have fallen in love with Albert Clees if he had not been deprived of a kidney. Amelia was pleased too. She whispered to me that she had seen it coming for a long time and that it was the best thing that could happen to her father.

The wedding was to be soon, for as Matilda said there was no sense in waiting, and Mr Clees gallantly added that he had waited long enough, which made Aunt Matilda blush prettily.

When the Clees had left Aunt Caroline let forth a burst of scorn and abuse.

'*Some* people thought they were seventeen instead of forty-seven.'

'Forty-five,' said Aunt Matilda.

'And what's the difference?'

'Two years,' said Aunt Matilda spiritedly.

'Making fools of themselves! I suppose there'll be a white wedding with bridesmaids in wreaths of rosebuds.'

'No. Albert thinks a quiet wedding would be best.'

'He's got sense enough to realize you don't want to make a fool of yourself parading in white, then.'

'Albert has a lot of sense, more than some I could name.'

And so it went on.

Aunt Matilda, who had become 'Matty', named thus by her devoted Albert, was excited about her wedding-dress. 'Nigger brown velvet,' she said. 'Jenny Withers will make it. Albert will come with me to choose the material. And a nigger brown hat with pink roses.'

'Pink roses at your time of life!' snapped Aunt Caroline. 'If you marry that man you'll sup sorrow with a long spoon.'

But in spite of her we grew quite gay over the wedding.

Amelia would come in and we would huddle together looking at patterns for the wedding-dress and for Amelia's grey silk which was being made for the occasion. Amelia was to be maid of honour.

We would all be laughing together when we would hear Aunt Caroline's stick outside the door (she had walked with a stick since her stroke, for one leg was useless). Then she would come in and say nothing but sit regarding us all with contempt.

But she could not spoil Matilda's happiness, although on the wedding-day she refused to attend the ceremony. 'You can all go and make fools of yourselves if you want to,' she said. 'I shan't.'

So Aunt Matilda was married and the wedding-breakfast was held in the rooms over the shop with just a few guests. Aunt Caroline stayed at home muttering and grumbling about mutton dressed up as lamb and people in their second childhood.

Two days after the wedding she had another stroke which rendered her almost incapable of moving at all. She did, however, retain her speech which was more venomous than ever.

There followed a very melancholy period which seemed to be devoted to the nursing of Aunt Caroline. Aunt Matilda helped; but her first duty was to Albert now and she was a happy wife determined to do her duty.

Often, when I was preparing a meal for Aunt Caroline, I would dream of a life I had once visualized during three blissful days. I thought of living in a schloss perched high on a hill, as so many of them I had seen had been; I thought of a gracious life with a husband whom I adored and who adored me; I thought too of children – my little daughter and a son. There would be a son. And often this seemed more real to me than the kitchen with its rows of bottles neatly labelled by Aunt Caroline and now often put back in the wrong place, until milk boiled over or something caught in the oven to bring me back to reality.

During this period there was great rejoicing in the Greville family becaue Anthony became vicar – not of our church but of another on the outskirts of the town. Mrs Greville was delighted with her clever son. I knew that she had already seen him in his gaiters presiding over his bishopric.

I had taken to going to church every Sunday with the Grevilles to hear Anthony take the service; and I felt more contented than I had believed possible. The fact that I did not hear from Ilse added to the sense of unreality and I began to feel that I had strayed into a strange world where events which would seem inconceivable in a logical world had happened. But at night I dreamed my dreams.

On Sundays after evensong I would go to the Grevilles' home for Sunday supper while Aunt Matilda or Amelia kept an eye on Aunt Caroline, who was more and more needing constant attention; and it was on one of the summer Sundays when supper had been cleared away that Anthony asked me to go for a walk with him. It was a lovely evening and we strolled out to the fields beyond the city and Anthony talked, as he loved to do, about the glories of Oxford. He loved to discover the history of the place and, like my father, he knew how all the colleges had been founded; on this particular Sunday he was telling me about the legend of St Frideswyde, which he said was something more than a legend. Frideswyde had actually lived and in the year 727 founded a nunnery. When the King of Leicester fell madly in love with her and tried to abduct her, he was struck blind. She lived so piously that when she died a shrine was dedicated to her. About this shrine a hamlet grew up, then a village and so began the ancient town of Oxford. There the owners of cattle drove them across the ford where the Thames and Cherwell met and thus the spot derived its name of Oxford.

He was so enthusiastic when he talked that he grew quite animated, which he was not in the normal way, and I was taken by surprise when he said suddenly:

'Helena, will you marry me?'

I was shocked into silence. If I had ever doubted it, I knew in that moment that I considered myself to be a married woman. It was so long since I had seen Ilse's kind face. It was so long since I had heard from her, that her image had faded and with it my fears that she, Ernst and Dr Carlsberg must have been right. The farther I grew away from that time the more vivid seemed my adventure in the forest and the less plausible their account of my lost days.

But marry! I was already married.

'Helena, is the idea so repulsive to you?'

'Oh no,' I said. 'No, no. It was just that I hadn't thought.' I stopped. How foolish this must seem. Of course it had been obvious for some time what Anthony's intentions were. The attitude of Mr and Mrs Greville had made it clear. I realized with dismay that they were expecting us to come back from our walk engaged.

I said quickly: 'Of course, Anthony. I'm fond of you.' Yes,

I was fond of him. I liked Anthony Greville as much as anyone in Oxford. I found his conversation interesting; I enjoyed
his company. I should be very lonely if he went out of my
life. But I wanted to go on as we were. It was his friendship
I wanted. There was only one man whom I could consider
as my husband and I believed he was that in spite of efforts
to convince me that I loved a phantom.

'It's just that I hadn't thought of marriage,' I finished
lamely.

'I should have led up to this, I suppose,' he said ruefully. 'I
know my parents expected. They are so fond of you and so
am I.'

I said: 'It would be very suitable of course, but . . .'

'Oh, Helena,' he said, 'get used to the idea. Think about it.'

'There is Aunt Caroline,' I said. 'I couldn't leave her. She
needs someone to look after her all the time.'

'We could bring her to the vicarage. My mother would help
to look after her.'

'I couldn't impose Aunt Caroline on you. She would disrupt
the household.'

I was talking round the matter, anything but to tell the
truth. I was really agitated because talking of marriage had
brought back so vividly that room in the hunting lodge, the
priest with the book and the ring, and Maximilian standing
beside me impatiently waiting for the time when we would
be alone.

I forced myself to think of Anthony. He would be kind to
me; we could have a pleasant life together. I could be of use
to him in his work; perhaps we should have children. I felt
the pain surging within me as I thought of that little face
framed in the white bonnet. How could I possibly marry
without telling what had happened to me – now six years ago.

I said quickly: 'I should have to have time to think . . .'

He took my hand and pressed it firmly. 'But of course,' he
said.

We were thoughtful as we went back to the house. I could
not tear my mind away from the past. I kept seeing Maximilian with the eager passion in his eyes. I had had no doubts
then; I would have made no excuses; I would have swept
them all away. And my child . . . I could not bear it. I must
control my feelings.

When we arrived back at the house I noticed at once the

expectancy in Mrs Greville's face. She was disappointed.

Anthony had now moved into the new vicarage, a charming Queen Anne residence with spacious, gracious lawns at both front and back. There was a south wall at the back – older than the house. It had been there since Tudor days. Peaches could be grown on it. There were apple and pear trees in the garden and a sundial inscribed with an old adage: 'I count only the sunny hours. 'They,' said Anthony, 'were the only ones which should be counted.' His parents had moved in with him.

'To make sure of his comforts,' Mrs Greville explained to me. 'Of course when Anthony marries we'll be ready to take a back seat.'

She spoke significantly. I knew she thought that although I was hesitant I should eventually marry Anthony. After all, what life was there for me otherwise? It wasn't right, said Mrs Greville, for young women to be cooped up looking after old ones. She implied that Aunt Caroline would be no less miserable installed in a room in the vicarage where she would help to look after her.

They were so good, so kind, and I loved them all dearly. Why did I hesitate? The answer was because I was clinging to a dream.

Either in reality or my dreams I had known the perfect union and I hungered for it. I knew that Anthony was a good man; it seemed very likely that Maximilian was not quite that; but one does not always love people for their virtues.

One day when we were in the walled garden, and I was alone with Anthony I blurted out: 'Anthony, I want to be absolutely truthful with you. I've had a child.'

He was startled and incredulous.

'You remember I was away for almost a year. It's the strangest story and the strangest part of it is that I don't know whether or not it's true.'

I told him what had happened, beginning with my adventure in the mist and the strong feelings that had been aroused in me that night. I wanted to keep nothing back. And then I went on to my adventure on the Night of the Seventh Moon.

'Everything was normal until then – and the rest . . . Anthony, I am not sure.'

He listened intently. 'It seems incredible,' he said. 'I should like to meet your cousin.'

'She was so good to me. She felt responsible. She couldn't do enough. She looked after me during those months . . . Then she ceased to write.'

'Some people are bad correspondents.'

'But I should have thought she would have sent me an address. Anthony, what do you think happened?'

'I know,' he said, 'that doctors are making rapid advances in this field and that experiments have been made. It must have been that this Dr Carlsberg used such an experiment on you, with the results we have seen.'

'Is it possible to forget six whole days of your life?'

'I believe it is.'

And then . . . this horrible thing happened to me . . . and I cannot remember it.'

'It is better that you don't. It seems that this was necessary to save you pain, humiliation and perhaps great mental stress which could have been dangerous.'

'I can see that you believe the marriage to have been a myth.'

'If it were not so, where is this man? Why did he not come forward? Why did he give a false name . . . a name that you had seen was one of the Duke's titles? Besides, why should your cousin lie to you? Why should the doctor do so?'

'Why indeed? Everything points one way. You as a practical man see that.'

'My poor Helena,' he said, 'it was a shattering experience. But it is over now. The child died, so any complications which might have ensued have been removed.'

I closed my eyes. I could not bear it when anyone talked of my child's death as this happy release.

'I wanted the child,' I said fiercely. 'I would not have cared for these complications.'

'You will have other children, Helena. That is the best way to heal that wound.'

How calm he was, how kind, how unshaken in his love for me.

I knew that I had told him this because the prospect of marriage with him was not an impossibility.

I was so pleased that I had told him. It was a great relief. I began to think how comforting it would be in the future to share my troubles with him.

The more I thought of marriage with Anthony the more rational it seemed. Anthony's calm reception of my revelation had shown me what a steadying influence he would have on my life; he was a man in whom I knew I could put my trust. Marriage with him would be like coming into a safe harbour after battling against the storms. On the very next Sunday he preached an eloquent sermon about the need to overcome past misfortunes, never to brood on what could not be altered but to try to profit from experience rather than to regret it. His text came from the story of the houses, one of which was built on sand, the other on rock; and the shifting sands of romantic dreams were doomed to destruction while the house which was built on the firm rock of reality would endure.

I was so moved by that sermon that I almost made up my mind to marry him; and yet that very night my dreams were as vivid as ever and I awoke to find myself call for Maximilian.

I found I could talk of my experience with Anthony more freely than I had ever believed possible. It was a pleasure to bring it out into the open. We discussed it at great length and went over every detail. He missed nothing; but he remained firm to his conclusion that I had been the victim of Dr Carlsberg's experiment and he believed that the doctor had been right to make it.

Mrs Greville was constantly busy helping with the work of the parish.

'My goodness,' she used to say, 'a man in Anthony's position can't get along without a woman to help him in his parish duties.'

She was just a little impatient with me. She once reminded me that I was no longer a young girl. I was nearly twenty-six. No longer young. People would soon be saying I was on the shelf.

How I should have enjoyed pleasing them! As it was, I did everything I could to help Mrs Greville. I was indefatigable in the organization of the sales of work; and social evenings. I made cups of tea which were distributed at the mothers' meetings.

'You have a flair for the work,' said Mrs Greville significantly.

Between my constant visits to the vicarage and the work I did and my occasional spells in the bookshop besides looking after Aunt Caroline, the time flew.

Aunt Caroline grudged every minute I was away from the house.

'Chasing after the vicar,' she used to say. 'I don't know. Some people are man-mad.'

She hated my going out but Aunt Matty insisted. She was very excited about my relationship with Anthony. She was so happy in her marriage that she would have liked to see everyone about her in the same blissful state – Amelia, myself and even Aunt Caroline.

She always came to the house while I was away.

'Now you go and enjoy yourself,' she would say significantly.

Then she thought it pleasant for me to be in the bookshop. 'Albert says you're better than anyone in the foreign department and it's amazing how many foreigners we get in.'

So the time flew past; there was never a moment to spare; and all the time at the back of my mind – and often to the fore of it – was the question: Could I be happy married to Anthony? Could I make him happy? Should I, if I married, cease to be haunted by nostalgic dreams?

I could see a very happy life ahead of me. Anthony's quiet charm would have been enhanced by a wife who had the enthusiasm I knew I could muster and once my old high spirits returned I would be a useful foil. Oh yes, I would tell myself again and again, it would be ideal.

Aunt Caroline continued to complain: 'Gadding about! Running after Anthony Greville. Hoping he'll marry you, I suppose. Making yourself cheap.' I wanted to shout at her: He has asked me; but I didn't. And always something held me back from accepting.

I was to have a stall at the sale of work and had been collecting for weeks to fill it. Members of the church sent in their donations. One parcel came containing half a dozen eggcosies from the Misses Edith and Rose Elkington.

I stared at the name for some seconds, and then I was back in the narrow street with the cobbled road, the overhanging signs; I was standing outside Dr Kleine's clinic and my body was heavy with my lively unborn child.

Two women had spoken to me on that occasion. Yes, their name had been Elkington. They sold teas and coffees, home-made cakes and home-made knicknacks like tea-cosy covers and egg-covers.

I shivered and felt vaguely apprehensive.

I was right to feel so. On the first afternoon of the sale of work they were there. Two pairs of bright eyes regarded me. They were like monkey's eyes – dark, living, curious.

'Why, it's *Miss* Helena Trant.'

'Yes,' I said.

'We sent the egg-cosies.'

'Thank you. They are very useful.'

'I hope you like the red and green combination,' said the younger.

I said I thought it was most effective.

The elder of the two said: 'Didn't we see you in Germany?'

'Oh . . . yes, I believe you did.'

'You'd gone out with your cousin, I believe, and stayed quite a long time.'

'Yes, that's right.'

'Interesting,' said the elder; and I did not much like the gleam in her eye.

It made me more uneasy.

Aunt Caroline worked herself up into a fury that night. Matilda had come in and hurried off early because she was worried about Albert. You had to be careful with one kidney, she kept saying.

I was late back. I had had quite a success with my stall and by the time I had added up the takings and packed away the unsold goods and gone back with Mrs Greville with this, it was beginning to get late.

Aunt Caroline screamed at me when I came home.

She really looked very wild, her hair in disorder, her face flushed.

She had been knocking on the floor with her stick for the last half an hour. No one had answered. Our maid Ellen was a lazy good-for-nothing, she declared; Matilda was besotted about that man next door; Amelia had gone to some concert; and I of course was busy chasing Anthony Greville. No one had spared a thought for her, but that was how it was when you were ill. People were so selfish.

She went on and on and I was afraid for her because the doctor had said that she must not become excited. He had given me some pills which should have a calming effect but when I suggested she take one, she cried: 'That's right, blame it on to me. I'm the one who has to calm down. I have to keep quiet. I mustn't say a word. You all go gadding off to enjoy yourselves in the grand man-hunt. First Matilda – Matty she calls herself now. Matty indeed! She's gone back to her second childhood. And as for you! You're brazen you are. I wonder the vicar can't see through you. Well, you're not a girl any more, are you? You're getting a bit worried. You're going to be left on the shelf if you don't watch out. But nobody could say you're not watching out. On the prowl, I'd say.'

I cried: 'Be quiet, Aunt Caroline. You're talking nonsense.'

'Nonsense. Nonsense that's as plain as the nose on your face. Nonsense indeed! Anyone with half an eye can see what you're after.'

I was goaded beyond endurance and I said: 'As a matter of fact Anthony has asked me marry him.'

I saw her face change, and I knew then that this was what she feared, and suddenly I saw clearly what her life had been. She had not had Matilda's more simple nature; Matilda had been interested in her invalids and sympathetic towards them: there was no sympathy in Aunt Caroline's nature. She had been the less attractive of the two sisters. She was the eldest of the family. My father had come in between. She had had to stand aside for him and envy had eaten into her soul. I saw it there on her face – envy of my father for whom sacrifices had had to be made, for Matilda, who had made other people's ailments her interest and who had now found a new life in her marriage; myself, as she thought, about to marry. Poor Aunt Caroline, robbed of everything; the education my father had had, the husband Matilda had; and in addition she was an invalid. I felt deeply sorry for her. Envy – that deadliest of the seven sins – had etched those bitter lines about her mouth, had tightened it and set the sneering glitter in her eyes. Poor, poor Aunt Caroline.

I thought: I must look after her. I must try to be patient.

'Aunt Caroline,' I began, 'I . . .'

But she was groping for her pills. I took one and put it into her mouth.

I said, 'You had better rest now. I am here if you want anything.'

She nodded; and that night she died.

No one could mourn her. Her passing could only be what was aptly and so commonly known as 'a happy release'.

'Her condition could only have worsened,' said the doctor.

Aunt Matilda reverted to type and talked endlessly about hearts which were such funny things but were going to get you in the end. I should sleep next door until after the funeral, she said. Mrs Greville immediately invited me to the vicarage, but I had already accepted Aunt Matilda's offer. So I slept in the room which had been mine as a very small child before my father had acquired the house next door.

There was that bustling which funerals always meant. Aunt Matilda was in her element. Funerals as the ultimate climax to illness were a matter of great interest to her. Everything must be done in a manner which she considered 'right'. Black had to be ordered and made at great speed; as chief mourner Aunt Matilda assumed a great importance. I was next and we should go together; she would lean on my arm and I would have to support her. Tears were necessary on such an occasion, and it was very strange, she told me, that some people did not always find it easy to shed them. One must not speak ill of the dead (an important point in funeral etiquette) but Aunt Caroline had been very ill and it was hard to regret her death. If tears should prove difficult, and she knew that I was by no means an easy shedder of them ('You never were,' she confided. 'It was something to do with being sent away from home when you were young'), she had heard a peeled onion concealed in the handkerchief was very effective.

I listened to the chattering and I thought how life had changed for her since Mr Clees had come along; and that she was a much pleasanter person than she had been under the sway of Aunt Caroline and a participator in the perpetual bickering that seemed inevitable.

Marriage had been a blessing for her.

And for me? I believed it would be the same.

The black arrived. Aunt Matilda was not pleased with Amelia's hat; her own, with its jet brooch and dead black satin ribbons, was a triumph. There were the wreaths which caused great consternation lest they should arrive too late. Aunt Matilda could not bear the thought of her sister's being carried to her last resting-place without the 'Gates of Heaven

117

Ajar' which she and Albert were contributing. In our little drawing-room the coffin stood on trestles; there was a funereal smell throughout the house. The blinds were drawn in all rooms and our little maid had gone home to her mother because she couldn't face spending the nights alone in the house with the dead.

At last the day arrived. The solemn black-clad, top-hatted men walking beside the black-velvet caparisoned horses provided mournful solemnity, and the necessary pall of gloom had been arranged even to Aunt Matilda's complete satisfaction.

Then back to the rooms over the shop to partake of funeral meats. Cold ham, Aunt Matilda said, was a necessity. At one funeral she had been given cold chicken, which in her opinion showed a certain levity out of keeping with the occasion.

The evening came.

'I should stay here one more night,' said Aunt Matilda. So I did; and in my little room that night, I thought: I should marry Anthony.

Just as I had almost made up my mind something happened to make me hesitate.

Ellen, our little maid, came back after the funeral looking very thoughtful. She was absent-minded and during the second day I asked if there was anything wrong.

'Oh, Miss Helena,' she said, 'I don't know whether or not to tell you.'

'Well, if you think it would help you . . .'

'Oh, it's not me, miss. It's . . . you.'

'What do you mean, Ellen?'

'It's you and the vicar, and I don't believe it and I don't think I should repeat it . . . but perhaps you ought to know. I'm sure it's just wicked gossip.'

'Do tell me.'

'Well my mum had it from someone who had been in their shop and she said there was a lot of people there and they were all saying it was shocking and that the vicar ought to be told . . .'

'But *what*, Ellen?'

'I hardly like to say, miss. They're saying that when you went away all that time it was because you was in trouble and that you had a baby.'

118

I stared at her.

'Who said this, Ellen?'

'It started with them Miss Elkingtons. They said they saw you there . . . and it was clear and you was coming out of some hospital.'

I remembered it all so clearly: the little street; the exultation I had felt because my child would soon be born; four curious monkey-like eyes regarding me intently.

'It's nonsense, I know, miss. But I thought you ought to know.'

'Oh yes,' I said. 'I ought to know. You did right to tell me.'

'Well, there's nothing to it but gossip. I know that, miss. So does anybody who knows you. Them Miss Elkingtons is terrible gossips. My mum says that's what they've got a shop for. Miss, when you get married, you'll be wanting someone up there and as I know your ways . . .'

I said: 'I'll remember, Ellen.'

I wanted to get to my room and think.

Of course, I said to myself, I can't marry Anthony. The Elkingtons would always be there to gossip. What a horrible sordid story! I had gone abroad to have a child . . . No, we could not live that down. Like Caesar's wife, the vicar's must be beyond reproach.

I told Anthony what Ellen had told me.

He brushed it aside. 'My dear, we'd live that down.'

'But it's true. I was pregnant when they saw me and it was obvious. I did have a child.'

'My dear Helena, that's in the past.'

'I know and with you I should be building the house on the rock. But it's not fair to you. A scandal like that could ruin your career. It could prevent your progress.'

'I'd rather have a wife than a bishopric.'

'I might fail you.' I frowned. I remembered the emotions Maximilian had stirred in me during that night in the mist. I remembered the slow turning of the door handle. If the door had opened, what then? I believed that I should have found him irresistible. What if by some miracle he came back? I feared that so strong would be my feelings for him that he would have the power to wreck that house – built on a rock though it might be.

Again I took refuge in prevarication.

'I must think,' I said. 'This has changed things in a way.'
He wouldn't agree, but I insisted.

It was at this time that I decided to write down what had happened to me in order that I might come to some conclusion as to what actually occurred on the Night of the Seventh Moon. But I must confess that when I came to this point I was no nearer the truth than I had been before.

I put the account away so that I would always have a record of it and as the years passed I could re-live that time of my life in detail.

But it was not long after this that I again stepped into that fantastic world and then I made up my mind that I would write down my adventures as they happened so that they would be clear and precise. I wanted the plain truth undistorted by time.

So when I once more arrived in the Lokenwald I started to record my adventures as soon as they began to happen.

The Reality

1870

ONE

With Aunt Caroline dead, life became calmer, giving one greater opportunity for reflection. How peaceful it was! I would hear Ellen singing as she worked. The days were full; I worked regularly at the bookshop which I found very interesting. When I was not working there I was helping with church affairs; but the Elkingtons had spoilt that for me and I was always apprehensive about meeting them. So I gave my attention to the shop and it was there that I encountered Frau Graben.

She came in one day – a comfortable, plump, middle-aged woman with streaks of grey in her wispy hair which escaped from under a plain felt hat. She was dressed in a rather dowdy brown and grey check travelling coat over a skirt of the same material. I was talking to Amelia and she made straight for us.

She said in a halting English with an accent which made my heart beat faster: 'You vill help me. Vot I vant iss . . .'

I immediately spoke to her in German and the effect was miraculous. Her plump face lighted up, her eyes shone and she answered volubly in her own language. In the space of a few minutes she told me that she was visiting England and that she spoke very little English – both of which facts were fairly obvious – and that she wanted a little book which would help her to understand the language.

I took her along to the German section in the foreign department, telling her that I had a phrase book she would find useful and I thought that a dictionary would be of great help.

She made the purchases and thanked me, but seemed loath to go and as we were not busy I was quite happy to talk with her.

She had arrived only a few days ago in England and had come to Oxford because a friend of hers had been educated there. She wanted to see the place of which she had heard so much. Was she enjoying England? I asked. Yes, was the answer but the language barrier was a difficulty. She felt lonely and she could not tell me how wonderful it was to find someone who could talk to her as I could.

I found myself explaining to her that my mother was German and that she used to talk to me in her native tongue, and that I had been educated in a *Damenstift* near Liechten-kinn.

The joy in her face was expressive. But that was wonderful. She knew the *Damenstift* well. It was not so far from where she lived. This was better than ever.

After half an hour she left, but the next day she was back again and made a further purchase. Again she stayed to talk.

She looked so wistful when she was about to walk out of the shop that I asked her to tea next day.

She arrived at the expected time and I took her into the little sitting-room which seemed so much more gay now that Aunt Caroline was dead. Ellen brought in the tea and some cakes which she had made. They weren't up to Aunt Caroline's standards, but neither of us cared for that.

The conversation was exciting, because Frau Graben knew the forest well. She told me that she lived in a small schloss perched on the mountainside and here she was the *Schloss-mutter*. She was in charge of the household and was the children's chief nurse. She was indeed the mother. She proudly told me that she was responsible for the management of the schloss.

The children to whom she referred with affection were Dagobert, Fritz and Liesel.

'Whose children are they?' I asked.

'They're the Count's.'

I felt dizzy with an excitement which had grown greater ever since I had met Frau Graben.

'Count . . .?' I reiterated.

'Well,' she said, 'he's the Duke's nephew and a gay young gentleman he is, too. Many people thought he was mixed up in his father's plotting. But now Count Ludwig has gone there's still my lord Count and no one can be sure what he might be up to.'

'What of the Countess?'

122

'She's a suitable wife for him and they have one son.'

'I thought you said there were three children?'

'I'm not actually in the Count's household. I have nothing to do with that son.' She shrugged her shoulders. 'You know how it is . . . But perhaps you don't. My lord was always after the women; Ludwig was the same. It runs in the family. They used to say that Ludwig was the father of a good many more than he owned to. And, my goodness, you can see the family features in the little ones playing about in the villages.'

'And these three?'

'He admits to them. Special favourites their mothers must have been. And the Count likes any connected with him to be well looked after. He's fond of them in his way and comes to see them now and then. He takes an interest in their future. And as our own state of Saxe-Coburg was allied with the royal family of England he wants them all taught English.'

'This Count,' I said, 'what is he like?'

'He's like all the family – tall and good-looking, and fond of his own way. No woman's safe once he's taken a fancy to her. Yes, he's just like all the family. I was nurse to them so I know, and I reckon that nursery was as difficult to control as a whole dukedom. The mischief those boys got into! I had my hands full, I did. And in their mid-teens it was the women they were after. But I will say this. He looked after the children. It's my belief that many a girl puts her trouble down to his door. He's careless. He'll see she's all right. He likes the fun, he says, and doesn't mind paying for it. The children think he's wonderful. Young Daggie will grow up just like him. I'm not so sure of Fritzi. There's something different about Fritzi. I worry about him. He needs a mother and of course that's just what he hasn't got.'

'Where is his mother?'

'She's dead, I dare say. But the mothers wouldn't come to the schloss in any case. Once he's done with a woman he's done with her. But I will say he takes an interest in the children. He didn't like the way some of the family couldn't speak English with the Queen's party when she came visiting us from England after her husband's death. "I want the children to learn English," he said. So now of course we'll have a new teacher for them. "An *English* teacher," he said. He's not going to have them talking with a German accent.'

'And the Count – does he speak English?'

'He's been educated here . . . in this place. He speaks English like you do. That's how the children will have to.'

'They'll have to have an English teacher.'

'Yes, that's what he aims at.'

She went on to tell me about the children. Dagobert was the eldest. He was twelve – and boys of twelve can be a handful; then came Fritzi, as they called Fritz. He was ten. He missed his mother. I thought: He would be a year older than my daughter, and the terrible yearning was back with me.

'Then there's Liesel. A haughty little piece she is. Five years old and very much aware of her noble blood even though her mother was a little dressmaker who came to the court to sew.'

Again I was being caught up in that fairy-tale atmosphere. The excitement had come back to me in force. I wanted her to go on talking to me about the schloss on the mountainside that looked down on the valley in which lay the town of Rochenburg, the capital city of Rochenstein, which was ruled over by the Duke Carl who was also the Count of Lokenberg.

It seemed a remarkable coincidence that Frau Graben had come into the shop and that I had been there to attend to her; that she had been so eager to talk in her own language that she was now sitting drinking tea in this house and bringing back so vividly that romantic adventure which had begun eleven years ago in the mist.

As she was leaving she said suddenly, 'Now you're the sort of person we'd want to teach them English.'

I felt a little faint. I stammered: 'But I'm not a teacher.'

She went on: 'It would have to be an English person. The Count was thinking of a tutor. But I don't think a woman would be out of place . . . better, I think. Women understand children more. I wonder . . .'

'I had no intention of teaching,' I said. 'You would want somebody qualified.'

'He'd want someone of education; but the main thing is someone who'd understand the children and speak German so well you could hardly tell it wasn't spoken by a native. Yes, I do reckon you're just the one.'

'If I had been looking for such a post . . .' I began.

'It would only be for a short time, of course. I don't know how long they'd take to learn. You love the mountains and the pine forests, don't you? You'd live in the schloss. I'd be there, as the *Schlossmutter*. I'm in charge of the children's household. There's something about you . . . *sympathetic* . . .

124

that's it. When the Count talked of having an English tutor I didn't like it at all. I don't want a man interfering in my household. I'd like a nice young woman, I thought. But not one of those stern, sharp-voiced English mistresses. Oh no! I wouldn't want that. I told the Count so. But my tongue's running away with me. If he engages a tutor, a tutor it'll be. Perhaps he has already done so. Well, it has been interesting talking to you.'

I said: 'You must come again.'

She held my hand when she said goodbye and there were tears in her eyes, as she thanked me for being kind and taking in the 'stranger within my gates'.

That night I scarcely slept at all. I was so excited. I thought of the schloss on the mountain looking down on the capital city and I longed to be there. I knew that I could never settle down happily with Anthony until I had made one great effort to discover the truth of what happened to me on the Night of the Seventh Moon.

I asked Frau Graben to tea again, just before she left Oxford. She talked of her home, of the children, of customs and feast days, of Rochenstein, of good Duke Carl who was stern and serious, so different from some of the previous rulers and members of his family. She told me about the visit of the Crown Prince and Princess of Prussia and I knew, didn't I, that the Crown Princess was Victoria who was named after her mother the Queen of England.

I was in a panic because she seemed to have completely forgotten her reference to the English teacher who would be wanted for the Count's children; I knew that I wanted to go, that this was an opportunity, a flimsy one it was true, and one which had come about as unexpectedly as . . . as the visit of Ilse and Ernst.

I had hoped that my cousin would ask me to pay another visit but she never wrote. Perhaps Ilse was not a good letter-writer and once she had assured herself that I had settled down after my experience she thought correspondence unnecessary. But she might have answered my letters.

It was I who had to make the reference. 'I should like to know that you return safely,' I said. 'Would you write to me? I feel you have become a friend and I should like to know how you get along with the tutor.'

'Oh, that tutor!' she cried. 'I hope he never comes.' She looked at me, her plump face earnest. 'Suppose I was to mention our meeting. The Count sets store on my opinion. Would you . . .? Just suppose he thought it might be a good idea.' She warmed to the subject. 'It would save so much trouble. We would have an Englishwoman and there wouldn't be the fuss of seeing you. I've done that already. I can think of no one more suitable . . . from my point of view. I could tell the Count . . .'

'I'd . . . I'd like to think about it.'

She nodded. 'Well, that's something. I'll mention you, and if he hasn't done anything . . . and if he agrees . . .'

'Well,' I said, trying to keep my voice steady. 'You might mention it.'

Now I could think of nothing but the possibility.

It was nine years ago since the day I left. Nine years! I should have made greater efforts to discover what had happened. I had accepted the solution given me by Ilse and Ernst; but they had faded into the past and seemed more unreal than Maximilian could ever be. Perhaps if I could go back I might discover the answer.

I *must* go back. I could take a holiday there perhaps with Anthony. No, that would not do. I should have to go as his wife and I must be free . . . free for whatever I should find.

I did not wish to go as a tourist. But to go to the schloss on the mountainside, looking down on the capital city . . . that was what I wanted. I knew then that I *must* go.

I lived in a fever of excitement. I was absent-minded in the shop. I kept away from the vicarage as much as possible.

'You are letting those Elkington women's gossip bother you,' said Anthony. 'You mustn't, you know. We'd face anything there was to face together.'

But it was not that. I was obsessed by the thought that I might find him. So it would be throughout my life. If ever I had known that marriage with Anthony would be unfair to him and perhaps wrong for me, I knew it now.

And at length there was the letter.

I was trembling so much that I could scarcely open it. The words danced before my eyes.

She had spoken to the Count. He agreed that the idea was excellent and as she had already vetted me there would be no need for any other recommendations. Would I let them know when I should be arriving and the sooner the better as far as they were concerned.

I was so excited I rushed into the shop and told Amelia.

'Go away to teach! You're crazy. What about Anthony?'

'Nothing has been settled between us.'

Aunt Matty was distraught. Just as she had thought I was nicely settled!

'Perhaps it won't last long,' I said. 'I might not like it.'

'Go for a holiday,' advised Amelia. 'Take a month or so and when you come back you'll have made up your mind to marry Anthony.'

But what could they know of this violent longing.

Mr and Mrs Greville were clearly hurt but Anthony understood.

'Go,' he said. 'This place meant something to you when you were young and impressionable. You see it different now you're grown up. You'll come back and then I'll be waiting for you.'

He understood as no one else could.

I did love him – but not in the wild unreasoning way I had loved before. I knew I was saying goodbye (but he said au revoir) to the best of men.

All the same, when the day of my departure arrived I felt more like the young girl I had once been than I had for nine long weary years.

TWO

It was dark when I arrived at the Schloss Klocksburg so that it was not until morning that I was able to take stock of my surroundings. I awoke to the sunshine of an early summer's morning which filtered into my room through two long narrow slits of window. A feeling of overpowering excitement was with me and for a few moments I lay still, saying to myself: 'I'm here. I'm back.'

Then I got out of bed and went to the window. From it I could look down on to the plateau from which the castle rose; I knew we were high because of the laborious manner in which the horses had climbed the previous evening; and I guessed that the castle had been built in the twelfth or thirteenth century, like so many I had seen in this part of the world, as a fortress, and had been added to as time progressed,

I was sure that the fortress in which I had my room was older than the buildings I was looking down on. These would be known as the *Randhausburg*, which meant surrounding house-castle, and they would contain the main living-quarters.

Beyond them I could look down into the valley to the town of Rochenburg which was the capital city of Duke Carl's domain. How beautiful it was in the light of early morning, with its mellowed roof-tops, its towers and turrets. Smoke was rising from some of the chimneys. Far above it on the hill stood another castle of imposing appearance. Like the Schloss Klocksburg there was the fortress with its turrets rising up stark from the mountainside, proclaiming its impregnability; I could make out the machicolated friezes which adorned the watch tower, and the round tower with the pointed roof and battlements from which in the past boiling oil and water would have been hurled down on attacking enemies. It was the most impressive of any among all the many castles I had ever seen.

A knock on my door made me turn from the window. It was a maid with hot water. Breakfast would arrive in fifteen minutes' time, she told me.

In a state of exultation I washed and dressed. I shook out my long dark hair in the way Maximilian had liked it to be when we had taken our breakfast in the hunting lodge. The magic was coming back to me so vividly that I don't think I should have been surprised to see him walk in, but when there was a knock on the door it was only the maid with my break-fast tray – coffee, rye bread and lots of fresh unsalted butter. It tasted good and while I was drinking my second cup of coffee there was another knock and Frau Graben came in.

She was beaming and looked as though she were very proud of herself.

'So you're really here,' she said.

It was gratifying to know that my presence gave her so much pleasure. 'Oh, I do hope you are going to be happy,' she went on. 'I've impressed on Dagobert that he must be a good boy because it is a great honour that an English lady should come all this way to teach him. If you have any difficulty with him just tell him that his father will not be pleased; that will quieten him. It always does.'

'When shall I see them?'

'As soon as you're ready. Perhaps you'd like to talk to them a bit about what you're going to teach them. You won't want to start lessons today. When you've seen them I will take you round the castle.'

'Thank you. I shall be most interested to see it. That's a very big castle I can see from my window.'

She smiled. 'That's the Duke's residence,' she said. 'Oh yes, it's more grand than little Klocksburg, which is only right and proper. I came to the royal castle when I was a young girl and looked after the boys. It became like home to me. And then afterwards the Count wanted me here. That was when Dagobert was born and he didn't know what to do with the child. After that Fritzi and Liesel joined us. But drink up your coffee or it will get cold. Is it to your liking?'

I said it was excellent.

'I believe you are quite excited about being here. I can see it's done you good already.'

I replied that I hoped I should give satisfaction. I had never taught before.

'This isn't ordinary teaching,' she said with that comfortable complacency which I had found rather charming. 'It's conversation that matters, so that they get the right accent. That's what the Count will look for.'

'I'm very eager to see them.'

'They'll have had breakfast. I'll send for them to come to the schoolroom.'

We left my room and descended a spiral staircase which led into a hall. 'This is where the schoolroom is,' she said.

'Are we in the *Randhausburg*?'

'No . . . we're still in the fortress. The children have their rooms here just below yours, but the rest of the household lives more in the *Randhausburg*.'

She opened a door. 'This is the schoolroom,' she said. 'The pastor comes to teach them. You will have to make your arrangements with him about the English lessons.'

'There should be a lesson every day,' I said. 'I am sure regularity is necessary. Perhaps an hour a day and very soon I hope to converse in English when I am with them, and perhaps take them for walks and give them easy lessons that way.'

'That sounds excellent.'

We went into the schoolroom – quite a large room with several embrasures in which were windows looking down on the town and across to the royal castle. The view from the windows was breathtaking.

There was a long table, rather scratched on its surface, and the legs were kicked. I guessed many generations of children had sat at that table. In the embrasures were window-seats on which lay books.

I remarked that it was a very pleasant room in which to work.

Frau Graben glanced at the watch pinned to her blouse.

'They will be here very soon,' she said. 'I do hope they are not going to be too difficult.'

There was a knock on the door and one of the maids entered; she was holding a little girl by the hand and behind her came two boys.

'This is Dagobert and Fritz and here is Liesel,' said Frau Graben.

Dagobert clicked his heels and bowed from the waist; Fritz, watching him, did the same; Liesel dropped a curtsey.

'This is Miss Trant who has come to teach you English.'

'Good morning,' said Dagobert in guttural English.

'Good morning,' I replied. Dagobert looked at his brother and sister as though expecting applause.

I smiled at them. 'We shall soon have you all speaking English,' I said in German.

'Is it easy?'

'When you've mastered it,' I assured them.

'Shall I speak it?' asked Liesel.

'You will all speak it.'

Frau Graben said: 'I will leave you with the children and then you can get to know them more easily. Perhaps they could show you the castle. That would be a good way of getting friendly.'

I thanked her. She was tactful, and I was sure that I could come to terms with my new pupils more easily on my own.

Liesel ran to the door as it shut on Frau Graben. I said: 'Come back, Liesel, and make my acquaintance.'

Liesel turned and put her tongue out at me.

Dagobert said: 'She's only a seamstress's daughter. She doesn't know how to behave.'

Liesel began to scream: 'I do. My papa is the Count. He will beat you. My papa loves me.'

'Our father would not have you forget your manners,' said Dagobert. 'So although you have the misfortune to be the daughter of a common seamstress, you have a noble father and you should not disgrace him.'

'You disgrace him,' said Liesel.

Dagobert turned to me: 'Take no notice of her, Fräulein Trant,' he said; but his eyes as they swept over me were contemptuous and it struck me that I should have more trouble with him than with the wayward Liesel.

Fritz – Frau Graben's Fritzi – had not spoken. He was regarding me with solemn dark eyes. It occurred to me that he might be the more difficult to understand. I had already decided that Dagobert was a young braggart, Liesel a spoilt child, but I had yet to form an opinion of Fritz.

'So you are Fritz,' I said.

He nodded.

'You're not to nod,' said Dagobert. 'Papa said so. You have to speak and say yes or no.'

I said: 'You are going to learn English. Do you know any yet?'

'I know Good afternoon, Mr.'

'Good afternoon, Mrs,' chanted Liesel.

Dagobert crowned it with: 'Good afternoon, ladies and gentlemen!' and watched me for applause.

'That is all very well,' I said, 'but will not get you very far. What else do you know?'

'God save the Queen!' said Dagobert. 'We shouted it when the Queen of England came here. We all had flags and had to wave them.' He waved an imaginary flag; then he started to run round the room shouting: 'God save the Queen.'

I said: 'Please be quiet now, Dagobert. The Queen is not here so it is not necessary. You have shown me how you shouted for her when she was here, so I know.'

Dagobert paused. 'But I want to shout for the Queen.'

'The rest of us might not want to hear.'

The children all looked expectant and Dagobert said craftily: 'But you've just come to teach us English, not to tell us when we can't shout for the Queen.'

The other two looked at Dagobert in admiration. I could imagine the state of affairs. He was Cock of the Nursery and as they looked up to him, I could imagine his spreading rebellion. He had too high an opinion of himself. That, I decided, must be deflated as soon as possible.

I said: 'If I am going to teach you I must have some authority. It is not a very admirable or clever thing to do to run round a room calling out a catch phrase even though it does show a hospitable sentiment towards the Queen of England. As I wanted to talk to you about your lessons, I would prefer you not to continue, Dagobert.'

Dagobert was astonished. I knew at once that he was not correctly disciplined and that he needed a firm hand more than the others. I could certainly look for trouble from Dagobert.

'My father went to Saxe-Coburg to see the Queen,' Fritz told me shyly.

'That was a long time ago,' said Dagobert scornfully. 'Prince Albert is dead and the Queen is a widow, God save the Queen. God . . .'

'Not again Dagobert,' I said.

'But if I want to I will.'

'In your own company then,' I said. 'I am going to ask Fritz and Liesel to show me the schloss, and I shall tell them about our English lessons.'

Dagobert looked at me coldly defiant; his legs apart, his head flung back, his blue eyes flashing.

I turned away and said: 'Come, Fritz . . . Liesel . . .'

Dagobert said: 'No. You're not to.'

I felt my future authority depended on the next few seconds so I took Liesel's hand. She tried to draw it away but I held it firmly. Her big blue eyes surveyed me with a kind of scared wonder. It was Fritz who decided.

'I'll show you, Fräulein,' he said.

'Thank you, Fritz.'

His eyes were large and expressive. I knew that he had scarcely stopped looking at me since they had come into the room. I smiled at him and he smiled shyly back.

Dagobert started to run round the room shouting 'God Save the Queen' but I shut the door firmly on him and said: 'In English we don't say Fräulein, Fritz. We say Miss. I'm Miss Trant, you see.'

'Miss,' said Fritz.

I nodded. 'Come on, Liesel. You say it too.'

'Miss,' said Liesel, and laughed.

'We shall have a short lesson every day,' I told them, 'and when we are together we will speak in English. We will surprise your father with your progress. Now you will tell me about the schloss. It is castle in English. Can you say castle?'

They both said it to my satisfaction and their own intense

delight. I contemplated that it would have been easy without Dagobert.

They showed me the rooms in the fortress – all with their embrasures in which were the long narrow windows. They took me up to the tower and Fritz told me that the tower was called the *Katzenturm*, the Cats' Tower, because the falling missiles which they used to throw down on the invading forces sounded like the screeching of cats. We stood up there looking down on the town and across the mountains and Fritz pointed out the Duke's castle high on the slope. Could I see the long buildings on the eastern side? They were the barracks and there the Duke's Guards lived. It was fun to see them standing there.

'They guard it all the time,' said Fritz. 'Don't they, Liesel?'

Liesel nodded. 'They have blue coats.'

'Dark blue coats, with gold on their sleeves and they have shining helmets. Sometimes they have feathers in them. They stand so still you think they're not real.'

'I should like to see them.'

'We'll show you, won't we, Liesel?'

Liesel nodded.

I felt I was getting on very well. Liesel was ready to go with whoever was the leader, I could see that. Fritz was quite different from Dagobert. He was much smaller but then he was several years younger; his eyes were dark whereas Dagobert's eyes were light blue; his hair was brown and straight, Dagobert's waved about his head like a glistening gold cap. Dagobert was the handsome one but Fritz interested me. He had a sensitive face and I remembered Frau Graben's saying that he missed a mother. I could well believe it. Dagobert would be self-sufficient; Fritz less so. I was sure, though, that Fritz was going to prove the better pupil.

I thought: He would be a year older than my own child. And I thought fleetingly how wonderful it would be if she had lived and all had gone as in those magic three days I had believed they would. Suppose this were my home – suppose instead of with these children I were here with my own . . .

I shook myself free of fancies. I must be firmly realistic – I must not allow the pine forests to put their spell on me.

'We'll go to the town together,' I said, 'and I'll tell you what everything is in English. That will be a lovely and easy way to learn.'

'Will Dagobert come?' asked Liesel.

'If he wants to.'

'Shall he be whipped if he won't?' asked Fritz. 'Would you whip him?'

I could not see myself so engaged so I smiled faintly. 'I shall just ignore him. If he doesn't want to learn he will be ignorant and when the Count comes he will say: "Well, what English have you learned?" And you and Liesel will speak to him in English and he will be pleased. Dagobert will know nothing.'

Liesel laughed. 'It'll serve him right,' she commented.

They took me down into the *Randhausburg*. This was of much later period – sixteenth or seventeenth century, I believed. It consisted of several turreted buildings on the mountain plateau above which the fortress rose. The sleeping quarters of the rest of the household were in one of these and in another was the *Rittersaal* – the hall of the knights – which would be used for ceremonial occasions. Beyond this was the stone-floored kitchen with its roasting spits and cauldrons. It smelt of sauerkraut and onions. During our tour we met one or two of the servants who bobbed curtseys at me when Fritz told them who I was.

It was in the *Rittersaal* that Dagobert appeared; he stood quietly listening to what I had to say and he was trying to pretend, I could see, that he had been with us all the time.

'This was where the knights used to be,' Fritz told me.

Dagobert said: 'Look at all the swords on the wall.'

'That one's the Count's,' said Fritz.

'No, that one,' contradicted Liesel. 'That's the biggest.'

'They're all the Count's, sillies,' declared Dagobert.

Liesel put out her tongue. 'We're going to speak English and you're not going to know any. Fräulein Trant said so.'

'No, that's not right, Liesel,' I corrected. 'What I said was that if Dagobert didn't want to be with us when we learn he would know nothing and then your father would wonder why he couldn't speak English like you and Fritz.'

'I'll speak English best of all,' said Dagobert.

I smiled inwardly. This was early victory.

'Can he?' asked Fritz almost anxiously; and I knew then that Fritz was hoping for an opportunity to excel the half-brother who beat him at almost everything he did.

'The one who works the hardest will be the best,' I said. 'It's as simple as that.'

Victory indeed! I had instilled in my pupils a determination to apply themselves and succeed.

After we had examined the *Randhausburg* we went back to the fortress, and the children showed me the hunting room. The ceiling of this room was decorated with groups of animals and there were some stuffed heads on the walls among guns of various kinds.

'We practise shooting,' Dagobert told me. 'I'm a good shot. Bang! Bang! I shoot to kill.'

'You couldn't,' said Fritz. 'The cartridges are all blank.'

'Yes, I could,' insisted Dagobert. 'Bang.'

'We have archery lessons too,' Fritz told me.

'We practise in the courtyard,' added Dagobert. 'I hit the target every time.'

'You don't,' Fritz disagreed.

'I would if I wanted to.'

'Well, I shall see,' I said. 'Now we'll go to the schoolroom and I'll see the Pastor.'

'The Pastor doesn't come today,' Dagobert said, scornful of my ignorance.

'Then I shall tell you what I hope to do about our daily lesson. Then I can arrange the time with the Pastor when he does come.'

We were mounting the staircase and came to a passage. I could turn right or left. One way led to my room, so I took the other and found myself at the foot of a spiral staircase. I started up this when Fritz called to me urgently: 'Fräulein Trant . . .'

I was about to say: 'It's Miss Trant in English,' when I turned and saw the fearful expression on his face. He was standing at the bottom of the staircase.

'What's wrong, Fritz?' I asked.

'You mustn't go up there.'

The other children came up. Their faces bore the same excited yet frightened look.

'Why not?' I asked.

'The haunted room's up there,' explained Fritz.

'Haunted? Who says so?'

'Everybody,' answered Dagobert. 'Nobody goes there.'

'The servants go to dust it,' contradicted Fritz.

'Never by themselves. If you go there by yourself something terrible will happen to you. You'd die and stay there for ever to haunt people.'

Fritz had turned very pale and I said sharply: 'That's nonsense. What could be in there?'

'The ghost,' said Fritz.

'Has anyone seen it?' I asked.

There was silence. I walked up a step or two then Fritz said: 'Come back, Fräulein, Miss . . .'

I said: 'There's nothing to be afraid of, I'm sure.'

An irresistible urge forced me to go on and besides I did not want the children, on whom I had made a good impression, to think me afraid, particularly Dagobert who, as I advanced, crept up behind me. .

All the children were watching me.

The staircase ended in a small landing on which was a door. I went towards it and took the door knob in my hands. I heard the gasp behind me.

I turned the handle.

The door was locked.

The rest of the day passed as though I were in a dream; I had to keep reminding myself that I was really here. I took luncheon with Frau Graben in a little room in the *Randhausburg* which she said was her sanctum. Her delight in my presence was very gratifying but I was a little afraid that I might not live entirely up to expectations. I had not had a great deal to do with children; yet although I had never thought to teach, when I had realized that I might have a child dependent on me and Ilse had suggested that I teach in the *Damenstift*, the idea had seemed possible. I had thought of Ilse quite often since I had known I was coming here and of how strange it was that after we had been so close during my months of waiting for the birth of my child she should have faded out of my life. For I really had no idea where she was now.

In the afternoon of that day I met Pastor Kratz, a shrivelled little man with very bright sparkling eyes. He thought it an excellent plan, he said, that I had come to teach the children English. He himself had toyed with the idea of introducing it into the series of lessons he gave, but his accent was not good. Nor was his English, and there was no one who could teach a language like a native of the land to which it belonged; and when that teacher had a good command of the pupil's language also, then it was ideal.

I was to give the children half an hour's lesson each morning and another half-hour's session in the afternoons, but I set greater store on what they would learn through conversation with me.

'The Count will expect quick progress,' said the Pastor, his eyes twinkling. 'He is a very impatient man.'

Frau Graben confirmed this. 'He was always like that, even worse than his cousin.'

'Who was his cousin?' I asked.

'The Prince, the Duke's only son and heir. They were brought up together as boys. What a handful! I can tell you all about that. I was nurse to them both.'

The Pastor invited me to call at the church, when he would show me the Processional Cross. The church was well worth a visit, he told me. The stained glass windows were famous throughout Europe. I must come and see them. The cross itself was kept strongly guarded in an oak chest which dated back to the twelfth century. Notice had to be given if one wished to see it, for the keys of the chest were locked away in a secret place and only the current pastor knew where; it was a secret passed on from pastor to pastor, a custom which had gone back all those years, for the cross with its lapis-lazuli and chalcedony, its rubies, pearls and diamonds, was priceless.

I said I should love to see it.

'Then you must let me know when and it shall be brought out for you. Two of the Duke's guards will be on duty at the church while we look at it.'

'So it is as priceless as that?'

'It's an old custom, really. The church has always had to be guarded when the Processional Cross was brought out. Old customs die hard in these parts.'

I thanked the Pastor and was sure that we were going to get along well. He was an unworldly little man but his zest for enjoyment was clearly great and both these qualities I found endearing.

In the afternoon the children took me for a little walk round the plateau on which the castle had been built. The scenery was magnificent. I was fascinated as always by the tall straight pines and firs and the little streams. We wandered a little downhill from the plateau, and the castle was soon hidden from our view by the trees; I loved it all – the sudden rush of a waterfall – the silver and spruce firs – the occasional woodcutter's hut; the sight of a little village below us and the sudden tinkle of bells which the cows wore about their necks to guide the cowherds in which direction to go to find them when the mist descended. I talked to the children as we went, giving them the English names for what we saw. They seemed to find this an exciting game and Dagobert was on his mettle trying to show that he could play this game so much better than the others. Fritz, however, seemed to learn more easily and I was secretly glad about this. I felt drawn strongly towards the quiet dark boy.

When we returned Frau Graben was waiting for us rather anxiously.

'I was afraid they would have taken you too far,' she said. 'Now, children, you just go off and Ida will give you your milk. Miss Trant, you come with me. I have a treat for you.'

The treat was tea. 'We know what you English are for tea,' she said, beaming; and I felt I could not have been made more welcome.

It was very pleasant to sit in Frau Graben's little room which looked on to a tiny cobbled courtyard.

'It's worked out so very well,' she said.

'It's so strange,' I replied. 'If I hadn't happened to be in the shop that day . . .'

'Don't let's think of anything so disastrous,' she cried. 'You are here and that makes me happy. What do you think of the children?'

'They are interesting.'

'They've all had such unconventional beginnings. Dagobert is the son of the Count and a lady of high quality. He would have married her but Count Ludwig his father wouuldn't give his permission. It was not the match he wanted for Frederic, and Frederic is near enough to the dukedom to have to obey orders. So he made the right marriage and now he has a fine boy of eight. He sets great store by him and I know he hoped he'd inherit the dukedom one day, because the Prince was so reluctant to marry.'

'So this boy is the heir.'

'Not he. And that's a sore point with Master Count. The Duke insisted the Prince, his son, marry and he couldn't hold out for ever. It was a necessary marriage; one of the terms in a treaty Rochenstein made with Klarenbock. So the Prince married Princess Wilhelmina. That was five years ago. There's a child – a boy; he's three years old, a son and heir. So our Prince has done his duty.'

'I suppose I shall learn the country's politics in due course.'

'They're frequently discussed. In a little country like this the reigning family lives close to the people.'

'Shall I see the Prince and Princess?'

Her expression was suddenly enigmatical; she seemed to be suppressing secret mirth.

'Oh, our ruling family's seen,' she said. 'Not like English Royalty, you know. We hear about England. It's because of our close ties since the Queen's marriage with one of our princes. I hear she shuts herself away since she lost him. She goes around in her widow's weeds and won't give up mourning, though it must be . . . how long since he died?'

'It's nine years,' I said. 'She was absolutely devoted to him.'

'Well, our Duke isn't allowed to shut himself away. He comes down from the castle into the town to attend certain functions; he hunts in the forests. The Prince is away at the moment. He's in Berlin at the Court of Prussia representing his father at a conference. Count Bismarck is constantly summoning heads of state to Berlin. I think he's of the opinion that we're all vassals of great Prussia. He is apt to forget that we are independent states and that is what the Prince is no doubt telling him now.'

'You know the Prince well, I suppose.'

'I should do. I was his nurse. He and the children's father were brought up together. And what a task to keep those two in order. The spirits! They were always fighting, those two boys. What a pair. The Prince is sure of himself, playing the Grand Duke almost in the nursery and Count Frederic determined to show he was as good as his cousin. They've been behaving like that ever since. But I'll have none of their old tantrums – I've told them both. I still think of them as my boys in the nursery and however grand they may think they are to others they're just my two boys to me.'

I asked if the children were like their father.

'There's a resemblance,' she said. 'Dagobert's got a look of him. That affair was more serious than the others. Liesel was the daughter of the sewing woman whom the Count took a fancy to.'

'And Fritz?' I asked.

'Fritz was two and a half when he came here. His mother had died, they said. She'd been a lady of quality and when Fritz was conceived she had disappeared. The Count was frantic for a while, but you know how these men are. He was quickly on with the next. Then the woman who had been

Fritz's foster mother died. I knew her; she was once one of the nurses under me. I had him brought here to be brought up with Dagobert. But Fritz was old enough to remember that he wasn't always here; I think it upsets him a bit. The woman who cared for him was like a mother to him and he missed her.'

'This Count seems to be very careless as to where he fathers children.'

'My dear Miss Trant, he's only following the tradition. They've always been ones for the women. They see them, they fancy them and there's no holding them back. If there are results they don't mind and nor do the women. Take Liesel. She's well looked after, she's being educated, a good marriage will be made for her. That wouldn't have happened to her if her mother had married a woodcutter, say. The child would be wandering the forest gathering sticks and not being sure where her next meal was coming from.'

I was silent for a while; then I said, 'I think I shall be able to teach them something. I want to be with them as much as possible. I'm already looking forward to the time when we can converse in English.'

'It'll come. You're going to succeed. I'm sure the Count will be pleased.'

'If he isn't,' I said, 'I shall go back to England.'

Then I thought of it: the shop, working for the parish, gradually clinging to the comfort which Anthony was offering. But at the moment I was in revolt against all that, for something told me that I was on the verge of discovery, that life was going to be exciting, though perhaps not happy – for happiness and excitement did not always go together.

Not yet, Anthony, I thought; and then I realized that although I had relegated him to the back of my mind I liked to think of him there.

'Don't say that, when you've only just come. What do you think of Klocksburg?'

'It's fascinating. I've seen many a schloss during the time I have spent here but I never thought to live in one.'

'The children showed you over it, I hope?'

'Yes, they took me everywhere, I think . . . except one part. It appeared to be locked.'

'Oh, the haunted room. There are haunted rooms in most castles, you know.'

'What is the story about this one?'

She hesitated. 'Oh, the usual, love . . . ending in tragedy. A young woman threw herself from the window to her death.'

'Why?'

'It was years ago. The present Duke's great-grandfather I think brought her here. She thought she was his wife.'

'And she wasn't?'

'It was a mock marriage. It was often done – still is. The girl would not give in to him so the marriage was arranged. The so-called priest who performed the ceremony was no priest at all, but one of the courtiers, so of course the marriage was no true marriage and the girl was tricked. Her scruples were calmed and the honeymoon followed. In these cases when the bridegroom grows tired of the liaison he passes on and the lady realizes the truth. It's been done many a time.'

'I see. And this girl?'

'Her lover was deeply enamoured of her. The story is that he might have married her if he had not been married already – as his position demanded.'

'So he deceived her?'

'Deceiving simple girls was one of their favourite pastimes. It meant more to them than ruling their lands. But he was more involved than was customary with this girl. He brought her to Klocksburg and she lived here thinking herself a countess. At first he came to visit her and then the visits grew less frequent. From the turret room – the one behind the locked door – so the story goes – she used to look for him. From the window you can see the road winding right down to the town. Day after day she sat there watching and waiting. Then one day he came, but with him he brought his Countess, who had insisted on accompanying him. The poor girl wondered who the lady was and when the Count entered Klocksburg the first thing he did was go up to that room to his mistress. The story is that when he told her the truth she wouldn't believe it. He insisted she keep quiet about their relationship. She must come down to the *Randhausburg* and behave as though she was here as the châtelaine of the castle to keep it in order for the time when the Count and his Countess should call. When he went away she locked herself in her room and, opening the casement window wide, jumped out to her death. Well, you can see how these stories start from that.'

'Poor girl,' I said.

'She was foolish,' said Frau Graben, pursing her lips. 'She

141

could have lived all her days in comfort. The Princes always looked after their favoured women.'

'I can well imagine the shock of believing oneself married and finding one was not.'

'They say she haunts the place. Some say they've seen her. If she comes back it must be because she realizes that it was a silly thing she did. She could have gone on living in comfort.'

'I understand her feelings.'

'Well, I keep the door locked. I don't want any of the maids getting hysterics. I go in with one of them once a week to dust and clean; then I see that it's locked up.'

I couldn't get out of my mind the thought of that girl watching for her lover and learning how he had deceived her. When she had told the story Frau Graben had seemed secretly amused, sly even. I felt for the first time that she might not be the simple warm-hearted woman I had imagined her to be. It seemed absurd to say there was something sinister about her – but that was how it seemed.

I quickly dismissed the thought as ridiculous.

I dreamed about that girl. I understood exactly how she felt. My dreams, as dreams so often are, were muddled, and I was the girl; and the man I saw riding up the mountain was Maximilian.

The children were very excited because Pastor Kratz was going to show me the Processional Cross. The road down to the town was about a mile long though there was a path, which could only be undertaken on foot or on horseback, which was much shorter. There was a surefooted little mare in the stables which had been put at my disposal, and the children had their ponies. Frau Graben said that Liesel should not ride all the way down to the town as she was not a practised enough rider, and as the little girl set up wails of protest at the thought of being excluded from the expedition, she promised to take her down in the horse carriage while I went down on my mare with the boys.

It was a beautiful afternoon; the sun was shining through the trees and one caught glimpses of silver streams glinting among the rocks. Dagobert rode ahead; he liked to see himself as a leader, but Fritz kept by my side as though he were taking care of me. He was ahead of Dagobert in his English and displayed a remarkable ability for remembering the words I taught. Already he had a small vocabulary, which was very pleasing.

As the trees grew less thick we could see the distant mountains and my eyes as ever went to the royal castle and I thought of Frau Graben as a young woman in her nursery there with the two boys on whom even now she clearly doted.

Below was the town taking on a definite character as we approached . . . a fairy-tale town with turrets, towers and red tiled roofs against a background of trees.

Although the main part of the town was in the valley, it was to some extent built on the slope and as we passed first through the *Oberer Stadtplatz*, with its fountain and arcades of shops, I was reminded vividly of Lokenberg, on the Night of the Seventh Moon. We were now in the month of June; very soon it would be the ninth anniversary of that night. I must ask Frau Graben whether the occasion was celebrated here.

We passed through narrow streets which sloped down to the *Unterer Stadtplatz* and here was the church with its baroque dome and Gothic walls.

Dagobert told me that we should stable the horses in the Prince Carl Inn which was close by the church. Delightedly knowledgeable, he led the way. The innkeeper received us with some deference, for he knew the boys. Dagobert haughtily accepted this and our horses were taken and we went to the church on foot, where Frau Graben and Liesel were already waiting.

Pastor Kratz said how pleased he was that he could show me the cross. Two soldiers from the Palace were already standing on guard in the crypt where the oak chest was kept.

'I'm afraid it's a great deal of trouble,' I said.

'No, no,' cried the Pastor. 'We like people to see the cross. Usually there is a small party of sightseers, but you, as a member of the Count's household, don't have to wait for that. I should be delighted to show you the church first.'

This he did. It was a fine old church dating back to the twelfth century; the stained glass windows were the pride of the town, the Pastor told me gleefully; and they were magnificent; the blues, reds and golds depicted the story of the Crucifixion and lit by the sun presented a truly magnificent sight.

There were memorial tablets on the walls and I read the inscriptions; these were scions of the old families of the district.

'The ducal family does not appear to be represented here,' I said.

'They have their own chapel in the castle,' said Frau Graben.

'They come here, though, for State occasions,' put in the Pastor. 'Coronations, royal christenings and such events.'

'Those would be great occasions for the people,' I added.

'Yes, indeed. Like everyone else we enjoy our ceremonies.'

' "The Family", as we call them,' explained Frau Graben, 'are not buried here. They have a special burial ground. It's an island.'

'I want to take Fräulein Trant to the Island of Graves,' announced Dagobert.

'*I* don't like it much,' said Fritz.

'You're afraid,' accused Dagobert.

'Now, now,' put in Frau Graben. 'Nobody's going to take anybody to the Island of Graves who doesn't want to go.'

'What a strange name,' I said.

'You children run on,' said Frau Graben. 'Go out and look at the tombstones.'

'It's not the same as the Island,' said Dagobert.

'It couldn't be because it's not an island.'

The boys had stopped to study an effigy in stone. Dagobert spelt out the inscription. Frau Graben drew me aside and I asked: 'What is this Island of Graves?'

'You should visit it. I think you'd find it interesting. But I don't want Liesel to go. She's too young. It's rather a morbid spot. But it's only the Family's burial ground. The island is in the middle of a lake and there is a ferryman who lives there and rows people back and forth. He looks after the graves.'

'And the members of the ducal family are buried there?'

'The family and those connected with it.'

'Servants, you mean?'

'No . . . no. People closer than that.'

'Closer?'

'Well, the dukes, the counts, they had their friends and sometimes there were children. There is a part of the island which is for people like that – close to the family, you might say, and yet not of it.'

The blue light from the stained glass window fell across her face as she spoke and again I was struck by the slightly mischievous light in her usually calm and simple face.

She went on: 'You must visit the Island of Graves. I'll take you myself.'

'I'd like to see it,' I said.

'We'll arrange it.'

We were ready to go down to the crypt and I was surprised by the little ceremony.

It was dank in the crypt; Fritz kept close to me and I wondered whether it was for my protection or his own; Dagobert's swagger was a little less convincing. There certainly was an eeriness about the place, perhaps because of the smell of damp and the dimness of the light. Our footsteps rang out on the stone floor, seeming to echo, and then I saw the great oak chest on either side of which stood a soldier in the blue and gold uniform of the Duke's Guards.

They stood at attention while three soldiers approached, one of these held the key.

I was astonished and a little embarrassed that all this ceremony should be for me.

The Pastor took the heavy bunch of keys. Opening the chest took a little time but the operation at length was completed. In it was the treasure of the church – I saw the silver goblets, the chalice and the crosses which were of silver and gold set with semi-precious stones. But the latter were not to be compared with the Processional Cross which was kept separately in its heavy wooden case which again had to be unlocked. It was at length revealed to me.

The children gasped as they gazed on it – lying on black velvet. It seemed to shine with an uncanny light and was intricately wrought in gold, enamel and precious gems. Each of the large stones which formed the centre had, I was told, a story attached to it. Each had been won in battle. In those days the country had been wild and the small dukedoms and principalities were constantly at war with each other. The centre diamond and the two rubies on either side had been set in the cross to emphasize the invincibility of the Dukes of Rochenstein. If the cross were stolen it was believed that would be the end of the line. This was why it was so guarded, not only because of its value but because of its legendary importance.

I was rather glad when the cross was back in its box and

the chest locked; so were the soldiers. They relaxed at once and ceased to look like stone statues. The children changed too; they began to talk in loud voices whereas previously they had whispered.

They appeared to know the soldiers well. One called Sergeant Franck was a particularly jolly fellow.

We came up from the crypt and were soon in the sunshine.

'There,' said Frau Graben, 'now you've seen the Processional Cross. You'll see all the sights in time.'

She seemed to be secretly amused and again I wondered whether I really knew her as well as I had thought.

THREE

It was the boys who took me first to the Island of Graves. Each afternoon during my first week at Klocksburg we went out into the forest – they on their ponies, I on my mare. I enjoyed these jaunts for they enabled me to get to know the children better and I was more fascinated by the forest than ever; every time I went out I felt as though I were on the verge of an adventure. As we were in summer the mountainsides seemed to be touched by a blue and pink mist which were the gentians and orchids flourishing there at that time of the year. They were breathtakingly lovely among the green.

On this particular day the boys had led me on to the downward slopes and as the land grew flat we came to a little wood in which the trees grew so close that the branches caught us as we rode beneath them. We came to a clearing and there to my astonishment was a lake, in the middle of which was an island. On the shore were two boats fitted with oars.

They had made up their minds to bring me here, I guessed, and were about to show me something of which they were rather proud.

We tethered our horses to one of the trees and both boys set about gathering the leaves and flowers which grew close to the water.

Then Dagobert cupped his hands about his mouth and shouted: 'Franz! Franz!'

I asked whom they were calling and they both exchanged secret glances. Dagobert said: 'Wait and see, Miss.'

I replied that I wanted to know what they were about and appealed to Fritz.

He pointed towards the island in the middle of the lake and I saw a boat being pushed out. A man jumped into it and began rowing towards us.

'That's Franz,' Fritz told me.

Dagobert was determined to be the one who disclosed the secret.

'Franz,' he said, 'is the keeper of the *Gräber Insel*. He is coming to take us over so that we can put flowers on our mothers' graves. You can row over yourself but Franz likes you to call him.'

The distance between the Island of Graves and the shore was, I guessed, less than a quarter of a mile. The man in the boat was very old and bent; his grey hair grew long about his face, which was almost covered by his beard so that little more than his eyes were visible and they were embedded in wrinkles.

'Franz,' called Dagobert, 'we want to show Miss Trant the island.'

Old Franz brought the boat on the shore.

'Well, young masters,' he said, 'I was expecting you.' His voice had a hollow ring; he wore a long black robe like a monk's and on his head was a tiny black skullcap. The little eyes were on me now.

'I heard you were here, Fräulein,' he said. 'You must come over to my island.'

'She wants to see the graves,' said Dagobert.

I was unaware that I had expressed such a wish but it seemed impolite to say so before their keeper.

'It was time you young masters came,' said Franz.

He took my hand to help me into the boat. His was dry, rough and cold. Something about him made me shiver. I thought of him as Charon, the boatman of the Styx. Fritz was close behind me as though to protect me, I thought; and I was touched.

Dagobert leaped into the boat. 'Are you frightened, Miss?' he asked gleefully, clearly hoping that I was.

'Why do you ask? Did you expect me to be?'

'Franz lives all alone on *Gräber Insel*, don't you, Franz? Most people are a bit scared when they go there because there's nobody there but the dead and Franz, of course. I wonder if you will be scared. Franz isn't scared. He lives there all alone with the dead, don't you, Franz?'

'For seventy years,' he said. 'Seventy years on the island. My father was keeper before me, and I knew I'd follow on.' He shook his head sadly. 'I've no son to follow me.'

'What will they do when you die, Franz?' asked Dagobert.

Old Franz shook his head. 'They'll bring someone else in. Before, it was handed down from father to son.'

'Oh Franz, the dead won't like it. I bet they'll haunt the next one and drive him away.'

'This is a very morbid subject,' I said. 'I'm sure Franz will be the keeper for many years yet.'

Franz looked at me with approval. 'My grandfather lived to ninety. My father to ninety-three. They say that the dead give the gift of long life to their keepers.'

'Oh, but you haven't got a son to follow you, Franz,' Dagobert reminded him. 'They won't like that.'

'Why are you so pleased at the prospect, Dagobert?' I asked.

'Well, they'll come out and haunt the next one, that's why.'

The oars lapped gently in the water. I could see the island very clearly now. There appeared to be avenues of trees and flowering shrubs. It was very beautiful; and among the trees was a tiny house which reminded me of the gingerbread cottage in *Hansel and Gretel*. I felt as though I were entering the fairy-tale world again.

The boat came to rest on the shore and we scrambled out.

'First show her the ducal graves,' demanded Dagobert.

'Come this way,' said Franz.

The two boys went off to lay their flowers on their mothers' graves and I followed Franz into one of the avenues between the flowers and the trees. There were the graves; they were magnificently kept and glowing with flowers; the marble effigies were beautiful; so were the statues of angels guarding the graves and on some were gilded caskets and ornamentations in gilt and wrought iron.

'These are the graves of the family,' Franz told me. 'After the memorial services and the burial ceremonies they are brought over to me to lie in their final resting-place. I tend the shrubs and keep the graves fresh. Members of the Family sometimes come here, but rarely young ones. The young don't think of death. These two boys come, though. That's because their mothers lie here . . . though not among the ducal avenues. There are two burial grounds here – that of the dukes and their legitimate families and those whom they have honoured, as they call it. Some might say dishonoured. The boys come because they like to remind themselves that they are connected with the Family. I will show you the other graves afterwards. First look at these of the Family. This one is Ludwig's grave. He is the brother of Duke Carl and a traitor. He was killed by the Duke's friends and just in time for if he had not been killed he would have killed the Duke.'

'I have heard something of Ludwig.'

'He will not easily be forgotten. And there is Count Frederic to follow him. Trouble . . . trouble . . .'

'Why should there be trouble between the Duke and Count Frederic?'

'There is often trouble in families . . . particularly our old German ones. In the old days when the estates were so poor the brothers drew lots to see who should have what there was. An estate divided would have brought very little to brothers if there were many of them – and there so often were – so that the only thing was to draw lots and let the winner take all. This has caused trouble through the ages. Those who have not inherited believe they owe their positions at the present day to the ill luck of their ancestors in the past. Many seek to win back by treachery what luck has denied them. Ludwig was such a one. He wanted to unseat Carl and rule Rochenstein himself.'

'And the boys' father is his son?'

'Yes, Count Frederic will have to be careful. He will have the Prince to answer to. But Frederic is clever. He'll bide his time.'

'So these are the dead ones,' I said. 'Well, if they suffered when they were alive they have been given due homage here. The graves are lovely.'

'It's my pride to keep them beautiful,' Franz said, his face lighting with a smile. 'I'll swear there are no more beautiful graves than mine in the whole of Europe.'

I walked down the line of graves and read the inscriptions. There were the Dukes of Rochenstein and Dorrenig and Counts of Lokenberg. 'Family titles all of them,' murmured Franz. As ever when I read that name I thought of myself back in the hunting lodge and the ceremony when Maximilian had slipped a ring on my finger . . . a ring which disappeared with my dreams . . . and the marriage lines which said I was his wife which had no substance either.

There were several avenues, all exquisitely kept – the grass weeded, the flowers blooming to perfection.

I saw the boys who called to me; and old Franz led me over to them. I passed through a gate and was in a walled graveyard. Here the graves were simple mounds with small grey stones at the head of them. I noticed some had no stones at all.

'These are the graves of those who are buried here with the permission of some member of the Family,' Franz explained.

'I'll show you my mother's grave,' said Dagobert.

I followed him, stepping cautiously between the graves to one with a headstone rather more elaborate than most of the others. On it was written Countess von Plinschen and the date of her death, 1858. Dagobert said: 'She died when I was born . . . she died having me.'

'That's sad,' I murmured, touched to see the reverent manner in which he laid the pink orchids on her grave.

Fritz said: 'My mother died too. Can I show you where she is?'

He took my hand and we walked away from the others. I was conscious of the eyes of Franz following me and I thought what a gruesome place this was, and it was a pity that the Family, as they were called, hadn't buried their dead in a churchyard like normal people.

I was deeply touched at the sight of Fritz kneeling by that grave. It simply said on it Luisa Freundsberg and nothing more.

'She loved me very much,' said Fritz, 'but of course I was an embarrassment to her.'

'My dear Fritz,' I said. 'You must have been a great joy to her.'

His eyes were suddenly touched by pain as he said: 'I don't remember her. I only remember Frau Lichen and then there was Frau Graben.'

'Well, I dare say they loved you dearly.'

'Yes,' he admitted shyly, 'but it is not the same as a mother.'

'There will be others in your life to love you,' I assured him; and that seemed to please him.

We went back and joined the others.

Franz offered us refreshments and we went into his ginger-bread-like house to partake of them. We stepped down into a room in which were several flowers in pots. The scent was almost overpowering. We sat at a table and from a cask he drew mugs of what tasted like beer. I didn't greatly care for it but the boys drank it with relish.

Franz told me he had made it himself. He looked after himself. He never went to the mainland; his provisions were sent over once a week by the Family, and sometimes he saw no one for weeks on end. The boys visited the island regularly once a month and every now and then when there was a burial the body was brought over by night and laid in its grave.

He was gardener and stonemason. In the old days it had been easier. He had helped his father; his mother had died when he was quite a boy. Women didn't take kindly to *Gräber Insel*. He himself had married a wife. He had gone to the mainland to find her, he said sadly. He brought her back and waited for his son. But there was no son. The island gave her the creeps, she said. She couldn't live there; and one night when he was asleep she crept out and rowed herself over to the mainland, and in the morning he awoke to find her gone. She was never heard of since, and he was unable to take another wife – even if he could have found one to share his lonely life on the Island of Graves.

I was glad when we were in the boat again. There was something uncanny about *Gräber Insel* and I couldn't stop thinking of the old man as Charon, the ferryman of the dead.

That night I awoke with a start. I had dreamed a great deal in the last eight years but never more vividly than since I had come to Klocksburg – except of course in the months directly following my adventures.

This time I had believed I was on the Island of Graves and in that avenue I found an inscription on which was written Maximilian Count Lokenberg, and as I watched the marble slab was lifted and Maximilian stepped out of the tomb. He came to me and took me in his arms and his embrace was a frozen one. I cried out: 'You are dead?' and woke up.

I had thrown off all the bedclothes. I was shivering. The window was wide open to the mountain air. I lighted my candle. I knew I shouldn't sleep for some time.

It was all coming back so vividly to me, as it always did after dreams, and with it that aching sadness with which I had become familiar. It brought with it a fearful sense of loss from which I believed I should never recover. There could never be anyone in my life to take his place.

Then I heard footsteps on the landing outside my room. I looked at my watch. It was just after one o'clock. Who could be walking about at this time? There were only the children and two maids in the fortress, the rest of the household had their quarters in the *Randhausburg*.

The steps were stealthy as though someone was carefully picking a way towards my room. They stopped. I saw my door handle slowly turn. I remembered that I had locked the door. Since my adventure in the mist I had made a habit of this and even at home I did it.

'Who is that?' I asked. There was no answer. I listened, then I heard the footsteps going on. They were mounting the stairs, I believed. I felt the goose pimples rising on my skin; if I was right and those footsteps were mounting the stairs they could only be going to one place – the room in the turret – the haunted room.

The two maids in the fortress and the children were all afraid of the haunted room. So . . . who could it be who was now stealthily making for it?

My curiosity was greater than my fear. Since I had come here the conviction had grown up within me that I was going to make some great discovery. I could not help feeling that I was a stranger to myself, and I must be so to a certain extent because I did not know whether I had actually lived through the greatest adventure of my life or dreamed it. I knew that until I could satisfy myself as to what really happened on the night of the Seventh Moon, I could never understand myself and therefore never know real peace of mind.

Why investigating uncanny footsteps on the stairs should help me, I did not know. All I was aware of was that these pine forests were the scene of my lost six days and somewhere here I would find the secret. So I must leave nothing unexplored, however remote it might seem to my personal affairs.

I hastily wrapped a dressing-gown about myself and picked up a candle; I unlocked the door; I looked out along the landing to the winding staircase. I could distinctly hear the footsteps on the stairs above.

I sped up there, holding my candle as firmly as my trembling hand would allow. Someone was there. Could it be the ghost of the woman whose lover had deceived her and who had thrown herself down from the turret windows?

The candle light flickered on the spiral stone stairs which were worn in the middle by hundreds of years of use. I was almost at the turret. There was the door. My heart leapt with fear, the candle tipped sideways and almost went out. A figure was standing at the door of the haunted room.

I saw a hand reach out to turn the knob.

Then I realized who it was. 'Fritzi!' I whispered, using the pet diminutive.

He did not look round.

I went up to him, all fear evaporated. '*Mutti*,' he whispered. He had turned to me and seemed to stare without seeing. Then I realized. Fritz was walking in his sleep.

I took his hand firmly in mine; I led him down the stairs and back to his room. I put him into his bed, tucked him up, and kissed him lightly on the forehead.

I whispered: 'Everything is all right, Fritzi. I'm here to look after you.'

He whispered: '*Mutti*? *Meine Mutti . . .*'

I sat by his bed. He was very quiet and after a while appeared to be sleeping peacefully. I went to my own room. I was very cold so I got into bed and tried to warm myself.

I slept little for the rest of that night; I kept straining my ears for the sound of footsteps. In the morning I decided to talk to Frau Graben.

'He was always a nervous child,' she said, beaming at me. In her sitting-room she kept a fire going most of the time and invariably had a kettle singing on it. She also kept what she called a stockpot and this provided a most appetizing-smelling soup.

She made tea for me. She always did this with a kind of smug delight as though to say, 'See how I look after you?'

As we sat sipping the brew I was telling her about last night.

'It's not the first time he's walked in his sleep,' she said.

'It's dangerous, I should think.'

'They say that people who walk in their sleep rarely hurt themselves. There was one of the maids . . . so the story goes . . . who got out of one of the windows and walked along the parapet of the tower without coming to any harm.'

I shivered.

'No, Fritzi's never come to any harm sleep-walking. They say they step over anything that's in their way.'

'But he must be in a disturbed state to sleep-walk, don't you think?'

'Poor Fritzi, he's the sensitive one. He feels things more than the other two.'

'Yesterday they took me to the Island of Graves.'

'Oh, that upset him. It always does. I don't like them going there, but don't like to stop it. After all, it's right they should respect their dead mothers.'

'I think it's a pity there has to be so much talk about the haunted room. The fact that it's kept locked makes them imagine all sorts of horrors behind those closed doors. Have the children ever been in the room?'

'No.'

'It's no wonder they're overawed. The fact that Fritz made his way up there shows that it's on his mind and he connects it in some way with his dead mother, because he was at the Island of Graves yesterday.'

'He seems to have been better since you came. Learning English agrees with him. Or perhaps it's you. He seems to have taken a real fancy to you – and you to him.' She gave me that rather sly look of hers. 'I reckon he's your favourite among the children. I'm glad, for Fritzi's sake.'

'I'm interested in him. He's a clever boy.'

'I'll agree with you.'

'I think he needs to be a member of a big uncomplicated family.'

'They say all children do.'

'I was wondering about that room. What is it like?'

'It's just a room. It's in the turret and so it's circular. There are several windows, the lattice type that open out. That was why it was so easy for her to open one and get out.'

'And this room has been locked for years and years.'

'I don't think so. The fortress wasn't used much before Count Frederic brought the children here. Then there was this story about the haunting and I thought it better to keep the door locked.'

I hardly liked to go against her authority so I was silent but she pressed me. 'You think it's wrong to keep it locked, then?' she went on.

'If it was treated just like an ordinary room people would

forget the story,' I said. 'Such stories are best forgotten, surely.'

She shrugged her shoulders. Then she said: 'Would you like me to leave it unlocked?'

'I have an idea it would be better. Then I'll try to make light of it and perhaps go up there occasionally with the children.'

'Come with me now and I'll unlock it.'

She kept her keys dangling from her belt like a good châtelaine; she delighted in those keys. I suppose she regarded them as a sign of her authority.

I put down my cup and we went up to the turret-room together; she unlocked the door. I must confess I caught my breath as we entered, though why I could not imagine. There was nothing eerie about the room; the windows and its extremely elevated position made it very light. There were several beautiful rugs on the wooden floor, a table, a few chairs, a settee and a bureau. It looked as though it had been recently occupied.

'It's not been used since . . .' said Frau Graben.

'It's a beautiful room,' I said.

'You can use it if you like.'

I did not know that I wanted to do that. Approached only by the narrow spiral staircase which led to the turret, it was isolated and although it was easy to feel comfortable here during the day with a companion I remembered the uneasy feeling I had experienced last night when I had followed Fritz up here.

'Perhaps we can use it . . . later,' I said. I imagined lessons up here; laborious conversations in English as to the beauty of the view, which was, as from all the windows in the fortress, magnificent.

'Which was the window from which the lady fell?' I asked.

She led me across the room.

'This one.'

She unlatched it and pushed it outwards. I leaned out. I was looking straight down the mountainside, for as in so many of the castles in these parts the mountain's side had been used to form a wall. The drop was sheer. I could see right down to the valley.

Frau Graben moved closer to me.

'Silly girl she was!' she whispered.

'She would have been dead before she reached the valley,' I said.

'Silly girl!' she repeated. 'She could have had so much and she chose to kill herself.'

'She must have been very unhappy.'

'No reason to be. This castle was her home. All she had to do was keep in her place and she could have gone on here . . . the mistress of Klocksburg.'

'Except when the owner called with his wife.'

'She should have had more sense. He was fond of her or he wouldn't have brought her here. He would have protected her. But she had to go and jump down there . . . to her end.'

I said: 'Is she in the Island of Graves?'

'She'd be there. There is one grave. It just says one name on the tombstone: "Gerda." They say that's the one. What a silly girl! It need never have been. It's a lesson to girls, though.'

'To make sure they can trust their lovers.'

She smiled her fat comfortable smile and gave me a little nudge in the ribs. 'To accept what's what, and make the best of it. If a count loves you enough to set you up in a castle, shouldn't that satisfy you?'

I said: 'It didn't satisfy her.'

'Some have had more sense,' she said.

I turned away from the window. I wanted to stop thinking of that girl who had discovered her lover to have tricked her. I understood too well how she must have felt.

Frau Graben understood my feelings. 'Silly girl,' she insisted once more. 'Don't go on feeling too sorry for her. You'd have had more sense in her place, I know.' Again that sly smile. 'It is a pleasant room. So you'd like it left unlocked and you'll come up here now and then. I think you're right. Yes, it's a good notion.'

The room fascinated me. I was soon feeling an urge to go there alone. I must admit that on the first occasion I went, I had to fight a lurking reluctance, but once I was there I experienced a certain excitement. It was a delightful room, perhaps the most attractive in the fortress. Even the view seemed more magnificent seen from these windows. I opened the one from which Gerda was alleged to have thrown herself. It opened with a little squeaking protest. It needs oiling, I thought, forcing myself to be practical.

How grand the ducal castle looked, a mighty impregnable fortress guarding the town. After frequent conversations with the boys who had on a very special occasion been allowed to visit the castle. I could make out the features which they had described. I could see the walls with their flanking turrets and the gate-tower fortress. There it stood, dating back in some parts to the eleventh century, guarding the town, ready to defend itself from marauders. What an uneasy life people must have led in those days when their greatest concern was to defend themselves. The boys had described the grandeur of the *Rittersaal* and the tapestries which adorned the walls; there were gardens with fountains and statues which their father had told them were like those of Versailles, for it had been the desire of every German princeling to follow the example of the great Sun King and, in his little domain, to see himself as the mighty French monarch.

I reminded the boys what had become of the monarchy of France. Dagobert replied: 'Oh yes, old Kratz told us all about that.'

Looking out across the sweep of the valley to the town and then up again to the royal castle, I could make out the outhouses of the *Randhausburg* where I presumed many of the outdoor servants lived; and there were the barracks too. Across the valley would come the trumpet call to wake them in the morning; I often heard it soon after dawn, and sometimes when the wind was in the right direction I would hear the band playing in the ducal gardens.

But as I sat in the room I wondered about the girl who had been so unhappy that she had decided to end her life. But I imagined her beautiful, with long flaxen hair, like a girl in the fairy-tale picture-book my mother had brought with her from her home. I thought of her sitting at this window awaiting the arrival of her lover and then seeing that other woman – the wife, when she herself had believed herself to be married to him.

The despair, the wretchedness, the horror would have been overwhelming. I imagined her to have been strictly brought up. She would have believed herself to be dishonoured and see the only way out of her wretchedness was to end her life.

Sad Gerda! Perhaps when anyone was as unhappy as she must have been, he or she left behind them some aura of the past. Was that what people meant by haunting?

What nonsense! It could well have been only a legend.

Perhaps the girl fell from the window by accident. People like to put dramatic constructions on perfectly ordinary events.

I decided that I would exorcize the ghost by making this a normal room so that in a short time no one would consider it any different – except perhaps more beautiful – than any other room in Klocksburg.

The next day I brought the children up and gave them a lesson there. At first they were overawed but when they saw that it was just like an ordinary room Dagobert and Liesel forgot about the ghost. Fritz, I noticed, kept looking over his shoulder and didn't like to move too far from my side. He was the sensitive one.

I took them to the windows and pointed out the various landmarks, giving them their English names. This was always a good way of getting them to learn and I really was becoming quite pleased with their progress. Fritz was by far the best, which pleased me because I thought it would give him the confidence he needed. Liesel was quite a fair mimic and although she couldn't always remember words her pronunciation was good. Dagobert lagged a little but there again I decided that would do him no harm; he really was a little braggart.

When I was alone with Fritz and we were in the school-room I said to him: 'Fritz, there's nothing to be afraid of in the turret-room.'

A puzzled frown appeared between his eyes. He said: 'A lady jumped out of the window.'

'That's just a story.'

'You mean it never happened?'

'It might have done but we can't be sure.'

He shook his head. 'A lady did jump,' he said. He looked at me as though wondering whether he could trust me.

'Yes, Fritz,' I said tenderly.

'I think it was my mother.'

'No, Fritz. If it did happen, it happened long ago. It couldn't possibly have been your mother.'

'She died,' he said.

'Unfortunately some people do die young . . . but never mind, you have Frau Graben, you have your father and now you have me.'

I felt very moved because he gripped my hand rather tightly and nodded. I was touched to think that already I meant something to him.

'There's nothing to be afraid of,' I said. 'It's only a story, you know. It may well not be true and if it is, it happened years and years ago.'

I had an idea that although he was comforted by my presence he didn't really believe that.

FOUR

Dagobert's eyes gleamed with excitement. 'There's going to be a stag hunt,' he told me. 'We're to go. It's exciting. Bang. Bang.'

'*You're* to go to hunt stag?

'This is a special one. My father will be there.'

I turned to Fritz. 'Are you going?'

Fritz didn't answer and Dagobert shouted: 'Of course he's going. Liesel isn't. She's too little.'

Liesel set up a wail.

'She can go in my place,' said Fritz.

'She can't,' cried Dagobert. 'Because you're frightened, that doesn't make her old enough.'

'I'm not frightened,' said Fritz.

'You are!'

'I'm not!'

'You are, you are, you are, you are!' Dagobert was dancing round Fritz like some irritating dervish. Fritz hit out at him.

'Please stop,' I said. 'It is most impolite to fight in front of your English teacher.'

Dagobert paused and said: 'Would it be impolite to fight behind your back, Miss?'

'You are being a little impertinent, Dagobert,' I said, 'which is equally impolite. Now stop being foolish. Where is this stag hunt to be held?'

'In the forest where the stags are.'

'In the Klocksburg forest.'

'No, in the ducal forest.'

'Do you mean to say that you boys are going to join the hunt?'

Dagobert tittered, and Fritz said: 'It's a different sort of hunt, Miss. They are all together, lots of them, and they come

159

in and they're shot dead and . . .'

'Bang, bang, bang!' said Dagobert.

I could see that I could not get from them what I wanted
to hear so I went along to Frau Graben.

She was seated in an armchair holding a basin in her hand;
she smiled at me when I entered. On the table beside her was
a piece of spiced cake such as I had discovered she loved and
which she kept in a tin in the cupboard in this room, with
various other food to take out at odd moments. She rarely
sat down to a meal, I had discovered, but was nibbling titbits
throughout the day.

She set down the basin as I entered and I couldn't help
seeing what was in it. Not the soup I had expected but two
spiders. She saw my astonishment and gave her fat comfortable laugh.

'I like to put them in together and see what they do,' she
said. 'They're scouting round at the moment. Don't know
what to make of it. There they are in this strange white
world. They'll fight, I shouldn't wonder. One will kill the
other.'

'But why . . .' I said.

'I like to see what they'll do. You put them together, you
see how they take it. Spiders are interesting. The way they
weave their webs . . . beautiful things, webs. One day I saw
a fight between a great bumblebee and a big spider.' Her eyes
gleamed with excitement. 'The bee was caught in the web and
you should have seen that spider get to work; he wrapped up
the bee in his sticky thread but the bee was too strong and the
web wouldn't hold him. He tore himself away and flew off
clutching the spider. I often wonder what happened to them.
It's like people. You put them down somewhere with someone else and you see what happens. But I'm being a silly old
woman. I'm afraid I'm often that. Now you're a nice kind
young lady and you're going to say I'm not, but you don't
know me, dear, do you? And you are a bit surprised at my
spiders, aren't you? Never mind.' She smiled comfortably.
'You see, dear Miss Trant, I'm so interested in everybody . . .
yes, everybody . . . even the spiders.'

I said: 'The boys say they are going stag-hunting, is that
true?'

'It's a form of hunt. You'll see, because you're to go with
them.'

'*I* go to a hunt . . .*'*

'It's not chasing the stag. You'll see what it is. The count wants the boys to go. It's tomorrow. It's the shooting festival. It's a pity the Prince won't be home for it. He always enjoyed the *Schützenfest*.'

'What shall I be expected to do?'

'Nothing. You'll just be there to look after the boys. You'll love the procession. It's pretty. We're very fond of these occasions here.'

'So it isn't chasing after the stag?'

'There's no chasing. Those boys will tell their tales.'

She was smiling her simple happy smile, which was meant to assure me that everything was well.

The next morning we set out for the shooting festival. I could get little sense out of the boys. Dagobert was too excited and kept running around shouting bang and killing, I supposed, imaginary stags. Fritz was silent, a little apprehensive.

As we were not coming home for food Frau Graben had told us we must stop at one of the inns in the town where we were to leave our horses. Here the very pretty innkeeper's daughter served us with a sort of cider ale, a long cool drink, and what was called a *Schinkenbrot*, which was several slices of boiled bacon on thickish brown bread and butter.

As we were eating crowds began to fill the *Oberer Stadt-platz*; wagons decorated with flowers trundled in from the surrounding country and in them sat the girls in their black skirts and yellow satin aprons. The men walked beside the wagons, dressed in various colourful costumes, reds, blues, blacks and yellows, calling to the girls as they walked. Some were on horseback; there were fiddlers to provide music, and some were singing.

Dagobert said that we were to go to the *Schützenhaus* without delay because we must be there before the procession came in. There was a special place which his father had said was to be kept for us.

Dagobert led the way and we came to a building near the town hall. As we entered a man in uniform approached us; he evidently knew the boys because he led us to seats near a platform, where we sat down.

We could hear the sounds of the band and singing as the procession was coming nearer. Dagobert kept looking at me to see how impressed I was. Now the hall began to fill with people. Tall men each carrying a rifle were then led in by a man in a green doublet. Dagobert whispered to me that he was the *Schützenkönig*. He was elected each year for his skill with his rifle and for the whole year he was king; and the medals he wore on his green doublet were given to him by the kings of other years. Into the hall began to file representatives from the surrounding villages, all come to see the shooting contest. Although the men and women in their colourful costumes kept crowding in, the centre of the hall and the space at one end opposite the dais were kept clear. In this space was a pole on which what appeared to be a bird was set up.

Fritz whispered that it was not a real bird; it was made of wood and the feathers had been stuck on. There was a new bird every year for the *Schützenfest*.

Now there was a great fanfare of trumpets because the ducal party was about to arrive. I was very excited. I should see the Count, the children's father, who, through them, had become a legendary figure to me. I noticed the effect the sound of the trumpets had on them. They sat in awed silence beside me.

Then a door which I had not noticed before was flung open. Two heralds came in – boys of about fourteen in the blue and gold which I knew to be the colours of the ducal livery. As they blew a fanfare on their trumpets all the people in the hall rose to their feet. The Duke entered. I recognized him at once as the man whose picture I had seen all those years ago. Even the cloak about him was the same as in the picture. It was of blue velvet lined with miniver. Immediately behind him were a man and two women. I felt my heart begin to hammer; the room swung round me, and for a moment I was afraid that I would faint. I had thought in that moment that I had found Maximilian. The man was like him . . . the same height, the same build. But it was not he. I had been mistaken. I had known him so well during those three days that every detail of his face was familiar to me, engraved on my memory for ever. I should never, never forget . . . nor could I mistake anyone else for him for more than a second or two. What I had seen was only a resemblance. But it was undoubtedly there. And one of the women who was with him reminded me of Ilse, though as I looked closer I saw that the similarity was by no means as marked as that between the Count and Maximilian.

This was like one of my dreams, I was going to wake up

in a moment. The hall had suddenly become unbearably hot but I was shivering. I felt Fritz gripping my hand. I returned the pressure and took comfort. I was not dreaming.

I looked at the boys; their eyes were fixed on the man whom I had momentarily mistaken for Maximilian. I had realized at once that he was the Duke's nephew and their father.

I thought then: I'm just imagining this. There is a slight resemblance . . . nothing more, and because above all things I want to see Maximilian again, I see him in this man because he has the same haughty demeanour and is of similar height and build.

The ducal group had taken their seats on the dais. I kept staring at the Count. Now I could see the differences; he was a little darker than Maximilian; his complexion was more ruddy; his expression was different; there was a touch of cruelty in his expression which I had never seen in Maximilian's. Had it been there, though? And had I refused to see it? This man had not the humorous expression which I had found so charming in Maximilian. His nose was longer; his mouth thinner. No, there was a strong resemblance but it was growing less the more I saw of him. And the woman who was with him – faintly like Ilse, yes, but that was all.

Dagobert gave me a fleeting look. I knew he wanted me to admire his father. I whispered: 'Who is the lady now sitting beside the Duke?'

'The Prince's wife, Princess Wilhelmina.'

'Where is the Prince?'

'He is not here. My father's his cousin and he's taking his place while he is away.'

I nodded.

The ceremony started, the object being to find the best shot of the year. The *Schützenkönig* of last year led the competitors in and presented them to the duke; they then began to shoot at the wooden bird, the object being to bring it off the perch.

The shots rang out as one by one of the attempts were made. Only two of the contestants succeeded in bringing it off its perch and loud applause followed these efforts; then the two had to undergo a further test and the bird was replaced. In a short time one of them was proved the victor and proclaimed the *Schützenkönig* for the next year. Up on the dais the Family congratulated him and the *Schützenfest* was over, but this was apparently only the beginning of the entertainment. The best was yet to come, Dagobert told me. The ducal party left the hall. As they came near us the Count looked in the boys' direction and his glance swept over me in a manner which disturbed me and aroused my indignation. I was in a strange mood. For a few moments I had believed I had found that which I now knew I had come a long way to seek, and a bitter frustration swept over me. Perhaps that was why I felt this indignation and imagined that there was something insulting about the manner in which he gave me that cursory glance.

'We're going out into the forest now for the real hunt,' said Dagobert.

'I don't feel well,' said Fritz.

I looked at him anxiously. 'Perhaps we had better all go home.'

'No!' cried Dagobert. 'Our father would be angry. You daren't, Fritz. You know it.'

'Yes,' agreed Fritz, 'I do.'

'If you are not well we should go back to Klocksburg,' I said. 'I will go with you and take the responsibility.'

'I won't go,' said Dagobert.

'I won't go either,' said Fritz.

But I could see that he wanted to.

We went to the inn where the horses had been watered and then set out from there. Many people were making their way into the forest. About half a mile in we came to a spot where a crowd had gathered and our horses were taken from us by one of the foresters. The boys seemed to be well known and the crowds parted to let us go through. Then I saw what looked like a large tent. There were four sides of canvas round an enclosed space which was open to the sky and as we approached a man who seemed to be standing on guard lifted a flap in the canvas and we went inside the enclosure. In the centre of this was a kind of pavilion which was beautifully decorated with flowers and leaves; some of these were made into garlands and wreaths and the effect was delightful.

There were seats in the pavilion and we were assigned to three of these.

'What is going to happen?' I whispered.

Dagobert put his fingers to his lips but I saw that Fritz had grown pale. I knew that something was about to take place which he knew would upset him.

I turned to speak to him but as I did so I heard the fanfare again and now others were coming into the enclosure. The Duke was not with them this time but the boys' father and the two women – one of whom had reminded me of Ilse – were there. They led the party. Again I received that quick appraising look and instinctively I knew that that was the manner in which he looked at every woman. I thought of the mothers of these two boys and little Liesel who had most certainly been assessed in the same way, and instinctively I disliked this man who had dared raise my hopes and filled me with great joy, only to let me discover that he was not the man I sought.

Fritz had moved a little nearer to me. I reached for his hand and pressed it. Dagobert's shining eyes were fixed on his father. All the seats in the pavilion were now occupied and the Count clapped his hands. Everyone stood up and I saw that they all had guns in their hands. Some of them standing near the canvas then let out bloodcurdling cries; the flap was lifted and numbers of stags and hinds dashed into the enclosure. I heard the rifles crack and I saw the beautiful animals stretched out on the grass; I could not bear to look. I glanced at Fritz whose eyes were tightly shut; he was swaying slightly.

I heard my own voice then. I was unaware that I had spoken. 'It's horrible – butchery!'

I took Fritz by the hand and, drawing aside the canvas, I dragged him away from the scene of the slaughter.

I had forgotten Dagobert. My one thought was to look after Fritz whose feelings were mine. I had rarely been so shaken in my life as when I saw those innocent beautiful creatures run forward to their deaths.

I found our horses. The man who was guarding them looked at me strangely.

I said: 'We are going back to Klocksburg. Will you go and tell Master Dagobert to come to us at once.'

Fritz was visibly trembling as he mounted his pony; I hope I managed to hide that I was similarly disturbed. In a very short time one of the foresters came out with Dagobert. The boy looked stunned. As we rode away he said: 'My father is very angry.'

I hope I did not show my dismay. I was well aware that both boys were watching me closely – Fritz as a kind of deliverer but one in whose powers he had little confidence; Dagobert as a stranger who had behaved in a reckless manner through ignorance rather than courage.

The journey back to Klocksburg was made in almost complete silence after that.

When we arrived I went straight to my room and it was not long before Frau Graben was knocking at my door.

'You left the pavilion! But nobody leaves the pavilion before the Family party!'

'We did,' I said.

In spite of the fact that she thought I had done something which might be unforgivable she could not hide her secret amusement. Her expression was like that I had surprised when she was watching the spiders in the basin.

'It's a mercy the Duke was not there.'

'That would have been *lèse-majesté*, I suppose.'

'That would have been a very serious matter.'

'And what would have happened to me? Should I have been put before a shooting squad?'

She smiled. 'I don't know what will come of this,' she said. 'We'll have to see. I heard from Dagobert that his father looked like thunder. I used to call my two when they were little, Donner and Blitzen. I never saw such rages as young Fredy could fall into. Talk about thunder! And the Prince, he was like lightning . . . into everything . . . wildly enthusiastic and all for it one minute and tiring quickly. Yes, Donner and Blitzen was my name for them.'

'I suppose I shall be asked to leave.'

'We'll see,' she said.

Then she began to talk about her two charges, the cousins – the Count and the Prince. There never had been such children, according to her. The mischief! It was one body's work just to get them out of that. I gathered that the Prince was her favourite. Little Lightning was slightly more lovable than young Thunder.

But I was not really paying attention; I was wondering what was going to happen. It was almost certain that I should be asked to pack and leave. The count would certainly not want someone who had shown him such disrespect to himself to teach his children.

I went up to the turret-room. Somehow it seemed to offer me a little solace. I looked across the valley down on the town where we had seen the *Schützenfest* that afternoon and

166

beyond to the forest where that nauseating slaughter had taken place, and terrible depression swept over me. If I left here now I would never know the answer I had come to seek. The manner in which Frau Graben had come into the shop and my arrival here had seemed to me like a pattern; it reminded me of the manner in which Ilse had appeared. There was something uncanny about it. It was like one of the fantastic adventures in which the gods and heroes of the forest indulged. I had changed since I had been here. I was growing more and more like that light-hearted girl who had wandered into the mist and I had felt certain that I was going to unravel the mystery and make the discovery which was necessary to my peace of mind. And if I were sent away that would be the end.

Perhaps I could go to the *Damenstift* . . . offer myself as a teacher of English as I had thought of doing once before. But I wanted to stay here; I was growing fond of the children, particularly Fritz. The restricted life in a convent was not appealing; its only virtue would be that I was here near that enchanted forest where once long ago I had walked into a dream . . . or was it reality?

I spent a sleepless night and the next morning when I was in the turret-room with the children, while we were at the window practising English vocabulary, we saw a little cavalcade of riders; they were coming up the mountain road which led to Klocksburg.

Dagobert shouted: 'It's my father.'

My spirits sank. He had wasted little time.

I said the boys should go to their rooms to wash their hands and prepare to receive him. I went to mine to prepare myself for the worst.

I was summoned down to the *Rittersaal*. I left the fortress, crossed the courtyard and entered the *Randhausburg*. My knees were trembling but I held my head high and I knew there was an unusual colour in my cheeks. I hope I did not show how agitated I was. I tried to calm myself. I was telling myself: You will be dismissed, but if they don't want you, you could stay on for a while living humbly perhaps in some mountain inn and then perhaps teach at the *Damenstift*.

He was seated there alone and rose when I entered. He bowed from the waist as the boys did, clicking his heels as he did so. He looked magnificent in the uniform of the Duke's guards. I felt like a drab little wren beside a peacock.

'Miss er . . .' he began.

'Trant,' I supplied.

'Miss Trant, we met for the first time yesterday.'

His English was good, there was only the faintest trace of accent. His voice unnerved me; it was very like Maximilian's.

'You are here to teach my children English,' he went on.

'That is so.'

'They do not appear to have made much progress.'

'On the contrary I would say that they are making excellent progress. They only had a word or two of the language when I arrived, their education in that direction having been entirely neglected.'

I was bold. I felt I had nothing to lose. He had determined to be rid of me; and because I found his bold glance offensive I could not prevent my voice taking on a firmness which I knew he would think of as insolent.

He sat down at the refectory table on which pewter utensils stood. 'You may sit,' he said.

I did so because although I resented the manner in which he gave me permission to do so, I could see that I should be at a disadvantage if I remained standing.

'So you found the children ignorant?' he said.

'As regards English, certainly.'

'And since you have come they have made such rapid progress in this that when I asked them to tell me in English what they had thought of yesterday's performance they were completely tongue-tied.'

'That might well be beyond their powers at present.'

'It was not beyond your powers to let us know what you thought.'

'I suppose I gave a good indication.'

'You left us in no doubt that you considered us a country of barbarians.'

He waited for my reply but I made none. He insisted, 'That was so?'

'I found the spectacle revolting.'

'Indeed?'

'Is it so surprising?'

'Ah, English susceptibilities! Your Queen was equally unimpressed . . . or perhaps impressed. I was present when she was entertained over here. Her remarks were identical. "Butchery!" she said.'

168

'Then I was in noble company.'

'You do not seem to set much store by that. You were in noble company yesterday but you behaved in an exceedingly discourteous manner. If it were not for the fact that you are a foreigner and can plead ignorance, it might be necessary to reprimand you very severely.'

'I realize that I have committed a breach of etiquette and for that I apologize.'

'That is indeed gracious.'

'Had I known what I was expected to witness I should not have come.'

'You were commanded to come.'

'Still I should have declined.'

'Those who serve us do not decline to obey commands.'

'I suppose not, and there is only one thing to do if one finds such commands unacceptable, which is to resign from the service.'

'Is that what you are doing, Miss Trant?'

'If it is your wish that I should do so, I have no alternative.'

'There is an alternative. You could plead to be forgiven. I might say you are a stranger, ignorant of our etiquette. Apologies could be made to the Princess, the Countess and other members of the court. On grounds of ignorance you might be forgiven, providing of course that you promise not to offend again.'

'I could not give such a promise. If I were asked to witness that sickening spectacle once more I should be obliged to refuse.'

'On your own behalf, perhaps. But you carried my sons with you. Do you imagine that I can allow you to instil into them ideas that are detrimental to their manhood?'

I had visions of his forcing Fritz to witness such scenes, of trying, as he would say, to 'make a man of him'. No wonder the poor child was nervous; no wonder he walked in his sleep. I was ready to fight for Fritz as I had not been to fight for myself.

I said earnestly: 'Fritz is a sensitive boy.'

'Why?' he cried. 'Because he has been brought up by women?'

'Because he has a highly-strung nature.'

'My dear Miss Trant, I have no patience with highly-strung natures. I want to make a man of the boy.'

'Is it manly to gloat over the slaughter of beautiful animals?'

'What strange ideas you have! I think perhaps you might do very well in a select academy for young ladies.'

'Perhaps,' I said. 'And you are telling me that I am dismissed? If that is so, I will make my preparations to leave at once.'

He stood up and came to my chair. He sat on the table very close to me.

'You are of a hasty nature, Miss Trant. I do not think impetuous people make good teachers.'

'Very well. I will go.'

'But *I* have no personal objection to that characteristic.'

'I am glad I do not displease you in all respects.'

'It is not *you* who displease me, Miss Trant. It is your action yesterday.'

I half rose. His great virility alarmed me at such close quarters. He was so like Maximilian and yet there was the subtle difference. Had I been with him that night in the hunting lodge I would never have been allowed to remain alone on the other side of that locked door. That was something I knew instinctively.

'I see that I have offended you,' I said quickly. 'There is no need to continue this interview. I will go.'

'You make a custom of taking your leave unexpectedly. It is *my* custom to give permission for those whom I employ to come or go.'

'I presume I am no longer in your employ so that does not apply to me.'

I turned away but he was beside me. I could feel his warm breath on my neck. He caught my forearm in a tight grip.

'You will stay,' he said. Then he smiled, his eyes slightly veiled as they swept over me. 'I have decided that you shall have another chance,' he went on.

I faced him boldly. 'I warn you that in similar circumstances I should act in the same way.'

'We'll see,' he said.

I took his hand from my arm and dropped it hastily; he was so surprised that he made no effort to check me.

I said: 'Whenever you wish me to leave your employ, please say so.'

And with that I walked out of the *Rittersaal*. I crossed the courtyard and entered the fortress. I was trembling but I felt elated as though I had won a battle, which perhaps in a way I had, because at least I was still employed at Klocksburg.

I sat by my window letting the air cool my cheeks. The encounter had shaken me because the bold message in the Count's eyes had told me he had marked me down for a victim. I was experienced enough to recognize his intentions. I was surprised. I had ceased to think of myself as an attractive woman. I knew I had been in my teens, with my somewhat inconsequential high spirits, my masses of dark hair and perhaps most of all my vivacious expression. But when I had believed myself to be married and had borne a child (at least I could be sure of that) and lost it, I had changed. I knew the change was remarkable because Mrs Greville and Aunt Matilda often said to me: 'I've never seen anyone change as you did when you came back from that long stay abroad.'

My gaiety had been overshadowed; the tremendous doubt was there. I had loved and lost my husband and my child; and who could be the same after such an experience?

Anthony, it was true, had asked me to marry him. I realized I had scarcely thought of him since I had left England. He had written twice – letters full of details about the parish and his work. I should have been interested a short while ago, but I had found my attention wandering even while I had been reading them.

Ever since I had come to Klocksburg I had felt an excitement that I had not known since I had awakened in my bed to be told that my marriage had been a dream, the result of Dr Carlsberg's treatment. There was a firm belief within me that if ever I was to find the solution to my mystery I should find it here. For a second when I had seen the Count I had believed I had found it. But that was a delusion; and now this very count was becoming an obstacle in my way.

I could guess what would happen. I was woman of the world enough to grasp the type of man he was; and because he was powerful in his little world he would have encountered little opposition and at first he would be attracted by it, but only for a while. It would soon begin to pall. Perhaps I should begin making enquiries at the *Damenstift*.

As I brooded I heard voices below, for one could hear very distinctly in that clear mountain air.

'Now, Master Fredy, you'll behave yourself. I'll not allow

any of your games.' That was Frau Graben, the lilt of laughter in her voice; I could imagine the fat comfortable smile.

'What was the meaning of this, eh, old woman? Why did you bring her here?' The Count! The arrogant powerful man allowing Frau Graben to address him in that way. But of course the old nurse had special privileges.

'It was about time those bastards of yours were given a bit of education.'

'They had it. We didn't need an English prude to give them that.'

'Not so prudish, Master Fredy. I'll promise you.'

'And who are you to make promises to me?'

'You remember your manners, Master Fredy. I was always telling you.'

'Good God, woman, I'm not in the nursery now.'

'You'll always be in the nursery as far as I'm concerned and that goes for your high and mighty cousin too.'

'He was always your favourite.'

'You get along with you. I had no favourites. You were both my boys and I wouldn't let you give me your sauce then and I won't now.'

'I should have had you turned out of Klocksburg long ago.'

'Then who'll look after your bastards?'

'Why, you old witch, there are hundreds who'd like the opportunity.'

'But you trust your old Nana, eh?'

'No farther than the end of the *Randhausburg*.'

'Listen to me, Master Fredy, you turn your gaze away from Miss Trant.'

'You brought her here.'

'Not for your amusement.'

'I'll decide where and when I'm going to be amused.'

'Not here, master.'

'Who's to stop me? You?'

'No. She will though. She's not for you.'

'Who said I was interested?'

'You were always interested in a fresh face – both of you. Don't I know you? Old Nana likes you to enjoy yourselves, but not Miss Trant, Master Fredy. She's in my care. So you give your thoughts to that little innkeeper's daughter I've been hearing about.'

'Trust you to hear everything.'

She gave a high-pitched giggle.

He said: 'Don't you dare try to dictate to me, you mischievous old woman.'

They went inside the *Randhausburg* and I heard no more.

I was indignant that I should be discussed in this way. I had already a notion of the count's intentions – which were, after all, only the same as he would have towards any woman – but what astonished me was the familiar manner in which Frau Graben addressed him and the inference that the decision to bring me out here to teach the boys English had come from her.

When the Count had left I went to the *Randhausburg* and knocked at Frau Graben's door. The air of excitement lingered about her; she looked as though she had just come from a highly diverting entertainment, the memory of which remained with her.

'Come in, my dear,' she said.

She was seated on her rocking-chair nibbling a piece of spiced cake.

'Sit down. Would you like some tea?'

It was as though she were placating me. Tea! The English could always be pacified with it!

'No, thank you.'

'I know. A glass of wine. I had some sent to me from the Moselle valley. It's good stuff.'

'No refreshment, thank you. I really wanted to talk to you seriously.'

'Oh, you're too serious, Miss Trant.'

'A woman on her own has to be.'

'You're not on your own. You've got that nice aunt of yours and the bookshop people and what about the reverend gentleman.'

She looked slyly knowledgeable. I was beginning to think that she knew more about me than I had imagined. But of course she had stayed in Oxford; while she was there she would have fallen into conversation with the shop people, and people at her hotel, anyone who might know something about me. But how could she? She spoke very little English.

I said: 'How did you know . . .?'

'One picks up these things. You must have told me during some of our little chats.'

I said: 'Did you decide that it would be a good idea for me to come over and teach the children? I mean, was it entirely your idea?'

'There'd been talk. And when I was in England I thought you were just the one.' She leaned towards me, nibbling. 'I took a fancy to you. I didn't want to lose you. I wanted you to be here. After all, we got on famously didn't we . . . from the moment we met.'

Those powerful men whose nurse she had been must clearly be fond of her, otherwise they would not allow her such power. I remembered the manner in which she had spoken to the haughty Count; and now it seemed she had the power to bring an English teacher into his household without consulting him.

There was evidently a softer side to the Count's nature since he was so affectionate towards his old nurse.

'So you are allowed to add to the household if you wish?'

'I was a mother to them. There's not always the time or inclination in people like them to look after their children. Those that are nurses to them are like their mothers. We're a sentimental race, you know. Those who have been mothers to us mean a great deal to us.'

I was surprised. I had always known that I owed my presence here to Frau Graben but I did not think it was so completely so as it evidently was.

'Don't you worry,' she said to me. 'I'm going to look after you.'

The words were comforting; but there was that glint in her eyes – something of the amusement and speculation which I had seen there when she was watching the spiders.

The Count lost no time in coming to Klocksburg. We were in the turret-room where I had made a habit of taking the children . . . not for the written exercises I gave them, but for our conversations. I would make them tell me about the ducal palace and then I would translate it into English. As they were greatly interested in the palace and everything that went on there, this meant that I had their full attention.

He came in and the children all rose to their feet – the boys bowing, Liesel dropping a pretty curtsey. He waved a hand indicating that he preferred them to be seated.

'Please continue, Miss Trant,' he said. 'I want to see how the lesson progresses.'

I was determined not to let him see how his presence disturbed me if I could help it. 'Now,' I said, 'there is the

174

Watching Tower. Fritz, will you please say that in English?'

He stammered a little but I was not displeased with the result.

Then I asked Dagobert in English to point out the barracks and tell me who lived there. He was particularly interested in the soldiers, so I felt safe there.

I asked Liesel to show me the big bell and tell me when it was rung.

They stammered through and I continued with the lesson, but I can hardly say that the children were at their best. Dagobert was soon trying to show off; Fritz grew nervous and Liesel was a little silly. The Count sat smiling superciliously. I could see that he was not impressed by the performance.

'You'll have to do better than that,' he said, 'if you want to be presented to Her Majesty Queen Victoria when she deigns to pay us another visit.'

Dagobert said: 'Is she coming again, sir?'

'Oh come, come. She was with us a few years ago. You must not expect too much from such mighty folk. I have no doubt that Miss Trant has told you that her country is the greatest in the world and we are just a poor little state in comparison.'

Dagobert stared open-mouthed at me and Fritz stammered: 'M . . . Miss T . . . Trant didn't tell us that. She . . . she likes our country.'

I was touched. It was an effort to protect me.

I said sharply: 'I have not come to teach politics, Herr Count. I have come to teach English.'

'With the natural assumption that the whole world recognizes without any prompting from its subjects the superiority of Britain.'

'You pay us a great compliment,' I said.

'I believe it was said you did the same to us when you allowed your queen to take a husband from one of our houses.'

'It linked our countries,' I said.

'And so great benefits were conferred.'

'Perhaps on both sides.'

'You are determined to be gracious.'

'It makes social life so much more comfortable.'

'Even when one does not say exactly what one means?'

'I try to say what I mean.'

'And only prevaricate for expediency. I believe that is a good old English custom.'

'It's frequently considered to be a diplomatic one, I believe.'

I looked at my watch.

'Pastor Kratz will be waiting for you,' I said to the children. They were surprised. I realized then that until the Count dismissed them we were supposed to remain where we were and Pastor Kratz could wait all morning if necessary.

I rose. To my surprise, so did the count.

'You speak German better than you teach English,' he said.

'It is unwise to judge on such slight evidence,' I retorted. 'My German could be better and I believe that in a few weeks your children will have quite a smattering of English.'

I took Liesel by the hand and led her to the door. The Count followed, so the boys came on behind.

We reached the schoolroom where Pastor Kratz was waiting. I went in to have a word with him and the Count sent the children in after me.

When I came out he had gone.

Encounters with him disturbed me. He was determined to be critical and yet at the same time he was interested in me. Our badinage amused him. I had always been able to hold my own in such conversations and when I was stimulated I felt these powers increase. I enjoyed my verbal battles. I had even enjoyed that one this morning, for I did not think I had come too badly out of it.

I knew what was going to happen. He was attracted by me. I must seem different from the women he would meet. I was a foreigner for one thing; he wanted to subdue me partly on this account. He had evidently been impressed by the dignity of our queen when she visited Saxe-Coburg, Meiningen and the surrounding states – and who would not be? Never had such a tiny person been able to display such regality. On the occasions when I had seen her I had been impressed by it – not that I had seen her often, for since the death of the Prince Consort she had shut herself away and had rarely been seen by her subjects. I knew, though, that she had visited Germany after his death; and I could imagine the effect that unconscious royal dignity would have on a man like the Count. Moreover, she was a great Queen, with a growing empire; and he was the nephew of the Duke of an insignificant state. How he would have revelled in her position! He would not see that it was natural acceptance of her royalty which gave her such presence.

How did I know so much about him? But he was easy to read. And this I knew: He was planning to seduce me. He betrayed that completely. He was ready to dally a little, but it would only be for a little while. He would enjoy being repulsed at first, but not for long. I thought of those beautiful deer; the destruction of the fleetest and most difficult to ensnare would provide the greatest enjoyment. But he would soon tire of the chase. And then he would be angry. He would find fault with me. I should be dismissed. This had happened to a friend of mine – one of the girls who had been with me at the *Damenstift*. She was exceptionally pretty and without means. She had become a governess. The master of the house had pursued her and when she had repulsed him at first he had been intrigued; but very soon she was looking for another post and had only a very indifferent testimonial to help her.

Life had become very uneasy since the appearance of the Count.

In the *Randhausburg* there was a garden. It was rather beautiful, shut in by stubby firs and containing a lawn with a fountain and seats painted white. Here the children practised their shooting and archery once a week. At one side was a sheer drop from the plateau, but the hedge of bushy firs made it safe for even little Liesel to wander in alone. It was a favourite spot of mine and I often went there. So this morning I took some books intending to work out my next lesson, but I suppose really to brood on my situation and to wonder whether I should begin making enquiries about a position at the *Damenstift*.

I was sitting with my back to the little gate which had been set up in the hedge of firs when I heard the latch click. Instinctively I knew who it was.

'Why, Miss Trant.'

He pretended to be surprised but I knew that he had seen me come here.

'Have you any objection to my sitting beside you?' he asked, with an irony which I pretended to ignore.

'Please sit here if you wish.'

'This is a pleasant garden,' he went on.

'Very pleasant.'

'I am glad you find it so. And what do you think of our

177

little Klocksburg?'

'I would hardly describe it as little.'

'Oh, but not to be compared with Windsor Castle, Buckingham Palace, and is it Sandringham?'

'There is such a palace and one could not really compare Klocksburg with them. They are quite dissimilar.'

'And much more grand, eh?'

'I find it difficult to make these comparisons. Personally I live in a small house next to a bookshop. I can assure you *that* is not in the least like Klocksburg either.'

'A small house next to a bookshop,' he said. 'But a very superior small house next to a very superior bookshop, I dare say.'

'I found it pleasant because it was my home. It is a good bookshop, too.'

'Do you think longingly of your home, Miss Trant?'

'Not yet. Perhaps I have not been away long enough.'

'I fancy you have a fondness for our mountains.'

I assured him that I had.

The conversation was running too smoothly.

He said: 'I was interested to see that you had decided to throw open our haunted room.'

'I thought it wiser to open it than keep it shut. Frau Graben agreed with me.'

'It has been locked for several years, but you sweep away our traditions with an imperious wave of your English hand.'

'I must explain about the locked room.'

'I look forward to your explanations, Miss Trant.'

'The room was kept locked,' I said. 'Therefore it was given a certain eerie aura. I believed that if it were open, the idea that it was haunted would be swept away. It would be shown to be just a room – nothing more. And this is what is happening.'

'Bravo!' he said. 'St George and the dragon – only this time we have a St Georgiana. With her cool common-sense broom she sweeps away our medieval cobwebs of superstition. That's the case, isn't it?'

'It was time that particular cobweb was swept away.'

'We like our fancies, you know. We are said to be so unimaginative, but are we really? You tell me, Miss Trant. You know so much about us.'

'I must dispute that.' I had half risen.

'You are not going?' He said it as a question but his eyes

178

made it a statement.

He took my wrist and held it so firmly that I could not release it. Rather than attempt and fail, I sat down.

'Pray tell me how you came here?' he said.

I told him about Frau Graben's coming into the shop, how we had spoken in German because her English was not very good.

'We grew friendly,' I said. 'She thought it would be a good idea if I came out to teach the children English, so I came.'

'What is she up to?' he murmured.

'I think she thought it would be good for the children to speak English.'

'English teachers are not very difficult to come by,' he mocked.

'Frau Graben thought a native would be best to teach the language.'

He narrowed his eyes. 'Well,' he said at length, 'I'm glad she brought you over.'

'I had the impression that you did not greatly admire my teaching ability.'

'But there are some things I do admire about you.'

'Thank you.' I rose again. 'If you will excuse me.'

'No,' he said. 'I will not. I have made it very clear that I wish to talk to you.'

'I cannot understand what we should have to talk about except the children's progress in English and we have discussed that already.'

'That was a not very inspiring topic,' he said. 'I am sure we have greater points of interest. I find you amusing.'

I raised my eyebrows.

'That is what I call mock surprise. You know you amuse me. I see no reason why we should not become good friends.'

'I see many reasons.'

'What are they?'

'Your elevated position, for one thing. Aren't you the nephew of the Duke? You have already seen that my knowledge of protocol is negligible.'

'It is easily acquired.'

'No doubt by those in the position to do so. As an English teacher – even though a parent of my charges is in a very exalted position – I could hardly expect noble etiquette to concern me.'

'It could concern you if I wished it.'

'Oh, but surely that would be another breach of the social code? After all, I am not even teaching your *legitimate* offspring.'

He leaned towards me. 'Would you care to? It could be arranged.'

'I am happy with the present arrangement.'

'Your cool English airs delight me. You behave as though I am a customer in the – er bookshop, was it?'

'Our encounter is not dissimilar. I have to sell my services as a teacher; you as my employer are buying them.'

'Ours is a more lengthy transaction, surely.'

'You would be surprised how many customers come back and back again in bookshops.'

'I think you and I are going to be on closer terms. What do you think? Or haven't you thought about it yet?'

'I do not have to think very long. I know that our respective positions and characters make a close acquaintance impossible.'

He was taken slightly aback and I felt the victory was mine, particularly as the gate clicked again and there stood Frau Graben smiling at us.

'I knew you were here,' she said. 'Miss Trant, Pastor Kratz wants to talk to you . . . something about changing the time of tomorrow's lesson. Fredy, I wanted a word with you.'

He frowned at her.

'Oh, you can frown, Herr Donner,' she said. 'You know I won't have tantrums.'

As I hurried through the gate, I saw her fat smile as she prepared to do battle with the Count. I was reminded of Hildegarde, my guardian angel of the hunting lodge.

My thoughts were in a turmoil for the rest of the day. I knew the relentless obstinacy of men like Count Frederic. I could picture his riding through the countryside, selecting the women who took his fancy briefly. He had believed that I would be so overawed by his importance, so beguiled by his masculine charm, that I would be the next victim. If, in spite of my attitude he still believed he could overcome my resistance, he was mistaken.

More vividly than ever there came back to me that day when Maximilian had loomed out of the mist. Could it really have been that he had been such another as this man? I was now ten years older than that girl who had been so deeply

180

impressed, who had fallen so much in love with the hero of the forest that she had never forgotten him, even though there were times when she feared he had been only another bold adventurer. Had I endowed him with the qualities of the heroes of his country's legends? Was the picture I had treasured for so many years only one of my own painting? If ten years ago the Count had shared that adventure, would I have believed him to possess those qualities with which I had endowed Maximilian.

When I went into the schoolroom after the Count had left there was a babble of excitement among the children. They were going hunting tomorrow with the Count.

'Who told you that?' I asked.

'The Count did,' said Dagobert. 'He is coming for us at nine o'clock.'

Dagobert's eyes shone with excitement but I detected a trace of apprehension. Even he was afraid that he could not match up to his father's expectations. As for Fritz, I could see that he was in a state of terror. I guessed that Fritz, after what had happened in the pavilion during the slaughter of the deer, would be expected, as his father would put it, to show his manhood. It wouldn't surprise me if this were not the purpose of the exercise. The child sensed this, I believed, and was very disturbed about it.

Liesel would not accompany them, of course. She was going to watch them ride off. There would be a party of them and they were going to hunt boar, the most dangerous creatures of the forest. Boars could be really vicious, Dagobert told me.

'My father likes hunting boar.'

'Say it in English, please, Dagobert,' I said automatically.

That night footsteps awakened me again. Stealthily they went past my door. This time I immediately thought of Fritz. I listened to which direction they were going. It was not to the turret-room this time.

Hastily I lighted my candle, put on my slippers and wrapped my dressing-gown about me. By the time I had done this I could no longer hear the footsteps. But I knew that they had descended the stairs. I went down the spiral staircase, through the narrow passages. A cold breeze sweeping into the fortress told me which door was open.

I hurried to it and I saw the small figure walking steadily

181

towards the stables.

I ran.

Fritz was at the stable door; he was trying to open it.

I caught him. The blank expression of the sleep-walker was on his face.

I took him gently by the hand and led him back to the fortress. Although it was summer and the days warm, the temperature dropped considerably at night and his hand was icily cold. I led him carefully to his room. He was shivering; his feet were chilled; he wore nothing but his nightshirt. He was murmuring something: 'No . . . please no.' And there was such fear in those words that I was sure I knew what was troubling him.

Tomorrow he was to go out hunting wild boar with his father: and he was afraid. That would explain why he had gone to the stables.

I felt a fury against this insensitive man who did not understand that he had a son who might well be brilliant. I had immediately assessed Fritz's mental capacity; but because of this he was imaginative in a manner which men such as the Count could not understand.

I leaned over Fritz. I said: 'It's all right, Fritz.'

He opened his eyes.

He said: '*Mutti* . . .' Then, 'Miss . . .'

'Hello, Fritz. Yes, I'm here.'

'Did I walk?'

'A little . . .'

He began to shiver.

I said: 'It's all right. Lots of people do it. I heard you and brought you back to bed.'

'You heard me last time. Dagobert heard them talking about it.'

'I've got a special pair of ears for you.'

That made him laugh.

'Tomorrow Fritz,' I said, 'you're not going to the hunt.'

'Did my father say . . .?'

'*I* said you're not.'

'You can't, Miss.'

'Oh yes, I can,' I said. 'Your feet are like ice. I'm going to put an extra blanket on. And tomorrow morning you're to stay in bed. You're a little chilled. And you won't get up until it's too late to go with the hunters.'

'Can I, Miss? Who says . . .?'

182

'I say,' I said firmly.

In some way I had won his confidence. He believed me. I stayed by his bed until he fell into a peaceful sleep, which was in a very short time.

Then I went back to my room and tried to sleep.

I must be ready for the battle which would surely come the next morning.

I watched the count and his party riding up to the schloss, and steeling myself, went down and out of the fortress to the *Randhausburg*. Dagobert was already there in his riding outfit.

As he was greeting his father, I slipped inside and waited in the *Rittersaal*. My battle with the Count must take place unobserved. I should never win if we had spectators because he was the sort of man who would never concede if observed.

He had seen me enter and, as I knew he would, he quickly followed me there.

'Good morning, Miss Trant,' he said. 'How gracious of you to come down to greet my party.'

'I did so because I wanted to speak to you about Fritz.'

'The boy, I suppose, is waiting to leave with us.'

'No, I have told him to stay in bed for the morning. He was chilled last night.'

He stared at me in astonishment. 'Chilled!' he cried. 'In bed! Miss Trant, what do you mean?'

'Exactly what I say. Last night Fritz walked in his sleep. I gather he does this when he is disturbed. He is a sensitive child, studious rather than athletic.'

'That seems to me all the more reason why he should take more physical exercise. Pray tell him to get up at once and that I am angry because he was not ready and eager to go to hunt the boar.'

'Would you have him pretend to feel something he doesn't?'

'I would have him hide his cowardice and pretend to a little courage.'

'He is no coward,' I said fiercely.

'No? When he cowers behind the skirts of his teacher?'

'I must make this clear. It was on my orders that he stayed in bed this morning.'

'So you give orders here now, Miss Trant?'

'It is essential for the teacher to tell her pupils what to do.'

'Even when it is to disobey a parent?'

'It did not occur to me that any parent would want to drag a sick child from his bed.'

'How dramatic you are, Miss Trant! I did not think that an English characteristic.'

'I dare say it is not, but I must make you understand that Fritz is different from Dagobert. Now *he* will enjoy the hunt and he will not be tortured by an over-active imagination. You can make of him the sort of man you admire – someone in your own image.'

'Thank you for that assessment of my character, Miss Trant.'

'I think you understand perfectly that I would not presume to assess your character on such a short acquaintance . . . or in fact at all. I came here to teach children English and . . . '

'And their father how to treat his children. His idiosyncrasies are no concern of yours, you say. Yet you belie this. Because now you are telling me how wrong my attitude is towards my son.'

'Will you do this for me?' I asked. His expression changed. He came closer. I held up a hand as though to ward him off and I went on quickly: 'Do not insist that Fritz goes to this hunt today. Please give me a chance with him. He is nervous and the way to disperse that nervousness is not to aggravate it, but to soothe it, to show him that a great deal that he fears lies only in his mind.'

'You talk like one of these new-fangled doctors one hears of nowadays. But you're a good advocate. What has Fritz done to deserve such concern?'

'He is a child who needs understanding. Please will you allow me to have my way over this?'

'I've an idea, Miss Trant, that you are a young woman who often gets her way.'

'You are wrong in that.'

'Then you should be grateful to me.'

I was suddenly thinking happily of Fritz's relief when he heard the party riding away into the forest.

'You are charming when you smile,' he said. 'It gives me pleasure to be responsible for such charm.'

'I am grateful,' I said.

He bowed. He took my hand then and kissed it; I took it from his grasp as soon as possible and he was laughing as he went out.

I went up to Fritz's room. He started as I entered.

184

I said, 'The party is just leaving. Would you like to see them go? We can watch from the window.'

He looked at me as though I were a magician.

He stood at the window and watched the cavalcade ride out of the schloss grounds down the slopes into the pine forest.

I sat by Fritz's bed and gave him a lesson in English. He sneezed once or twice and I went down to Frau Graben to tell her I thought he had a cold. She brought up her own remedy – a cordial she made herself. She smacked her lips as she took a spoonful of it.

'Lovely!' she said, beaming.

Fritz knew the cordial well and took it with relish. It made him sleepy, so I left him and went for a walk in the woods, but not very far from the schloss. I had no desire to run into the hunting party.

It was a lovely afternoon. I came back and went to sit in the garden to prepare next day's lesson; it was peaceful there, shut in as it was by the short thick firs.

One of the two girls, Ella, who looked after us in the fortress, came down to tell me that Frau Graben had sent a message over to ask me to her sitting-room.

I went; she had a little spirit lamp which she used in the summer and the kettle was boiling.

'Tea,' she said once again, as though I were a small child to whom she was offering a treat.

I noticed the new addition to the room – a blue gilded cage in which was a canary.

'Look at my little angel,' she said. ' "Angel", that is his name. Tweet-tweet. Isn't he a little treasure? I saw him in a shop in the *Unterer Stadtplatz* yesterday. I couldn't resist buying him and bringing him home. They say some of them can talk. Wouldn't I love to hear him talk? Come, little Angel. Say "Frau Graben . . ." Say "Hello Miss." Stubborn, eh? Well, my little man, we'll see.'

'You like . . .' I was going to say animals, but I suppose one could not call canaries or spiders animals . . . I substituted 'living things'.

Her eyes sparkled. 'I like to know what they'll do. You can never be sure. I like to see for myself.'

'What happened to your spiders?'

'One killed the other.'

'And then?'

'I let the winner go. It seemed only right. I guessed that's what would happen but you never know . . . with living things they can do just the opposite to what others in the same case have done before them. Tweet, tweet, my Angel. Come on, talk for Frau Graben.'

The canary gave voice to a few notes, which delighted her. 'More!' she cried. 'But what I really wanted, my pet, was for you to talk.' She smiled at me. 'Well, if he won't that doesn't mean we can't. There. The kettle's boiling. I'll make the tea and we'll get cosy.'

Over the cups she said: 'Well, so Fritz didn't go. You could have knocked me down with a feather. What did Fredy have to say to you?'

'I told him that Fritz was a sensitive child. This sleep-walking worries me. It happens when he is disturbed. He was worried last night about this hunt . . . so he walks in his sleep. He is a very clever boy. We don't want him upset.'

'And you told Fredy all this?'

'I did.'

'And he gave way! It's a bad sign. It shows that he likes you.'

'Is it so bad to be liked by the Count?'

'If you're a young woman, it's tricky. He's a libertine of the first degree. It's a way of life with them. They've heard the stories of their parents and grandparents. We're a lusty nation, Miss Trant; and we're divided into these states which seem small to you but the heads of them have great power . . . they and their families. It's not good for young men. In the past they've had their pick of the village maidens and took it as a right. The boys have been brought up to this. The history of our reigning families is one of seduction in various ingenious forms. The most popular through the last century or so was the mock marriage. There's our legend here of the haunted room that you decided to unhaunt. You see what I mean about taking the Count's fancy? A young woman's not safe when she does that.'

'I am not a particularly young woman.'

'Now, Miss Trant, you're not old. And if you are somewhere up in the twenties you've gained something on the way. But I must warn you about some of our gentlemen.'

'I think I know how to deal with them.'

'Fredy can be forceful.'

'I think I shall know how to behave.'

Frau Graben seemed satisfied. She beamed and handed me the spiced cakes. I took one and nibbled at it. It was very rich.

'Well,' she said, 'he'll soon be on duty at the Duke's schloss. The Prince is coming home. There's to be a special procession to the church to welcome him back. I think it will be in a week or so.'

'Where has he been?' I asked.

'He's been to Berlin to take part in a conference there. There's talk about the French getting very obstreperous.'

'And Rochenstein would fight with Prussia?'

'If the French attacked us all true Germans would stand together. So that's what the Prince has been doing. You'll see him ride to the thanksgiving service. That'll be a day.'

'Very soon, I suppose.'

'As soon as he gets home the Chamberlain will arrange it. You'll see some crowds then. You'll want to see the procession from the palace in the town to the church and back to the palace.'

'Is the Prince very poular?'

'You know how it is with royalty. Sometimes they're popular, sometimes not. You'll see them riding through the streets and people shouting for them and the next day they have a bomb thrown at them.'

'Does that often happen?'

'Shall we say it happens. They're not safe. I was always terrified when my boys used to go out with their parents. In the first carriage would be the Duke and his lady and their son the Prince and in the next the Duke's brother Ludwig and Fredy. Of course Ludwig was a traitor and came to his end; Fredy swore loyalty but I reckon the loyalty of most people is to one person – themselves. You'll have to go and see the thanksgiving service. They'll get the Processional Cross out, and as you know that's quite a ceremony.'

'It was indeed and I thought what a lot of trouble they had gone to just to show me. I shall never forget how they guarded it. There was a very pleasant soldier – Sergeant Franck I believe he was called. Someone must have mentioned his name.'

'Oh, I know Sergeant Franck. A pleasant fellow. He was put to soldiering when quite a boy and I remember how proud his family were of him when he got into the Duke's Guard. Then he married that wife of his. She's changed. It just shows

187

187

you what can happen. She was a poor frightened little thing when she married Franck. There'd been some sort of past . . . but he took care of her and now she's got two children and is very pleased with herself. The change in people! It always makes me laugh. There they are and then life picks them up and puts them somewhere with someone else and you watch what happens from there.'

'Like soldiers,' I said.

'Oh, people are a lot more interesting than them.'

I agreed.

'I'm glad he's coming home when he is – the Prince, I mean,' she went on. 'It's the right time, when you come to think of it. Oh, he's a one, he is. Fredy always declares he was my favourite. "I never had a favourite," I said. But that wasn't really true. Thunder and Lightning, I said. I couldn't imagine one without the other. The flash and the roar. That's how they always seemed to me. I'd like to be back in the days when they were little. The joy of my life they were! Of course Ludwig, the Duke's younger brother, wanted young Fredy brought up in the palace. Secretly he thought he had as much right there as the Duke. Fredy's Ludwig all over again. He always wanted to excel in everything, and just as Ludwig wanted to outshine the Duke, so Fredy wanted to do better than his cousin the Prince. What the Prince had, he wanted – all their toys, I mean. It frightened me then. Toys when they're young, and when they grow up, I used to say, what then? It'll be more than toys then. But you won this morning, didn't you? You got your way about young Fritzi. My goodness, you've done something for that child. You understand children. That's strange really, because there you are, a spinster . . .' Her smiling eyes were intent on my face, '. . . and never having had one of your own.'

I felt a slow flush creep into my cheeks. I couldn't help it. She had conjured up so clearly a vision of that nursing home – the pregnant women chatting on the lawn – the poor girl who had died – Gretchen I think her name was. Gretchen Swartz.

I had hesitated a second too long; those bland smiling eyes missed very little I was sure.

I said: 'Understanding children is something one is born with, perhaps.'

'Oh yes, of course, that is so. But when a woman has a child something happens to her, I think. I've seen it happen.'

'Perhaps,' I said coolly.

'Well, the Prince will be home in time for our great night. Oh, you wouldn't know about this. We're regular ones for celebrations. This is Loke's land here. The Lokenwald, you see. And in two weeks' time the moon will be full. That's the night for mischief. I shan't let you go out on that night, Miss Trant.'

I shivered a little; memories were unbearable.

She leaned towards me and took my hand in her rather damp hot one.

'No, I wouldn't let you go out. It's not safe. Something gets into people on that night. It's Loke's moon – the seventh of the year; and there are people here who will be good Christians every night of the year except the night of the full seventh moon. Then they're pagans again just as they were centuries ago before Christianity came to tame them down. Why, Miss, I believe I've frightened you.'

I tried to laugh. 'I've heard of it, you know. I've read of the gods and heroes.'

'So you do know something about our Night of the Seventh Moon after all?'

'Yes,' I said, 'I know something.'

The afternoon was hot and sunny.

'We'll all go down together,' said Frau Graben, 'there'll be such crowds I don't want anyone to get trampled to death.'

'Surely it's not as bad as that,' I protested.

'They're all excited to know he's back.'

We drove down into the town through the mountain roads which never failed to delight me. The orchids and gentians were in bloom, brightening the mountain slopes; every now and then we came upon a plateau with a small farmhouse and heard the familiar tinkle of the cowbells. Down in the town the sun was shining on the mellowing roof-tops; the bells were ringing and as we came into the *Oberer Stadtplatz* we were greeted by the gay sight of flags fluttering from every place where it was possible to put them. The men and women were in their native costume and I guessed that hundreds of them had come in from the neighbouring countryside.

I was glad we had Frau Graben with us, for the children were very excited and I should have been afraid that they might stray away and get hurt in the crush.

We drove to the inn where we had stabled our horses on

another occasion and there a window looking on to the square in which was the church had been kept for us. From there we should be able to see the procession undisturbed.

The innkeeper treated Frau Graben with great respect. She evidently knew him well for she asked after his daughter. His eyes lit up at the mention of her and he clearly doted on her. 'The prettiest girl in Rochenburg,' commented Frau Graben, and I was aware of the sly speculative look in her eyes and wondered what it meant.

Wine and little spiced cakes, at the sight of which Frau Graben's eyes glistened, were brought out and there was some sweet drink for the children.

Frau Graben was clearly as excited as the boys and Liesel. Dagobert kept telling me what everything signified; Fritz, now completely devoted to me, kept near me and I was delighted because this was a spectacle he was going to enjoy; Liesel could not keep still; but Frau Graben seemed absorbed in some secret mirth which delighted her to such an extent that I got the impression that she was debating whether she would be more amused to share her mirth or keep it entirely to herself.

Everywhere was an air of expectancy; people called excitedly to each other. The flags gaily fluttered at the windows. I recognized that of Rochenstein of course, and the Prussian flag, but most of the Austrian and German states were represented. A band started to play. In the *Oberer Stadtplatz* a choir was singing. I recognized the words which began:

'*Unsern Ausgang segne Gott*'

'God bless our going out nor less our coming in.' My mother had taught me this. They sang it, she said, when they moved into a new house. I suppose it could now refer to the Prince's visit to Prussia and his return home.

In the distance I could hear the military band.

'They'll be coming from the palace now. You'll see the Processional Cross, Miss Trant,' chortled Frau Graben.

'I dare say there was a big ceremony getting it out of the crypt.'

'Yes, and taking it to the palace. Sergeant Franck was telling me about it.'

'I shall look forward to seeing it in use. I hope nobody tries to steal it.'

Dagobert looked excited. 'If they did I'd run after them.

I'd kill them. I'd get it back.'

'Single-handed?' I asked.

'All by myself,' went on Dagobert. 'Then the Duke would send for me and he'd say you're my true son and you'll come before Carl . . .'

'Poor Carl!' I said lightly. 'It's hard on him. After all, to be set aside because he didn't recapture the cross. Is that fair?'

'Nothing's fair,' said Dagobert. 'My father could be the Prince . . .'

'Now,' said Frau Graben comfortably, 'that's enough of that talk, Dagobert. The Prince is the Duke's son and true heir and little Carl the heir to follow him. That's how it's been arranged. You're getting more like your father every day. Oh look, here's the beginning. My word, don't the soldiers look fine in their uniforms!'

They did indeed; the brightly caparisoned horses with their waving plumes; the blue and gold uniforms and the glitter of helmets; the marching tunes of the band; the waving flags. The crowd was reduced to a momentary hush. Then the cheers broke out.

On came the brilliant cavalcade and behind it members of the church in the long black and white robes. A soldier on horseback held the Processional Cross. It scintillated in the bright light; the emeralds, rubies and sapphires shone and the diamond sparkled with red and blue fire. This was the way in which to see it. I recognized Sergeant Franck riding on one side of it; there was another stalwart soldier on the other.

The silence as the cross passed could only be construed as an awed hush.

After the cross came the ducal coach. It was not unlike the pictures I had seen of our queen's coach, elaborately gilded and drawn by eight white horses. There was the Duke and on one side of him the Prince and on the other the woman whom I had seen at the pavilion and who had reminded me of Ilse.

I hardly saw the Duke, nor the Princess. I felt as though I had stepped back into a mad fantastic dream. I stared; for there, seated between the Duke and the Princess, was Maximilian.

FIVE

Frau Graben was saying, 'Are you all right, Miss Trant? My goodness, you do look queer. Is it the heat?'

'I . . . I'm all right,' I said.

The sound of brass bands seemed a long way off; the crowds below me seemed to sway; I looked at the goose-stepping soldiers without really seeing them.

I could never mistake him. I knew him too well. In his uniform he looked more splendid than he had in the woods. But I would have known him in any costume.

I sat there, aware of Frau Graben's anxious glances which were somehow eager and excited. I was sure she knew that it was something more than the heat which had disturbed me.

The crowds were sweeping forward; the ducal party and its retinue had now gone into the church; the service was in progress.

Frau Graben had brought her smelling-salts from the capacious pocket of her skirts.

'Have a sniff of these, my dear,' she said. 'And, Fritzi, run and tell the innkeeper to come to me.'

I repeated: 'I'm all right.' But my voice sounded strange, shaky.

'I think you felt a bit faint, dear. Would you like us to go back now or would you like to wait?'

Dagobert's mouth was a round O of protest. Liesel began to wail: 'I won't go home.' Fritz looked at me anxiously.

'I want to stay,' I said.

Indeed I wanted to stay. I wanted to see him again. I wanted to assure myself that I had been right. I kept saying to myself: When you first saw the Count for a second or so you thought he was Maximilian. Perhaps you've been mistaken again. But no. I had not been. It was true I would know him anywhere; and the reason there was a resemblance between him and the Count was because they were cousins; they had been brought up together and it was not only their looks which were similar.

The innkeeper came and Frau Graben asked him for brandy. When it came she said: 'Here, Miss Trant, sip this.

It'll do you the world of good.'

'There's nothing wrong,' I protested.

'I don't think you're right, dear.'

She was smiling, faintly complacent. She didn't seem to take her eyes from my face.

'There,' she said, when I had taken some brandy, 'that's better.'

I wanted to shout: It makes no difference. It's not the heat. I've seen Maximilian and Maximilian is your Prince of Rochenstein.

The children were chattering. 'I liked the cross best.'

'I didn't. I liked the soldiers.'

'I liked the drums.'

'Did you see papa?'

'Papa was the best. He was the most handsome.'

And so on. I wished Frau Graben would not show such concern.

'Perhaps we should have left,' she whispered.

'No, no. It'll be all right.'

'It's too late now. The crowd's growing more dense. They'll all be there till after the return procession back to the palace.'

The service was over at last. They rode through the streets. Once more I saw him. At one moment I thought that, as he acknowledged the shouts of the crowd, he would look up at our window, but he did not.

I felt dizzy and bewildered; but there was a great singing gladness in my heart. I had found Maximilian.

I was silent as Prinzstein, one of the coachmen, drove us back to Klocksburg.

When we arrived, Frau Graben said: 'I should go and lie down, dear. That's the best thing after a turn like that.'

There was nothing I wanted to do so much as to be alone. My thoughts were in a whirl. I had to see him. I must let him know that I was here. Whatever had happened during those three days following the Night of the Seventh Moon I knew that it was the Prince whom I had met in the mist and that he was the father of my child.

Little scraps of Frau Graben's conversation came back to me. Her boys had been 'ones' for the women; they had seen them and fancied them and let nothing stand in the way of their desires. She had impressed that upon me.

I was suddenly reminded of the Princess Wilhelmina – the

woman who had a look of Ilse. His wife! But how could she be if he were married to me? Unless of course they had been married before. No, I remembered something Frau Graben had said. Four years ago the Prince had married . . . reluctantly . . . a woman who came from a more important state than Rochenstein. So it was a good match. They had a child, who had followed in one of the carriages. I had not noticed him. I could see nothing, think of nothing but Maximilian.

A great desolation came to me. It was nine years since we had met. What place could I have in his life now?

But I must see him. I might mean nothing to him, but I must see him. I had to know what had happened to me during those six days of my life.

How did one see a Prince? One could not, I supposed, go to the schloss or the palace and ask to see him. Perhaps one asked for an audience. My life was once more taking a dramatically fantastic turn.

Frau Graben was knocking at the door.

'Ah, lying down!' she said. 'That's right. I've brought you some of my special wine.'

'You are very good,' I said.

'Stuff and nonsense.' She laughed as though something had secretly amused her. 'This will do you good. I made it myself. It's made with dandelions and a touch of the sloe, but I'm not giving any more secrets away, not even to you, dear Miss Trant. Poor Fritzi's very anxious about you. My goodness, you've wormed your way into that boy's heart – no mistake. And he's not one to give his affection easily either. You frightened me.'

I sipped the wine. It made my throat tingle.

'It'll warm the cockles of your heart, as they say. There now, doesn't it? What did you think of our Prince?'

'Very handsome . . .'

'Well, I'd say Fredy was the more handsome of the two but young Maxi had a charm of his own.'

'So you called him Maxi.'

'Oh, he's Carl Ludwig Maximilian like his father – so is the little one. They're all Carls when they come to power but they have their own family names. The boy's called Carl in the Family and in public, like his grandfather. It did me good to see Maxi. He looked well, I thought, after his stay in Berlin. I'll warrant he enjoyed that. They say the Berlin girls are very smart.'

'Did he go to see the girls?'

She laughed her loud abandoned laugh. 'Well, he'd always do that; but it was this conference as well. He'll have to show himself now round the countryside. I'll bet he'll be off on a tour of some sort soon. He's been away some time. It was a good procession, wasn't it? Nothing like royalty to draw the crowds. And of course a young Prince is always an attraction. Prince Charming, you know. The people like a young Duke and they say his father's not long for this world. He had a bad illness last year. It was a wonder he survived. Fredy's a trial. He doesn't want to see his cousin come into the title – the boy I brought up with him in the nursery.' She shook her head. 'Fredy was always a handful. They both were.'

While she spoke she was watching me with her bright, humorous but intent gaze.

I wanted to say to her: Go away. I must be alone to think.

She went to the window. 'There's his own flag flying from the tower. Blue on green with the eagle in the corner. That means he's there. The Duke's flag is there too.'

I got up and went to the window and looked out. There were the two flags as Frau Graben had said.

'Fredy flies his flag from his own schloss and it's very similar to Maxi's. Fredy had the design altered slightly so that the difference between them is not all that easy to tell. Mischief!'

I stood at the window looking at the fluttering flags.

'He's come home in time for the Night of the Seventh Moon,' she observed.

I spent a sleepless night and the next morning was determined to see him soon. If I wrote, would the letter reach him? There were probably secretaries who screened his correspondence. Suppose I presented myself at the schloss and said: 'I must see the Prince. I am an old friend of his.'

It would not be easy. There were guards at the entry to the schloss. They would not let me through. I could consult Frau Graben. If she were on such familiar terms with Maximilian as she was with the Count, she would advise me; but she would ferret my story from me and I did not wish to speak of it to anyone.

I remembered how it had upset me when I had talked to Anthony. No one could have been more sympathetic, too much so perhaps.

Frau Graben came to my room before breakfast to see how I was. Why didn't I take a day's holiday? she said. Get into the forest with the children. It would do me good.

I said: 'Is the Family accessible?'

She looked puzzled.

'I mean, do they meet people?'

'They're meeting people all the time.'

'I mean spontaneously. Do people call on them . . .?'

'Call on them! Well, not exactly. They'd have to wait until they were asked, wouldn't they?'

'I see. And I suppose there are secretaries and so on to protect them?'

'Well, would anyone be able to call on *your* queen?'

I said I was sure that would have to be arranged too.

She went to the window. 'Oh, the Prince's flag is no longer flying. That means he's set off on his tour already. I shan't see him now until he gets back. I'll give him a good talking to. He knows I like to see him when he gets back from his stays away from us.'

I felt a sense of frustration. I was on the point of telling Frau Graben that I was planning to see him; that I must see him on a matter of great importance to me. But I felt it was wiser to say nothing. In any case I could take no action until he came back. Perhaps in the next few days some solution would occur to me.

So I continued to fret and brood and yet sometimes I was so happy that my moods were unpredictable. I fluttered between despair and a wild unreasoning hope.

The children were excited. Soon it would be the Night of the Seventh Moon. They had pointed the moon out to me when it was no more than a slim crescent lying there in the sky, seeming to hang over the ducal schloss. When it was full there would be the great night.

There would be firework displays in the schloss gardens and the whole town would be able to see them. Frau Graben had said that we should look from the turret-room where we would get the best view.

'The children would like to go into the town,' she said, 'but I'm not having that. As for you, Miss Trant, I'd strongly advise you to stay in too. I wouldn't like to think of you out there. People seem to go quite mad on this night. You wouldn't understand.'

'I think I do,' I said.

'My goodness, ordinary decent Christians behave like barbarians. Something happens when the moon is full, they say. We go right back to the days before Jesus Christ walked this earth. Then there was a different religion here and this is Loke's land . . . the land of mischief. I reckon it's time this was abolished. The Duke tried to once, you know, but the people wouldn't have it. Whether the night was recognized or not, they were still out in their masks and costumes. There's many a girl meets her ruin on the Night of the Seventh Moon.'

'I shall be content to watch from the turret-room window,' I said.

She nodded smiling.

'I'll feel happier to know you're there.'

All day long there was a mounting tension. On the previous afternoon the Prince had returned to the schloss. Before I went to bed I saw his flag flying from the tower.

I could not describe my feelings; they fluctuated between despair and elation, between frustration and hope. One thought filled my mind: I must see him soon.

In the afternoon the children, Frau Graben and I drove down into the town to see the preparations. Flags were hanging from the windows of the houses and I had never seen the flower-boxes at many of the windows so colourful. Some of the shops had boarded up their windows.

The sun was hot; people were laughing and joking; they were all talking of 'Tonight'.

'I want to come down here tonight and see the dancing,' announced Dagobert.

'You're going to see the fireworks,' Frau Graben told him firmly.

'I want to come too,' said Liesel, who followed Dagobert in everything.

'Now, now,' said Frau Graben comfortably, 'the fireworks will be lovely.'

'I'll come out and put on a mask and ride down,' cried Dagobert.

'I dare say, my lad, in your dreams,' laughed Frau Graben.

'Now, who'd like to go to *The Prince*'s for spiced buns?' She gave me a gentle nudge. 'That sounded funny, didn't it? Go to the Prince's for spiced buns. The inn, I mean, of course, not His Highness.'

She went on chuckling at her joke and I made up my mind that the next day I would come down to the town when the children were with Pastor Kratz and ride up to the schloss and tell the guards that they must let the Prince know that Helena Trant was asking to see him. At least if I did not see him, then I might discover how I could do so.

The children chattered over their buns and Frau Graben said we'd better be getting back. The crowds started coming in early, and we didn't want to get caught in the crush.

The evening came. I kept thinking of that long-ago day, of going forth into the town – another town, it was true, but that afternoon I had been struck by the similarity between the two – of losing Ilse and plunging straight into fantasy.

The children were allowed to stay up a little later than usual to see the fireworks. 'Providing,' said Frau Graben, 'that as soon as they are over, there are no protests about going to bed.'

So when it was dark we went to the turret-room – the children, myself and Frau Graben. Candles in sconces stood on either end of the mantelshelf and on the polished table was a small candelabrum. The effect was enchanting.

We ranged ourselves round the window and the display began.

It was taking place in the grounds of the ducal schloss, which was an excellent spot as it would be visible from almost every point. The children shrieked with excitement as the fireworks flashed across the sky and when the display was over there were groans of disappointment, but Frau Graben hustled them all away and as she did so she whispered to me: 'Stay here. I'll join you later. There's something I want to show you.'

So I stayed and, looking round the room, remembered the unhappy woman who was alleged to have thrown herself from the window and haunted the room ever since. In candle light it did seem eerie. I wondered how desolate one had to become before one took such a terrible step; I could imagine her feelings so acutely in those moments.

I felt a great desire to go to my comfortable room below; here I felt remote from the rest of the fortress, although only

198

the spiral staircase separated us.

I turned away from the window and sat at the table. Footsteps were mounting the spiral staircase – two sets of footsteps. My heart began to beat wildly. I wasn't sure why. I sensed that something tremendous was about to happen. Frau Graben was with the children – she could hardly have had time yet to see them in bed. There were just the two maids in the fortress. The steps were not light enough for those.

The door was thrown open. It *was* Frau Graben, beaming, her hair slightly ruffled, an unusual flush in her cheeks.

She said: 'Here she is.'

And then I saw Maximilian.

I stood up, my hand touching the table for support. He came in; he stared at me unbelievingly. Then he said: 'Lenchen! It can't be! Lenchen!'

I went forward; I was caught in his arms. I clung to him. I felt his lips on my brow and cheeks.

'Lenchen,' he repeated. 'Lenchen . . . it can't be.'

I heard Frau Graben chuckle. 'There. I brought her for you, couldn't have my Lightning fretting, so I went and got her for you.'

Her laughter broke in on our wonder in each other and we were only vaguely aware of what she was saying. Then the door shut and we were alone.

I said: 'I'm not dreaming, am I? I'm not dreaming?'

He had taken my face in his hands; his fingers caressed it as though he were tracing its contours.

'Where have you been, Lenchen . . . all this time?'

'I thought I should never see you again.'

'But you died . . . You were in the lodge . . .'

'The lodge had disappeared when I went back. Where had you gone? Why didn't you come for me?'

'I'm afraid you'll disappear in a moment. I've dreamed of you so often. And then I wake to find my arms empty and you gone . . . You were dead, they told me. You were in the lodge when it happened . . .'

I shook my head. All I wanted for the moment was to cling to him. Later we could talk.

'I can only think of one thing at the moment. You're here . . . with me.'

'We're together. You're alive . . . my darling Lenchen . . . alive and here. Never leave me again.'

'*I* . . . leave *you*.' I laughed. I hadn't laughed like that for years – abandoned, gay . . . in love with life.

And for the moment there was nothing for us both but the joy of this blissful reunion. We were together; his arms were about me; his kisses on my lips . . . our bodies calling for each other. A hundred memories were back with me – they had never really left me, but before I had never dared look back at this perfect joy because to know that it had gone, to have that lingering doubt that it had ever existed, would have been unbearable.

But there was the mystery between us.

'Where have you been?' he was demanding.

'What happened on the Night of the Seventh Moon?' I had to know.

We sat side by side on the couch – before us was the open window; the smell of burning bonfires was on the air; we could hear the shouts of the people far away in the town.

I said: 'We must start from the beginning. I must know everything. Can you imagine what it is like to believe there is a possibility that you have lost six days of your life and three of them the happiest you have ever known? Oh, Maximilian, what happened to us? Start at the beginning. We met in the mist. You took me to your hunting lodge and I stayed a night there and you tried to come to my room but the door was locked and Hildegarde was there to protect me. That was real enough, I know. It is the next part. My cousin Ilse and her husband Ernst came to Oxford and brought me back to the Lokenwald.'

'She was not your cousin, Lenchen. Ernst was in my service. He had been an ambassador to the court of Klarenbock, the home of the Princess.'

'She whom they say is your wife. How can she be? I am your wife.'

'My Lenchen,' he cried fervently, 'you are my wife. You . . . and you only.'

'We were married, were we not? It's true. It must be true."

He took my hands and looked at me earnestly. 'Yes,' he said, 'it's true. The people around me thought I was repeating the practices of my ancestors, which are sometimes carried out now, I fear. But it was not so in our case, Lenchen. We were truly married. You are indeed my wife. I am your husband.'

'I knew it was true. I would not believe otherwise. But tell me, my dearest husband. Tell me everything.'

'You came to the lodge and in the morning Hildegarde took you back to the *Damenstift* and that was the end of our little adventure – so I thought. It did not turn out as I intended for I saw that you were so young, a schoolgirl merely. It was not only Hildegarde who looked after you that night. But you had done something to me, aroused feelings I had not experienced before. And after you'd gone I continued to think of you and I wanted to see you again. Try to understand how things have been. Perhaps I have been over-indulged, not refused often enough. You became an obsession with me. I thought of you constantly. I could not stop thinking of you. I talked of you to Ernst. As an older man of rich worldly experience, he wagered that if my affair with you had progressed as so many had before, I should have forgotten it in a few weeks. So we planned to bring you out here that you and I might meet again.'

'And Ilse . . .'

'She had married Ernst when he was ambassador to Klarenbock. She is the sister of the Princess – but a natural sister, so that marriage with our ambassador was a good one for her. Ernst was ill; he needed medical advice and the best to be found was in London. He wagered me that he and Ilse would bring you back. And so they went to Oxford; they told this story of the relationship between Ilse and your mother and they brought you out here.'

'A plot!' I cried.

He nodded. 'A not very original one.'

'I did not see through it.'

'Why should you? It was made easy by the fact that your mother was born here. But that I suppose is the pivot on which everything turns. You had our forests and mountains in your blood. That I sensed from the moment we met. It drew us together. It was simple for Ilse to assume relationship. She could talk of the home life she had alleged she shared with your mother. Homes of the sort from which your mother would have come are very much alike. That part was easy. So you came, and then on the Night of the Seventh Moon . . .'

'You were there waiting when she brought me into the square and that was her cue to disappear?'

'I was there. My intention was to take you to the lodge and to stay there with you until such a time as one of us should wish to leave. I even had plans for keeping you there altogether. That was really how I hoped it would turn out.'

'But it was different.'

'Yes, it was different. Nothing like it had ever happened to me before. As soon as I saw you again I knew how different. I didn't care for anything. I knew that whatever happened afterwards we were meant for each other and that I would face anything rather than lose you. There would be immense difficulties, I knew, because of my position – but I didn't care. I could think of only one thing that mattered to me. I was going to make you my wife.'

'And you did! It's true that you did. They lied to me – Ilse, Ernst and the doctor. They said . . . oh, it was shameful . . . that I was carried off into the forest by a criminal and that I returned to the house in such a state that they had to put me under sedation to save my reason.'

'But they knew what had happened.'

'Then why . . . oh, why . . .?'

'Because they feared the consequences of what I had done. But how could they? Like the rest of my staff, they believed that our marriage was no true marriage. They did not believe it possibly could be. How could I, my father's heir, marry except for state reasons? But I could, Lenchen, and I did, because I loved you so much that I could contemplate nothing else. I could not deceive you, my darling. How could I deceive my own true love? I knew – and they knew – that my cousin had on one occasion deluded a girl into thinking that he was marrying her and that the man who performed the ceremony was no true priest, thus making that ceremony without meaning. A mock marriage. That was what they thought ours was. But I loved you, Lenchen. I couldn't do that.'

'I'm so happy,' I cried. 'So happy!' Then: 'Why didn't you tell me who you were?'

'I had to keep it secret, even from you, until I had made my arrangements. I alone must explain this to my father, for I knew that there were going to be all kinds of difficulties. He had been urging me to marry for some time – for state reasons. It was not the moment to tell him that I had married without his consent and that of his council. There was too much trouble in the dukedom. My Uncle Ludwig was seeking an opportunity to overthrow my father and could well seize on what he would call a mésalliance as a reason for deposing him and setting up my cousin as heir. I could not tell my father then . . . and when I could have done so, I believed you to be dead.'

'I must tell you what happened, because I can see that you have no idea. Ilse and Ernst came and took me away from the lodge after you had gone.'

'And told me that you were there when the place was blown up.'

'We must follow it bit by bit as it happened, for it all seems so incredible. After you went, Ilse and Ernst took me back to the house they had rented in the town. The next morning I awoke in a dazed condition and they told me I had been unconscious for six days after I had been criminally assaulted in the forest.'

'Impossible!'

'This is what they told me. They had a doctor there. He said he had kept me under sedation to save my reason, and that the days which I believed I had spent with you had actually been passed in my bed.'

'But how could they hope that you would believe that?'

'I didn't, but they had the doctor there. And when I went back to the lodge it was gone.'

'The lodge was blown up on the day I left. Hildegarde and Hans had gone into the town for provisions. It happened while they were away. I believed it was a plot to kill me. There have been such plots before and my Uncle Ludwig was at the bottom of them. It is not the first time that I and members of my family have escaped death by a very small margin. Ernst came to tell me that the lodge had been blown up and you were in it at the time.'

'I went there to look for it,' I said, 'and found it was a shell. So it had only just been demolished. Oh you see how I have been deceived.'

'Poor, poor Lenchen. How you must have suffered! How we both have! There must have been times when you wished we had never met in the forest that day.'

'Oh no, no,' I said fiercely. 'I never felt that . . . not even in the most wretched and desperate moments.'

He took my hands and kissed them.

I went on: 'So I stayed with them and they looked after me . . . and when the child was born . . .'

'The child!' he cried.

'Oh yes, we had a child. She died at birth. I think I was

never so unhappy as when they told me. At least, I thought, I shall have her, and I thought I would take a post at the *Damenstift* and I planned our future together . . . hers and mine.'

'So we had a child,' he repeated. 'Oh Lenchen, my poor sweet Lenchen. And Ilse and Ernst . . . why did they do this? Why should they have done this? I must discover what this means.'

'Where are they now?'

'Ernst is dead. He was ill, you know . . . very ill. Ilse went back to Klarenbock. I heard she married again. But why should they tell me you were dead? What motive was there in this? I shall find Ilse. I must have the truth from her. I will send someone to Klarenbock to bring her here. I want to know from her what this means.'

'She must have had a reason.'

'We'll find it,' he said.

Then he turned once more to me; he touched my hair and my face as though trying to convince himself that I was really there.

I was so happy to be with him, I could think of nothing beyond the glorious fact that we were together. I was bewildered – still groping in the dark, but Maximilian was with me and that for the moment was enough. And I had learned the truth of what happened on the Night of the Seventh Moon; I had taken back those six days of my life; they belonged to me and I had been wantonly deceived.

What could have been the motive of Ilse, Ernst and the doctor? Why should they have deceived me so utterly that they had almost made me doubt my own reason in order that events might appear in the light they wished them to.

Why?

But Maximilian was there, and as happened long ago, I could think of nothing else. So while the moon shone its light into the turret-room I was happy as I had not been since the days of my honeymoon.

There was a light tap on the door and Frau Graben came in carrying a tray on which was a squat lighted candle, wine and glasses, with a dish of her favourite spiced cakes.

She said, her eyes gleaming with delight: 'I've brought you these. I thought you'd be hungry. Well, Master Lightning,' she went on. 'You can't say you're not old Graben's favourite now, can you?'

'I never did,' he replied.

She set the tray on the table. She said: 'Oh, Miss Trant, I knew how he was fretting for you. I could tell. He was never the same again. He used to be so gay . . . he was the gay one . . . always up to tricks, laughing, joking . . and then suddenly he changes. It's a woman, I said. Then poor old Hildegarde Lichen told me. She turned to me. We'd worked at the schloss together in the nursery. She was my under-nurse. She thought the world of the boys and in particular Lightning here. And she told me all – about how the little English girl came to the lodge one night and how he was never the same since. It was such a romantic story and how they blew up the lodge so that it would look as though she had died there.'

'Hildegarde told you that?' cried Maximilian. 'Why didn't you tell me? Why didn't you?'

'It was a secret, Hildegarde insisted. She told me with her dying breath. And she said, "Tell no one unless it's necessary to his happiness, for it is better that he should think her gone."'

'You were always an old meddler,' said Maximilian. 'But how dared you keep this from me?'

'Now don't scold me. I brought her back, didn't I? I planned it all. I went and found her and played the tourist looking for books and making it all seem so natural. All the time I was thinking, I'll surprise Master Lightning, and how right it was that he should have his surprise on the Night of the Seventh Moon. I'll have a glass of wine with you, shall I?'

She did not wait for the invitation; she filled three glasses and sat down, sipping, and nibbling one of her spiced cakes.

She talked of how poor Hildegarde had worried about what had taken place in the hunting lodge. She had made Hildegarde tell her all she knew – and Hildegarde knew a great deal. She had been as interested in everything concerning the Prince as Frau Graben herself. She had kept her eyes open. She knew that the young lady was a pupil in the *Damenstift* when she first come to the lodge, and that when she returned she had been brought out by Ilse and Ernst and that her father had kept a bookshop in Oxford. She knew her name.

'I noted that,' said Frau Graben. 'I liked to know what my boys were up to and this was no ordinary affair. Hildegarde knew that it was different right from the start, she said. That was why she was so upset. She didn't like it. And that ceremony she didn't like at all. She said it wasn't right. The girl was so innocent that she believed it was a true marriage.'

'It *was* a true marriage,' said Maximilian.

Frau Graben stared at him and then at me. '*Mein Gott!*' she cried. 'It's not true. It's one of your larks. I know you, Master Lightning.'

'Dear Graben,' he said solemnly, 'I swear to you that I was married to Lenchen in the hunting lodge nine years ago.'

She shook her head and then I saw her lips begin to curl. *She* had brought me here; *she* had presented me to him. This was the kind of high drama she liked to provoke. But if we were truly married! I could imagine her delight in the possibilities this was suggesting to her; and for the first time since Maximilian had walked into the room I was fully aware of the complicated situation which confronted us. Until that moment I had thought of little but the fact that Maximilian had come back to me. My reason was vindicated; I had been the victim of a wicked plot but I was not unbalanced. I had imagined nothing and I had regained my husband.

Frau Graben was saying: 'It is so, then?'

'It is so,' answered Maximilian.

'And Miss Trant is your wife.'

'She is my wife, Graben.'

'And the Princess Wilhelmina?'

A shadow crossed his face. I believed he had forgotten her existence until that moment.

'She cannot be my wife since I have been married to Lenchen for nine years.'

Frau Graben said: '*Mein Gott!* This will shake the dukedom. What have you done, Maxi? What will happen to us all now?' She chuckled, not without a degree of delight, 'But you don't care, do you? You're bemused both of you. You don't see anything but each other. Oh Maxi, you love her, don't you? It does me good to see you together, that it does. Don't forget I found her – I brought her to you.'

'You meddling old woman,' he said, 'I'll never forget you brought her back to me.'

'Tomorrow,' she said, her eyes sly, 'that'll be the time to face the music.' She laughed. 'Tonight is the Night of the Seventh Moon. We mustn't forget that, must we? Oh, you're going to be grateful to me, Maxi . . . and you too, Miss Trant. All these years . . . fancy! And you two pining for each other. I said to Hildegarde, "You tell me about that room in the hunting lodge" and she told me, for she knew every piece that was in that room. So I said to myself: I'll make another room here in Klocksburg and tonight we shall put the clock back. We'll bring the lovers together again. The bridal chamber awaits you, my chicks. You can't say that old Graben doesn't look after you.'

'You brought Lenchen here, Graben,' said Maximilian, 'and I shall bless you for ever for that. But now we want to be alone.'

'Of course you do, and you're going to be. I've got the bridal chamber ready myself.' She grimaced and tiptoed to the door, looking back as though loath to leave us. 'We always got on like a house afire, didn't we Miss Trant? We'll have some talks . . . '

She shut the door on us and we were in each other's arms. I knew that he was, as I was, recalling those days in the lodge and the intensity of our need for each other was unendurable.

'Tomorrow we can talk,' he said. 'We will make our plans. We have to consider very carefully what we must do. Of one thing I am certain. We shall never be parted again, whatever may come. But that is for tomorrow . . .'

He opened the door. Frau Graben was waiting there with a candle. We followed her down the stairs and she opened a door. The full moon shining through the window showed me the four-poster bed. It was a faithful reproduction of the room we had shared in the hunting lodge during our honeymoon.

And now, after nine long and weary years, we were together again.

The great moon hung heavy in the sky and I was happy as I had never thought to be again.

When the dawn was in the sky we were both awake. I knew that he felt as I did. We did not want a new day to come for we knew that it must bring with it problems. I kept thinking of the cold proud face of the woman who believed herself to be his wife.

But no matter how we wished it, the magic night was over

and the day had begun.

'Lenchen,' he said, 'I shall have to go back to my father's schloss.'

'I know.'

'But tonight I will come here.'

I nodded.

'If I had not allowed them to persuade me to this marriage with Wilhelmina it would have been so much easier. I shall have to tell her.' He frowned. 'She will never understand.'

'You can prove it to her,' I said.

'I have our marriage lines. Do you remember? There was one set for you and one for me. I can produce the priest.'

'They took my lines from me,' I said.

'It will not be easy, Lenchen. There is my father who is very sick. I don't think he has long to live and this could hasten his death.'

'I begin to see what it will mean. How I wish that you had been – say, a lawyer, a doctor or a woodcutter in your little cottage. How happy I should have been then!'

'Ah, Lenchen, how fortunate these people are! *They* are not watched at every turn. Their actions are not the spark that sets off mighty conflicts. This is the worst possible time. Klarenbock will consider this an insult to the ruling house. It could mean war with them . . . at a time when the French are threatening to march against Prussia, which would involve the entire German states. I must have time to think. I can only be sure of one thing. I love you, Lenchen. You have come back to me and we shall never be parted again.'

'As long as you tell me that, as long as I may be with you, I am content.'

'It must be settled soon, my dearest. I can't bear the uncertainty. Whatever happens we must be together . . . and not in secret. But I must go. They will be missing me.'

I went with him out into the early morning and watched him ride away.

As I came back into the fortress and mounted the stairs to my bridal chamber I heard footsteps behind me and I guessed who it was. Frau Graben's hair was in iron curlers under a sleeping cap; her eyes were sparkling and she was smiling secretly, delighted with herself, with me and her Master Lightning. I thought fleetingly that she must always have lived vicariously through her boys, and therefore this must be one of the most exciting occasions of her life.

She said: 'So he's gone.'

She followed me into the room. I sat on the bed while she settled comfortably into a chair. 'Well,' she said, 'he's happy again . . . happy as he hasn't been for nine years. You have a big responsibility, Miss Trant. Oh, I mustn't call you that now, must I – but just for old times' sake until your title's known. Well, you've got a lot to answer for. You've got to keep him happy.' She laughed. 'My goodness, I've never seen him so pleased with life. Fancy that!'

'And you knew who I was all the time.'

She was overcome with secret mirth. 'You must admit I did it well. I said, "I want a phrase book . . . something to help me along with the language." And you hadn't a notion. And weren't you frightened, eh, when you thought I wasn't going to ask you to come along and teach the children!'

'Yes,' I agreed.

'And when you came I was hard put to it not to confide in you. And he was away in Berlin! I couldn't wait for him to come back. Mind you, it's a bit more than I bargained for. Hildegarde thought it was a mock marriage and it would have been a lot easier if it had been. That's something people understand. But married to the Duke's heir and him having made a state marriage to a princess that's brought us closer to Klarenbock and that being so important . . . well, I don't know!' Then she laughed as she studied me. 'But you can't think of what's to be, can you? You can only think of him and that you're together again. Well, that's how it is. But the reckoning has to come. What a man our Lightning is! They still talk about his great-great-grandfather, Maximilian Carl. He was a great duke and a great lover, too. He's a legend in these parts and I used to say to Hildegarde when Maxi used to go off riding in the forest or practising his archery and shooting in the courtyard, I'd say: "Look at him, Hildegarde. There's another Maximilian Carl. A legend, eh?" And so will he be. The Duke who found a schoolgirl in the forest and married her. What a story! And that's not the end, eh?' Her shoulders shook with secret mirth. 'We've got to wait for that. Now what's going to happen?' Her eyes sparkled at the prospect. 'We shall see . . . in time. But my word, this is going to take a bit of untangling.'

The thought of the tangles stimulated her, though. I had

never seen her quite as excited as she was on that night.

'You won't sleep, will you?' she went on. 'No more will he. No more will I. In any case, it's morning. They'll see him riding back to the schloss – some of them. "Oh," they'll say. "His Highness has been out for the night!" And they'll laugh and nudge each other and they'll say "Another Duke Maximilian Carl, he is." They won't know, will they, that he was with his wife.'

I tried to speak calmly. 'We must wait, and Maximilian will know what is the best thing to do.'

'Well,' she said, 'it could be your secret, you know. You could live here, or in one of the castles, and he could call on you. Very romantic like. And no one need ever know that you were the true duchess . . . because that's what you'll be soon. The old Duke is failing fast, believe me, and soon our Maxi will be in his shoes. And what of you then, eh? And what of Wilhelmina?'

'We shall have to see,' I told her. 'Now I think I should try and sleep for an hour or two.'

She took the hint and left me. I did not sleep, of course. I lay awake thinking of the wonder of that night just passed and the undecided future.

As soon as I was up Frau Graben was knocking at my door. Her hair was out of its curlers and was now crimped about her head; her rosy cheeks shone and she was as lively as ever.

'I didn't think you'd sleep long,' she said with a chuckle. 'I've got something for you. A message from him. My word, he *is* impatient. Always was when he really wanted something.' She handed me the note as though I were a child and she a benign nurse offering a special treat.

Eagerly I took it.

'Read it,' she said unnecessarily. I knew she had already.

'My darling Lenchen,

'I'll be in the forest at eleven o'clock at the first copse from Klocksburg by the stream. M.'

It was like a command but then, I supposed indulgently, he was accustomed to giving commands.

'You've got two hours,' beamed Frau Graben.

'What of the children's lesson?'

Frau Graben flapped her hand at me. 'Bah! The old pastor

210

can take them through their history.' She laughed like a conspirator.

Not that I wanted to make excuses. The thought of seeing him again was an intoxicating one.

I dressed with care, realizing that this would be the first time he would see me in daylight for nine years; but the prospect of seeing him made me radiant.

I saddled my mare and rode out. I found him waiting at the appointed spot on a white horse and I was taken back all those years to when he had loomed out of the mist.

I said: 'You have changed very little.'

'You have grown more attractive,' he replied.

'Is that really true?'

'Experience has left its mark. You are more exciting. There is so much I want to discover. The young girl from the *Damenstift* was a promise . . . now that promise is fulfilled.'

He leaped from his horse and lifted me down from mine We stood in a close embrace and I was so gloriously happy that I should have liked to hold that moment for ever: the forest smells; the faint sound of the breeze as it moved in the trees; the distant lowing of cows and the tinkle of the bells about their necks.

'Never to part again,' he said.

'What is going to happen, Maximilian?'

'I don't know . . . yet. There is so much to consider. I have been trying to work out a way, but last night I could think of nothing but our being together again.'

'That's how it was with me.'

We tied up the horses, and, arms entwined, walked through the forest as we talked.

Here was the position: He had thought me dead; he had seen the charred remains of the lodge; he had listened to the account Ernst had given him and believed it. He had not cared after that what had happened but he had had an abhorrence for marriage with anyone else. His father had tried to persuade him, implore him and even threaten him with the loss of the dukedom unless he married. Klarenbock had been an antagonistic state and more powerful than Rochenstein. The marriage had been one of the clauses in a treaty, and a few years ago he had allowed himself to be drawn into it.

'That is the story, Lenchen. If only I had known . . .'

'And while I was in Oxford looking after Aunt Caroline, you were thinking of me, longing for me, as I was for you . . .'

211

'If I had come to England to look for you I should have found you as Graben did. I can't forgive myself for not doing that.'

'But everything seemed so clear to you. You had always trusted Ernst and there was the burned-out lodge. And surely there was something *I* could have done? But it's no use blaming ourselves . . . no use looking back. I can forget all that now.'

'We'll put it behind us, Lenchen. It is what we have to do now that is important. My father is very feeble. Trouble with Klarenbock now would be fatal. I believe the French, too, are determined to make war on Prussia. If they did all the German states would be involved. They say that Napoleon III has the best army in Europe and he is determined on conquest.'

'Does that mean that if there was war you would have to fight . . .'

'I am the Commander-in-Chief of our army. Oh, Lenchen, I've frightened you. There may not be war. Let us hope not. But we must waste no more time. We have been apart too long. But I do believe the French are determined on war. You have seen our people. They are gay and pleasure-loving; but we of Rochenstein are not typical of our race. The Prussians under Bismarck have become a militant people. His slogan of "blood and iron" speaks for itself. We shall defend ourselves if the French should attack us, and military opinion throughout Europe is that war is imminent. We have a treaty with the Prussians. It was to ratify this that I was so long in Berlin. But I will not bore you with politics.'

'They are your concern and therefore they must be mine.'

'Yes,' he said solemnly. 'Now that we have found each other you will share my life. I shall bring my burdens to you. I will discuss affairs with you. But our task now is to make plans. We must. I long to have you with me, Lenchen, all the time . . . and openly. But I fear this is not the moment to let it be known. I almost told my father this morning but he was so ill . . . so feeble. He is overcome by the burdens of state. He is afraid of Napoleon. Only this morning he mentioned Klarenbock and said that since I had married Wilhelmina at least we need not expect trouble from that quarter. I fear, Lenchen, that my father cannot have long to live.'

I understood well the effect such an announcement would have on an ageing man weighed down with responsibilities, and for the time being it was enough for me that I had found Maximilian.

I said: 'Let us wait awhile. This is something which cannot be decided in a few minutes. But the Princess . . .'

'A marriage of convenience . . . that was no marriage.'

'How will she take this?'

'I am unsure. I have always been unsure with Wilhelmina. It was a marriage of convenience for her as for me. There is no doubt that when she learns that her marriage was no true marriage she will feel . . . degraded. There may well be trouble. We have to face that, Lenchen. We must give a lot of thought to how it should be done.'

'With as little heartbreak as possible to everyone concerned,' I agreed. I longed to be with him, to share his life completely, but I could not be entirely happy, I knew, and nor could he if, by making the truth known, it brought about the death of his ailing father and discredit to the Princess. I was conscious of a twinge of jealousy for that proud woman whom I had briefly glimpsed and who had been accepted as his wife. Proud, cold and royal as she was, I could imagine what her feelings would be when she was confronted with the fact that she, a princess, was no true wife. Oh yes, indeed we had to tread with the utmost care.

'For the moment,' decided Maximilian, 'it is best for us to keep this secret. I shall come to Klocksburg tonight. I shall think of nothing but you and how best we can arrange our lives. I long for us to be together.'

'In the meantime,' I replied, 'we shall have to be careful. It would never do for your father or the Princess to learn the truth through another source. You will visit me frequently . . . Promise.'

'I swear it and never did I more gladly swear anything.'

'And we must act as we have been acting . . . as though things were as before.'

'Ah,' he said tenderly, 'I can see what a help you will be to me, Lenchen.'

'It will be my mission in life . . . to care for you, to give you every comfort.'

'Ah, dearest, when I think of all those wasted years . . .'

'Don't think of them. They are past. The future is before us. Perhaps they have not been entirely wasted. We have learned something from them. To be with you again . . . to have found you . . . I care for little beyond that.'

213

We clung together; we could not bear to separate. He wanted to ride back to Klocksburg with me, but I thought the children would see him and wonder why we were together. I pointed out to him that we had to be careful. The future was gloriously inviting, but to reach it we had to hurt other people. I wanted – and I knew Maximilian did too – to hurt them as little as possible.

So we said goodbye, with assurances that that night we should be together.

I turned towards Klocksburg. I didn't want to leave the forest yet. I was considering our problem, trying to discover a solution, when the sudden rustle of undergrowth startled me; the sound of a horse's hoofs not far off was unmistakable. For the moment I thought he was coming back. But it was the Count who came through the trees.

'Miss Trant!' he cried. 'I am charmed to meet you. But I do wonder why you have deserted your duties to ride through the forest at this hour of the morning.'

I replied: 'The children are busy with the Pastor.'

'I hope their English is not suffering.'

'I think you will find great improvement if you care to question them in that language.'

'One thing, Miss Trant, you have great confidence in your own powers.'

'Confidence is necessary to succeed in teaching.'

'As in most things, I think you will agree.'

'I dare say you are right.'

'You are gracious this morning, Miss Trant.'

'I hope I am never ungracious.'

'Shall we say there is a little touch of asperity now and then?'

'I had not noticed it.'

'I did. Perhaps because I was the target. I wonder whether you served it to my cousin. I think not, from what I observed. Oh yes, I did see you. You seem to have become well acquainted in a short time. Unless of course you knew each other previously.'

'Your cousin . . .?' I murmured to gain time.

'His Royal Highness, the Prince. I have the honour to be his cousin.'

'Oh . . . congratulations.'

'Condolences would be more acceptable. Imagine if I had

214

been the Duke's son instead of that of his brother . . .'

'Why should I imagine it?'

'Then you could picture me in his position. Perhaps that would mean you would be as affable to me as to him.'

I wondered how much he had seen, from where he had been watching us; and I thought that there would always be people to watch the actions of a man in Maximilian's position.

I said: 'The Prince and I discovered that we had met some years ago. I was a pupil at one of the *Damenstifts* in his country.'

'And you came back to us. That is a compliment, Miss Trant, I am sure. You must have liked our country very much.'

'I find it very interesting.'

'I should like to show you my own castle. You must bring the children over to it one day. Better still, you could come alone.'

'It is kind of you to suggest it.'

'But you think it unwise to come?'

'Did I say that?'

'You don't have to speak always for me to know what you are implying. Your cool English manner does that very adequately.'

'I am sure you must find it extremely unattractive. So I won't burden you with my presence . . .'

'On the contrary, I find it . . . interesting, and I assure you that if I found your company a burden I should not seek it.'

'Have you sought it?'

'But surely you know the answer to that?'

'I'm afraid I don't, Herr Count.'

'I should like us to be better acquainted. I really don't see why we shouldn't be on such pleasant terms as you are with my cousin? We are very much alike. You must have noticed it.'

'There is a facial resemblance.'

'More than that. Some can't tell our voices apart. We have the same arrogant manner, don't you think? We have the same vices. He has always been a little more diplomatic than I. It's rather necessary in his case. He suffers restrictions which don't bother me. In some ways it is better to be the Duke's nephew than his son.'

'I dare say you are right.'

He had brought his horse close to mine and caught my arm. 'I have more freedom,' he said, 'to do what I want.'

'I am sure you find that very gratifying. Now I must get back.'

'I'll ride with you.'

I could not refuse to ride with him and we went back to Klocksburg.

'It will be a surprise for the children,' he said. 'I'll take them out. I want to see how they are progressing with their English. How is your special protégé?'

'What do you mean by my special one?'

'Now, Miss Trant, you are prevaricating. You know I refer to Master Fritz. Do you remember how concerned you were that he should not ride and how, because you pleaded so prettily, I gave way to your request.'

'I remember your realizing that the boy had a chill and was better at home.'

'I realized no such thing; and boys who are going to grow into strong men should not be coddled by devoted but misguided teachers of English. I agreed that he should stay behind because you asked it, and you must believe, Miss Trant, that I am very anxious to please you, although if my efforts were so misconstrued and quickly forgotten I might not consider it necessary to make them.'

There was a cruel smile on his lips. I trembled for Fritz. There was something sadistic about this man which could be terrifying. Was he implying that unless I became what he would call 'friendly' he would wreak his frustration and anger on Fritz because he knew that was what would hurt me most?

I could think of nothing to say. I could not plead with him now. I had an idea that if I did he would make conditions.

I was glad when we reached the schloss.

The children had seen our arrival and Dagobert came running out to do homage to his father.

'And Miss, where have you been?' he demanded.

'Miss has been enjoying the solitude of the forest,' said the Count.

I took my mare to the stables and went in. I wanted to see Fritz.

I found him in his room. I said: 'Your father is here and he is taking you and Dagobert riding.'

I was pleased to see that he did not look nearly so frightened as he used to. I had done that for him. I had assured him that if one feared something one must look it straight in the face and try to overcome that fear. He was very familiar with his pony, and it was only when he showed fear that the pony sensed it. If he felt perfectly at home, so would the pony. I had driven home that lesson.

Half an hour later I was in the schoolroom watching them ride away when Frau Graben came in.

'There they go,' she said, 'off to the hunt, I dare say. My word, Fritzi sits his pony well. He seems to have lost some of his fear of his father.'

I nodded, smiling.

She looked at me anxiously. 'I saw you ride back with Fredy.'

'Yes, I met him in the forest.'

'It was Max you went to meet.'

'Yes.'

'And you saw him?'

I nodded.

'Well, I expect you'll be leaving Klocksburg soon.'

'I've not made any plans yet.'

'You will,' she said confidently. Then she looked less happy. 'Did Fredy see you with Max?'

'Yes, he did.'

She stuck out her lower lip, a habit which implied consternation.

'You'd better be careful. Fredy always wanted what Maxi had. The fact that it was Maxi's gave it special value in his eyes. The trouble I had with that boy! There was a lovely little horse and carriage Maxi had. His mother gave it to him one Christmas. They had their own tables at Christmas. That was the great day of their lives. They'd talk about it for weeks. And then there would be their tables with their little fir trees all lighted with candles. Their presents were on the big tree and there was this carriage and horses for Maxi. It was a fine thing. It was painted like the royal carriage with the crown on it and the Duke's arms and Fredy saw it and wanted it. That night he took it away and hid it. We found it in his cupboard and back it went to Maxi and the next day we found it smashed up. The wicked boy had destroyed it rather than that Maxi should have it. I've never forgotten it.

217

I don't think he's changed much.'

There was a faint glint of anxiety behind the bland smile. She was afraid. She wanted me to understand that because the Count was interested in me and had discovered that Maximilian and I were in love, he was now quite determined to become my lover.

Perhaps I should have been warned but I could not take this threat seriously. If I were careful never to be alone with him, there was nothing he could do. I was not a horse and carriage to be smashed, though he could of course make life very unpleasant.

I was in my room when they came back. I went to the window and saw them. My first glance was for Fritz; he was happily sitting his pony and riding with ease.

All I had to do was make him understand that he must not show fear. It seemed he had learned that lesson.

But I soon discovered from Frau Graben that the Count had decided the boys should now have done with ponies. They were to ride horses. He had been to the stables and chosen which they should have.

I knew something of the horses there and when I realized which was to be Fritz's mount, I was afraid. It was one of the friskiest horses in the stables.

What sort of man was this who could endanger his son's life on the pretext that he was making a man of him and at the same time showing his displeasure towards a woman who had flouted him?

I had to try to see him against his own background. Was I perhaps unable to visualize what the rather wild upbringing had made of him? The outlook here would be very different from that in a peaceful English town. That was why everything seemed a little fantastic and unreal. These men took what they wanted and didn't count the cost to others. They were so ruthless that even when they loved they could deceive with a mock marriage. What were they capable of when they were prompted by lust alone?

My fears for Fritz did at least stop my brooding exclusively on my own problem.

I went into the town that afternoon while the children were having a drawing lesson from a young artist who came up to the schloss to teach them once a week.

I saw the hat in the window and afterwards I thought it

was fate or instinct or something like that which led me to that window.

It was a boy's hat in pale grey rather like a bowler and there was a small green feather stuck into the ribbon. Beneath the hat was a notice. 'The Safety Riding Hat'.

I went into the shop. Yes, it was designed to give extra protection to the head. The hatter had heard only that day that a young fellow had fallen from his horse and avoided a serious accident because he was wearing his safety riding hat.

I bought it.

If I were going to give Fritz a present I must buy gifts for the others. The toy-maker's shop was always a delight to all the children. There were cuckoo clocks and dolls' houses and dolls' furniture, humming-tops and toy horses and riding whips. It was not difficult to find something. For Dagobert I bought what was called a weather detector. It consisted of a little wooden house with two figures, a man dressed in sombre clothes and a woman in bright colours. The woman came out when the sun was going to shine, the man when it was going to rain. I guessed that would please him. Liesel's gift was a double-jointed doll.

When I returned to the schloss the children were back from their art lesson, which had been given out of doors. They were delighted with their gifts.

Fritz put on his hat.

'It's a safety hat,' I told him.

'Is it magic?'

'It means that while you're wearing it you'll be much safer than you would be without it.'

He regarded it with awe. Dagobert was delighted with his weather-house but his eyes did rest rather longingly on the safety hat. It was astonishing really, because I had thought a toy would have been much more desirable than an article of clothing; but it seemed that they had already endowed this hat with some special magic.

Inside it was a silk tab on which was inscribed the words 'Safety Hat'. They read it with awe. Fritz put it on and wouldn't take it off.

'It's really for riding,' I told him; but he wanted to keep it on all the time.

I wished that I had bought them both one.

'Why is it a present day?' asked Liesel.

'Oh, just because I felt like it,' I told her.

'Do they have present days any sort of time in England?' asked Fritz.

'Well, yes, any time can be present-giving time.'

'I want to go to England,' announced Dagobert.

I was at the turret window watching for Maximilian to come. Across the valley I could see the lights of the ducal schloss, and I thought of that woman who, legend had it, had thrown herself from this window because she had discovered that she had been tricked into marriage and could not bear to go on living since she had been so deceived. How different was my position! I glowed with exultation because he loved me so much that he had jeopardized his future for my sake. I had lived in this community long enough to realize the feudal state of life here. The people's rulers belonged to them; they were powerful overlords yet they existed in power only through the approbation of those they ruled.

I knew that I could never allow Maximilian to suffer through me.

When he had married me (and I shuddered to think how easily he could have followed the custom of his ancestors and gone through a mock ceremony, for how should I have known the difference?) he had proved his all-embracing love for me. I was determined to show mine for him.

At last I saw him. He came alone without attendants. I leaned from the window and caught my breath because of the sheer drop below, and again I was thinking of the desperation of that sad woman who had been less fortunate.

I could hear his footsteps on the stair. I was at the door to greet him and we were in each other's arms.

In the early morning before he left, we talked again of our future.

He had wondered whether to tell Wilhelmina and had come to the conclusion that his father should be the first to know.

'Again and again I am on the point of telling him. I want to take you to him. I want to tell him everything that happened. Yet I fear the effects of the shock.'

'And Wilhelmina?' I said. 'I think a great deal of Wilhelmina.'

'It was a union of convenience. Since the birth of the child

220

we have lived apart. I was grateful for that reason when the child came . . . so was she because it meant that we need not live together.'

'I had forgotten the child.'

'The complications are so great,' went on Maximilian. 'It maddens me. It might have been so different. I was once on the point of telling my father what had happened to try to make him understand that I had met the only woman I could love and had married her. He could have borne it then. There would have been trouble and because I believed you dead I saw no point in raising it. These people had lied to me. I shan't rest until I know why. I shall have Ilse brought here. I shall discover from her what it all meant and why she and Ernst interfered in my life.'

'You had commanded them to interfere in the first place.'

'I had commanded them to bring you to me. They were the witnesses of our marriage. But they lied to you and to me. Why? I shall soon know, for she is to be brought here. We will confront her and have the truth.'

'Do you think she will come?'

'My cousin has to visit Klarenbock on state business. I have told him that I want Ilse, if still living, to be brought here.'

'Your cousin?'

'Count Frederick.'

I felt uneasy. The Count always made me feel so.

'Does he know the reason for which you want Ilse?'

'Good God no. I wouldn't trust Frederick with that. Heaven knows what use he'd make of it. He's getting as troublesome to me as his father was to mine.'

'And he is the one whom you have asked to bring back Ilse!'

'She would know she must obey him. She might even think it is her half-sister Wilhelmina who wishes to see her. I have not specifically said it is I.'

'How I wish she were here now! I should like to meet her face to face. There is so much I want to ask her. She seemed so kind to me. I don't understand why she should have tried to ruin my life.'

'We will discover,' said Maximilian.

The dawn was with us and it was time for him to leave. How happy we could be even though we could not look more than a day or so ahead and had come no nearer to finding a solution to our problem.

The next day Frieda, the wife of Prinzstein, the coachman, who had joined the two maids we already had in the fortress, brought in letters from England – one from Anthony, one from Aunt Matilda and one from Mrs Greville.

Anthony wanted to know how I was faring. It was a long time since he had heard.

'Is everything well there, Helena? If not, give it up and come back. I miss you very much. There's no one to talk to as I can talk to you. The parents are very good of course, but it isn't quite the same. Every day I look for a letter from you which will tell me that you have had enough of it. Come home. I do understand that you are restless. What happened to you there makes that very understandable. Don't you think that dwelling on the past only keeps it alive? Wouldn't it be better to try to forget it? Do come home, where I shall do everything possible to make you happy.

My love as ever,
Anthony.'

What peaceful calm that conjured up: the new vicarage with those lovely green lawns which had been maturing for more than two hundred years; the lovely house which was Elizabethan and built to represent the letter E as so many had been during that Queen's reign. A fascinating house with its buttery and stillroom, its walled garden, its little orchard which would be a glory of pink and white blossom in May. How far away it seemed from the schloss in the mountains!

Suppose I wrote to Anthony and told him I had found Maximilian. Perhaps I owed that to him. I did not want him to go on thinking that one day I would return to him. But I must not do so yet. Maximilian's father must be the first to know.

There was a letter from Aunt Matilda too.

'How are you getting on, Helena? Have you had enough of that teaching job yet? Albert says he reckons you'll be back before the summer's over. The winter wouldn't be good there. I believe they have a lot of snow. Take care of your chest. There are some that say mountains are good for chests, but chests are funny things. We miss you in the shop. On busy days Albert says "We could do with Helena, particularly in the Foreign Department." He works like a slave, which isn't right with one kidney . . .'

How those letters brought it all back!
And Mrs Greville's:

'We miss you very much. When are you coming back? It's been such a lovely spring. You should see the shrubs in the vicarage garden. And now the lavender's a picture. The grass was a bit trampled by people at the fête, but it was a great success. Anthony is very popular. There are so many willing helpers. A very nice lady, a Mrs Chartwell, has come to live close by. She has a pleasant daughter who is being so useful in the parish. Anthony was saying what a great help she is. She's quite nice-looking too, is Grace Chartwell, gentle personality, gets on with people . . .'

I smiled. In other words, a perfect vicar's wife. I understood Mrs Greville was telling me: Come back before it's too late.

A hush had fallen over the town, over the schloss and over the mountains. The Duke was very ill.

There was a note from Maximilian for me which told me that he was unable to leave the schloss. The doctors were in attendance on his father and it was feared that the end was not far off.

Frau Graben couldn't hide her excitement.

'Our Maxi will soon be Duke,' she whispered to me.

I avoided her eyes.

The children were affected by the general solemnity for a short while, but they soon forgot it.

Fritz was rarely seen without his hat although Dagobert had long grown tired of telling people whether it was going to rain or shine and one leg of Liesel's doll had come off.

I should have given them all hats.

Through the next day the Duke lingered on. In the streets there was a hushed silence; people stood about on corners talking in whispers.

He had been a good ruler, they said, but ailing for a long time. It was a mercy they had a strong Prince to follow, with the country and the surrounding states in such a turmoil.

Those days of anxiety over the Duke were not allowed to interfere with the life of the schloss.

In the courtyard twice a week the children practised archery when other boys of noble families came in to join them, and very often there were as many as ten or eleven taking lessons. It had been considered that there would be greater competition for the boys if others were there; and there was always a great deal of activity and noise in the courtyard where they practised.

I was in my room when Fritz came running in. He was carrying his hat and protruding from it was an arrow.

'It hit me on the head,' he said, 'but it went into my hat. It'll have to be pulled out carefully or it might tear. Herr Gronken said I could bring it to you when I told him you would know how to get it out. Oh, Miss, do be careful with my magic hat.'

I took it in my hands: the thought immediately came to me that if he had not been wearing a hat, the arrow would have struck him in the head.

I withdrew the arrow very carefully and laid it on the table.

We examined the hat together. It had made a hole in the fabric.

'Never mind,' I said to Fritz, 'that makes it more interesting, more your very own. Battle scars are signs of honour.'

That pleased him. He put the hat on again and went off to finish his lesson.

I picked up the arrow. The point was sharp. It had to be, of course, to hit the target. What struck me was that there was a faint discoloration at the tip. I wondered what it was.

I thought no more about it then, for a few hours later news came that the Duke was dead.

All the flags in the town were flying at half mast.

'Of course it had to come,' said Frau Graben. 'This will make a difference to our Prince. My goodness, he'll be busy for a few days. And then of course there'll be the funeral. That will be an occasion for sure.'

A disturbing incident happened. The following afternoon Dagobert went into the forest on his new mount. We were unperturbed during the first hour or so when he didn't return, but when it grew dark and he had still not come back we grew alarmed.

Frau Graben sent the servants out to look for him. Herr Prinzstein, the coachman, formed a party which he divided into two and they went off in separate ways.

We sat together in Frau Graben's little sitting-room and anxiously talked of what could have happened to him.

Fritz came in and said: 'My hat's gone. My magic hat. I've looked everywhere.'

'You can't fret about a hat when your brother's lost,' said Frau Graben.

'I can,' said Fritz. 'I think he's taken it.'

'Oh, Fritz, why do you say that?' I asked.

'He's always trying to take it.'

'Never mind about that hat,' I said. 'Let's think of Dagobert. Have you any idea where he's gone?'

'He likes to ride out to the Island of Graves.'

While we were worrying over the mystery of what had happened to Dagobert there was a shout from outside. 'He's here.'

We rushed out and there was Dagobert, hatless and sheepish. He had a wild story to tell. He had been kidnapped.

Frau Graben said: 'Never mind about that now. You're damp.'

'It was misty,' said Dagobert.

'So we'll get those clothes off and you'll get in a hot bath with mustard. That's it. You can't beat mustard. And some of my soup and cordial.'

Dagobert was bursting to tell of his adventures but he was shivering with cold so he allowed himself to be immersed in the mustard bath, and it was later when wrapped in a warm dressing-gown after having drunk hot soup that he told us what had happened.

'I was in the forest,' he said, 'when two men came up to me. They had masks on their faces. One of them came on either side of me and they got hold of my horse's bridle. I wasn't frightened. I said: "Who are you? I'll kill you if you touch me." So I drew my sword . . .'

'Now, Dagobert,' said Frau Graben, 'no stories please. We want to know what really happened.'

'It was a sort of sword . . .'

'You know it was nothing of the sort. Now tell us what really happened.'

'They made me get off my horse and I lost . . . my hat, and I said I must find my hat . . .'

'Your father will want to know what really happened,' said Frau Graben, 'so you'd better try to remember. And no stories about swords because you haven't got one.'

Dagobert regarded us soberly. 'They led my horse away right into the forest where the trees were thick . . . it was near the lake . . . and I think they were going to kill me, honestly, Miss . . . honestly, Frau Graben. And I was frightened because I'd lost the hat and the magic wouldn't be there without it . . .'

I said: 'You were wearing Fritz's hat?'

'Well, I thought he wouldn't mind just once . . . and I said, "I've lost Fritz's hat. Miss bought it for him. I must find it because it's not mine. I only borrowed it." And they said: "You *are* Fritz and it's your hat." And I said "No, I'm Dagobert . . ." Then they whispered together and after a long while let me go.'

'My goodness,' said Frau Graben, 'it must have been someone playing a sort of game. There are people who think that kind of thing funny. I'd flay them alive. Frightening the life out of people.'

'Oh, I wasn't frightened,' said Dagobert. 'I would have killed them both. I soon escaped. It was only because I lost my way in the mist that I was late.'

We let him go on boasting of what he would have done. I was silent, so was Frau Graben.

A sudden fear had taken possession of me.

When the children were in bed I went down to Frau Graben's sitting-room.

She was sitting thoughtfully staring into the fire.

'Oh, Miss Trant,' she said, with that little smirk which always appeared when she used my name, 'I was just thinking of coming up to you.'

'What do you make of it?' I asked.

'You never know with Dagobert. He might have decided not to come in, have forgotten the time and then try to make excuses about masked men.'

'Oh, I don't think so.'

'You believe two masked men really took him away. For what purpose?'

'Because they thought he was Fritz.'

She stared at me in blank amazement. 'But why Fritz?'

'I don't know. But he was wearing Fritz's hat. Now Fritz has rarely been seen without that hat since I gave it to him. It's possible that, seeing Dagobert riding in the forest wearing it, these men thought he was Fritz.'

'That's very likely true, but why should they want to take Fritz away?'

'I don't understand it. Frau Graben, will you come to my room. I want to show you something.'

When we were there I took the arrow out of a drawer and laid it on the bed.

'What's this, dear?'

'It's an arrow which was aimed at Fritz. The hat I bought for him stopped its penetrating his skin.'

'It's one of the arrows they use for their practice.'

'Yes, and it was aimed at Fritz while they were doing their practice in the courtyard.'

'Who aimed it?'

'I don't know. I wish I did.'

'They wouldn't do much harm, surely.'

'In certain circumstances they could.'

'You're being a bit mysterious, Miss Trant.'

'Look closely at the tip. That's the part that penetrated Fritz's hat. Do you notice the tip?'

She bent over it and when she raised her eyes to mine her expression had lost its habitual cosiness.

'Why,' she said, 'it's been dipped in something.'

'Do you know what?'

'I've an idea. I remember in the old days they used to hunt the wild boars and stags with arrows. They dipped the tips in some sort of solution . . .'

'Poison,' I said.

She nodded. 'I've seen them. It leaves a stain like this.'

I felt rather uneasy. 'If someone deliberately aimed a poisoned arrow at Fritz; if two men tried to kidnap him, what does it mean?'

'You tell me, Miss Trant, for I can't say.'

'I wish I knew.'

'Perhaps we're mistaken about that stain. It could have been something else. The children do aim rather wildly now and then. Someone might have hit Fritz unintentionally.'

'And then tried to kidnap him?'

'But it was Dagobert.'

227

'Dagobert in mistake for Fritz.'

'Well, Miss, it does sound a bit like romancing to me.'

'I think these two things happening together make it too much of a coincidence.'

'What can we do about it?'

'We must watch over Fritz. We must make sure that any other attempt does not succeed. That hat I bought for him has saved him twice. It's been a warning to us . . . or so it seems. And if we are wrong . . . if the arrow was just a stray shot and the discoloration was not made by poison, if it was merely two bandits who decided to kidnap one of the Count's sons and then thought better of it . . . well then, no harm will be done.'

'I can see that you are really concerned, Miss Trant. You can rest assured that I will do everything I can to help you watch over Fritz.'

A letter came from Maximilian. He wanted to see me at the royal schloss and Frau Graben was to come with me. He thought it would be less conspicuous if we came together.

Frau Graben was beaming with satisfaction when she came to my room.

'A command from the Duke,' she chuckled. 'I thought that wouldn't be long in coming. We'll leave in half an hour. Pastor Kratz will stay here with the children for the morning and Frieda's a good girl. I've told her to keep her eyes on them. You can trust Frieda. It's always a good thing to have wives and husbands working for the same household. It makes a certain stability . . . or that's my experience.'

She went on to tell me how Prinzstein the coachman had asked if there was a place for his wife Frieda and how she had decided that there was work enough to the fortress for her because Ella had developed an unexpected talent for the concocting of wine and cordials and she could make use of that.

I believed she was talking just to tease me. She knew how impatient I was to prepare for the journey.

We skirted the town and took the road up to the ducal schloss. I had never been so near it before, having seen it only from the windows of Klocksburg and from the town.

As we approached I was aware of its magnificence. It seemed to rise out of a wooded park and one wall seemed like a continuation of the mountainside. Above us loomed the great towers and turrets; impregnable in grey stone which had stood against time for hundreds of years. I looked up at the *Katzenturm* and imagined the boiling oil tumbling down on any invaders.

At the gates of the castle soldiers in their uniforms stood on duty. They glared at us as our carriage approached and when Frau Graben called out 'Hello, Sergeant!' I saw them visibly relax.

'We're here on orders,' she cried with a chuckle, and we were allowed to pass through the gates and into a courtyard.

'My goodness,' chuckled Frau Graben, 'this reminds me of old times. You see that window? That's where my nurseries were.'

I thought: There is a child up there now. His child! Perhaps he is watching us. He in his turn has become the heir to all this.

Frau Graben walked with the confidence of one who knows her way. More soldiers stood at attention at the great oak door. They looked at us intently. Frau Graben grinned at them and I saw the answering response. Her position at the schloss in the old days must have given her special privileges.

'We've had orders to come here,' she announced happily.

A soldier came forward. I remembered Sergeant Franck who had been present when I first saw the Processional Cross. He bowed to us both.

'Will you come this way, ladies,' he asked.

Frau Graben nodded. 'And how are the children?' she asked. 'And the new baby?'

'Everything well.'

'And Frau Franck?'

'Very well, thank you.'

'Was it a good confinement?'

'Fairly comfortable. It was because she was not so much afraid this time.'

Frau Graben nodded. 'This is the hunting room,' she said.

I realized that. There were implements on the wall – guns and spears and the heads of stuffed animals. The hunting room in the *Randhausburg* at Klocksburg was a replica of this one. We went through another room and another. The ceilings were lofty; each had the old Gothic panelling and circular windows – some with window-seats – looking over the town and beyond the valley to Klocksburg.

In the *Rittersaal* there was a huge pillar round which had been painted a tree so lifelike that it looked like a real one. I noticed that lettering in red and green had been added.

Seeing me look at it, Frau Graben explained. 'It's the family tree. The male line is in scarlet, the female in green.'

Had I not been so eager to see Maximilian I should have enjoyed examining that tree. I told myself that in the near future I should have an opportunity of doing so, and that my name would be added to it.

We mounted a staircase and facing us was a door on which was painted the royal arms and the flag of the country.

These were the ducal apartments.

Sergeant Franck opened the door and we were in a thickly carpeted corridor. Frau Graben was invited to step into a room, which she did with a grimace, and I was alone with Sergeant Franck.

He led me along the corridor to a door; he knocked; Maximilian bade him enter. The door was opened and Sergeant Franck, clicking his heels and bowing smartly, announced that I was there.

Then the door shut on me and we flew to each other and clung together with that wonder which the appearance of each other never failed to inspire.

'I had to see you,' he said at length. 'Hence this ceremony. Nothing I can do avoids it now.'

His presence banished the faint depression which my walk through the castle to this room had given me. When I had passed the soldiers at the gate and entered the great rooms I had felt years of tradition close in on me. I understood then how difficult it was going to be for Maximilian to bring me forward as his wife when his people believed him to be married to Wilhelmina. I understood then how right it was – particularly at this time – to preserve a secrecy.

He held me against him. 'It seems so long, Lenchen.'

'A day and a night is like a year when you are not with me.'

'It shall not be so much longer. When the funeral obsequies are over, then I must act.'

'Be careful, my love. Remember that you are now the ruler of this state.'

'It's a very small one, Lenchen. It is not like France . . . or Prussia even.'

'But to these people it is as important . . . as important as

France to the French or Prussia to the Prussians.'

'The situation is explosive at the moment. It always is when a ruler dies and a new one takes over. There are inevitable changes and the people are wary of them. They suspect a young ruler until he proves himself to be a worthy successor to the old one. My father was popular. You know that my uncle rose against him and tried to depose him. That was at the time of our marriage. You remember Ludwig's followers blew up the lodge at that inopportune moment. If they had not our lives would have been different.'

I gripped his arm in my sudden fear for him.

'Be careful,' I said.

'As never before,' he assured me. 'There is so much to live for now. My cousin has returned. He could not find Ilse. She seems to have disappeared completely. No one could give him any news of her.'

'Could she be dead?'

'We should have known if she had been. As soon as I can get away I shall go myself. I shall find out what has become of her and if she is alive I shall have the truth from her.'

'Perhaps it is not so important now that we have found each other.'

'Oh, Lenchen, how I long to have you here with me! When I ride out it is you I want beside me. You will find so much that is ceremonious. It is not an easy way of life.'

'If we are together I shall want nothing more.'

The meeting was over all too soon. It must necessarily be short. I realized that already his position had changed. He was no longer as free even as he had been.

We found it difficult to leave each other. He said that he would, if it were possible, come to Klocksburg that night. If he could not we must arrange for Frau Graben to bring me to the ducal schloss, although too frequent visits would give rise to comment and he did not want people to draw the kind of conclusions which they certainly would. He wanted everyone to know that I was his wife, and nothing would content him but that.

It was what I had wanted, but I was aware as he was of the delicacy of the matter and that we must tread with the utmost care.

Frau Graben was waiting for me somewhat impatiently and Sergeant Franck escorted us back to the carriage.

'Tell your wife that I'm happy to hear she came through all

right. I've got a bottle of cordial for her. I shall see that she gets it in the next few days.'

Sergeant Franck thanked Frau Graben; and we got into the carriage and rattled down the hillside to the town and then back to Klocksburg.

In the church the Duke was lying in state. I took the children down to see his catafalque which was displayed in the church. This was draped in black velvet on which the Duke's emblem had been embroidered in gold thread. Candles burned at either end of the coffin and the church was full of the scent of flowers.

The light filtered through the stained glass windows and in the semi-gloom people filed past the coffin.

The children were suitably solemn and I suspect rather relieved when we came out into the sunshine.

People whispered together.

'How impressive it was!'

'Poor Carl, he was a long time dying.'

'The Prince will have to settle down now that he's Duke.'

'Oh, he was serious enough. Let him enjoy himself while he's young.'

'Women! You all make excuses for him. Oh yes, he'll have to settle down now. If there's war . . .'

My heart was touched with a cold fear at the thought. He would have to go off to fight at the head of his army. I shivered. I could not bear to lose him to war.

The children quickly recovered from the gloom of the church.

'Let's go and look at the shops,' suggested Dagobert.

'Is it present time in England now?' Liesel wanted to know.

I answered that birthdays and Christmas were really time for presents. But there were Easter eggs at Easter.

'It's not Easter now,' said Fritz.

I said I would buy them all a safety hat. What about that?

'There was only one magic one,' sighed Fritz sadly. 'And Dagobert lost that.'

'I didn't really lose it. A troll came and picked it off my head.'

'There aren't any real trolls, are there, Miss?' pleaded Fritz.

'Oh no, they disappeared long ago.'

'Dagobert just lost my hat.'

'I want a magic hat,' wailed Liesel.

They should all have one, I said. And perhaps they would all turn out to be magic.

So we went and bought hats – even little Liesel had hers, and the children enjoyed swaggering along with them, glancing sideways at themselves in shop windows. They laughed at each other until I reminded them that the town was in mourning for the dead Duke.

'It's not a real mourning,' Dagobert told me, 'because there's a new Duke. He's my uncle in a way.'

'Mine too,' said Fritz.

'And mine,' insisted Liesel.

'Of course,' whispered Dagobert, 'it ought to be my Papa who is Duke.'

'Now Dagobert,' I said, 'that's treason.'

Fritz looked alarmed, but Dagobert was rather delighted with the prospect of treason. I wondered where he had picked up the idea that his father ought to be in Maximilian's place.

When we reached the schloss they played a new game: lying in state. Dagobert thought he ought to be the Duke in the coffin, but that was very dull; he much preferred the game of robbers in the forest.

All through the morning the bells tolled from my room. I saw the flags of the royal schloss flying at half mast; our own was lowered in the same way.

The children were excited, though silent. They had been caught up in the general air of solemnity. Frau Graben and I were taking them into town to see the funeral procession.

'We'll go early,' she said, 'you won't be able to move in the town in a few hours' time.'

It had been arranged that we should see the procession from the window of the inn where we had seen that other cavalcade which was to celebrate the return of Maximilian from Berlin.

We all wore black clothes and there was a black rosette on the horse which drew our trap.

Liesel started to sing as we drove on the downhill road but she was reprimanded by Fritz.

'You don't sing at funerals,' he told her; and for once Dagobert joined in to agree with him.

Frau Graben somehow made it seem almost like a festive

occasion; she couldn't hide her excitement; her eyes darted everywhere, but she drove with a competence which was surprising.

Crowds were already filling the *Oberer Stadtplatz*; they were taking their stand on the steps which led to the fountain in the middle of the square; strips of black crêpe fluttered from the windows; and with the flags at half mast it was clearly a town of mourning.

'We'll get along to the inn while we can,' said Frau Graben; and I was quite relieved when we arrived there. The trap and horses were taken care of and we took our seats in the window as we had before.

The innkeeper came to chat with us and talked about good Duke Carl who was dead and young Duke Carl who had succeeded him.

'Times are troublous,' murmured the innkeeper. 'We miss the good old days. Let's hope the young Duke gets a long peaceful reign, though I'm forced to say the signs go against that.'

I felt very uneasy and said: 'What is the news?'

'They say Napoleon's getting more and more pugnacious.'

'And you think he'll declare war?'

'That's the way things are going.'

Dagobert cocked an imaginary gun. 'Bang! Bang!' he cried. 'You're dead.'

'Let's hope it won't come to that,' said the innkeeper.

Dagobert started to march up and down, singing the National Anthem and saluting as he came past us. Fritz fell in behind and Liesel joined them.

'Now children,' said Frau Graben comfortably, 'we're not at war yet, you know.'

'I'm going to the war,' said Dagobert. 'Bang! I shall lead you all into battle. My father will go.'

'He's not the Commander-in-Chief,' said Fritz.

'Oh yes he is, really.'

'No, he's not. That's the Duke.'

'He is really, only he lets the Duke pretend. He could be Duke if he wanted to.'

'Now, children,' said Frau Graben, 'don't let's have nonsense!'

'It's not nonsense, Grabey. My father . . .'

'We'll have no more guns or wars or dukes or it will be no funeral procession for you. Now, Liesel, you'd better

234

come over here with me or you won't see a thing there.'

We arranged ourselves at the window and the innkeeper brought wine for Frau Graben and me; the children had a sweet drink and the inevitable spiced cakes.

The guns booming from the tower of the royal schloss announced that the procession was about to begin. Slowly the cavalcade descended the mountain into the town on its way to the church where the late Duke had been lying in state.

There was the carriage on which the coffin would be placed and taken to the shores of the lake when Charon would row it over; only a few of the nearest relatives would cross to the Island – led by Maximilian and Count Frederic.

There was the Processional Cross glittering in the sun as I had seen it before, and there was Maximilian remote as a hero of the forest, seated in his carriage, wearing his robes of state – purple velvet edged with ermine – and as I gazed at him I said to myself: Is he really my husband? But when he looked up, for he knew I should be at the window, and smiled, he was no longer remote, and not even the sound of the ominous funeral march nor the guards with black feathers in their hats in place of the habitual blue ones, could curb my joy. Slowly they filed past.

'There's my father,' said Dagobert in an awed whisper.

And there he was, the Count himself, in military uniform, medals glistening on his chest, a black feather in his helmet.

He too looked up at the window and I fancied there was a supercilious smile about his lips.

The duration of the church service seemed interminable to the children; they fidgeted and Dagobert wanted Fritz's seat because he thought it was better than his own and as the eldest he should have it. He tried to jostle Fritz out of it, but Frau Graben in her comfortable way controlled them.

At length the service was over. The coffin was laid in the carriage for its last journey to the Island. The band struck up a Dead March, and slowly the horses, caparisoned in heavy black velvet, black plumes waving on their heads, drew the carriage through the streets. On either side marched the soldiers.

The crowds were silent as the cavalcade went winding its way though the town towards the forest and lake. When it came back the carriage which had contained the coffin would be empty, and the chief mourners would no longer be there;

235

the Processional Cross would be taken back to the church and locked away in the crypt.

Dagobert announced that he wanted to go to the Island to see his mother's grave.

'Now you know nobody is allowed on the Island today,' said Frau Graben. 'If you're very good I'll take you to see the Duke's grave.'

'When?' Dagobert wanted to know.

'Not today because you wouldn't be allowed. This is the day of the burial.'

'When my father dies it'll be a better funeral than this,' said Dagobert.

'Good gracious alive, what a thing to talk of!'

'I didn't want him dead,' said Dagobert, ashamed, 'only I wanted him to have a better funeral.'

'There's not a better funeral than the Duke's,' said Fritz.

'There can be,' insisted Dagobert.

'Now no more talk of funerals or there'll be no trip to the Duke's grave for some people.'

That quietened them but they were restive.

I suggested a guessing game which we played with moderate concentration until the Processional Cross was brought back and the crowds started to disperse.

Frau Graben thought we might be leaving soon, but when we descended to the inn parlour it was to find the crowds were so thick that we could scarcely move.

'We'll make our way to the stables,' said Frau Graben. 'By the time we're ready to leave it'll be less congested.'

Dagobert slipped out of the inn yard to look at the crowds and I was anxious because of what had happened to him in the forest. I followed him, calling him.

I then saw Sergeant Franck who had caught Dagobert by the arm. He pulled him round and indicated me.

I went up.

Sergeant Franck clicked his heels and bowed.

'It's too crowded out there,' he said. 'Give them ten minutes and it'll be considerably less crowded. You want to be careful no one picks your pockets in a crowd like this. All the beggars and thieves come in for miles around. It's a field day for them.'

Frau Graben came up.

Again he clicked and bowed. 'I was just telling the Fräulein here that it would be better to wait for a few minutes. Why don't you pop in and see Gretchen and the children? She'd be glad to see you.'

Frau Graben said it was a good idea, and she wished that she had brought the cordial she'd promised.

'Never mind, she'll be better pleased to see you than all the cordial in Rochenstein.'

'I don't know that that's very polite to my cordial,' beamed Frau Graben.

'Better still,' I said, 'it's very complimentary to you.'

Sergeant Franck made a way for us through the crowd and we left the main street. There was a small side alley made very pretty by window-boxes on the sills; it was like a little court.

Frau Graben told me that the married guards had their homes in little squares like this throughout the town, though the single ones were in barracks close to the schloss.

The door of one of the houses was open; one stepped straight into a living-room. There were two children sitting on the floor – one, about six years old, drawing, the other, about four, was playing with bricks.

'Visitors, Gretchen,' said Sergeant Franck; 'and now it's back to duty for me. You'll make the introductions, Frau Graben, I know.'

'You can trust me,' said Frau Graben. And she said something which I didn't hear. For I could only gaze in shocked amazement at Gretchen Franck, for I recognized her at once; she was Gretchen Swartz whom I had met in the clinic when I was going to have my baby; the girl who had been in great distress and who they told me was dead.

She curtseyed to me, but I saw the startled expression in her face and I was aware that she knew me, even as I knew her.

Frau Graben was smiling at us, watching us – as though we were two spiders in a bowl.

Then she said: 'And how is the new baby, eh?'

'He's sleeping,' said Gretchen.

'I hear he's going to be the image of his father. So you didn't come out to see the show, Gretchen.'

'I couldn't very well take the children,' said Gretchen, her eyes still on me.

'You could have joined us at the inn window. There was plenty of room. If I'd known I should have brought that cordial. Are you all right? You look a bit . . .'

237

'I'm all right,' said Gretchen quickly. 'And Mrs . . .'

'Miss Trant,' said Frau Graben.

'Miss Trant.' Her eyes held mine. 'You would like some . . . refreshment?'

'We had wine at the inn. I dare say the children would like something.'

'Yes,' said Dagobert, 'we would.'

While she brought the refreshment I was thinking: I must speak to her alone.

When she came back, she put a tray on the table and served the wine. Her eyes held mine as she handed me my glass. She was telling me that she recognized me and was refraining from saying so for fear of my embarrassment.

There was some cordial for the children and the inevitable spiced cakes. Dagobert said to the children: 'Two bandits tried to kidnap me, but I frightened them away.'

The children listened intently to his imaginary adventures in the forest.

'He wore my magic hat and lost it,' Fritz told.

Then they talked of the magic hat.

Frau Graben sat listening; then she said: 'How are your roses coming on, Gretchen?'

'Very well,' replied Gretchen.

'I'll have a look,' said Frau Graben. 'No, don't bother to come with me. I know where to find them.'

Gretchen looked at me. She moved through the open door into the kitchen. I followed.

'I knew you at once,' she said in a low voice.

'And I you. But I couldn't believe it. They told me you had died and that your grandmother had taken the little boy . . .'

She shook her head. 'It was my baby who died. She was a little girl.'

'Then why . . .?'

She shook her head.

'I don't understand why Dr Kleine should have deliberately lied to me.'

She seemed bewildered. 'And you?' she said. 'What happened?'

'My baby died. A little girl. I saw her in her coffin. A little white face in a white bonnet.'

She nodded. 'Mine was like that. I dreamed of her for a long time.'

'And what really happened?'

'My grandmother took me back after all and I came home. Hans was the greatest friend of my Franz and he courted me. He said that Franz would have wanted him to take care of me and he had always loved Franz and me too. So we married, and my grandmother was pleased because Hans was in the Duke's Guards and gradually I began to forget that nightmare and be happy again. What did you do?'

'I went back to England.'

'You did not marry again?'

I shook my head.

'It is a pity. When our first baby came I stopped dreaming of that little face in the white bonnet. I told Hans about it and how that day I had wanted to kill myself. And how a strange English girl came to my room and because of her I went on. I never forgot you. And it is strange that we should meet like this.'

'I came back here,' I said, 'to teach the children English. Frau Graben visited England. I got to know her and she offered me the post.'

'How strangely life works out,' she said.

'It is all so bewildering.'

She touched my hand gently. 'I shall never forget what you did for me. I would have jumped from that window . . . I know . . . if you had not come in that day. I don't know what it was about you. I knew that you had suffered some tragedy as great as mine; you did not talk of it. There was something stoical about you. It gave me courage . . . and to you I owe this happy life which is now mine. I have often told Hans of you . . . but have no fear; I shall not mention that I have seen you . . . not even to Hans. I think perhaps you would rather not.'

I nodded.

'Then I shall tell no one.'

I said: 'I must find out why Dr Kleine told me you were dead.'

'Perhaps he mistook me for someone else. There were many people at his clinic.'

'I don't think that was so. There could not have been a mistake. He distinctly told me that you were dead and that your grandmother had taken the child. And yet . . . it was the other way round. Why?'

'Is it important?'

239

'I'm not sure, but I have an idea that it might be . . . very important.'

Frau Graben was standing in the doorway.

'Ah, having a cosy chat. I knew you two would get on. Yes, Gretchen my dear, they're coming on well. But you watch out for the greenfly.'

She was smiling slyly, blandly. I wondered how long she had been standing there.

I was impatient for Maximilian to come that I might tell him what I had discovered. This was yet another strange aspect of the mystery which overhung my life.

I waited at the turret window and when I saw him riding up the road I was filled with relief.

He ran up the stairs and I was in his arms. He could not stay, alas; he had ridden over from the ducal schloss in all haste to tell me that he had to set out without delay with some of his ministers for Klarenbock. A tense situation was arising for war with the French seemed inevitable. There were certain clauses in the treaty with Klarenbock which had to be clarified in the event of such a war and it was imperative that he leave.

The thought of his going away terrified me. I suppose I was unduly anxious because once before I had lost him.

He would be back in a few days, he assured me, a week at most, and as soon as he returned he would come to me.

As I watched him ride away a terrible feeling of desolation and insecurity swept over me. It would always be thus, I feared, when he went away – even for such a short time.

It was some while afterwards that I remembered I had not mentioned what I had discovered through Gretchen Franck that day: and to stop myself brooding on Maximilian's departure, I wondered whether I might not go to the clinic, see Dr Kleine and discover whether he could throw any light on what had happened.

The more I thought of the idea, the better it seemed to me. I should have to tell Frau Graben that I was going but I did not wish to tell her for what reason. She was far too inquisitive and I could not bear her to ask questions.

I said there were some people I had met in the town of Klarengen and that I had often wondered about them.

'Have you written to them?' she asked.

'No, but I should like to go to see them.'

'There's a train which would get you there in an hour or so. I wouldn't like you to travel alone. My word, if anything was to happen to you I'd have His Highness to answer to, wouldn't I? No, I'm all against your going alone.'

'I could ask Gretchen Franck to go with me.'

'Gretchen Franck! Why her?'

'The outing would do her good. All this talk of war seems to worry her. She's upset thinking of Hans going to the front.'

Frau Graben nodded thoughtfully. 'It would do her good. I'm glad you liked her. I'll get her children and bring them back here. I'll look after them while you're away.'

'The baby is young, of course.'

'Do you think I can't handle a young baby?'

Gretchen was surprised at first when I suggested the trip; but she quickly agreed to come with me when she heard of Frau Graben's offer to look after the children.

She was puzzled as to why I wanted to go back there, and I couldn't explain to her. I just said I wanted to see my baby's grave and she said that she would like to see hers.

We caught the train at ten o'clock. Prinzstein drove me to the town and we picked up Gretchen there. The train journey was through beautiful mountain country which, had I been in a less absorbed mood, I could have greatly enjoyed.

We went straight to an inn for a meal. The town was very small and there were only two. The one we chose was practically empty; and here, as in Rochenburg, the imminent war was the great topic of conversation.

When we reached the clinic, Gretchen shivered as she looked up at the window and I knew she was thinking of that day when she had planned to throw herself out. There was the spot where I had met the Misses Elkington.

I said: 'We are going in to see Dr Kleine.'

'But why?' asked Gretchen.

'I must see him. I want to ask him where my baby is buried.'

She didn't demur and we mounted the steps to the porch and rang the bell. It was answered by a servant and I asked to see Dr Kleine.

I was expecting her to say that he was no longer there, in which case it seemed that my journey would bring no results, but to my relief we were ushered into a waiting-room.

241

'I want you to wait here, Gretchen,' I said, 'while I go in and see Dr Kleine.'

Aften ten minutes or so I was taken to the room where Dr Kleine received his patients. I remembered it so well: here Ilse had brought me when we had first come here.

'Please sit down,' he said benignly.

I sat down. 'You don't remember me, Dr Kleine. I am Helena Trant.'

He was too late to hide the shock I had given him. I had taken him completely by surprise, for he had scarcely looked at me as I entered and it was so long ago since he had seen me.

He wrinkled his brows and repeated my name. But somehow I sensed that he remembered me very well.

'Mrs Helena Trant,' he said.

'Miss . . .' I said.

'Oh. I'm afraid . . .'

'I came here and had a child,' I said.

'Well, Miss Trant, I have so many clients . . . How long ago was this?'

'Nine years.'

He sighed. 'It's a very long time ago. And you are again . . .'

'Indeed not.'

'Perhaps there is some other purpose for your visit?'

'Yes. I want to see my child's grave. I would like to see that it is tended.'

'For the first time in . . . nine years did you say?'

'I have fairly recently come back here.'

'I see.'

'Do you remember me now, Dr Kleine?'

'I believe I do.'

'There was a Miss Swartz in the clinic at the time.'

'Oh yes, I remember now.'

'She died, you told me, and her grandmother adopted her child.'

'Yes, I do remember that. There was quite a fuss about it. The girl was in a sad state.'

'She tried to kill herself,' I said.

'Yes. I remember. It was small wonder that she did not survive her confinement. We were astonished, I remember, that her child lived.'

'But she did survive, Dr Kleine. It was her child who died.'

'No, I am sure you are wrong.'

'Could you make sure of it?'

'Miss Trant, I should like to know what is your purpose in coming here?'

'I have told you. I want to see my child's grave, and to confirm what happened to Gretchen Swartz. She lived in this neighbourhood and . . .'

'You thought you would like to meet her again. But she is dead.'

'Could you look up your records and tell me for certain? I do particularly want to know.'

My heart was beating wildly. I wasn't quite sure why. I felt I had to go carefully, and that if I did I might discover what had happened to Ilse. And if I could find Ilse I should have the key to the mystery which still obscured my past. Of one thing I was certain. Dr Kleine was not telling the truth. He knew who I was and he was disturbed because I had come back.

'It is very unorthodox to discuss my patients,' he said.

'But if they are dead it does not matter?'

'But since Miss Swartz died how can you possibly see her again? And it is no use going to visit the grandmother. I heard that she died too and the child was adopted by people who went out of the country.'

He was getting more and more involved and worried.

I went on: 'If you could assure me that Gretchen Swartz actually died I should be satisfied.'

He sighed and hesitated. Then he went to the bell-rope. A nurse appeared. He told her that he wanted a certain ledger.

While we were waiting for it to come he asked me what I had been doing in the last years. I said I had gone home to England; then I had had an opportunity to come out here and teach English.

'And it was then that you decided you would like to visit your child's grave?'

'Yes,' I said.

'Graves such as that of your child which are never tended are naturally hard to find. In the cemetery you will see many small mounds which are almost obliterated by time.'

The ledger was brought in. The date . . . He turned it up. 'Ah yes. Gretchen Swartz died in childbirth. The baby was adopted.'

'Your ledger is wrong, Dr Kleine,' I said.

'What do you mean?'

'Gretchen Swartz did not die.'

'How can you be sure of that?'

'I can be very sure. I have met her.'

'You have met her?'

'I have. She is now married to a Sergeant Franck and lives in Rochenburg.'

He swallowed; the silence seemed to go on for several seconds; he stammered: 'That's impossible.'

I rose. 'No,' I said. 'It's true. I do wonder why you have recorded the death of Gretchen Swartz and the adoption of her child. What is your motive?'

'Motive? I don't understand. There may have been some mistake.'

'There *ha*s been some mistake,' I said. 'Excuse me one moment. I have a friend whom I should like you to meet.'

Before he could protest I had gone into his waiting-room and come back with Gretchen.

'I want you and Dr Kleine to meet,' I told Gretchen.

He stared at her. 'Who . . .' he began. 'What . . .'

'This is Frau Franck,' I said. 'You remember her as Gretchen Swartz. But you thought – or you told me you thought – she was dead. You see, she is alive.'

'We both had children in your clinic, Dr Kleine.'

'But I don't understand. You and she . . . here together. You . . . planned this?'

'Oh yes, yes . . .'

'You told me that Gretchen's child lived and was adopted.'

'There has clearly been a misunderstanding. You did not tell me that Fräulein Swartz was here.'

'She is Frau Franck now, but you were so certain that she was dead. Your records said so.'

'It is obviously a clerical error. I am glad Fräulein Swartz did not die, but as I say, it is so long ago.'

'How did you come to make such a record?'

He shrugged his shoulders, his composure almost regained. 'Mistakes happen, Miss Trant, as you must be aware. I'm afraid I can't help you further.'

'Perhaps you can,' I said. 'I wonder whether you can give me the address of Frau Gleiberg.'

He wrinkled his brows but he did not deceive me. 'Wasn't she your friend?' he asked.

'I have lost touch with her.'

'I too. And now, Miss Trant, you will understand that I

am a very busy man. I am sorry that I can be of no help to you.'

He ushered me out of his clinic with alacrity. I was excited because a sudden notion had come to me that just as he had deceived us into thinking that Gretchen's child had lived, might he not have deceived me into thinking that mine had died?

He could give me no details. He could not tell me where my child was buried.

How I wished Maximilian would come back. There was so much to discuss with him.

A letter came from Anthony:

'Things look a little unsettled over there,' he wrote, 'I don't like the idea of your being there. The French are very bellicose, and they and the Prussians are such old enemies. If there was trouble – and opinion here seems that there might well be – I shouldn't like to think of you there. If you send word, I'll come out and bring you back . . .'

It seemed unfair not to tell him that I had found Maximilian. I was so fond of Anthony that I wanted him to stop thinking of me. I hoped that the girl to whom his mother had referred would be all that he needed in a wife and I wholeheartedly wished that he might fall in love with her and forget me.

As soon as I possibly could I should tell him.

Frau Graben came into the schoolroom in a flutter of excitement. I was taking an English lesson and trying to keep my attention on what we were doing. It was not easy. I kept thinking of my visit to Dr Kleine's clinic and asking myself what it meant. I was beginning to believe more and more that there was some mystery about my little girl's death.

Every time I heard the sound of horses' hoofs in the courtyard I started, desperately hoping it would be Maximilian. I yearned to talk to him, to sift the reason for Dr Kleine's strange behaviour from all the mass of mystery which surrounded me.

Frau Graben said: 'It's the Duchess. It's Wilhelmina.'

I heard myself say in a voice which sounded haughty but this of course was due to nervousness: 'What does she want?'

245

'She's come to see you.'

'To see me!'

'That's what she says. She's over at the *Rittersaal*.'

Dagobert said: 'Is the Duke with her?'

'No,' answered Frau Graben. 'She's all alone . . . at least she's alone in the *Rittersaal*. She has two of her women waiting in the carriage.'

'I'll go at once to her,' I said. 'I can't imagine why she wants to see me.'

I told the children to go on reading from the book of fairy stories which we were studying.

As the door shut on us Frau Graben looked at me, her eyes dancing with excitement, and lifted her shoulders.

'What does this mean, I wonder,' she whispered.

'She did say she wanted to see *me*?'

'She certainly did. And there's a look in her eyes . . .'

'What sort of look?'

'Reminded me of icebergs,' said Frau Graben. 'Not that I've seen an iceberg. Cold. Very cold. Shivery cold, I'd say. And I've been told that there's a lot more ice in icebergs than you see on the surface.'

'I wonder if . . .'

'She knows anything? Couldn't say. News leaks out . . . particularly bad news and this could be bad news to her. Still, you'll soon know. Just go in and call her Your Grace and show the proper respect. You can't go wrong then.'

I found that I was trembling. I had seen this woman on one or two occasions, but only from a distance. The fact that she believed herself to be Maximilian's wife made her alarming, to say the least. I felt that I was wronging her, which was not so. It was neither her fault nor mine that we were in this position.

She was seated at the table when Frau Graben opened the door.

'Here's Miss Trant, Your Grace,' she said, and I stepped into the room. I was aware that Frau Graben had not shut the door. She would be standing very close, listening. The eavesdropper in this case was rather a comfort.

'You are Miss Trant?' The coldest blue eyes I had ever seen were appraising me. They were expressionless and it was impossible to tell from them what she knew. She was beautiful in a certain style, I noticed with a pang of jealousy. How absurd to feel that! He loved me and he had never loved her.

246

She was beautiful as a statue is beautiful – remote and so cool. Her fair hair was swept up from a pale, rather long face, her nose was aquiline and patrician; her mouth matched her eyes – unsmiling. Her velvet cloak fell back to display the lace ruffles at her wrists and neck. Diamonds sparkled on her fingers and in the lace at her throat. They suited her. I could not imagine her ever glowing with passion; yet aloof as she was there was something deadly about her as there is about a snake.

But I believed she was feeling more interest in me than she would normally have for a teacher of English. She knows, I thought, if not all – something.

'I hear you teach the children English.'

'That is so.'

'And are they good pupils?'

I replied that I was satisfied with them.

She said: 'You may be seated.' She pointed to a chair close to hers and added: 'There.'

'How long have you been in Klocksburg?' she went on.

I told her.

'Why did you come here?'

'Frau Graben came to England and we met. She thought I would be suitable to teach the children English.'

'Frau Graben! Why should she decide that the children should be taught English?'

'Perhaps she could tell you that.'

The eyebrows were imperceptibly raised. I hoped I did not sound impertinent. I did not mean to be. I was merely horribly nervous because she was in the position which should be mine, because she believed herself to be married to Maximilian and was not. I could not imagine what her reaction would be when she knew the truth. She was proud and haughty and I should think would be very humiliated. The loss of dignity would mean a great deal to her.

'We are living through difficult times, Miss Trant,' she said. 'It might be well if you returned to your country.'

I was sure there was an even colder glitter in her eyes.

She knows! I thought. She is telling me to get out. I had the impression that she was offering me escape or the consequences of remaining here.

Go home! Leave Maximilian! As if I could! Was he not my husband? But I was sorry for her. I would be sorry for any woman in her position, be she proud princess or humble

247

woodcutter's daughter.

I knew in that moment that I was going to fight for what was mine. Because my visit to Dr Kleine was fresh in my memory, I thought of the children I should have; and it must be my son, not hers, who should be his father's heir. For myself I did not seek great riches. I knew that I should have been happier if my husband had been in a less exalted position; but for my children I would fight as any other mother would.

'I have no wish to return to my country,' I said. 'I propose to stay here.'

She bowed her head. What secrets those eyes held! Indeed she was like a snake. Her eyes were steady; her mouth cold; one sensed the poison dart was ready, waiting.

'We could be at war at any moment. The Duke, my husband, is most concerned.'

I felt the colour flush my cheeks. I wanted to say: No! *My* husband. And do you think *I* do not know of his concern?

This was foolish, of course. I was not being reasonable. She had no notion that I was Maximilian's wife. This cold appraising manner was the one accorded to all those whom she considered far beneath her.

'I should advise all *foreigners* to go,' she said. 'But you do not wish to. You are enthralled by your post.' Her lips curled, but there was no smile in her eyes; it was as though she were shrugging her shoulders at my folly, telling me that if I were wise I would go; but if I would not, then stay and take the consequences.

'I prefer to stay. It is good of Your Grace to concern yourself with me.'

That was hypocritical for I knew very well that there was nothing good about her concern. She was not in the least anxious for my welfare. She wanted something.

'Since you will stay,' she said, 'I will call upon your help. I wonder whether you will do as I ask.'

I sensed that she was playing with me – tormenting me in some way. I was convinced in that moment that she knew; but in the next I was telling myself that I was fanciful.

'The war is coming,' she went on. 'There is no doubt of it. I plan to turn one of the smaller schlosses into a hospital. We shall need all the helpers we can get. Are you prepared to join us, Miss Trant?'

I was astonished. What an absurd imagination I had! Had she after all merely come to ask my help in a hospital! And here I was imagining that she was planning to murder me!

I was tremendously relieved and I think I showed it.

'I would do anything I could to help,' I said warmly. 'I must tell you, though, that I have had no experience of nursing.'

'Few of us have. We may have to learn. Then, Miss Trant, can we count on your help?'

'If this war should take place then I should be eager to give my services.'

'Thank you, Miss Trant. That is good of you. I have the schloss in mind. It is called the Landhaus because the Government used to sit there years ago. You have seen it?'

I said I had not.

'It is on the other side of the mountain and easily accessible. I trust that we may not need it, but we have to be prepared.' The cold eyes looked straight into mine. 'It's no use waiting for events to catch us. We must be ready to meet them when they come. You agree, I am sure.'

'Yes, I do.'

She waved her hand rather imperiously to denote that the interview was over. I rose and went to the door.

When I reached it she said: 'I shall be calling on your help . . . soon.'

I said I would be ready.

As I went out I almost fell into Frau Graben.

'Come to my sitting-room,' she said, 'and I'll give you a cup of tea.'

I followed her there; the kettle was already on the boil.

'There,' said Frau Graben as she poured out. 'What do you make of that?'

There was no need to ask how she knew the gist of the conversation. I knew – and she knew I knew – that she had been listening all the time.

'I suppose it's wise to be prepared. If there is a war there will be casualties and it is well to have hospitals.'

'I wonder why she came to see you.'

'She will want as many helpers as she can get.'

'I know. I know. But why come to see *you*? Is her High and Mighty Grace going to interview all those who will be called in to help?'

'Perhaps she thinks as I'm a foreigner my case is different.

249

She warned me I should leave, as you heard.'

Frau Graben narrowed her eyes. 'I wonder what she *knows*. They've got spies everywhere. You can depend upon it Maxi's visits here have been noted. And why should he come here, they'll be asking themselves, and when they ask themselves a question like that they come up with the same answer every time. A woman!'

'She gave no indication that she knew.'

'As if she would! Close, she is. Cold as ice on top. And what's underneath? I wonder what she'll do. People! They're worth watching. If she thinks you're just another woman she might plague you for a bit, but if she knew you were his true and lawful wife . . .' Frau Graben began to laugh so much I thought she would choke.

'It seems to amuse you,' I said coldly. 'Sometimes I think you're a wicked woman.'

'I have my parts like everyone else. People – you never can be sure, can you?'

How true that was! One could never be sure – only of the one who was closest to you.

Oh Maximilian, I prayed, come back soon.

The next day a messenger arrived from the Count. He came in a carriage with the arms blazoned on it. They were so like the ducal arms that at first I thought that Maximilian was back. My disappointment was intense.

Frau Graben had, of course, seen the carriage and ascertained the reason for its coming.

'It's from Fredy,' she told me. 'You're to go to his schloss. He wants to consult you about the children's lessons.'

I stared at her in dismay. She nodded grimly.

'We can't disobey an order from the Count . . . not until you're recognized, you know.' She giggled. 'But he didn't say anything about your going alone. Though I doubt not that he has that in mind. I know Fredy. I'll come with you.'

I was glad of her company; she always brought a touch of lightness into everything that happened. Her intense interest in what was going on and her determination to extract the ultimate excitement from it was infectious.

'Fredy won't be very pleased to see *me*,' she chuckled. 'But Maxi left you in my care, remember, and I'm not one to forget my obligations.'

Her eyes danced with excitement. I believed she would

rather have something tragic happen than nothing at all.

We reached the Count's schloss. It was not unlike the ducal one, being only slightly less grand.

'Fredy imagines himself the Duke,' grunted Frau Graben. 'As I've said to him more than once in the old days, as long as he keeps it to his imagination I'll not quarrel with that.'

We passed the sentries who all knew Frau Graben, and went into the *Rittersaal* where a servant in the splendid livery of the Count's household – as grand as the traditional ducal one and scarcely any different – took us into an ante-room.

The Count himself joined us there. His eyes narrowed when they saw Frau Graben.

'You! You old meddler,' he said.

'Now, Fredy, remember whom you're talking to.'

'I did not send for you.'

'Naturally I came. I can't have young ladies from my household visiting unescorted.'

Although he was angry, I saw that she could still extract some sort of obedience from him. She could by a word or a look transport both the Count and Maximilian back to their childhood. She must have been a powerful force in the nursery, and that power lingered. She exasperated them but still kept that hold on their affections. This undoubtedly proved the truth of her observations about people. There were so many different sides to their character and the Count, who was undoubtedly an unscrupulous man, could remember the affection he had for his old nurse.

'You wanted to see Miss Trant. Well, I've brought her to you.'

'You will wait here,' he said to her. 'Miss Trant will come with me.'

She could say nothing to that and I must go with him; but it was a great comfort to know that she was waiting for me.

He shut the door firmly on her and I followed him up a wide staircase to a small panelled room. There was a window in the embrasure with window-seats, and the magnificent views, which had become almost a commonplace, were evident.

'Now, Miss Trant,' he said, 'pray be seated.' He brought a chair for me and placed it so that the bright light from the window was on my face. He seated himself in the window-seat, the light behind him. He folded his arms and studied me intently.

'How are the children progressing with their lessons?' A

question which he had not brought me here to answer, I knew.

I told him that they were progressing satisfactorily.

'I have become very interested in their studies . . . since you arrived.' There was a gleam of humour in his face. He was implying of course that he was interested in me.

'It is a fair distance to Klocksburg and I am a busy man. I should like to see more of them, so I am going to suggest that they come here.'

'I think it would be a mistake to move them,' I said quickly.

'Indeed. Why so?'

'Klocksburg has always been their home. The servants are familiar to them.'

'They can always visit Klocksburg and I do not wish them to become attached to servants.'

'They feel very secure under Frau Graben's rule.'

'I don't doubt it,' he said grimly. 'But I want the boys to be men, not little chickens cowering under the old hen's wing. Moreover, it would be pleasant to see more of you, Miss Trant. You are a very interesting woman.'

'Thank you.'

'Don't thank me. Thank the powers above that made you so.'

I stood up. 'I think I will leave now.'

'Spoken like a . . . Duchess! My God, you have the air! You have acquired that since you've been here. Of course, you were always ready to express your disapproval. Remember our first meeting? But you have changed since then. It is since my cousin returned.'

I moved towards the door but he was beside me. He had gripped my arm.

'I should be glad if you would remove your hand.'

'Come, Miss Trant, it is not the first time you have been touched.'

'You are insolent.'

'Forgive me . . . Duchess.' He brought his face close to mine. 'I know a great deal about you, you see.' He did not release my arm and I was uncomfortably aware of his brutal masculinity. I thought gratefully of Frau Graben.

'If you do no release me this instant . . .'

'What will you do?'

'I will see that the Duke . . .'

'My noble cousin is far away. When he returns you will

report to him that I have dared lay hands on what is his. Is that so?' His cruel face was close to mine. 'I know a great deal about you, my dear mock-Duchess. You were acquainted with our Maximilian years ago, were you not? You came here to seek him out. You wanted to renew that interesting liaison which took place a number of years ago. It seems an unusual story to you, but to us it is common enough. I have even played it out myself. A simple country maid who is ignorant of the ways of the world. She guards her virtue as a sacred thing, and so a mock marriage is necessary.'

'You are wrong,' I was stung into reply. 'There was no mock marriage.'

'Still deluded, Miss Trant?'

'How do you know of this?'

'My dear Miss Trant, I have a way of discovering what I want to know. I have my spies and they work well for me. You surely do not believe that my cousin is really married to you!' I did not answer and he went on: 'Ah, I see you do. You really believe that. Do you think that even he would be such a fool? How easy it is . . . you would not believe how easy. A simple ceremony, a friend who obligingly poses as a priest. My dear Miss Trant, it has been done a thousand times in the past and will doubtless be done a thousand times more.'

'I cannot discuss the matter.'

'Much as I wish to please you, we cannot always talk only on what gratifies you.'

'Why have you brought me here to tell me this?'

'This was just *en passant*. I have brought you here to tell you that the children are to take up their quarters here and you, as their teacher of English, will naturally accompany them. I can promise you as pleasant a time here as you enjoy in Klocksburg. What have you to say to that?'

'I have nothing to say.'

'That means you will prepare to leave Knocksburg immediately.'

'I shall not leave Klocksburg.'

'Do you mean you are resigning your post?'

'I should do so if you insisted on the children coming here.'

'And what of Fritz . . . your special protégé?'

I flinched. I couldn't help it. I had a horrible vision of what his sadistic treatment could be to that boy. In the joy of Maximilian's return had I neglected Fritz a little?

I had no fear for myself. Maximilian would protect me from this man; but even when there was no longer need to keep our marriage secret, Fritz would still be in his power. I had allowed myself to become deeply involved with the boy. He needed me and I knew I had done a great deal for him.

The Count was watching me slyly, reading my thoughts. He put his face close to mine. 'You have a deep feeling for that son of mine, Miss Trant,' he said. 'I like it. It shows me what a warm-hearted woman you are. It increases my admiration for you. You will come here and continue to look after him. There is no reason why you and I should not become great friends. You could reason with me, if you thought I was too harsh with the boy. You would be able to apply your maternal instincts . . . would you not? Oh, Miss Trant, you are a wonderful woman. I will tell you frankly – I adore you.'

'I wish to leave now.'

'And you will consider my proposition. Don't think too much about that incident of the past, will you? Max and I are very much alike. We always were. Brought up together, we developed similar tastes. That diabolical Graben will tell you that. As for that affair in the hunting lodge – be reasonable. I shouldn't like you to attach too much importance to it. It was a commonplace in the past and is not so very unusual in the present. And just suppose it were not a mock ceremony. What do you think would be the result of *that*? I can tell you. Trouble! Big trouble! And with Klarenbock. Do you think the people of that state would stand calmly by and accept the degradation of their Princess? And even if they did, what would be the reaction of the people here? They would never accept you . . . a foreigner of no rank, however attractive you might be. Do you know what would happen? The end of Maximilian. At best he would be deposed. You would not want to make such a disaster for him . . . for our little Rochenstein. But praise be, it was not so. The ceremony in the hunting lodge was like others before it. *They* never shook the foundations of the dukedom, so why should this.'

It was our secret no longer. It was out and known to the man who was, I felt certain, our most dangerous enemy.

I must get away to think.

I heard him say: 'In due course a carriage will come for you and the children. I look forward to receiving you here. You and I will then be able to continue our interesting friendship more comfortably. That will give me the greatest pleasure.'

I told Frau Graben as the carriage took us back to Klocksburg.

'Take the children! I never heard of such a thing.'

'He says that is what he will do. And he knows about the ceremony in the hunting lodge! He said that was a mock marriage!'

'He's lying. Maxi was never a liar. Fredy would lie himself out of any trouble. I know him well.'

'He was very offensive to me and I am afraid for Fritz.'

'He wants you because Maxi loves you. He was always like that. He must have what Maxi had. It was an obsession with him. But you'll not go to that schloss of his.'

'No,' I agreed. 'But what of Fritz?'

Frau Graben narrowed her eyes. 'He'll not have the children there. The Countess would never allow it. She's the one person he's afraid of. She'd never have her husband's illegitimate children in her schloss. I'm certain of that. He's a bluffer, our Fredy.'

'He knows about the ceremony. How could he have discovered?'

'Spies . . . everywhere. He's as troublesome as his father was. We're going to have trouble with him. I wasn't stern enough in the nursery.'

'He has a certain respect for you that he doesn't seem to have for anyone else.'

She nodded, smiling.

'And,' I went on, 'he says that if it were known that I were Maximilian's wife the people would revolt. They'd not accept me and Maximilian would be deposed.'

'Indeed! And Master Fredy would step in to take the dukedom, eh?'

'He did not go so far as to say that.'

'It's in his mind. It's always been there . . . rankling. That's what he's after and he'd stop at nothing to get it. He wants you, too, you and the dukedom. Everything that's Maxi's must be his. I've heard too that he's tired of his innkeeper's daughter. That was one of his longer affairs. Her father didn't like it at all, poor man. He doted on her; she's the only child. But Fredy comes along and must have his way. Poor girl. Oh, we've got to watch Master Fredy.'

'I long for Maximilian to come back.'

'Well, that,' she replied with her bland smile, 'is right and proper, seeing that he's your lawful husband. All we can do is wait. Something's going to happen soon. I feel that in my bones – and it's going to be something big.'

I heard her chuckle. I had rarely seen her so excited.

I was very anxious that the children should not hear that the Count had said they were to leave Klocksburg. The more I thought of that, the more inclined I was to agree with Frau Graben. His Countess, whom I had glimpsed briefly, had the appearance of a very determined woman, and I did not think Frau Graben was far wrong in saying that she would never accept the Count's illegitimate offspring in the schloss where her son was being brought up. Yes, he was bluffing. But there was no doubt that he had learned something and that was that there had been some ceremony between myself and Maximilian all those years ago.

The boys were clamouring to see the royal tomb and the afternoon following the day I had been summoned to the Count's schloss we went to the Island of Graves. Liesel had not come with us but had stayed behind with Frau Graben.

There was a boat at the moorings and the boys declared they wished to row across themselves rather than wait for old Charon to come and take them over. There was a bit of a squabble as to which one should take the oars.

I suggested that we should toss a coin and decide who should row us over and the other one could row us back. This they agreed to. Dagobert won the toss and rowed us over, with Fritz watching him carefully to make sure that his strokes were perfect.

As we scrambled ashore Charon came out of his house to greet us. He stood before us, his eyes peering at us through the wrinkled flesh.

' 'Tis been a sad day since you were last here,' he said, looking at me.

He gave me his hand. I remembered how dry and cold it had been on that other occasion. It still was.

'And you've come to see the royal grave.' I remembered the hollow ring of his voice. 'We've had visitors lately. 'Tis always the same when one of the Family comes to the last resting-place.'

I was one of the Family now, and it might be that one day

256

what was left of me would be lying on this Island.

'Come with me,' said Charon. 'Come, young masters. I'll show you where the old Duke lies. May God rest his soul.'

I walked beside him, the boys following. They were unusually solemn. No doubt they felt as I did – that we were in the presence of Death.

Dagobert said: 'Have you found someone to train to take your place, Franz?'

'I'm all alone on the Island as I have been these many years,' was the answer.

'I do wonder who's going to look after all these dead people when you're dead too.'

'It will be solved,' said Charon.

'All these dead people,' mused Dagobert. 'They do want someone to look after them. I reckon everyone would be afraid to live here . . . except you, Franz. Are you afraid?'

'The dead have been my companions too long for me to fear them, master.'

'Would you like to be here alone when it's dark, Fritz?' demanded Dagobert. Fritz hesitated and Dagobert accused him: 'You know you wouldn't. You'd be frightened. You'd scream when all the ghosts got out of their tombs.'

'You know you wouldn't like to be here alone after dark either, Dagobert,' I said, 'and as neither of you is going to be, there's no point in talking about it.'

'I wouldn't mind,' boasted Dagobert. 'I'd sit on the gravestones and I'd say "Come out and see me. I'm not afraid of you!" '

'And you would be just like the rest of us,' I told him.

'Perhaps they're afraid too,' said Fritz. 'I wouldn't like to be down in the ground with a lot of earth on top of me.'

'That's no way to talk,' I admonished. 'Those flowers are very beautiful.'

'Planted only a few hours after His Grace was laid to rest,' said Franz.

We had come to the grand avenue and there was the new grave covered with flowers. The grand effigies and statues had not yet been erected.

The boys stood and gazed solemnly at it.

'Do people ever get buried who are not dead?' asked Dagobert.

'What a question! Who would bury people before they were dead?' I said lightly.

'Some people *have* been buried alive. In monasteries they used to put them in a wall and build round them.'

'Now you've seen the Duke's grave. Wouldn't you like to visit your mothers'?'

They would naturally do so and we left the grand burial ground for that other. Charon accompanied us; he looked as one would imagine the boatman of the Styx with his black robes flapping round him and grey locks straggling out from under his skullcap – a messenger of Death.

'I want you to be careful of the new grave,' he said.

'A new grave!' Dagobert's eyes sparkled. 'Whose grave?'

'I dug it this morning,' said Charon.

'May we see it?' asked Fritz.

Charon pointed. 'It's close by. There are wooden planks across it.'

'May we see it?' asked Fritz.

'Young masters, be careful. Don't go falling down. Why, you could break a leg.'

They were eager to see. I followed them over to the grave and Charon lifted the planks and we looked down into the deep dark hole.

I felt the goose pimples rise on my skin. I suppose it was due to the thought that soon a coffin would be lowered down there and another life would be over. I felt, as they say at home, that someone was walking over my grave.

'Who is to be buried there?' I asked.

'A young woman,' replied Charon shaking his head. 'Too young to die. She's the daughter of the innkeeper in the town.'

I knew who she was then – another of those unfortunate women. The Count had favoured her for a short while and then discarded her. I knew that she had taken her own life and the favour shown her had led her, as it had led others before her, to the Island of Graves.

I felt a great desire to get away from the place.

All that day the tension seemed to be mounting. I was waiting for I knew not what. Of one thing I was certain. This state of affairs could not last. I was listening for the sound of a horse's hoofs on the road. Maximilian might come. How I longed for him – not only for the joy his presence always gave me, but because I desperately wished to tell him of my mounting fears. And if the sounds from without should be those of a carriage and there should be an imperative demand from the Count that the children should leave, what should I do? I would not go – and yet how could I allow Fritz to go without me? My mind was working on wild plans to keep Fritz behind. I must pretend he was ill. No, that would not work again. But I must find a way.

'My goodness,' said Frau Graben. 'You're all of a jump.'

'I'm thinking of the Count's taking the children.'

'I tell you he daren't. The Countess wouldn't have it – particularly now there's this fresh scandal. That girl of his, the innkeeper's daughter, she was to have a child and she has taken her life.'

'I saw her grave . . . freshly dug,' I said.

'Poor soul! It's the end for her. And what a way to die. She threw herself from the topmost attic of the inn into her father's courtyard. They say he found her there. He's nigh demented. She was his only child.'

'What a terrible tragedy!'

'She was a fool. He would have taken care of her and the child even though he was tired of her. There would have been another little one to join us. These poor girls. It's so romantic in the beginning and then there's the reckoning.'

'But not for him,' I said angrily.

'Fredy looks upon it as his right. And she knew that from the start. It's happened to others before. Poor, poor child. It had to end, though. Fredy wouldn't stay faithful for ever. But it's over now – a warning to young girls. Now cheer up. I tell you, he won't take the children. How can he? The Countess won't have them under the same roof as the future Count. No, here they'll stay. You'll see. And now all we have to do is wait for Maxi to come back.'

How I yearned for that day!

It must have been just past midnight. I had retired to bed as usual and was in a deep sleep when I was awakened to find Frieda standing by my bed with a candlestick in which was a lighted candle.

'Miss Trant,' she cried. 'Wake up. Fritz isn't in his bed.'

I started up and hastily put on slippers and a dressing-gown.

'He must be walking again, Miss Trant. I went in because I thought I heard a sound . . . and he wasn't there. His bed is empty.'

Frieda was trembling so much that the box of matches in the saucerlike base of the candlestick fell on to the bed. She replaced them with shaking fingers.

'We'd better look for him,' I said.

'Yes, Miss.'

I ran out of my room; she followed holding the candle high.

I went to Fritz's room. His bed was empty.

'He can't be far,' I said.

'Miss,' said Frieda, 'there's a draught on the turret stairs. I couldn't understand . . .'

'A draught! But that would mean a window was open somewhere.'

I started towards the turret stairs. I realized at once what she meant. If the door was shut there would be no draught. It could only be if the window was open . . .

I was frightened. Fritz walking in his sleep . . . into the turret-room, to the window . . . the window from which long ago poor Gerda had flung herself. Gerda's story had caught his imagination; I believed I had suppressed the children's unhealthy fear of ghosts, but how could I be sure of what went on in their innermost minds, and if Fritz were sleep-walking . . .

I ran up the stairs; the door was open; there was no doubt that the draught came from the open window.

Frieda was close at my heels with the candle, which was a good thing for it was a dark night; there was a certain amount of mist in the air, but the candle light showed me the room with the open window, the window from which Gerda had thrown herself and from which there was a steep drop to the valley below.

I ran to it and leaned out. I could just make out the shadowy shape of the mountainside. I sensed a presence behind me. A warm breath seemed to touch my neck. In that instant I thought; someone is going to force me out of the window.

There was a sudden scream and a blaze of light illuminated the room. I saw Frieda cowering against the wall. She no longer held the candle but was staring in horror at the velvet table-covering which was on fire. I forgot my terror of a few moments before. I rushed to pick up a rug and started to beat out the flames.

Frau Graben appeared, a candle in her hand, her hair in

260

iron curlers under a nightcap.

'*Mein Gott!*' she cried. 'What is happening?'

I continued to beat out the smouldering remains of the table-cloth. My mouth was parched and for a moment I could not speak. Then I said: 'Frieda dropped the candle . . . and I think there was someone here. Frieda, did you see anyone?'

She shook her head. 'I dropped the candle . . . the flame caught the matches . . . the whole box went up in flames . . .'

'Where were you, Frau Graben?' I asked. 'Did you see anyone? You must have.'

'There was no one on the stairs.'

Frieda cried: 'It must have been the ghost.'

'You're shaking like a leaf,' said Frau Graben to me. 'But why did you come up here?'

'Fritz!' I cried. 'I'm forgetting Fritz. I came to look for him. He's sleep-walking again.'

'Well, he's not here,' said Frau Graben.

I stared fearfully at the window. 'We must search everywhere . . . everywhere,' I cried frantically.

'Come then,' said Frau Graben. 'Frieda, damp down that cloth just in case. Make sure there's no danger.'

We went down the stairs to Fritz's room. His door was open. To my great relief he was in his bed.

'Fritz,' I cried, bending over him, 'are you all right?'

'Hello, Miss Trant,' he said sleepily.

I kissed him and he smiled happily. I felt his hand. It was warm. I remembered how icily cold his hands and feet had been on that other occasion when I had found him walking in his sleep.

'I've been to see a horse,' he murmured. 'All polished it was . . . and shiny and there was a man sitting on it with a gold crown on his head.'

'You've been dreaming, Fritz,' I said.

'Yes,' he murmured, closing his eyes.

Frau Graben said: 'Well, we'd better get to our beds.'

She came back to my room with me.

'You've had a nasty shock, Miss,' she said. 'I didn't want to say too much in front of Frieda. She was near hysteria. You say someone was behind you?'

'Yes.'

'Yet Frieda saw nothing.'

'I can't understand it. But it all happened in a moment.

She dropped the candle and the matches caught fire. That saved me, I think.'

'They'd say it was the ghost. That was why we kept the room locked. They used to say that if anyone went up there and leaned out of that window they wouldn't be able to stop themselves going over.'

'That's nonsense. Someone was there – behind me.'

'Can you be sure? When Frieda saw nobody?'

'Do you think I imagined it?'

'I don't know what to say, but I reckon you ought not to go on brooding on it. I'll bring you a drop of hot cordial; it'll put you to sleep; and if you lock your door you'll feel safe. Then after a good night's sleep you can start worrying about what really happened.'

She slipped out and shortly returned with the cordial. It was hot and warming. She took the glass away; I locked myself into my room; and to my surprise I was soon fast asleep. Her cordial must have been very potent.

I woke in the morning feeling heavy-headed. I washed and dressed hurriedly, thinking about last night's terrifying incident. By daylight it no longer seemed fantastic; I had had an anxious time and may have imagined that someone was behind me and that had Frieda not dropped the candle I should have been forced out of the window. It seemed the most logical conclusion. The innkeeper's daughter's death was in my mind, and she, poor girl, had fallen to her death. Was I becoming fanciful? It was unlike me, it was true, but possible, I supposed.

I told myself that I must be calm and behave normally so I went to the schoolroom to find Fritz and Liesel there alone. They told me that Dagobert was not up.

'He's lazy,' said Fritz.

'No, he's not,' contradicted Liesel, protecting Dagobert as usual. 'He's an old sleepyhead this morning.'

I said I would go and wake him.

'We've had our breakfast,' said Liesel. 'Fritz was naughty.'

'I wasn't,' retorted Fritz.

'Yes, he was, he left half his milk.'

'I always leave half my milk. You know Dagobert drinks it.'

'He drinks it for you.'

'No he doesn't. He drinks it because he likes it.'

I left them arguing and went into Dagobert's room. The boy was lying flat on his back. I bent over him and a great fear struck me. 'Dagobert!' I cried. 'Wake up, Dagobert!'

He did not open his eyes. I bent over him, studying him intently. This was no ordinary sleep.

I ran as fast as I could to Frau Graben's sitting-room.

She was eating a slice of pumpernickel sprinkled with the caraway seeds which she liked so much. Nothing that happened could affect her appetite.

'Frau Graben,' I said. 'I'm worried about Dagobert. I wish you'd come and look at him.'

'Isn't he up?'

'No. He's asleep. It's rather peculiar.'

She left her pumpernickel and came with me.

She took one look at the boy and felt his pulse.

'Mein Gott!' she cried. 'What goes on in this place? He's been put to sleep.'

'Dagobert! Put to sleep!' I cried.

She shook her head gravely.

'Something strange is going on,' she said. 'I don't like it. I wish I knew who was responsible for this.'

'What shall we do?'

'Leave him to sleep it off. We'll tell the children Dagobert's not feeling well and will spend the morning in bed and they're not to disturb him.'

'Has this anything to do with last night, I wonder?'

'What could it have? Do you know, Miss Trant?'

'I've no idea. All I'm convinced of is that last night someone was waiting in the turret-room to kill me.'

'Have you any idea who?'

'No. But it has something to do with my relationship with Maximilian.'

'Ah,' she said, 'but we don't want to get ideas and fancies till we're sure, do we?'

'I feel very uneasy.'

'That's a good sign. You'll be on your guard.'

'So many strange things are happening. Fritz walking in his sleep . . .'

'He's done that often.'

'What of Dagobert?'

'The young monkey got hold of someone's laudanum bottle and took a swig or two. Nobody would be very surprised at that. We know what he is. He's into everything.'

'It's too glib an explanation,' I said, 'following on what happened to me.'

'We'll let him sleep it out. He'll be himself before the day's out.'

We went back to the schoolroom.

Fritz was telling Liesel: 'And I dreamed that someone came in and picked me up and I was carried away and away . . . and I was in a new country and there was a horse . . . a horse with a man on it and the man had a crown on his head . . . all polished it was.'

That afternoon I was in my room when there was a tap on the door. I called 'Come in' and Prinzstein entered.

'I have the carriage below, Miss Trant,' he said. 'The Duchess sent a message that I was to take you to the Landhaus. She is holding a meeting there of those who are to help her in the hospital.'

'I had no message,' I said.

'It came some time ago. I told Freda to tell you. I believe Frau Graben called her away for something. She must have forgotten it. I hope you will not be too angry with her. She is of a nervous nature and the fire in the turret-room upset her, so she is not herself.'

'I understand, of course, but I am not ready.'

'Perhaps you will be as quick as possible, Miss Trant. We must not keep Her Grace waiting.'

The idea of meeting that woman again made me very apprehensive. This time, however, there would be others there – her helpers. I knew that war was very close indeed. It seemed inevitable now; and she would naturally wish to get her hospital into working order as soon as possible.

I changed my dress and combed my hair. I wanted to look as attractive as I could. That would give me courage in the presence of the woman who believed herself to be Maximilian's wife.

Fifteen minutes after Prinzstein had knocked at my door we were driving to the Landhaus. We drove to the town and then through the valley to the other side of the mountain. There it stood – a yellowish-gold coloured castle, smaller than Klocksburg but beautifully perched on the hillside among the pine woods. We drove through the gates under the castellated tower into a courtyard.

We entered the castle and I saw that the *Rittersaal* had already been made into a ward and several beds had been placed side by side.

Prinzstein led me to a small room at which was a table with chairs placed round it. On the table was a bottle of wine and several glasses, with a plate of little spiced cakes.

'It seems that I am not late after all,' I said.

'Her Grace and the other ladies have not yet arrived. Or perhaps they are inspecting another part of the castle. Equipment is being brought in every day. Her Grace's instruction was that I was to offer you refreshment as soon as you arrived.'

'Thank you. I prefer to wait for the others.'

'Her Grace said immediately you arrive. She will not be pleased if you refuse. This wine is from the vines of Klarenbock. She sets great store by it and I will warn you she likes everyone to praise it. She will no doubt ask your opinion. She says it is better than anything that comes from the French wine-growing country or the Moselle district.'

'I would rather wait.'

He poured a glass. 'Just taste it,' he said, 'and as soon as you see her, take an opportunity of telling her how good is the flavour.'

I sipped it. I could taste nothing special about it. He offered me one of the spiced cakes. They were similar to those which Frau Graben ate in such quantities, and I refused.

Prinzstein went on to say that it would not be long before war was declared. He reckoned he would have to go. There would be changes. Wars were terrible.

He left me sipping the wine and said he would go and see if anyone was arriving. He left me in the room for a few moments and when he came back said that Her Grace had arrived and had gone straight up to the rooms at the top of the castle which would be used for those who were not badly wounded; and she wished me to join her and the others there.

Prinzstein led the way. We climbed a broad staircase to a landing and then mounted a spiral stair. This was very similar to Klocksburg and the room I entered bore a resemblance to the turret-room there.

She was there and, to my surprise, alone. There was something different about her. Her expression was as cold as it had been on that other occasion but there was an excitement behind it. She appeared to be suppressing some inner emotion.

'Ah, Miss Trant,' she said, 'it was good of you to come so promptly.'

'I feared I might have kept you waiting. I understand you are calling together several of those who will help in the hospital.'

'There is someone here. She will come in shortly. Perhaps you would like to see the view while you are waiting. There is a door leading out to a little tower. It's called the Cats' Tower. You have seen such towers before, I am sure. Boiling oil and missiles used to be thrown down on invaders from them. The noise it made was like screaming cats. You can imagine that, I am sure, Miss Trant.'

'Yes,' I said.

'The view is magnificent, is it not? Straight down the steep side of the mountain to the valley. Do you wonder what it would be like to plunge straight down to . . . death.'

'Such a thought had not entered my mind.'

'Had it not? It is a way to die. You know, of course, of the legend at Klocksburg. A young woman years ago threw herself out of the window there. The room is said to be haunted.'

'I know of that – yes.'

'Well, you know Klocksburg well. But you are not superstitious. You are practical . . . the sort I shall need in my hospital, I am sure. That girl killed herself because she had been deceived . . . a mock marriage with one of the Dukes. One can understand in a way. Can you understand, Miss Trant?'

She was standing very close to me, her eyes inscrutable; and for the second time I had the alarming feeling that I was in great danger. I grasped the stone balustrade firmly. I saw her eyes go to my clenched hands.

'It's a strange afternoon,' she said. 'Do you feel it? There's a humidity in the air. Does it make you feel sleepy?'

I replied that on the contrary I felt very wide awake.

'Let us go inside for a moment,' she said. 'There is something I have to say to you.'

I was relieved to get away from the tower. She sat down and signed to me to take a chair.

When we were seated she said: 'You are aware, Miss Trant, that I know a good deal about you.'

'I have no idea what you know about me.'

'About you . . . and my husband. I have learned that there was a ceremony in a hunting lodge. Do you really believe that

266

was a true marriage?'

I knew I had to speak then. 'It *was* a real marriage,' I said. 'I am his wife.'

'In that case, who am I?'

'You are not his wife.'

'It is not possible for a Princess of Klarenbock to be in the position you suggest I am in.'

'It is possible. Moreover, it is a fact.'

Her eyes narrowed. 'I mean that it is not possible for such a slur on our house to be accepted. Do you understand that you are in acute danger?'

I stood up. 'I think we should discuss this when Maximilian returns.'

'We are going to settle it now.'

'How can we without him? He is planning to tell you. It is no fault of his, yours or mine that we are in this position.'

'I am not concerned with faults. I merely tell you that it cannot be.'

'But if it is . . .?'

'It may be now but it must not be tomorrow. What did you think of the wine? We are proud of it in Klarenbock.'

She was looking at me steadily and a horrible possibility dawned on me.

'Yes,' she said, 'the wine was drugged. Don't think we have poisoned you. Not at all. You are just sleepy . . . nothing more. When you are so far gone that you know nothing at all, you will be carried out to the Cats' Tower and gently dropped down into the valley.'

I cried: 'This is madness.'

'It would be madness to let you live, Miss Trant.'

I could not stop staring at her, although my greatest impulse was to run as fast as I could down the spiral stair and out to Prinzstein and the waiting carriage.

'It will be the old story,' she said quietly. 'The deceived woman . . . the plunge to death. It is becoming so usual. Even inkeepers' daughters do it now.'

She laughed in an odd way. Then she looked up at me and went on: 'The wine is taking care of you.'

'I scarcely touched it,' I replied.

'A little would suffice. You will feel nothing. It is an easy way out. Easier than it would have been because this time you will know nothing. They should have managed better. It was a simple thing. Frieda is quite stupid.'

'You mean that Frieda was aware . . .'

'People are aware sometimes, Miss Trant. Why don't you sit down? You must be feeling very strange.' She passed her hand over her eyes and murmured: 'The fools. They should have managed better. Where are you going, Miss Trant?' I was at the door and about to leave her when she added: 'It is no use. Prinzstein will not let you go. He failed in the Klocksburg room. He will not fail in this one.'

'Prinzstein,' I stammered. 'He is a good servant.'

'A good servant to me. He has served me well and would have done so last night but for that stupid wife of his.'

My hand was on the door handle. I tried to turn it but could not. The horrible thought struck me that I was locked in. But I was wrong. The reason the door would not open was because someone was holding it, trying to turn it and come in.

'Who is there?' I called.

The door opened and Ilse walked in.

'Ilse!' She hobbled towards me with the aid of a stick. I stared at her in astonishment, for I could not believe in the first seconds that it was really Ilse.

'Yes,' she said. 'It is. You are right, Helena.'

'What are you doing here? I have so much to say to you.'

'Yes, of course, Helena. You see I have grown infirm since we last met, I cannot walk very easily.'

She sat down in the chair I had vacated.

'I have so wanted to find you,' I cried.

She looked at the Duchess, who was staring into space in an extraordinary manner. She smiled at her fondly but the Duchess did not appear to see her. 'She is my sister,' said Ilse, 'my half-sister. I was the result of one of those light love-affairs which are so prevalent in high places. I was brought up in the shadow of the palace, but never being part of it. I always loved my little sister, though. She is fifteen years younger than I.'

'I think she is ill.'

'She is heavily drugged. She has taken the draught that was meant for you. It should be you who would be sitting there, Helena. That was the plan. You were to be unconscious, in a stupor, and then we were going to take you out to the tower and let you fall over. Prinzstein was to have done it in the turret-room at Klocksburg. It would have been so much more

appropriate there. But they bungled it. Her Grace was furious
with them.'

'I don't understand,' I said. 'Have you brought me here to
murder me?'

'You have guessed aright, Helena. You were brought here
to be disposed of. But I am not a murderess. They would say
it was a weakness in me.'

'You are talking in riddles,' I said. 'Explain to me. She
wants me dead because I am Maximilian's wife – that's true,
I know. She brought me here to kill me.'

'You must not judge her harshly. She does not regard it as
murder. It is a state of affairs that cannot be allowed to
continue. She . . . the Duke's mistress! It is impossible. His
having a wife already cannot be tolerated. It is statecraft, she
would say. Sometimes people have to die for it and in strange
circumstances. She plans that when you are dead she and the
Duke will be secretly married and few will be the wiser as to
what has gone before. I have been brought up more rigidly. I
see the deliberate killing of one person by another as murder.
So I am here to look after you both. I looked after you once
before . . . you don't realize what I did for you. I could so
easily have . . . disposed of you then. But I didn't. I looked
after you, I made everything easy for you . . . '

'Easy! That . . . easy! Listen, Ilse, I want to know exactly
what happened . . . right from the beginning.'

'I'll tell you. A husband was found for me. Ernst – ambassador from Rochenstein. I married him and persuaded him to
work for my country, Klarenbock. This sometimes meant
working against Rochenstein. Ernst was a friend of Prince
Maximilian before he came to Klarenbock and when he went
back to Rochenstein with me as his wife, he had a post in
the Prince's entourage. He learned of Maximilian's meeting
with you and his obsession. Ernst had to go to London to see
a heart specialist and he offered to bring you back.'

'So you posed as my cousin.'

'The fact that your mother was a native of these parts made
that easy. We brought you back and arranged that you and
Maximilian should meet on the Night of the Seventh Moon.
There was the marriage. We believed it would be a mock
marriage with a pseudo-priest, and when we discovered that
Maximilian was so besotted that he had gone through a
genuine ceremony we could see that this was disaster to the

269

treaty which was being made between Rochenstein and Klarenbock. I was working for my native country and I realized that I had to act quickly. The Prince went away after the brief honeymoon because a rebellion was brewing and he had to be with his father. I should have left you in the lodge to be blown up, but I couldn't do it. My sister says that was the greatest mistake I ever made. From her point of view, I dare say it was, but I had come to look upon you as my little cousin. I was fond of you. I thought I would get you back to England and no one would be the wiser. So I destroyed the evidence of the marriage – your lines and ring; and with the help of the doctor who was working with us we tried to convince you that you had lost six days of your life when you lost your virtue. I don't know how we did it.'

'You never did,' I said. 'You never convinced me.'

'I feared not. And then you discovered you were going to have a child – a child who would be the legitimate heir to the dukedom! Ernst said I was a fool. I should first have kept you in the lodge when we blew it up, for after all it was blown up that we might convince Maximilian that you were dead. You should have been dead in truth, Ernst said. But I couldn't do it. I preferred to take a chance in building up that fabric of lies, as you call it. But when the child was coming and all the terrible complications with it, even I began to waver. But I saved you, Helena. It would not have been difficult to get rid of you at that time. But I couldn't do it, and because we had people placed strategically over the country who could be used in any situation to work for Klarenbock I believed I could delude you and so save your life.'

'You were good to me, Ilse.'

'I don't think you realize even now how good. My sister will never forgive me. I saved your life and then I allowed her to marry – or go through a form of marriage – knowing of your existence. I am not going to let her kill you now. Maximilian and you must proclaim the truth without delay, whatever the consequences. For the sake of you and the boy . . .'

'The boy?'

'Your son.'

'My son. I have no son. My daughter, they told me, died.'

'You know now that was untrue. You went to Dr Kleine. He reported to me at once and I could see that things were reaching a climax. My sister discovered what had happened. Frederic knows. You and the boy are in acute danger. I have

270

saved you today. Good luck has saved you both before. Neither can go on doing so.'

'My son . . .' I repeated.

'Fritz.'

'Fritz . . . my son! My child was a girl. She would not be as old as Fritz.'

'He is your child. We had to make it appear that he was older so that he was not connected with what happened at Dr Kleine's clinic. Oh, if you had stayed in England this would never have happened. My sister's son would have inherited; the marriage in the lodge would have been of no importance. But because I am a sentimental woman who grew fond of you, because – spy that I am – I have never killed and cannot kill – I have ruined my sister's life.'

'What will happen now?' I asked.

'You will take the greatest care if you are wise. You will guard your life as you never guarded anything before. And you will watch over your son because he is in even greater danger.'

'There have been attempts on Fritz's life.'

'They will not always fail. My sister was determined to remove you. But there is a more powerful force which seeks to remove your son.'

I could only stare at her in speechless horror.

'Count Frederic!' she said. 'He has learned the truth. He has discovered the priest who performed the ceremony. He has spies everywhere . . . even as we have. He has been suspicious for some time. He will now try to discredit Maximilian with the help perhaps of my father. I don't know whether he will succeed in that. My father is an honourable man but the thought of what has happened to his daughter will incense him. But Frederic will think that it is useless to depose Maximilian while he has a son to follow him. Frederic wants the dukedom for himself. He has always wanted it . . . as his father did; and it is very likely that in view of the scandal which this is inevitably going to bring about, the people of Rochenstein will reject Maximilian. But the Duke will then be Fritz because he is the direct heir. The boy is too young to rule and his father might well be appointed Regent. That would not suit Frederic. If Fritz did not stand in his way when Maximilian was deposed, the dukedom would almost certainly fall to Frederic. You must realize the importance of these politics, because you are involved in them –

271

your child is involved in them. For God's sake watch over him. He is in imminent danger from the most ruthless man in Rochenstein.'

'I must go back to Klocksburg,' I said. 'I shall tell Fritz I am his mother. I shall care for him. And I shall never let him out of my sight.'

She nodded.

'I will tell Prinzstein to drive you back immediately.'

I looked at the Duchess. 'I shall care for her,' said Ilse, her face softening. 'Oh, Helena, what a lot of trouble would have been avoided if you had not got lost in the mist that day when you went out on the school picnic.'

She called Prinzstein. He looked astonished. Doubtless he was surprised to be ordered to drive me home instead of to assist in throwing me down to death from the Tower of the Screaming Cats.

As the carriage clattered into the courtyard, Frau Graben came running out.

'It's you. Where have you been? He's back.'

My heart leaped with joy. I could have forgotten everything in that moment but that Maximilian was back and that he would be here under this roof with me and our son.

'Where is he?' I cried.

'Come along in,' replied Frau Graben, 'and calm yourself. He's back, I said. Back in Rochenstein. I didn't say he was here in Klocksburg. He *was* here. He's gone looking for you.'

'Where has he gone?'

'Now, now, be calm I said. It's not like you, Miss Trant, to be otherwise. Maxi came here shortly after you'd gone. He's just home and the first thing he did was come to you.'

'But where is he now?'

'It was Dagobert. He said he'd heard Prinzstein say you were going to the Landhaus to see the Duchess. My goodness! He was in a fret then. He was as bad as you. He wouldn't stop a minute. He was off.'

'He would have been too late if . . .'

She looked at me oddly. 'Here, you'd better come and sit down. I'll get you a cup of tea.'

'Not now. I couldn't drink it.' I had to talk to someone. I had to tell the news that I had a son and he was alive and that I already loved him dearly. I wanted to tell Maximilian, but Frau Graben would have to do.

I blurted out: 'I have just heard that Fritz is my son.'

'There,' she said beaming. 'I guessed that. It all fits, doesn't it? I knew a good deal, but there were things I wasn't sure of. You sit still for a minute. You're shocked or dazed or something. What happened up at the Landhaus? *She* sent for you. I was worried and, by the looks of him, so was Maxi. He wouldn't stop a minute. He was off and no explanations either. Yes, I guessed about Fritzi. Hildegarde put two and two together. She knew it was a true marriage, I suspect, and she thought it best that you were spirited away to England and forgotten. That was what she would think was best for Maxi and what was best for Maxi was what she wanted.'

I was scarcely listening. I was thinking of Maximilian's arriving at the Landhaus. He would find his wife drugged and helpless . . . and Ilse. She would explain to him and send him back. So there was nothing to do but wait until he came. But I must see Fritz. I must tell him that he had a mother after all. Perhaps Maximilian and I ought to tell him together. We could all three share the wonderful moment.

Frau Graben went on talking. 'Hildegarde took Fritz when he was born. She knew who he was and loved him dearly. She connived at the gunpowder affair and she confessed a good deal to me when she was dying. That was when I took over Fritzi. Then of course I began to learn things. What a situation!' She chuckled. How she loved to interfere in people's lives, to bring about dramatic situations and watch people's reactions to them. 'You were for Maxi . . . there was no doubt about that. He changed after he lost you. One night he was ill . . . feverish . . . rambling. It was all about you . . . your name . . . that bookshop and the town where you lived. I got it all by degrees and I thought: My Maxi will never be the same without her and so I brought you here to him – my gift to Maxi on the Night of the Seventh Moon. Of course I planned for you to be happy in some little schloss. No one would have known what it was all about . . . except me. You would have been his true love. Princes lead their state lives with their state wives and have their loves in secret. Why not Maxi?'

'Oh, Frau Graben, how you have meddled in our lives!' I cried.

'But what have I brought you but good, eh? And now what will happen? This could be trouble with Klarenbock. They'll say we've insulted their Princess. Maxi never wanted her,

273

though. Cold as an icicle. She was no wife for him. I thought we'd all be happy together and there'd be the babies, and no one know the truth but me and what a chuckle I'd have over that. And up at the big schloss there'd be the Duchess and her son who'd be the heir and none the wiser. That was how I'd planned it. And then things started to happen. There was the arrow in Fritzi's hat and the bandits who took Dagobert by mistake, and there was that silly affair in the turret-room that gave them away. They put a sedative in Fritzi's milk and he only drank a little which didn't put him to sleep properly. Dagobert took the rest and went off altogether. Then Fritz went on about the horse and the man with a crown. I know that it's in their room. It's a carving Prinzstein made himself and polished and is very proud of. It was Prinzstein who was waiting for you up there when Frieda took you up, but the silly creature by good luck dropped the candle and the matches caught fire. If you'd turned and seen Prinzstein the game would have been up. So he fled. He was hiding behind the door as I came up and slipped down the stairs after me. But I knew what had happened. I'd suspected he was working for Klarenbock and that silly little Frieda would do as he said.'

'They were going to kill me,' I told her, 'and she was going to do it this afternoon. I wish Maximilian would come.'

'He'll come straight back here when he finds you left the Landhaus.'

'I must see Fritz. I can't wait to tell him. This is going to make him so happy.'

'He loves you. I'll swear if he could choose a mother she would be you. Talk about dreams coming true! You took to him from the start, didn't you? I wonder if it's true that mothers would know their own no matter what had separated them.'

'I was drawn to him and he to me. I must find him. I'm going to him now.'

I left but she followed me out to the *Randhausburg*, into the fortress. I went up to Fritz's room. He was not there. He was nowhere in the fortress.

As we came down the stairs and out to the courtyard I saw Dagobert. 'Have you seen Fritz?' I called.

'Yes, he's gone off. It's not fair.'

'Not fair? What's not fair?'

274

'My father took us into the forest riding and then sent me back.'

I felt as though my blood had turned cold.

'Sent you back,' I repeated.

'Yes, and Fritz was to go alone to the Island of Graves . . . to the empty grave with the planks across.'

'Why?' I stammered.

'Because he's a coward and he's got to learn not to be. He's got to row over there by himself and wait there and stay till it's dark.'

I didn't wait for any more. I ran to the stable.

Frau Graben was behind me. 'Where are you going?' she demanded.

'I'm going to the Island of Graves. Tell Maximilian, there's not a moment to lose. Fritz may be in danger.'

I rode through the forest seeing only Fritz, my son, a forlorn figure alone on the Island of Graves with a man who was determined to kill him. I myself had faced death twice in a very short time. Who knew? I was probably coming face to face with it again. I did not care. All I thought of was my son.

'On the Island of Graves . . . alone!' I kept hearing those words.

Oh Fritz, my son! I prayed: 'Let me be in time to save him.'

I did not ask myself *how* I could save him from a man who had determined to kill him. I only thought that I must be there. If Maximilian had not gone to the Landhaus . . . if he had waited, but how could he wait when he believed me to be in danger?

I had reached the lake. There were no boats there. I stared in desolation at the Island. Then I saw Charon emerge from his house.

'Franz!' I called. 'Franz!'

He heard me and shaded his eyes to look. I waved frantically. He got into the boat and – slowly, it seemed – rowed towards me.

'Why,' he said, 'it's Miss Trant.'

'I must get to the Island quickly,' I cried.

He nodded. 'Where are the boats?' he said. 'There is generally one here. They must all be on the other side. One should always be there. But few are in a hurry to get to the Graves.'

Oh hurry, Charon, I thought. He sat there bent over the oars, his dark robes falling about him, eyes peering out from under the grey straggling brows.

'Why are you in a hurry, Fräulein?' he asked.

I replied impatiently: 'Did you see Fritz?'

He shook his head. 'There are people on the Island today. I don't see them come but I know. I sense them. Sometimes there is the peace . . . the quiet of the dead . . . and then it changes and though I see no one I know. I never fail to know. Today there is no peace. Perhaps because tomorrow it is a burial day.'

'Someone is to be buried tomorrow?'

'The daughter of the innkeeper. She killed herself, poor soul, but she's entitled to a place in the burial ground. She carried a child . . . a child of the Family.'

'Poor girl,' I said.

'She's past all earthly suffering now. She will lie in her grave and I will plant a flower for her. A rosemary because someone will remember her.'

We had reached the shore. I leaped out of the boat.

'I am going to look for Fritz,' I said by way of explanation; and I ran as fast as I could to the burial ground and that spot where the new grave had been dug. The planks were still across the dark hole.

I called: 'Fritz! Where are you, Fritz? I have come for you, Fritz.'

There was no answer. Could it be that he had disobeyed the Count's orders and not come? He would not dare. Besides he would want to prove that he was not afraid.

'Fritz, where are you? Fritz!'

No sound at all. Nothing! I could not see Charon now. He must have gone into his little house. I felt as though I were alone on this island of the dead.

I did not know which way to turn and I stood for a few seconds staring down at the grave in which tomorrow a young girl would be laid to rest.

And then I knew that I was not alone. I turned sharply. The Count was standing a few paces from me. It flashed into my mind that he had been watching me from behind one of the bigger tombstones.

'Where is Fritz?' I demanded.

276

'Do you expect me to know?'

'He was told to meet you here.'

'Who told you that?'

'Dagobert. You told Fritz to come here alone. I want to know where he is.'

'That is what we should both like to know. The little coward didn't come. Of course, he wouldn't. He was afraid to.'

'He was more afraid of you than of the dead. I believe he is here somewhere.'

'Where? Please tell me.'

'I should think you'd be better able to tell me.'

'Why should we concern ourselves with the tiresome child? Here we are together – you and I. So quiet it is. No one on the island except the old man and he does not count. A strange meeting-place . . . but at least we shall be undisturbed. Old Franz is half dead in any case.'

'I came here to look for Fritz.'

'And you found me. Much more interesting, I do assure you.'

'Not for me. I ask you again, where is the child?'

'And I tell you again I have no idea. Nor do I care. I was going to teach him a lesson. I would rather teach you one.'

I started to walk away, but he was beside me. He caught my arm.

'I have grown weary of the chase,' he said. 'It ends here.'

I tried to wrench my arm free but I could not. His evil laughing face was close to mine.

I said: 'I know you lured my child here.'

The change in his expression was obvious. The lust was tinged with a certain apprehension.

I went on: 'I have learned this day who Fritz is. I know what is in your mind. You want Maximilian's heritage. You are hoping to discredit him because of his marriage to me. But you can't discredit his son. You have lured him here. What have you done with him? I have come here to take him away to safety. I am his mother.'

'You are hysterical,' he said.

'I want my son.'

'And I want you. I wonder who is going to be satisfied. There seems to be scarcely a doubt. Do you realize, my dear Duchess, that you are alone with me on this Island for as I said we cannot count that feeble old man. I would throw him

277

into the lake if he dared interfere.'

'I despise you,' I said.

'That is of no consequence. You are caught. There is no escape for you. You are wise enough to know that.'

'Please keep away from me.'

'Why, when I am pleased to be near you.'

'You are wicked. Do you know for whom that grave has been dug? For a girl who trusted you, whom you have betrayed, a girl who has taken her life because you have made it intolerable for her. How dare you! How can you . . . Here . . . beside her very grave.'

'Don't you see, it adds a touch of piquancy?'

'You disgust me.'

'I find that amusing too.'

I was trembling. I looked towards the shore. There was no sign of anyone. I knew that if I attempted to run he would overtake me. There would be a struggle and although I should employ every bit of strength I possessed, I knew that he would overcome me.

I cried out: 'I want Fritz. What have you done with him?'

'Now you are being tiresome.'

'I insist . . .'

'*You* insist? You are in no position to insist. Come, let us be friends before you die.'

'Before . . . I die.'

'You are not your usual clever self today. You have accused me of treason. The penalty for treason is death. I do not want to die. So I cannot allow you to live after making such an accusation against me.'

'You are mad,' I said. And then I cried out in sudden fear: 'You have killed my son.'

'And now you are going to force me to kill you. I shall not enjoy that one little bit. I shall hate killing a woman whom I admire, especially one whom I have never really known and who has not become tiresome to me.'

'You have no regret for the death of those who have become tiresome, I see. Tell me,' I cried, 'have you killed Fritz?'

He kept his grip on my arm and forced me towards the grave.

'You are a fool after all,' he said. 'Perhaps I should have tired quickly of you. You need never have died. You could have lived in retirement with Max. I should have allowed that.'

'You *are* mad,' I said.

I could see that this was so. He was mad with ambition, with the love of power and the burning desire to take from his cousin all that he had ever had.

'You will not live to see me rule Rochenstein, but before you die I am going to show you what kind of lover you turned your back on. Then I shall kill you and you shall join your son.'

Still gripping me, he kicked aside one of the planks. I looked down into the grave. Fritz was lying there.

'Oh God,' I cried, trying to struggle free. I wanted to go down there, to bring him up . . . my own son who had been taken from me at his birth and now that he had come back to me was in the grave.

I heard a shout from the bank then. 'Lenchen! Lenchen!'

'Oh thank God,' I cried. 'It's Maximilian.'

'Too late, cousin,' muttered the Count. 'By the time you are here I shall have been both your wife's lover and murderer. Then I shall be ready for you. A triple funeral with some honours . . . and in the royal avenue, I suppose.'

He had seized me. I fought with all my might. And then suddenly a shot rang out. The Count's hold on me was relaxed. I sprang back in time to see him stagger like a drunken man before he fell. Then I saw the rich red blood staining the grass.

'Maximilian,' I whispered, 'you have killed him.'

I ran as fast as I could to shore. Maximilian was getting out of the boat. I fell into his arms and he held me against him. I stayed there only a second. I heard myself babbling something about Fritz, my son lying in a grave.

It is difficult to remember clearly what followed. I think I was in too great a state of shock to realize exactly what was happening. Maximilian had descended into the grave; he held up Fritz; and another man had appeared on the scene. He carried a gun which he laid on the grass while he took Fritz from Maximilian.

He set him down gently on the ground and then Maximilian was beside me and we were kneeling down beside our son.

I was suddenly aware that the man who had joined us was the innkeeper.

'He's not dead,' said Maximilian. 'We'll get him back to Klocksburg without delay.'

'We'll make a stretcher for him,' said the innkeeper. 'I'm glad I was there.'

'You shot him through the heart,' said Maximilian.

'And I'd do it again,' replied the innkeeper. 'I meant to get him and I did.'

We took Fritz back. Thank God it had not been the Count's intention to kill the boy outright, for he could so easily have done so. He had knocked Fritz unconscious and thrown him into the grave, to be discovered the following day when the coffin of the innkeeper's daughter was brought for burial. By that time Fritz would have died of his injuries, exposure or fever; and if he were not quite dead the Count's spies would have found some way of killing him. It would appear, of course, that the boy had fallen into the grave and injured himself in the fall.

I would not let him out of my sight and I was at his bedside when he regained consciousness so that I was the first person he saw when he opened his eyes. I put my face close to his and whispered: 'Fritz. I am here with you. We're going to be together for evermore.' He stared at me wonderingly and I went on: 'You always wanted a mother, Fritz. Now you have one. I am your mother.'

I don't think he understood but my words had a comforting effect on him. I longed for the day when he would be well enough to understand fully the wonderful thing that had happened to us.

The day after that on which the Count had been murdered the French declared war on the Prussians and all the German states were involved.

These events dwarfed everything else into insignificance. As the Commander-in-Chief of the army, Maximilian had to prepare immediately to leave for the front. I was left behind and nursing Fritz back to health gave me something to work for during those dark days. I think the fact that I was his mother was such wonderful news that it speeded his recovery.

The Prince of Klarenbock, to whom Maximilian had told the whole story during his visit there, behaved magnanimously. He said his daughter must return to Klarenbock; and this she did in the company of Ilse; I heard later that Wilhelmina had entered a convent where she hoped to expiate the sin of attempted murder.

Soon after the outbreak of war the innkeeper was tried for the murder of the Count. Maximilian had asked for special leniency to be shown, for as the father of a girl whom the Count had seduced and deserted and who had killed herself because of this, he had committed the act under great provocation.

There was a war, said Maximilian, and all good men were needed at the front. He would personally vouch for the innkeeper.

And this he did.

While I was nursing Fritz back to health I used to talk to him of the wonderful time we would have when the war was over and he, I and his father were all together.

We used the Landhaus as a hospital and those were grave and anxious days when it was good to have plenty to do; but when the terrible casualties started to come in I was filled with terror lest one day they should bring in Maximilian. I don't know what I should have done without Frau Graben. I have since discovered that I owe that woman a great deal.

At last came news of the great victory, the bells rang out from the *Pfarrkirche*. The French were in retreat and the Emperor was cornered at Sedan.

What joy there was on the day Maximilian came marching home.

We were together again. I was the first to greet him openly now. No more secrets. The story of our marriage, the death of the Count, the retirement of Wilhelmina into a convent, the discovery of our son – these were legends of the past. They had been swallowed up in the great event of war.

Maximilian was home! There was the great joy of bringing him and Fritz together. My son not only had a mother but a father whom he could love and respect.

The day I was able to say to my son: 'Fritz, this is your father!' and I saw how it would be with them, I said: 'This is the happiest day of my life.'

'So far,' added Maximilian.

1901

ONE

What followed the battle of Sedan is well-known history. The French were utterly defeated; and the result was the unification of the German states as the German Empire under the leadership of the King of Prussia who had become the Emperor. He lived only a few months as Emperor and then his son William took the imperial title. The little principalities and dukedoms were absorbed in that great Empire. There were no longer rulers of small territories; a duke in his schloss was of little more importance than an English country squire.

This is what happened to Maximilian and that was years ago.

As I write this we are in mourning for the death of Queen Victoria, for we have strong ties with England. It is over thirty years since the battle of the Sedan and I am no longer a young woman. I have my family around me. The eldest is Fritz, nearly a dozen years older than Max. Then I have my two daughters and another son. A big family which gives me great satisfaction.

Fritz is a gentle boy and clever too; he lectures at Bonn University. The others are married now, with the exception of William, my youngest. Dagobert and Liesel joined us and when Princess Wilhelmina of Klarenbock left for her own country her son – who is Maximilian's too – came to live with us. Dagobert climbed rapidly in the army, and Liesel is happily married.

Frau Graben naturally remained with us. She bullied us, watched over us and now and then would try to embroil us in those dramatic situations which so delighted her. We grew so accustomed to her as part of our household that when she died at the age of eighty it was like losing part of ourselves.

We had had a good life.

Several years after Maximilian returned from the front, Anthony Greville came to visit us with his wife Grace – a pleasant, mild woman, a typical vicar's wife; she was devoted to Anthony and it was not difficult to see why. He was so kind and considerate to everyone. When I saw them together I wondered whether I should have been like Grace if I'd married Anthony, living an easy pleasant life where the great moments of decisions were whether the mothers' meeting should be held on Mondays or Wednesdays and who should have which stall at the sale of work.

Anthony looked at me a little wistfully when I took him round the schloss garden.

'Are you happy, Helena?' he asked.

And I replied fervently: 'I could never have been completely happy in any other life.'

And when I look back I know that to be true. I have had my fears and anxieties; there have been differences between us and great difficulties to overcome; Maximilian had known what power meant and it had left its mark on him for ever; he was born to dominate and I don't think I was born to be dominated. But whatever our differences we knew that we belonged together, that there was no true happiness apart from each other. I was right when I told Anthony that I could never have experienced those moments of complete and utter happiness in any other life; I have known great joy; perhaps I should say fulfilment – those moments when one realizes that anything that has gone before is worth while to achieve them.

So here I am an old woman, yet I can still recall that terrifying day on the Island of Graves where I looked straight into the face of death and learned then how precious life was. I am immersed in the affairs of my home; not the political affairs which are no longer our concern but the domestic ones of those who farm and live on our estate. I have my family; I have Maximilian – I never quite got used to the diminutive form of his name, for to me he was always the hero of the forest, and he has never lost that magic quality which enchanted me on our first meeting.

In January of this year Queen Victoria died and this night is the Night of the Seventh Moon. Since the unification more than thirty years ago, the ceremony has not been celebrated, though many remember it and tell their children of it, and are afraid to go out on that night in case the God of Mischief

283

should be abroad.

What a beautiful night! With the full moon high in the sky paling the stars to insignificance and throwing its calm brilliance over the mountains.

I was at my window watching it, when Maximilian came and stood by my side. We are two who will never forget the Night of the Seventh Moon and we shall continue to celebrate it as long as we both shall live.